To Simon And Rich,

Hoping You Can Find This To Help Me Finding A Good Literary Agent Or Publisher And/Or Having This Reaching Netflix Interest So To Be Able To Realize My Dream

ANGEL ROSES

KING OF KINGS

THE HERO OF THE FOX

angelroseshollywood87@gmail.com

+447464792969

To myself, that I keep finding even more questions after the answers.

To my mom and my dad that I love in a Universal kind of way.

To Victoria, thank you for the sensations.

To Johnny, for everything you have always been doing for me without even knowing it.

Text Copyright © 2022 by Angel Roses

Illustrations Copyright © 2022 by Angel Roses

All rights reserved.

No part of this publication may be reproduced, or stored in a retrieval system, or transmitted in any form or by any means, electronic, mechanical, photocopying, recording, or otherwise, without written permission of the publisher.

Roses, Angel

King Of Kings – The Hero Of The Fox / by Angel Roses

ISBN 9798825458755

First edition, May 2022

CONTENTS

- I. BEDLAM
- II. MOON HILL
- III. ADRIEL
- IV. NIGHTMARE
- V. QUEEN LAYLEEN
- VI. SOLEMN SQUARE
- VII. THE SWORD ON THE TABLE
- VIII. REVELATIONS
- IX. THE CIRCLE
- X. SLOW MOTION
- XI. THE COLOUR OF BLOOD
- XII. THE PRINCESS WITH THE RED EYES

- XIII. THE BRIGHTEST LIGHT IN THE SKY
- XIV. BLEEDING TOGETHER
- XV. THE SACRED ANIMALS
- XVI. THE DREAM
- XVII. THE DRAGONS' TREE
- XVIII. THE WALK
- XIX. UNCONSCIOUS POWER
- XX. SACRIFICE
- XXI. THE BLACK HOLE
- XXII. LANDSCAPES
- XXIII. INSIDE A DIFFERENT DIMENSION
- XXIV. LION-LIKE
- XXV. DARK PARTICULARS
- XXVI. LUMINOUS CONNECTION
- XXVII. THE POWER OF HOPE
- XXVIII. THE SAD FATHER
- XXIX. THE DEEPEST FEELING

XXX. THE MEETING

I

BEDLAM

-It's beautiful. - Said the grave voice. That kind of grave, mystical voice, that sounds like it comes directly from Hell.

But, in fact, we are very far from Hell at this point of our Story.

Misty and gloomy was the air and the whole area all around.

Thick grey cirrocumuli were the only sight from the knees to the invisible but present ground.

The only gleaming presence was given by bright white spherical lights. Hundreds. Thousands. Millions of them. Floating all around and all over that undisturbed and surreal location at an astonishing speed, only hesitating at some rare times, when getting close to the two men that were standing in there, in the middle of that silent and indeed remote place at the Northwest limits of The Circle.

-Well... Now... How the process has to be done, Your Unique Majesty? - The words came out slowly from the mouth of the same man with the deep, grave, and solemn voice.

The silence all around was somehow rowdy. Outlandish.

-Just wait and see. -

The words that broke that gaping stillness sounded like the howl of a breezy wind.

The other man's voice had a completely different sound.

Calm. Crystalline. Firm and proud.

Apparently not releasing any particular feeling.

It was impossible to understand if the main feeling in his voice was happiness or anger, or if he was expressing excitement or boredom.

The man with the grave voice was shorter, much shorter, and definitely older.

His presence was a pleasant encounter of the grey of his hair and his beard and the golden yellow of his long and soft tunic.

He was presenting a small amount of jewellery, with his few rings and the bracelets that were covering his wrists.

Both of his ears were exhibiting an earring.

But it was, without any doubt, the necklace he was wearing at his neck, the item that was attracting the whole of the attention if anybody was going to be standing right in front of him.

A White Gold Cross with, in the middle, a charming dark stone, a kind of dark that was shining vividly at every minimum flash of light.

Hard for me, at this very beginning of our Story, to properly describe you the appearance of the taller man with the crystalline voice, as due to some singularity of the lights coming from the floating spheres combined to the otherwise complete darkness of that location, he was somehow remaining less visible than the older man, standing tall few feet away from him.

I can only say it was the matter of a second, maybe less, when the tall man unsheathed his sword, placing it right in front of himself, holding it with both of his hands, the blade pointed to the invisible sky eaten up by the soundless darkness.

To try to describe the sword is impracticable due to the already mentioned dark spot its Master was standing in, the darkest spot of the whole place.

The invisible ground underneath the cirrocumuli trembled for a few seconds.

The air was smelling fresher… Like fresh roses.

The entire location started to get an unusual combination of trembling, like if ready for an imminent earthquake, and a sensation of crisp and warm smell of the air, the kind of air normally present in the most beautiful Spring nights.

A mellow wind started to embrace the remote area all around, whispering serene through the lightful spheres.

Suddenly, it started to be audible, lovely and hopeful, the chants of many someone coming from somewhere around and above.

-They are singing… I can hear them… This is the first time that you, Your Unique Majesty, are doing this… But it seems like is going perfectly…-

The old man, while saying that, raised his voice a bit, as the wind and the trembling sound of the whole shaking place was getting louder and louder.

-Remember. - The tall man said, still hidden by the playing of the darkness mixed with the floating lights that now started to move around at a very incredible speed.

-It's the first times that always define the result of who we are. -

Now the chants were clearly filling the whole surrounding, the wind was running fast, hot as fire, the smell of roses was strong, more chants, Latin…

"Recordare Domine quid acciderit nobis."

("Remember Lord, what we have upon us.")

"Intuere et respice opprobrium nostrum."

("Consider and behold our reproach.")

Now the trembling was a shaking and then the shaking became an earthquake, with nothing, nothing all around to demolish and destroy.

"Recordare Domine quid acciderit nobis.

Intuere et respice opprobrium nostrum."

The blade of the sword turned light blue and little thunders were then crossing the whole of it making a bit clearer few details of the tall man's face.

It was two seconds, but his brown eyes turned light blue too, then the attention back to his glorious sword which blade happened to give birth to two more, shorter lateral blades, as well lightened up, so that the sword got the form of a magnificent and thundering Cross.

"Recordare Domine quid acciderit nobis."

Then, something unbelievable happened.

The spherical lights stopped, not running fast anymore, motionless in the air and then, all at once, they disappeared.

All of them. Except one. Only one of them was still part of the scene, still present, brighter than ever.

The sphere started to move, floating, getting closer and closer to the sword then with the form of a Cross, until being right in front of it and right in front of its Master, his face now lightened up by all of that elation, his eyes still shining of that unreal light blue, the long blond hair moved by the wind still running wild.

"Intuere et respice opprobrium nostrum."

He then closed his eyes, all those phenomena at their maximum level of intensity, the earthquake was massive, even the invisible sky was shaking, the darkness were screaming for mercy, the wind was so strong the cirrocumuli got wiped away, then the ground was visible, ready to break forever, the chants were so loud the whole Circle was able to hear them… Chaos, disorder, confusion, mayhem, bedlam…

Then his eyes opened, brown again, and everything ceased.

The wind was howling no more, the ground was not trembling anymore, the chants were in the Past, the cirrocumuli restarted to take form, covering the miraculously still existing ground.

Silence.

The Cross, the triple bladed sword, between the eyes of the tall man and the only lightful sphere remained, still there, shining without a move.

Then he spoke, in a Language known by few.

-Seistere gonamun tekil atoari. -

("From Light to Life.")

A shine from the Cross, a beam of white light colliding with the spherical light, a flash, then this last one vanished, leaving a little sparkle behind, on the spot where it used to be a few instants before.

The two men were in there no longer as well.

Dark. Extremely dark.

Then, one by one, first slowly and then faster, the other hundreds, thousands, millions bright spherical lights started to reappear, restarting their floating in the air, starting to recreate what seemed to be the regular process of Life in that surreal, silent, and indeed remote location at the Northwest limits of The Circle.

II

MOON HILL

The Silvery Lands were the pleasing meeting of the grey and the white of the stony mountains that were reigning over the Towns of those acreages and the brilliant green of the valleys where, not too often, it was possible to spot the presence of Life.

These Towns had the particular detail that no other colours apart of the grey, the white and the black was present on any of the buildings, even the light bulbs of the streetlamps were giving a grey light, opaque and mysterious, instead of a nice and bright kind of luminescence.

The Silvery Lands were located in the exact middle of The Circle.

However, they were divided in two different Kingdoms.

At East we had the Kingdom Of The Wolf.

The people of that Kingdom were living happy, but they were never really smiling. Their saying was that to show a smile to another person had to happen only when that other individual was able to succeed in gaining respect and trust from the other fellow.

And that was where the main Principle that was characteristic of that Kingdom, was always having its beginning.

Loyalty.

That was the main Principle of the Kingdom Of The Wolf.

That was where all the belief of every single person of that Kingdom was laying.

Loyalty.

Being constantly supportive and helpful and trustworthy to the other Being that was having that special exchange of real and honest sensations.

The Kingdom Of The Wolf was all about that.

The few Towns at the limits of the Kingdom were presenting buildings and houses of a very intense black colour. All of them.

The other few Towns located in the more middle areas were presenting a shiny grey colour, making the structures look like they were big awesomely shaped stones made of Silver.

But the most beautiful Towns were the ones closer to Moon Hill, the hillock where the Castle was brilliantly showing its majestic presence to the people that had the luck to live close enough to that spectacular white and shiny, beautiful Fort.

Shaw was the largest Town of the Kingdom and the closest one to the Castle.

In that area, the buildings were white, which was the main colour everywhere, even if instead of appearing bright as the Castle was, the houses and the structures of Shaw and the other Towns not extremely far from Moon Hill were presenting a more pallid type of white.

King Adalwolf was reigning with kind strictness.

He was a good King, but all about order and organization.

The way he became King was unknown as, apparently, he was the first and only King the Kingdom Of The Wolf did ever have.

Sometimes it was possible to hear the sound produced by his fingers on the piano keys he was playing from a very tiny room in one of the upper floors of his Castle.

When this was happening, the people that were walking around Shaw were usually stopping whatever they were doing, and they were focusing their ears on direction of the Fort on Moon Hill.

It was very easy to spot him at the window having a look outside when the snow was happening to fall on his Kingdom.

In fact, another particularity of the Kingdom Of The Wolf, it was that it was very common to have every type of weather even only in a day.

The people that were living there were able to experience an amazing sunny morning resting on the green areas around the cold coloured Towns, before having to run looking for a shelter once the rain was suddenly starting to make the whole location wet and watery.

After the rain it was possible to even assist to some electrical phenomenon, maybe the few raging minutes of a storm and right after that, finally, that was the occasion when the most favourite atmospheric beauty of the King was happening in all its candid presence.

Snow… It was able to last for hours, or maybe even only for seconds, but whatever its duration was, that was going to keep King Adalwolf at his window for all that long or short time.

At the current point of our Story, it was night and the lights inside the houses of Shaw were switched off.

The most of them.

But not all of them.

A very pale grey light was coming out from the semi opened window of a very tiny house, where somebody was definitely crying, loud enough to make few cats that were running around there stop and point their curious eyes to the window, searching for the reason of that noise, but it was impossible to spot someone as the window was open enough to just permit some of the light inside the house to pale away out of it.

A strange noise from inside the place and the clatter of something falling on the floor, a bit of silence, and then the strong and unexpected opening of the door, that made the cats that previously stopped by, run away in panic.

A thin and tall guy appeared on the entrance and looked around.

It was late at night. Nobody was around. Not even one person.

The guy, apparently quite young, quickly closed the door behind of himself and he started to run.

He was panting and he did stumble a few times during his attempt to run fast in direction of Moon Hill.

The Castle was the most luminous spot of the whole area, the white of its walls shining under the gleaming of the Moon in the sky over it. Also, there was a huge Cross on the top of the highest of the towers, with, in the middle of it, a breath taking, magnificent blue Sapphire, which was, however, not very luminous, a detail that was very strange considering that the Moon was rising exactly, precisely, all over it and the rest of the Castle.

The guy stopped.

He gave a better look. There were few lights coming out from some of the windows of the Fort, which it was meaning that possibly somebody in there was still awake, despite of the time, so late at night.

He started to walk slowly, panting again, starting to make his way up to the Castle, but that hillock was far from being easy to walk.

It was not particularly high, but the ground was presenting holes and parts of it where it was very slippery and ruined, even a bit stony. Being totally honest, way more than just a bit.

Even if it was not a dangerous attempt, it was still a very uncomfortable one and the result, in most of the cases, was for whoever that was making his way up there to find himself about to present his figure at the Castle of King Adalwolf with dirty clothes, broken boots and, in few rare cases, even with some bleeding wounds.

And that was exactly what happened to the skinny guy that that night decided it was the right moment to go to visit the Castle on the hill over the Town of Shaw.

Once he found himself in front of the shiny building, he had a look at the Moon.

His eyes had a sparkle.

He walked to the huge main doors, and he pushed them. They were open. But he already knew that. They were always open for him.

The massive hall was so cold the guy thought he was going to die frozen in there.

-No... -

He was barely able to pronounce a word.

The enormous statue in the middle of the hall was great and powerful.

The shape of a huge wolf all made from Silver with two very luminous blue Sapphires that were his eyes.

It was stronger than him. Every time he was seeing it, it was almost impossible to go away from that view.

Almost.

In fact, when the Hall was happening to be that freezing, he always had to make a move faster than what he really wanted.

He ran to the opposite side of the hall, and he took the stairs, leaving the grey and black floor and walls of the hall behind himself.

One floor. Two floors. Three floors... Finally... He was panting so much he thought he had to put his head out of a window to try to catch some air, but, unfortunately, there were no windows in that part of the Castle.

One little wound he procured to himself while making his way up the hill, started to get a bit too itchy.

He scratched it a little bit.

The door he was standing in front of was not entirely closed.

The temperature on that floor of the Castle was back to normality, but the guy was still warming himself up, mainly patting both of his hands on his arms.

What he was wearing was probably not helping in his trying to get warm, as he was showing himself with a vest and a pair of trousers, both of an extremely thin material.

His boots were very consumed. To walk up Moon Hill always had its price to be paid.

He knocked on the door.

No answer.

He knocked again.

A little chatter came from the inside.

Few steps not too far and then the door got completely opened.

-You. -

The man that opened the door was very short and he had a very upset expression on his face.

-I will be quick… Please… Let me in…-

The words of the young guy came out slow and full of tension.

The short man looked at him with his eyes full of disappointment, but, ultimately, he moved on one side so to let the tall guy entering inside that room.

It was very dark inside with the only exception of few candles here and there that were giving an even more sinister atmosphere to the whole environment.

Not too far there were few steps just to lead to an upper side of the white marble floor, where a big, imponent Throne made from stone, was starring over the rest of that atypical room.

And sitting on that Throne there was a man whose eyes were stabbing through the darkness of that place, to end right inside the frightened eyes of that guy that, suddenly, restarted to cry for the first time since he left his house down in Shaw just to run all the way to Moon Hill and then the Castle of the King of the Kingdom Of The Wolf.

-You. Again? -

The words of the King came out like a whisper. The loudest whisper ever.

-I was only... I was only wondering... If you had the time to think about my... My request...-

It was very difficult for that young man to talk while trying to do not share the view of his very own tears crossing his not particularly beautiful face.

He was, in some way, glad the tears were covering his features.

He hated his face. He hated everything about his own appearance.

-Yes. - The King answered.

-Yes... Sure, I did...-

The young man stopped to cry for a moment.

He was only waiting for the answer.

King Adalwolf passed his hands on his Crown, fixing the position of it on his head.

A big Crown made out of Titanium that was presenting in the middle front the face of a wolf with two tiny little blue Crystals where the eyes were supposed to be.

-And my answer is no. Again. -

The tall guy fell on his knees, expressing a strange look of his eyes that were not focused anymore, at that point, to anything or anyone specific inside the Throne Hall of King Adalwolf.

The short man that previously opened the door to him, got close to his King.

-What is happening, this time, Your Majesty? -

The King was looking at that scene not too many feet away from him with his sparkly yellow eyes.

-Bring him outside. -

He ordered without answering to the question.

The short man bowed down.

He then walked his way to the young man that was still on his knees, the eyes lost in the nothing and apparently not conscious anymore of his own Existence.

Even if the light dressed boy was taller than him, the older man easily managed to drag the other fellow outside the room and he kept dragging him down the stairs, without any caring about the fact especially the legs of the still mind lost guy were slamming down the stairs step by step.

When finally in the Main Hall, the short man with a very angry face looked at the guy that was finally restarting to blink with his own eyes, trying to stand up, feeling the pain on his legs that his being dragged all down the three floors caused on him.

-I suggest you will never come back here. You are unwanted. -

The will to answer to those words was strong, but the strength to do that was not.

The man wearing his thin clothes made his way to the main doors, restarting to feel an unbelievable cold.

And the Main Hall was so dark…

Right before opening the doors, he gave one last look at the other man at the other side of the hall.

-Why? -

And he restarted to cry. Once again.

The man by the angry expression on his face looked at him with a mean pleasure.

-Because he will never give you what you are asking. You are not good enough. You have never been good enough. And you will never be. -

The crying man was freezing, but he was not able to move due to the pain those words were causing inside of him.

The shorter man spoke again. Blood of hate in his eyes.

-You are not wanted, Cobalt. You do not belong to these walls. -

And Cobalt strangely noticed the man, while saying that, pulled the sleeves of his dress up and he clearly saw him passing a hand on his sweaty forehead.

How was that possible? The Main Hall, in that moment, was like the coldest spot in the whole vastity of The Circle...

But he didn't have much time to think about that.

The short man raised a hand and suddenly, without even understanding how, Cobalt found himself outside, in the still dark blue light of the night, not freezing, just a mild wind that was giving a smell of Spring to Moon Hill and the closest Towns of the Kingdom Of The Wolf.

The Moon was still there, bright and beautiful.

He started to walk, slowly.

To walk Moon Hill on the way down was tricky as much as on the way up.

But that was the last of his thoughts in that moment.

His mind was lost inside the Throne Hall.

The King saying "No" to him, again.

His request not even, he was sure about that, seriously took in consideration by the King. King Adalwolf. His King.

He tried to close his mind at least for few minutes to those very sad thoughts, starting to walk his way down the hillock, but all at once he stopped and he turned his head, to give another look at the Castle.

All the lights inside of it were then switched off, without exceptions.

Not even one little gleam was coming from the Castle, apart of the natural shine its outside walls were giving to whoever was able to spot and to enjoy that superb view.

Cobalt put a hand on his heart. It was beating slow. Hurting. Once again. Maybe once per all.

By the King... King Adalwolf... The King Of The Wolf...

His King.

His father.

III

ADRIEL

-I can feel something coming from you... But it is not intense enough...-

Adriel was really trying his very best to follow the instructions of Crevan.

The amount of time he was spending training was impressive, but somehow, he was always ending up feeling like he was blocked, stuck, in some remote area deep inside of his mind.

It was a stunning warm and sunny day in Renard, the second largest Town that was part of the Kingdom Of The Fox, in the West side of the Silvery Lands.

There were more fields than buildings, in that exact area and all of them were presenting a very rarely cut orange and yellow grass that was often caressed by the wind, reminding the precious fur of hundreds of foxes moved while running in the wind.

And those areas were very much based on that. Calm. Nature. Connection with the wild.

And it was in the Nature, in that total calm, that Crevan was trying to make Adriel finally having a true, real connection with himself.

Adriel was pointing his sword at Crevan, while, at the same time, was holding it as well, but from the edge of the blade.

He was not holding it too hard, but he really had his hand well closed around it.

Contrarily, the very young man had a very strong hold on the hilt of his sword.

He was concentrating, trying to give out of all of his energy, to release at least a little part of it, and that was all Crevan wanted from him.

-I can feel… I feel your potential… But it's always like, God knows why, you have your head somewhere else. Or maybe… You don't want it enough. -

Those words were not meant to have a kind effect on Adriel, and, in fact, they worked on him pretty quickly.

But, as much as that boy was swimming in his own pride, he was also very smart.

He really wanted to hit back the man that was training him with a proper good answer, but he knew that if he was going to do that, Crevan, the Commander of the Kingdom Of The Fox would have decided to do not train him anymore.

He knew that. He knew that too well. And he needed him. He needed him like he needed the air he was breathing.

-Yes… I am sorry, Commander. I have… I must concentrate more… I know I can do better… And you know that, too…-

Crevan rolled his eyes. He then stopped holding the blade of Adriel's sword and he gave him the back.

-However…-

Crevan stopped, as, apparently, Adriel still had something to say.

-However, I would appreciate if you don't say anymore that I don't want it enough… As we both know… That it is not true… You know… Very well… You know better than anybody else how much I want it, Commander. -

It was stronger than him. As much as he decided to contain himself in his answer, he still had to make a point on that very important, for him, kind of topic.

The Commander Of The Fox looked at him.

-You are right. You see, you are very right, Adriel. - He said while easing the leather belts that were keeping the whole of his black and handsome gear all together.

-In fact, when, one day, you will know that more than I do… That will be the exact moment when you will reach the power you need to just even try to become who you decided you want to become…-

This time Adriel didn't feel any need to answer back. Mainly, it was because he knew, inside of his heart, that Crevan was right.

He really wanted it so badly… But… Maybe still not enough?

The boy threw his sword on the ground.

He looked at the sky, mastered by the Sun, so that it was appearing of a more yellow colour than the actual very deep blue it was.

-You see…-

Adriel looked at Crevan, listening to him.

The Commander was gently caressing the warm coloured grass that probably didn't see a cut since at least two if not three months before.

-You see how beautiful this grass is, Adriel? -

Adriel looked at it, starting to caress it as well, and he nodded his head.

-It grew up strong and tall, look… But sooner or later, somebody will come to cut it down… It's inevitable…-

The young man tried to don't look confused, as he really had no clue where Crevan was going with that sentence, but he kept listening, waiting for the rest of that speech.

-But it doesn't matter, because then, this grass will grow up once again, it always does, and even this, my dear boy, is inevitable. -

Crevan walked closer to Adriel keeping his hands down, passing them through the soft grass of one of those mesmerizing fields that were located close to the Town of Renard, in the Kingdom Of The Fox.

-Answer. What is the difference between you and this grass, Adriel?-

The way Adriel looked back at Crevan with his green eyes was of pure perplexity, but he tried to hide it passing a hand on the hair that were covering his forehead.

He was still sweating from his training, a training where he did put a lot of effort, but that gave nothing as a result.

-I guess…- He tried.

-I believe the main difference between me and this grass is that I can always find a way to escape from my Destiny. While this grass obviously cannot. -

The Commander of the Kingdom Of The Fox had a severe look on his face.

-To escape? - He said, repeating that part of the sentence that Adriel just expressed.

-To escape from your Destiny, you say. -

Adriel felt straight away the Commander was probably not happy with his answer.

He remained silent, maybe a bit embarrassed, waiting for what Crevan had to say.

-You cannot escape from your Destiny, young man. Nobody can. There were plenty of wrong answers you were able to give me. But this one was by far the most wrong one and, not surprisingly, is in fact the one you decided to pick. -

It was frustrating at that point for Adriel to try to bite his tongue but, somehow and quite greatly, he managed to refrain the strong instinct to answer back very badly to Crevan.

-And… What is it, then? -

He limited himself to these words.

Crevan was then in front of him.

-The difference, Adriel… The main difference between you and the grass we are caressing in this moment, is that if somebody will ever try to cut you apart, you will be able to fight back. You will always be able to have the chance to do not fall, broken, on the ground. -

The young boy was paying a lot of attention to Crevan's words.

-And if you will ever succeed in not succeeding… Then, at least, in that case you will always have the opportunity to learn from it, understanding that even if you fall you might still have another chance of building yourself up again, even stronger than the previous time, stronger than ever before. -

Those were powerful words.

The kind of words that have the great characteristic to be able to have a double effect on the person that is receiving them, with one of the two meanings being the exact and total opposite of the other one.

-So…-

Adriel found back the will to try to have that kind of very uncomfortable conversation with Crevan.

-In this sentence, now, you are saying I can be the Master of my own Destiny, after all. -

Crevan looked at him, deep in the eyes, with his brown eyes that were always gaining a lovely hint of orange inside of them when the Sun was that strong.

-I've said you cannot change your Destiny. I've never said you can't be the Master of it. -

The two walked down the field, directed to the not too far buildings that were meaning the presence of Renard.

Multicolour buildings, very noticeable even from a considerably distance.

Some of the houses were literally having at least bricks of five different colours.

It was the only Town in the Silvery Lands that was not just white, grey, or black.

There was a house right close to a shop that was selling armours and gears, and other types of clothes, that was presenting a lovely pink colour on the front, then red on one of its sides and blue on the other.

All of those colours around the Town, were giving a lot of vitality to the people that were busy living in there, and for Crevan was always a bit unusual going to Renard.

-In Vixen we don't have all these smiley faces going around the Town…- He stated, while stopping with Adriel in front of the armours' shop.

-What are you looking at, Adriel? -

But Adriel was already inside.

Inside that shop the atmosphere was different, the air was different.

-Hello. - A voice said.

-Can I help you? -

The figure of a purple haired woman appeared in front of Adriel, that, however, was not ready for that extreme change of his breathing.

-I only… I only wanted to have a look inside… I always see your shop and I have never entered… But… What's wrong with the air inside of here? -

The eyes of the woman, just for a moment, had a little strange movement and then a very clear sparkle, that revealed, for another second, very thin black pupils over bright green eyes, but right before anything else was being said or done, Adriel found himself back on the gritty road in front of the shop.

-What!!-

Crevan was shaking him.

-What are you doing?! Adriel, what are you doing?!-

The boy focused better his eyes on Crevan's face.

-What… What am I doing? -

He was visibly disoriented.

-You were grasping for air! - The Commander Of The Fox said, with vivacity.

-I saw you from the door, you were like choking… But when I tried to enter, something was holding me outside. I had to enter in that other way…-

At that point the young man was more confused than ever.

-In that other way…- And he remembered.

-Commander!! Let's get inside the shop!! The woman… The woman with purple hair… She works there… Commander, she was not Human, her eyes…-

But right when he was about to say to Crevan what he just saw, a tiny little man came out from the shop.

-You little disgrace!!- He yelled at Adriel.

-You've never entered inside this shop and today you decided to come to scare my customers away!!-

Adriel got back on his feet, properly and he yelled back at the man.

-Scaring your customers away?! Are you serious?! That woman that works in there is the only reason why your customers get scared, little man!!-

The tiny man had a confused expression on his face for a moment and he then said.

-Woman?! What woman?!-

-The woman with purple hair! - Adriel said, then more nervous than upset.

-Yeah, she shouldn't work in there, trust me! -

The man was even more confused than Adriel has ever been since the previous vision of the purple haired woman with the green eyes.

-You are drunk, young boy! Go home! - He said, angrily.

-This is my shop. And I am the only one working in here, not a woman with purple hair has even ever been inside of my shop since I have opened a few months ago! -

Adriel really wanted to run back inside the armours and gears' shop, but Crevan grabbed him by the arm, and he dragged him away, with the little man still yelling.

-Punish him, Commander!! Punish him!! Coming into my shop getting short of breath and choking like he was about to die, scaring everybody away!! Punish that little bastard!!-

The Commander was literally still dragging Adriel away through the streets of the Town.

-What was that?! Can you explain? I really thought you were about to pass away. -

The young green-eyed boy finally freed himself by the hold of Crevan.

-A woman inside the shop just showed up out of nowhere, Commander. She asked me if I needed help, but I was not able to talk well because of an impressive shortage of air… And her eyes changed…-

-Her eyes? - Crevan repeated, now a bit more interested.

-Yes. - Adriel answered, actually satisfied by the fact he understood he somehow got the Commander's attention on that topic.

-Yes, Commander. Her eyes changed. It was only for a moment, but I saw clearly… Thin black pupils… And very big and sparkly green eyes…-

At that point the Commander Of The Fox changed his expression.

-Don't go inside indoor places alone anymore, with the only exception of your own house, Adriel. -

The answer came out straight and very direct.

-Do you understand? -

Adriel understood very well, but obviously he was not quite understanding the reason why Crevan was saying that to him.

-Why? -

-Because I say so. - Crevan cut the conversation.

-Well, that's not very useful for me to understand, right? - Adriel complained, walking behind the Commander.

-It doesn't have to be. Just do what I say. -

They walked another couple of minutes, until they ended up in front of a still colourful house, but with less colours than the one that was close to the armour's shop.

-Here. You are home, young man. I will see you in few days. -

Adriel looked at his house, half red and half dark blue.

-I don't want to go home. Bring me to Vixen. -

-Adriel. Go home. I know it's hard. But go home. - The Commander seemed to literally beg the good-looking boy.

-Please. - He added to his sentence.

Adriel didn't say anything, but right before entering the gate, he looked at Crevan.

-Tell me. - The man said, understanding there was a question about to come out from Adriel's mouth.

-I want to be the next Hero Of The Fox, Commander. - The boy said, putting his hand on his heart.

-And I will make it happen. -

Crevan had the instinct to smile, but he made that smile disappear very quickly.

Adriel needed a stricter treatment in the continuously researching of his hidden power and he was so proud and full of himself that even only smiling to some of his words, would have happened to make him feel comfortable. Too much comfortable.

And Crevan certainly didn't want that to happen.

The Commander nodded his head, and he was about to leave, but Adriel was not done, yet.

-Listen, Commander. - He said with unusual malice in his voice.

-What, Adriel? - Crevan replied, without really having any clue about what was about to come in terms of questions from Adriel's obviously always very busy mind.

-You once told me... Since how long the Kingdom Of The Fox has not its Hero? -

Crevan was very surprised by the question as he was expecting something way more complicated, but that was something he already talked about with the boy, he remembered that.

-It's twenty years. Twenty years that the Kingdom Of The Fox doesn't have its Ultimate Protector. -

Adriel thought about something only with himself, then he said.

-It seems like is about time, then...-

Crevan looked at him with a muddled expression.

-Yeah... It is about time, indeed...-

-And what happened to the last Hero Of The Fox? - Adriel asked.

That question was unexpected.

-He died. - He answered very calmly.

-How? -

The Commander Of The Fox expressed all of his feelings on his then sad and scared eyes.

-I have killed him, Adriel. I had to. Somebody asked me to. And there was no way for me to even only think to refuse to do that. -

IV

NIGHTMARE

-My Queen… My Queen, please, wake up!!-

-Pass me the water, Evangeline… Careful… We need to wake her up! -

It was then the twentieth year in a row that Layleen, the Queen of the Kingdom Of The Dove, was found sleeping in the forest not too far from her Castle and it was always happening in the same periods of the year.

It was always happening in the nights of every single Equinox and every single Solstice.

Her long dark hair was laying with her on the white and fresh grass of the forest, her forest, but her breathing was not serene or peaceful at all.

-It seems like is bad again! - One young woman said.

-Well, it never seemed to be quite good, right, Evangeline? -

The voice and the way to talk of the other woman was very strong and it had something masculine in it.

The same woman passed some water on the Queen's lips.

In the same moment, a very strong wind started to move their vests and the candid white leaves of the trees around there, and a thunder was audible far, very far away from where the three women were.

-What's happening, Ailana? - The youngest girl asked, with a clear sound of agitation in her voice.

And then, all at once, it seemed like the day was back right in the middle of the night, as a blinding and massively powerful flash happened to light up the forest and the whole Kingdom Of The Dove.

-Oh, come on, my Queen!! Please... WAKE UP!!-

Queen Layleen softly passed her tongue on her lips.

-Oh... She is waking up...- Evangeline was feeling very excited.

And, suddenly, it was like the two brightest stars of the sky decided, for once in a Lifetime, to shine of the deepest blue colour and the grass of the Kingdom Of The Dove, pure and immaculate, was the most beautiful sky that was able to be seen from every Region of The Circle, when the Queen Of The Dove opened her eyes.

-Ailana... Evangeline... Where am I... Oh... Obviously...-

The voice of the Queen was dreamy and serene, quite surreal considering it was coming from someone that just found herself waking up again, since twenty years, four times every year, in the middle of the forest, without any kind of logic explanation.

Ailana and Evangeline went to help the Queen to stand up, but Layleen pushed, very gently, their hands away.

-Don't worry, both of you. I can stand up by myself. -

She then had a look at that night's starless and Moonless sky.

Ailana and Evangeline kept their eyes on their beautiful Queen.

She was indeed genuinely remarkable.

Her eyes were like two Oceans.

Her hair, tied up, of a colour that was matching the dark of the most secret of the sins.

Lips that were getting humid only by the shy touch of a gust of the wind.

A figure that was expressing love and wildness, all together.

She was Queen Layleen, and she was the beyond belief Queen of the Kingdom Of The Dove.

-Please, leave me alone for now. I wish to spend some more time in here. - She said to the two girls.

-Alone. - She specified.

Ailana had a very impressive muscular figure and she grabbed, in the gentlest way possible, Evangeline by her shoulder.

-Let's go. Let's leave the Queen alone as she asks, Evangeline. -

The younger girl had extremely long sandy yellow hair and the calm and lovely wind that was hanging around the forest in that moment was moving them so tenderly that it was almost hypnotic to look at them.

-Fine. - She said.

-If that's what Queen Layleen wants…-

-It is what I want, my lovely Evangeline. - The Queen confirmed with a smile that was sweet enough to make every man and every woman falling in love with her.

A very little bowing down from the two girls and the Queen looked at them walking away, directed back to the Castle, not too well visible from that spot in the middle of the White Forest, the forest of the Queen Of The Dove.

That was where she was using to hang out by herself, thinking, thinking and still thinking… So many things were making Layleen's mind busy… Too many…

When Ailana and Evangeline were not able to be spotted anymore, she left herself falling on her knees, in tears.

The emotions that were accumulated inside of her heart were too much to be kept hidden.

She was not able to refrain the tears anymore.

-Why… Why me… All these nightmares… All these visions in my dreams… So realistic… So painful… And so powerful…-

She walked few steps just to get closer to a little lake that was pleasantly offering its surface to the soft touch of the wind.

The face of the Queen was welcoming enough tears already, so she tried to get a very deep breath, looking for the way to calm down at least just a little.

Her eyes went then more serious, focusing on the lake.

She needed to do it. She needed to go back and see…

She also knew, however, that it was not the best decision to take.

But she needed to go back and try to notice every possible detail able to explain at least a little bit more than the very few she already knew.

She had to do it. And she was ready for that. Once again. Like every Equinox and every Solstice every single year since twenty years.

She was wearing a red silk dress and it was sensational. It was like even the wind was trying to don't run too strong just to avoid ruining that perfect figure.

She was that lost in her thoughts and focused on what she had to do, that she realised she forgot something very important.

She was not even sure it was there, this time, but it normally was, so she didn't see any reason why it would have not been there that time, too.

She had a little search around the area where the lake was, she literally walked around it for a good couple of minutes.

It was a dark night, as already mentioned, so a great focus of the eyes was very much needed.

She was so impatient, but she tried to remain relaxed as much as it was possible to be.

And then, right there, few steps away from her feet, she saw what she was looking for, laying on the ground.

A shiny sword was there, waiting for her, the hilt confounding itself with the grass, as white as the lawn was, with a circling spot right before the base of the blade that was presenting a beautiful green Amazonite.

Two dove's wings were intertwining with each other, but only to not even the half of the length of the blade, where four letters were forged showing the powerful word that was also the main Principle of the Kingdom Of The Dove.

Hope.

And that sword was exactly what Layleen needed.

That very distinctive and milky white sword.

Her sword.

When the event of her waking up in the White Forest was happening, she was never able to remember how she ended up there.

She literally never had any lucid remembering of what she was doing before that, as the last thing she was able to recall was always her lunch time and her total blackout was always happening in the night where the Equinox or the Solstice was having its new birth.

That means she always had several hours of total loss of her memory regarding the day that was preceding the night that was when the change of the Season was happening.

However, somehow, when she was going out from the Castle directed to her forest in an absolute state of unconsciousness, she was always managing to bring her own sword with her.

That was a clear matter of fact as every time she was getting awaken by Ailana and Evangeline, and then, once alone again as she requested that same night too, she was always finding her sword not too many feet away from her and always very close to the lake's shore.

And that night was there, once again, waiting for its Queen to pick it up.

And that is exactly what Layleen did that night.

She went down on her knees to pick her sword up and she had a look at it.

Beautiful sword.

Absolutely unique.

And that word... That word forged on the blade... The only word she really needed to read with her starry blue eyes in that moment... The word that was representing the only thing she was really in need especially in that very particular moment of her Life.

Hope.

She stood up and she walked back down the lake.

She was not sure about what time it was, but she was sure she was still finding herself in the real fullness of the night.

She had no time to wait anymore.

She stopped thinking and she raised the sword pointing it to the lake.

Her eyes closed.

Her heart open.

And the familiar feeling that was generating between her Soul and her sword didn't take too long to manifest itself in all of its greatness.

A silent explosion.

The Amazonite lighted up and a white beam of energy collided with the watery surface of the lake, making it shake.

And in a matter of few seconds the result was successful.

The Amazonite lost its light, and the Queen relaxed the hold on the hilt, also lowering her arm and so her sword.

At a very first sight, apparently nothing was changed.

But with a better look it was possible to notice what happened.

The surface of the lake was not made of water anymore.

There was just a misty amount of smoke, very similar to thin and small grey clouds and even being that hazy, it was however interestingly dazzling.

The Queen left her sword on the white grass, laying it down very gently and with genuine care.

She moved few steps and she stopped only when on the limit of the shore.

She took another deep breath.

And she entered inside the smoky lake.

She floated inside… Only the upper part of her body was then visible, but it was seeming like she was flying inside that obviously not ordinary lake.

She reached the middle, slowly, and once there she stopped moving.

She kept her eyes open for a moment and then she spoke.

-Donaiesti pertura evin fintlico. -

(-Dream again and wake up brighter. -)

Dark.

When Queen Layleen reopened her eyes, the level of confusion inside of her head was very high.

She was finding herself in a very inky place, somewhere far away from her Kingdom, her beautiful Kingdom known as the Kingdom Of The Dove, located at the Northeast side of the Regions Of Light, in the North areas of The Circle.

Wherever she was finding herself, was definitely very far away from home.

Very far from her stupendous lilac coloured Castle, majestic as much as its extremely merciful Queen.

The place where she was standing in that moment was a mysterious location and she was able to feel, once again, the sensation of fear she already experienced when she found herself in there during her last dream.

She was able to experience again the intolerable sensation of being very well aware of the fact she was in a place way far from being safe.

-Where am I?!- She screamed.

All around there, there was nothing.

Not even the sky.

Just a dusty and burnt ground under her feet, that was all that was able to be felt and seen.

She walked for a moment, but it was pointless, as wherever she might have been going was presenting nothing to see.

Everything was looking the same in that place.

-Is there anybody in here?!- She started to scream again.

-I want to go back!! I want to go back to my Kingdom!! Someone has to come here and help me!!-

She was screaming all those words so loud that she felt like her voice was about to abandon her throat.

-PLEASE!!-

And she tripped and fell on that barely visible naked ground while attempting to run away from that spot she was in that moment, even if running around would have been meaning finding herself somewhere else around there with the same thing to look at.

Nothing.

-Why are you screaming, Layleen? -

The Queen Of The Dove was then in silence, staring at the darkness that were as well swallowed by the nowhere.

-Who are you? - She asked, then with a whisper.

-Please, I need to go back to my Kingdom… Please…- She was talking slowly, her voice reduced to a low sound produced by her tremulous mouth.

She remained silent for a moment, waiting for an answer that didn't happen to be pronounced.

-I WANT TO GO BACK TO MY KINGDOM!!-

She yelled so loud that she thought her voice, after that last, blaring scream, was gone forever.

-What Kingdom, Layleen? - the mysterious voice said, something in between a whisper and a scream.

-You have no Kingdom… Not anymore… Layleen… Come to me… My Queen…-

The howls of an apparently decent number of wolves became very much audible, coming from somewhere, out of nowhere. And probably far. But not that far.

-NO!! Where are you?! I can't see you!! Who are you?!-

Her throat was in pain, her eyes full of tears with the taste of fear.

-You cannot see me, Layleen… But you can hear me… Follow my voice… Layleen… Follow… My voice…-

The occult voice was everywhere. All over the place. Above and around.

Impossible to understand where it was coming from.

Then, suddenly, the Queen Of The Dove started to feel her body getting tired… Even just staying stand was starting to be difficult…

-How... How can I come to you if I can't see you? - She then said.

-Your voice is all around... I can't understand from where is coming from...-

-Close your eyes...- Then the voice said, magnetic and dark.

-Close your eyes and follow my breath, Layleen... I am waiting for you... My Queen...-

Layleen closed her eyes. She was too tired to only even think about anything else in that moment, she was giving up on resisting that inscrutable voice, she had no interest in fighting it anymore, everything was changing and very quickly inside her mind... All she wanted was to end that never ending feeling of confusion and, sometimes, pain, that was never leaving her until the moment when she was waking up from her unusual and unwanted dreams every Equinox and every Solstice since twenty years.

And then she felt it. His breathing. Low and deep...

-Follow me... Come to me... Listen to my breathing... Follow it... Walk, Layleen... Come to me...-

That was the moment when everything changed.

Not just the moment when something happened, but literally the moment when everything happened.

As Layleen started to move with the intention to follow the deep and perilous breathing of the mysterious talking presence that was calling for her, she felt like the hand of someone grabbed her from behind, holding her left shoulder.

The hold was too strong even to try to move.

A hold that was not even just strong.

It was absolute.

She was not even able to move her feet. Not able to talk.

She was completely immobilized, unable even to think.

A bright golden light started to slowly appear around the whole scene.

The luminosity of it was increasing fast…

It was not only around Queen Layleen, but it was especially around her…

And then completely all around that dark location.

Suddenly, that dark and intimidating place was literally shining, due to that mystical golden light appeared out of nowhere.

Even if unable to speak, to move, or to do anything else, Queen Layleen was still able to feel.

And the sensation of ultimate and unmatchable protection she was feeling in that moment was something she did already experience, a very long time ago, but not in her dreams, no… That happened in the real Life…

She had a moment of lucidity where she thought she was realizing what was happening…

And then.

The escalation.

The entire location started to shake, trembling ground under her feet, she was about to fall, but she didn't, as still held, strongly, by that superior power.

Way superior of any other kind of power she did ever witness in all of her Life.

It felt strange, but all at once she started to feel safe… Calm… And, more than anything else, happy.

And all of those warm and beautiful feelings were taking form inside of her while, in that exact meantime, the whole area was seeming to be about to collapse inside the ground, deep down, to the centre of Hell.

And then she heard them.

Chants.

Chants coming from far away, Chants coming from hundreds of voices, the whole place was full of those singing voices, so far, but somehow so close.

"Sanctus Dominus Deus…

Dona Eis Requiem…

Qui Tollis Peccata Mundi…

Dona Eis Requiem…"

("Holy Lord God…

Let them rest in peace…

You, who takes away the sins of the World…

Let them rest in peace…")

At that point it literally looked like the End Of The World was about to begin.

The Planet was shaking, the grimy ground was cracking, and the golden light was enlightening the entire vastity of that vexatious location…

Then the wind started… The strongest wind ever been felt by any Being that had the unique gift to have at least one Life in the unbelievable process of that Universal Existence…

The raging wind was making almost impossible to have a good view of whatever was happening all around, but Layleen was safe, tranquil, in her spot where that mystical and absolute power was keeping her, forcing her to do not make a move, to avoid having her involved in all that violent madness that was happening in that unknown location.

In fact, while all of that insanity was happening all around, literally, all around her, that piece of ground where she was standing, immobilized, was a peaceful and serene shelter, with not a feeling of the Planet shaking, not a view of the ground cracking, and no wind raging… She was seeing all of that happening… But where she was located was the only safe spot of the whole area, untouched, in the middle of that great mayhem, but, somehow, at the same time, it was like she was somewhere else, being able to see what was happening as she was physically there, but not able to be affected by it as Spiritually she was far, very far away from there…

And she saw it. Somehow, she managed to see it.

The face of a man, long black hair, the eyes that were seeming to be entirely, fully black, but all the rest of his body was blurry and confused with the wind and the total destruction that was happening all around.

Even if able to see his face, everything was too confused for Layleen to manage to properly see the details of it.

The man screamed with the same voice of the mysterious talkative Entity that was calling for Queen Layleen since she found herself in that place.

-Aaaaaaahhhhhhhhh!!!!!!!!!!!!!! NO!! NO!! YOU!!!! I'M SORRY!! NO!! PLEASE!!!!-

While screaming those words with clearly signs of incredible pain, his image started to vanish…

-PLEASE!!!! LEAVE ME!! DON'T HURT ME!!-

It was unpleasant to listen to his voice, that changed so much from when it was sounding charming and seductive while trying to convince Queen Layleen to follow him, to that moment, screaming in agony and begging for mercy clearly to someone, but it was totally unclear who this someone was.

-Please… DON'T HURT ME!!!!-

He was crying in pain, his image vanishing more and more…

And the Queen was still there, assisting at that incredible scene, completely secure and out of danger, while all around her, but not where she was finding herself in that moment, it was like the entire World was about to meet the end of its Existence.

"SANCTUS DOMINUS DEUS…

DONA EIS REQUIEM…

QUI TOLLIS PECCATA MUNDI…

DONA EIR REQUIEM…"

The chants were louder, the wind was about to wipe the World away, the entire Planet was still shacking, just even more, the ground was starting to definitely crack, opening in huge and deep cavities, and then, literally appeared out of nowhere, the Queen Of The Dove noticed the presence of a lake not too far from the spot where she was, but she was not able to see its surface very well, but what was surely easy to see was the unbelievable amount of smoke that was firing out of it.

The golden and luminous light that expanded itself for the whole vastity of the location, started to surround the mysterious man with the fully black eyes and what was remaining visible about him.

-DON'T KILL ME!!!!-

That was his last desperate scream.

And then…

A very loud thunder.

And the biggest and brightest flash of light that ever happened to appear in the History of the Existence.

Blinding.

Extraordinary.

Silence…

Everything was quiet, then…

Layleen opened her eyes.

It was a bit cold then and she was breathing deeply.

The lake's water was back where it was supposed to be, and Layleen's legs and arms were moving instinctively to be able to keep her staying afloat.

She stayed few instants looking in front of her but without really seeing what was in there.

Her mind was still living the events that happened in her last dream, the dream she went back to, trying to experience one more time the sensations and also the view of the many unusual and singular happenings that ended with that blinding flash of light that was the last thing she saw in her very mystical dream, before getting awaken by Ailana and Evangeline.

In particular, she was remembering the part of her dream where the powerful hold grabbed her shoulder.

When in that moment she felt, and she also realised that she was not only about to be safe…

She was safe already.

She calmly moved in the water and started to make her way to the shore.

Once out of the water, her red satin dress was still completely dry.

And her sword was there, right where she left it before entering inside the then smoky and misty lake.

She picked it up. The weapon, from the base of the hilt to the edge of the blade, shivered between her hands.

She then had a look at the sky, and she felt amazingly surprised when she realised the stars were back to populate the night, and she felt even more in ecstasy when she saw, up there, the only view that was always making her feel in the only way she wanted to feel herself.

Happy.

Up there in the sky the brilliant and sublime presence of the Moon.

It was easier then to spot the way through the White Forest that was leading back to her Castle.

Layleen's eyes were literally stolen by the beauty of that Full Moon.

She would have been able to stay there, without even moving her neck, for the next at least two hours.

But as much as she was enjoying the feeling of her lips giving birth to one of the sincerest smiles she did ever produce before, her attention got caught by what in particular all that light coming from the inhabitants of the sky was making stunningly visible.

Although her Castle was not easy to be seen from the spot where she was, it was still possible for her to distinguish the huge purple Cross that had its location on the top of her Castle's highest tower.

So luminous under the Moonlight that was making even more luminous the incredibly stunning green Amazonite that was stuck right in the middle of the Cross.

Normally it would have not been extremely bright, it never really was, but the stunning Gem was of a very attractive kind of green, like the one on Queen Layleen's necklace, but however of an opaque class of light.

But that night it was shiny, not because of its natural characteristic, but due to the incredible Moon that was in that sky, even brighter than the Sun.

The Circle.

Queen Layleen loved The Circle.

But her mind was not easy to empty to be able to only enjoy the beauty of the World.

Sometimes she was not even able, actually quite often, to even enjoy the greatness of her own Existence.

She tried anyway, at least for few instants, to don't think too much and she started to walk to finally lead herself back to her Fort, when, all of a sudden, she realised something unusual.

She was able to smell it very clearly.

A strong and very intense smell of roses.

The unmistakable fragrance of hundreds and hundreds of roses.

The White Forest, as all the rest of the Kingdom Of The Dove, had the characteristic, the unique characteristic, to present all of its vegetation's colour of the purest kind of white.

However, classic types of flowers were growing easily and happily in there and there was a very remarkable selection of those.

Orchids, peony, gardenias, daffodils, daisies… Even some violets, but only a few bunches of them around the whole forest.

And, possibly, few more types of flowers, beautiful and full of many different colours.

Actually, the White Forest had a very good variety of flowers.

There were so many flowers in there…

So many flowers…

Countless of flowers…

Except roses.

V

QUEEN LAYLEEN

The days at the Castle of the Kingdom Of The Dove, were usually starting very early.

Inside the Castle there was movement since the first hours of the morning and mostly was due to the people that were serving for Queen Layleen, that was typically sleeping until the later morning, or sometimes the very early hours of the afternoon.

The day after she got found asleep in the forest in the night of the Spring Equinox, Ailana and Evangeline were giving instructions to the people working in the Castle.

-Roy, please, be sure all those clothes are clean and dry for tomorrow morning, please, no delays! - Ailana was ordering to a lovely chubby man that smiled with very genuine happiness.

-I will, of course, Commandress! -

And he ran away, very fast, honestly impatient to go to start his duties.

-Commandress, can I be the one that cooks for lunch, today? Please, please, please! -

-All right, all right!! Calm down! - Ailana answered to a young lady that was jumping with a lot of emphasis all around her.

It was always like that, every single morning at the Castle, and every single person was very well capable to do everything and to take care of every single duty.

Ailana was giving orders and instructions to everyone, while, instead, Evangeline was very busy talking with a woman in a corner of the Great Hall, the spot of the Castle where they all were in that moment of the day.

-Evangeline, what are you doing? You should help me instead of chatting around...-

But the young girl with the extremely long and sandy yellow hair, looked at her and answered.

-Ailana. I'm sorry. I am having a very important conversation in this moment. -

That answer surely surprised the Commandress Of The Dove.

Evangeline was a shy girl, and she did never answer to her like that before.

Not in terms of way to speak, Evangeline was always very kind and respectful in her talking, but normally, in any other kind of situation, the girl would have just apologised to Ailana and she would have got back to her allegiances.

But that morning her very polite answer was however a clear desire to let Ailana know that she was currently occupied in doing something else and, for her, more important.

Ailana didn't like that.

-Evangeline. Don't make my day starting not well...-

-How? - The young girl asked.

-Because, for once, I am doing something that is not listening to you? -

At that point, the Commandress was confused more than upset.

She had a look at the person Evangeline was talking with.

She was sure she did never see that person before.

A very tiny woman like she had never seen before in all of her Life.

Her skin was strange. She was supposed to be young, but some of her characteristics in terms of presence, in terms of figure, were not very clear.

Literally.

While she was looking completely normal, every now and then her skin was getting blurry and unclear to the eyes, to then, in a matter of instants, being again of a very regular appearance.

-Who are you? - Ailana asked to the woman.

Her eyes were rarely blinking.

-Hi… My name is Siah. -

Her voice sounded very deep, too deep to be associated to such a small woman like that.

-Siah… And what are you talking about in here, away from everyone else in this corner, if you two don't mind me ask? -

The girl called Siah, started to giggle with a weird kind of excitement.

It was a very surreal moment.

-Evangeline… What is going on in here…? -

The young girl looked at Ailana in the eyes.

-We are talking about him, Ailana. - She said.

-Siah wanted to know if we heard something about him recently… Or, definitely way less possible, from him…-

Ailana grabbed Evangeline by the arm.

-Him? - She asked with her eyes stabbing Evangeline's strangely lost ones.

-You mean… Him?!-

The woman was still giggling, just with more animosity.

-Ailana, you are hurting me… Ailana! -

Evangeline freed herself from the Commandress.

-Ailana!! What is wrong with you?!-

But before Ailana was able to answer, the giggling little woman, started then to laugh with a very deep and not Human voice.

Her brown eyes looked black for a moment.

-Evangeline, out of the way!!-

Ailana pushed Evangeline away and she unsheathed her sword and without even giving the time to the other people in the hall to understand what was happening, the Commandress tried to pierce Sinah in the chest.

And the reaction of everyone in that place was something between the being surprised and the being scared, all at the same time.

The little woman was laughing no more.

Her eyes were completely black and not only she was not laughing or giggling anymore, but also, she was not even smiling.

And all of that with her little finger in front of her, on the top of the blade that Ailana tried to use to stab her, but that she stopped only with one finger and without any sort of difficulty.

-Do you really want to kill me? -

Her smile got back on her face. Her voice was like it was coming directly from a tomb.

Ailana stepped back, the sword still pointed in front of her.

-I have understood it since I saw your skin blurring...-

-Very intelligent, Ailana. - The woman mocked her.

In that meantime, the air was full of negativity and the few people that were still in the Great Hall, previously waiting for the Commandress to give them orders and duties for the day, were waiting to see what was about to happen, without really understanding what exactly was in fact happening.

Ailana felt, like everyone else, that negativity entering under her skin, inside her veins.

-Ailana, leave her alone…-

Evangeline was standing there, the eyes lost and confused.

-What have you done to her? - Ailana asked to the woman that in the meantime had the whole of her eyes completely black, without even one tiny white spot to be part of them anymore.

The woman only smiled, and she then spoke with the same voice, dark and grave.

-Nothing. - And then she laughed.

The more she was laughing, the more her body was seeming to grow up…

The not anymore tiny woman opened her mouth and a black vapour started to come out of it.

And at the same time, inside her mouth, a brilliant purple kind of light was pulsing.

Ailana's hands held the hilt of the sword and fetching the air, she produced a lightening that electrically went to impact with the woman's body, but the effect inflicted to her resulted to be inexistent.

The pulsing light inside the Being that was then very obvious to be way far from being a woman, seemed ready to get released and it became clear once Sinah took a big breath to then be able to make all that energy explode, but everything changed when all at once everything became not audible anymore, like the whole place had been thrown down into the deepest spots of a very gaping Ocean.

A light blue sparkling light was surrounding the whole hall expanding itself in slow motion.

And then, without any kind of way to predict anything, the whole scene got hit by a massive spark of light, bluest than the most serene of the skies, and for all the presents became impossible to be able to see anymore for the following instants.

Everything was unclear and muddled when the Commandress of the Kingdom Of The Dove restarted, like most of the presents, to be able to be graced by the already hugely missed capability to hear and to see.

Everyone was still there.

Evangeline ran to Ailana.

-Ailana!!- And she hugged her.

The Commandress looked straight away at the spot where previously the Being called Sinah was.

Nobody was there anymore.

The negativity in the air was not part of that Environment anymore.

-Evangeline, are you feeling fine? -

-Yes, Ailana. I don't remember much… Just… I saw a woman I've never seen being part of the people that work at the Castle… And I went to question her about who she was… And… Then I do not recall anything else…-

Ailana caressed her face.

-You were controlled. Your mind was acting without you being aware of it. -

She then had a look around. It was hard to tell what happened to that Entity and even more difficult was to give an explanation regarding what that previous great flash of light was and how did it happen.

-Ailana! Evangeline! Are you both all right? -

A young girl with red hair ran to them.

She was probably on her teens, and she had beautiful green eyes that were hesitating on the two women.

-Edme. We are fine, thank you. Is everything good with you? - Ailana asked.

-Sure. - Edme answered. Her eyes were studying the two girls.

Then, she smiled, very happily.

-Very well. I can see you really are all right. -

And she then looked at the ceiling.

-The Queen is fine too. - She stated.

Evangeline's eyes got thoughtful.

-How do you even know that? Actually, let's check if she really is feeling well. -

The three of them left the few people that still were in the Great Hall in there, leaving them unable to be aware of what was going on at the Fort that morning, but after all, not even Evangeline or Ailana had any real clue about the nature of the events of that very troubled day.

And surely, not even the young girl called Edme was aware of anything more than anybody else.

They really reached the fourth floor where the Queen had her bedroom very quickly and the Commandress knocked at the door.

The answer from the inside came straight away.

-The door is open. -

The three girls entered in the room.

The Queen Of The Dove was sitting on her bed, one hand on the other hand, the hair tied up leaving her beautiful face very well visible and illuminated by the bright Sun that was hitting through her open window.

-My Queen, how do you feel, is everything fine up here? - A very concerned Ailana asked, while massaging the hilt of her sword that earlier failed twice, firstly with an ordinary kind of hit and secondary, with an attempt of throwing an attack made of energy. Pure energy.

-I am feeling very well. - The Queen said.

-Why? -

That answer relaxed both Ailana and Evangeline, while Edme didn't seem too surprised or excited by Queen Layleen's answer, like if she already knew the Queen Of The Dove was completely fine.

The Commandress explained to the Queen what happened in the Great Hall, reporting every single detail she was able to remember from the scaring events that had place inside her Castle few minutes before, including as well the detailed description of the appearance of the Being that was firstly having the figure of a woman and then the aspect of still a woman but with her eyes of a total dense black colour and her clearly not natural growing up in terms of height.

But all of those descriptions seemed not to be the main interest of the Queen Of The Dove, that, still looking outside, out of her window, asked very calmly.

-She wanted to know about… Him? -

The three presents in that room noticed very easily the way the Queen said the word "Him".

Her eyes shined a little and her hands did hold each other in a visibly strong way.

And her voice while saying that, got lower, similarly to when a voice is going down before exploding in tears.

-My Queen. - Ailana said.

-Yes. She was asking to Evangeline… But Evangeline's mind was obscured by Sinah's power, and so she is unable to remember whatever she might have been said. -

Layleen showed a smile without happiness.

-Well. Nothing, then. As there is nothing we have ever heard, recently, about him... And...-

And she closed her eyes before finishing her sentence.

-Certainly, we didn't hear anything from him. Since forever. -

While reopening her eyes, Layleen was able to feel the wetness caused by the part of herself that she was hating the most.

Her heart.

-Very well. Ailana. Evangeline. Thank you, as always. Go back to our beautiful people down in the Great Hall and reassure them everything is under control now and there is not any kind of danger. -

She then looked ad Edme, and she added.

-You stay. -

While Ailana and Evangeline were about to leave the room, Layleen called one more time.

-By the way, Evangeline. -

-Yes, my Queen? - the young girl answered.

-You are the Leader of the Kingdom Of The Dove. You help Ailana to also train our Warriors. I do expect you to be way more clever than today. -

Those words hit a bit, but the Leader Of The Dove knew her Queen was right.

-Yes, Queen Layleen. -

-Great! - Layleen then said with a big smile.

-Don't worry. I still love you! -

That made Evangeline not only smile, but also look at Ailana with visible relief.

They both bowed down, quickly, and they disappeared exiting the bedroom of Queen Layleen.

The Queen then stood up from her bed and she stretched her arms.

-Beautiful day outside today, right? - She asked to the young lady called Edme.

The girl pointed her green eyes on Layleen.

-Yes. It is. - She answered without interest while studying the Queen.

-Is it all good? -

Queen Layleen noticed the weird stare of the girl on her.

-Yes. All good. -

Another very quick answer that made the Queen a bit confused.

But she also realised that the vibrations that she was receiving from Edme were very good… She was able to feel the good in her presence, even if that morning she was seeming to be acting a bit stranger than usual.

-Edme? -

-Yes, my Queen? -

The Queen thought a second or two to how to formulate the question she wanted Edme to hear.

-What do you know about Astro Innocent? -

The girl finally had a little light of surprise in her eyes.

-Astro Innocent… Your father, Queen Layleen. -

The Queen smiled.

-I know who he is… Was… My question is what do you know about him? -

Edme walked closer to the Queen, closer to the window that was giving a great view of the Town of Umbriel, the biggest Town of the Kingdom Of The Dove.

It was also possible to spot the White Forest, white and shiny under the warm Sun.

-What I have been hearing about him is all very good. People always had lovely words when talking about the King, my Queen. -

Layleen put a hand on Edme's shoulder.

-And tell me, Edme. Do you know how the King found the end of his days? -

The little lady looked at her Queen.

-Yes. -

Green eyes and blue eyes were mixing with each other, and it was a spectacular kind of greatness to be able to witness.

-Would you tell me how? -

But Edme got tense.

The Queen saw that and felt that with her hand on the girl's shoulder, that got rigid and uncomfortable like all the rest of her body.

-Don't worry, Edme. Go back downstairs. I want you to have a fun day enjoying your duties. - The Queen then said.

Edme was a bit confused for the very first time that day.

Actually, she was very difficult to find her confused about something in general.

Layleen grabbed her other shoulder too and she got down a bit to be able to kiss the cheek of the girl with the red hair.

-Thank you to be here. -

Edme didn't really expect that, but she smiled.

-Queen Layleen. Can I ask one very little favour? -

Layleen was the one that appeared surprised by that question, but she kindly answered.

-Well. If I can, why not? Try. -

The young lady opened her hand in front of Layleen and then she said.

-Hold my hand, my Queen. Please. -

The Queen Of The Dove didn't seem bothered at all by the request even if it sounded a little bit strange to her.

-I mean... Sure...-

She then closed her hand around Edme's one and the girl tightened the Queen's one to lock the hold between the two hands.

And the feeling coming from the Queen was of pure love.

Edme was feeling her Queen's vibrations entering inside the complicate structure of her Existence as a Being.

The Queen was really loving her.

She really cared about her.

And Edme, in that moment of love, beauty and passion, saw everything.

She was looking into Layleen's eyes, and she saw him.

She saw his eyes.

She saw his look. Powerful. Invincible.

And she understood even more what she already knew.

But maybe for the first time Edme understood, totally and truly, the reason why her Queen based her Kingdom on Hope.

She understood, finally and very clear, from where, or better, from who, all the Hope that Queen Layleen had inside of herself was coming from.

VI

SOLEMN SQUARE

The very colourful Kingdom Of The Fox was extremely quite that day.

The people around were not many, and they were all looking like they were in a rush, walking fast and looking at the ground while doing that, doing their best to do not get across any eye contact with anybody to avoid having to stop and finding themselves in the middle of an unwanted conversation.

The reason behind that strange behaviour, was unclear.

Few kids were running dodging other people while on their dash.

-Faster, faster!! Hello!! We are sorry!! Oh, hey, out of the way!!-

They were running that fast that to even only try to tell them to slow down or paying attention, or both, was probably the biggest waste of time in the Universe.

But those kids were not the only ones running, speeding up, obviously leading somewhere that was in the same direction for everybody that was sprinting that madly, that early morning.

It was appearing to be a promising very sunny day.

Where all of those people were directed?

Why were they speeding that much?

What was about to happen in the Kingdom?

Why the shop that few days before saw Adriel gasping for air was there no more?

Not just the shop as a Business was gone.

The entire building was not there anymore and not just like it had been dismantled, but like it never been there, like it never actually existed.

That was the Town of Renard, the second biggest one part of the Kingdom Of The Fox.

The biggest one was Vixen, not extremely far from there.

Finally, it started to be more clear where all those people were heading to and the main square, Solemn Square, was the place of interest.

Everyone was gathering in there and circling the scene of whatever it was actually going on.

-Ladies and Gentlemen. It is a pleasure to have you here, present, all of you, great people of Renard. Sly people of the Kingdom Of The Fox.-

Crevan's voice was loud, enough to be herd by all the presents.

At that point probably at least the most of the habitants of Renard were all in there, facing Crevan and the two boys that were on both of his sides.

Adriel on his right. Dawako, a young boy older than Adriel, that was smiling smartly to everyone that was there assisting at the whole scene.

He was occasionally even wave at them with his hand, the white teeth well shown to the people in front him and in front of all the three of them.

-Adriel and Dawako, my great people. The best of the best. The ultimate selection of our youngest Warriors, the two that showed and proved that more than anybody else they deserve a chance. Still so young and they already have to face the most incredible opportunity of all of their Existence. -

The people were very silent.

Adriel looked at Dawako and he smiled at him, but with brashness.

The older boy saw that with the corner of his eye, but he ignored him pretending he was not seeing or noticing him at all.

-One between the two of them, my dear friends, will become the next and new...-

Crevan took a breath, not because he needed it, but just to create more suspense on the big audience that were circling the entire area where that speech was having place, in the middle of the very radiant Solemn Square.

-One of them will become the next and new Hero Of The Fox! -

From the silence of the spectators to their applauses, the rise happened very quickly.

Crevan then looked at Dawako.

-Dawako. You want to say something to these people that came here just to assist at this official statement regarding the battle that will have to take place between you and Adriel this coming Summer?-

Dawako smiled at Crevan and then at all of the listeners, keeping his charm at a very high level.

-Commander. People of Renard. Habitants of the Kingdom Of The Fox. - He introduced with warm and serene voice.

-I have to say two things only to all the presents. First, my name is Dawako Kettu. Second, in this moment you are listening to the voice of the Warrior that will become the next Hero of the Kingdom Of The Fox! -

Many applauses fulfilled the air around the square.

And, after few seconds, even more.

It was quite easy to understand the people of Renard were liking the dark-haired guy called Dawako.

When the applauses ceased, Crevan spoke again to the audience.

-That was a warm round of applauses for our Dawako. Thank you for that. -

And then, the silence went back to be the main sound in the beautifully coloured Solemn Square.

-And now. - The Commander restarted saying.

-Adriel. It is your turn, now. What do you want to say to the people of Renard? You are from here. I am pretty sure you want to say something to this amazing listeners. -

Adriel had a look at the presents that were in front of him.

Their eyes were all pointed at him. But they were far from being eyes of good thoughts about him.

The young boy scratched his forehead, passing a hand through his long brown hair.

He had an entirely grey coloured gear, with chains all around of it, vest and trousers, the boots were black and tough.

-Honestly…- He said.

-Honestly, the only thing I want to say is that if you all are so cheerful for Dawako over me, then you should all move to Vixen so you can see his annoying smile every single day. -

First there was the little surprise for those words, everybody was silent, still, trying to understand if that saying actually really happened. Crevan and Dawako were not speaking as well.

Then, first low, then definitely very loud, the people that were attending that official presentation that day, started to boo Adriel.

The boy looked at Crevan and said.

-I am going. -

But Crevan grabbed his arm.

-No, you don't. -

The presents were still booing while Dawako was laughing over the reaction of all of the people in Solemn Square.

-Leave me alone. They don't like me, it is fine, not a problem for me. That makes me even more hungry, that makes me want to train even more so I will silent them all when I will succeed. -

But Crevan had another opinion.

-You have a very good brain, Adriel. I expect you to be way more mature when it comes to having to deal with the people. -

The spectators seemed like not even thinking to low down their disappointment for Adriel's words and they were definitely very far from being in the mood to completely stop with it.

-What do you mean? - Adriel asked to Crevan. -

-I mean…- And the Commander got sure Dawako was not listening, and he really was not, too busy in his laughing and smiling to the people in front of him that were quite obviously supporting him and only him regarding the challenge against Adriel to become the Hero Of The Fox.

-I mean, Adriel, that if you go, they will like you even less. I also mean that your target doesn't have to be to succeed to silent them. Your target has to be to succeed to make them talk even more. You have to succeed to make them talk forever. About you. -

Those words hit right.

The boy by the long hair had a nice and big smile on his face, almost to match Dawako's one, and he said.

-Thanks. -

Crevan smiled, but quickly got serious again, while the booing finally vanished, and the people restarted to applause for Dawako that in the meantime was back talking to them.

-This Summer… This Summer!! The Solstice!! All together, me and all of you, my people!! My friends!!-

Adriel, suddenly, walked to where Dawako was, and he put a hand on his shoulder and said to all the presents.

-Don't you worry, everybody! When I will win the challenge against your favourite one, I will get sure he will still keep all of his teeth on so he will still be able to please all of you with his annoying but apparently very effective smile! –

There was a moment of hush.

Then, all at once and all very out of nowhere, the crowd started to laugh unbelievably loud, that loud that Adriel was honestly unable to hear what Dawako yelled at his hear while pushing his hand away from his shoulder.

Crevan was looking at Adriel, while most of the presents were still laughing.

He was looking at him extremely pleased and even him seemed genuinely amused by what Adriel just said to the load of presents that then, in a very surreal moment, started to give him a very shy round of applause.

They were not cheering for him.

They were not giving him a huge and loud motivation.

But, at least, they were clapping their hands, yes, diffidently, but still, they were positively reacting at him.

Dawako was staring at him not smiling anymore.

He was stabbing him with his grey eyes.

But Adriel's green eyes were pointing somewhere else.

They were focused on the people.

The crowd that, for the first time, was expressing a positive reaction to something he said, even if honestly not very full of any kind of deep meaning.

-Very well, people of Renard! - Crevan said, inviting everyone to get silent again to be ready to hear what he had to say to them.

-There is something you don't know. And to be honest, what I'm about to reveal is something that not even Adriel and Dawako know, yet. And they are about to discover this exactly like you, right here and right now. -

A very lively murmuring fulfilled the air following Crevan's unexpected sentence.

Dawako's expression was far from being the smiley and cheeky one he was normally showing off in public.

Adriel's eyes were not sure if looking at Crevan or at the ground, totally empty in terms of ideas regarding the statement the Commander Of The Fox just declared.

-Adriel. Dawako. - Crevan called.

-Come closer to me, please. -

The two boys got closer to their Commander as they have been asked.

Crevan put a hand on Adriel's shoulder, and he did the same with Dawako.

-Initially you might not like this. But, if you will take few minutes to think about it, you will realise you should actually feel hyped about it. -

Everybody was waiting to discover what Crevan, the extra special Commander of the Kingdom Of The Fox had to say.

-We all know…- The speech started…

-The Silvery Lands are an amazing location right in the middle of The Circle and these are our lands. The lands we defend, firstly taking care of our Kingdom, the Kingdom Of The Fox. Secondly, but not less important, as part of the Silvery Lands as well is our duty to keep an eye on the Kingdom at East of our Fatherlands.

The Kingdom Of The Wolf. As two Kingdoms, yes different, but part of the same piece of our beautiful World, it is a must being sure we are ready to help the Kingdom Of The Wolf as much as they will always be ready to help us if in absolute need. -

The Commander took a pause to be sure everyone was following and that everything that have been said until then was clear and understood well enough.

Seeing that the whole of the audience was all ears and both Adriel and Dawako, while looking at him, had nothing to say or to ask, he carried on with his speech.

-Now. Many things you don't know, my dear boys. Both of you are born in here, in the Kingdom Of The Fox, and never been out of it. Let me be honest with you two, you know a very small percentage of the secrets of The Circle, as we are called Neutral Regions, due to our not taking part of one particular side between the Regions Of Light at North and the Regions Of Darkness at South. -

Crevan took another pause and this time someone had something to say.

A woman from the crowd asked.

-Commander. Is it true that because of that we, as Silvery Lands, are not totally, completely aware about the whole mechanism of the Existence of The Circle? -

-Indeed. - Crevan answered straight away.

-Well, I do. The King obviously does. Few other people do. Some people know. And they also know they absolutely cannot share that kind of knowledge with anybody else living in the Silvery Lands unless they are ordered to do so. -

He took both boys under his arms.

-I don't want to keep you on a bed of nails for too long. Let me be real and clear. One of you two will be the next Hero Of The Fox. The other one, even if losing that opportunity, will most likely become the next Leader Of The Fox, the last figure in terms of guide and protection of the Kingdom, but still one of the most important roles of our World. -

The Commander looked first into Dawako's eyes.

-You two are the personal choices of King Balgair. And my two choices too. But. We might be wrong. -

And he then put his eyes inside Adriel's ones.

-That is the reason why we need to go to the Kingdom Of The Wolf. For the Meeting. -

In the exact meantime the Commander finished his last sentence, he rapidly winked at Adriel, that didn't understand the reason behind of it. Or, maybe, there was not any particular purpose behind that wink of the eye Crevan threw at him.

At that point, one man spoke, out of the listeners that were still massively making Solemn Square the most populated spot in Renard, that day.

-The Meeting?! I thought that was just a Legend regarding how the Hero of a Kingdom of The Circle was chosen. -

Crevan focused on the man that was standing not too far from them.

-That is unquestionably way more than a simple Legend, I believe, my friend. -

-Hey. - Adriel interrupted.

Crevan and Dawako both looked at him.

-What are you all talking about? Would you mind to explain? What is it? The Meeting…? -

Dawako remained silent but it was obvious he wanted to know the answer to that question too.

-The Meeting…- The Commander said.

-You will know more about it, properly, both of you, during our journey. For now, be satisfied with just knowing that this very extraordinary event will sign your Life, young man. Forever. -

He then faced the people that were starting their very characteristic murmuring once again.

-Ladies and Gentlemen. People of Renard. Inhabitants of the Kingdom Of The Fox. Dwellers of the Silvery Lands. Proud Beings of The Circle. I extremely thank you for your presence and your interest, today. It has been a great exchanging of vibrations. -

He released Adriel and Dawako by the hold of his arms.

-Go back to your duties. Your work. Your home. Whatever you like. And feel glad. It is just a matter of time until we will have our new and amazing Ultimate Protector.-

-Yeah… If they will agree…- The same man that questioned the Commander few minutes before said, while walking away from the scene.

One by one, all of the presents started to get back on their own way, getting then back to whatever they were doing before the official statement regarding the next Hero of the Kingdom Of The Fox, that took place there in Solemn Square.

When everybody left and Crevan, Adriel and Dawako remained the only ones in the multicoloured square, Dawako spoke.

-Journey? A journey you said, Commander? To the Kingdom Of The Wolf?!-

Crevan answered without looking at him.

-Exactly. Tomorrow. -

-But… Commander…-

-Any concerns, Dawako? - The Commander Of The Fox asked with a tone of his voice that sounded not happy about Dawako's talking.

-No… No. Commander. Not at all. I was just… Not imagining we were going to go… I mean, how will we even get there? -

Crevan did not answer, and he just fitted his gear a bit tighter.

-You will realise it. Tomorrow. - Crevan said making that "tomorrow" sound like there was not room for any other questions that day.

-Commander. -

This time was Adriel's voice the one that did break the silence while Crevan already started to walk his way away from the spot where the speech had place.

He stopped, without a word, obviously waiting to hear what the young man was about to say.

-Will we meet here? In Solemn Square? -

The Commander found the question logic enough to turn his head and answer to it.

-Yes. Me and Dawako will rest tonight here in Renard, in a Boarding House not far from here. In the morning we will head to Vixen all together and from there we will start our journey. -

Adriel didn't want to look like he was disappointed, but he probably did.

-So, I have to go back home now… And spending the night there…-

-I do believe so. - Crevan replied.

-And…- He kept saying.

I also do believe you should sort things out before you leave home tomorrow. I know it's not easy. But you need to. You have to. -

Dawako passed close to Adriel and whispered in his ear with his iconic and annoying smile.

-Good luck…-

And he then left him there, alone, walking his way out away from Solemn Square with the Commander Of The Fox.

It started to rain.

Adriel's hair were gently touched by the lenient rain, that was also making the coloured ground of Solemn Square wet and filmy.

And he stayed there, standing, then sitting on that picturesque ground, thinking. And thinking. And thinking again and again.

He stayed there for several minutes, or maybe hours, not easy to tell.

What was sure, however, was the fact that the emptiness of the Square, the colours, the rain, the silence… They were, all together and all at once, making him realise the Commander was right.

He needed to sort his things out. He had to.

He stood up and he walked few steps, looking at the ground without seeing it, still busy inside of his own head, cogitating about the huge situation he was about to face once back at home.

But he was ready for that. Or, at least, he thought he was.

He was on his way home, not too far from it anymore, when he noticed the change of light happening.

It was still late afternoon, not fully evening yet, but he was able to see, pale in the sky, the presence of the Moon.

The rain stopped instants before, and the sky was already clear once again and that soft image of the Moon appeared quite pleasant to Adriel's spectacular green eyes.

Then, suddenly, he had a strange feeling, starting from his feet and ending inside his brain.

Out of nowhere, the Moon looked like something that was not belonging there. It was like his eyes were then looking at something that was there, up in the sky, but it was not supposed to be where it actually was.

He had the inexplicable feeling that the Moon was there because it had been put in there.

He clearly had the mystic feeling that the Moon was where it was because someone decided so.

VII

THE SWORD ON THE TABLE

The evening's air was already pretty much present in the environment when Adriel finally found himself in front of the door of his house.

The lights were still turned on inside, it was possible to spot that due to the open curtains at the windows.

Even if he made up his mind about the fact he had to face his issues at home, Adriel spent some time outside after the speech that had place in Solemn Square.

He pushed the door and he got inside.

It was nice and warm in there, and the wooden floor was giving a serene atmosphere to whoever was entering inside the house.

Somebody was laughing in one of the rooms not far from the corridor at the entrance of the building.

Adriel left his upper gear on the pavement and entered the kitchen where a woman was sitting on a chair, reading a book.

-What are you doing naked? - She asked looking at the boy.

-I am not naked, mom. Anything refreshing in the fridge? -

Adriel made his way to the refrigerator, thirsty and wet because of the rain that still was falling outside all over Renard.

-Where have you been? I haven't seen you the whole day. -

The voice of the woman was firm but somewhere inside of that voice there was a little hint of fear and relief at the same time.

-I was in Solemn Square. And I'm sure I told you I was going to be there... The speech... The Commander...-

-Oh... Right...-

There was insecurity in her voice.

-You didn't come. - Adriel said, straight into his mother's eyes.

Brown eyes. Deep. Mysterious. Sensational.

-You know, Adriel... It was... Not possible...-

Adriel did bite his own lip.

Then, somebody laughed again.

It was coming apparently from the room right opposite the kitchen.

Adriel took a big breath.

He left his mother in the kitchen and he entered inside an enormous room, that was presenting three different sofas and a very big rectangular table where a sword was laying over.

It was a simple sword at the appearance. Apart of the top of the blade. It was presenting a little incision on one of its sides, but it was very small, and Adriel was not interested at all to study it or even look at it.

His attention was on a man sitting on one of the sofas, laughing by himself, apparently unable to even raise his arms, not even his hands.

But he was able to use his legs and once he realised Adriel was inside the room, he stood up immediately.

-Adriel... Adriel... Adriel... Adriel...-

The young boy stayed where he was and he looked at that man, wetness covering his eyes.

-Adriel... Good boy... Safe... Brave...-

The man walked close to the boy.

-Green eyes… Beautiful boy… Beautiful eyes…-

Adriel tried then to take a bit more of distance and he spoke to the man.

-I will have to go. Tomorrow. I go away. With the Commander. And Dawako. -

The man that previously was laughing by himself, started to cry without any single way to predict that.

It really happened out of nowhere.

-Hey… What's happening…-

Adriel said caught by the surprise of that.

-My son… My son… Where are you going… You can not… You will stay in Renard… You will stay in Renard…-

Adriel scratched his eyes with both of his hands and replied back to the mind lost man.

-No. I have to. I go to the Kingdom Of The Wolf. -

It happened fast, but slow enough to see it.

The entire figure of the man released a black vapour that vanished almost immediately.

Suddenly the expression of confusion on the man's face, seemed to be way more controlled and attentive.

He was looking at the pavement and he then looked at the boy.

-The Meeting. - He said.

Even his voice was different.

-Yes. - The straight and simple answer of his son.

The man walked close to the table that was presenting the sword on it.

-Do you know why I am dying, Adriel? -

The lucidity that was existing in the voice of the man that only few minutes before was talking in a state of total confusion and with a psycho expression on his face, was somehow way scarier.

He kept staring at the sword, waiting for Adriel to answer to his question that left the beautifully green eyed boy in a condition of pure surprise.

-No. I don't know. -

-I know you don't. -

-So why are you asking? -

The man went silent for a moment and then he spoke slowly, like to be sure Adriel was able to get every single word correctly.

-I know your head is busy. I know you are sad. I know you are upset. But one day you will understand the reason why my days reached their end. -

Adriel felt himself way more confused than ever before.

He looked at his father that was still looking at that sword, still without the possibility to move his arms and his hands.

They were just pending at the sides of his body, lifeless.

-Right... I go to sleep. Tomorrow will be a long day...-

Adriel gave his back to the room, but he had to stop.

-Adriel. -

His father called his name and the boy had to stop where it was.

-Adriel. Thank you. I needed this as much as you did... I know... It is not easy to see your father in these conditions... Lost... Destinated to die... But you see...-

And he started to silently cry.

-I was not having a moment of awareness since the past six long months, Adriel...-

And he openly started to cry. Loudly. Honestly. With painful tenderness.

-It was last time you came to talk to me… To see me…-

Adriel looked at his crying father and he started to cry as much as him.

-Because you stopped to talk to me!! You stopped to come to see me when I was training, or even at the door when I was coming home from an entire day outside with the Commander, trying to give out my very best to reach my desire, to draw the line of my own Destiny!!-

-Adriel…-

The two of them were eyes in the eyes, green eyes, both of them, crying and looking at each other.

-You didn't even tell me… You were dying… Now you are not even telling me why you are dying…-

And with these last words Adriel grabbed his father, he held him, he held him more and even more.

And his father's impossibility to physically hug him, to hold him as well, was not a barrier, it was not an obstacle in any single kind of way, as the parent was hugging and holding his son with the sensations, the feelings and all the vibrations of love that were coming from the deepest insides of his Soul and that was an absolute unique way to express love and passion, one of the rarest ones, and it was tighter and greater than any hug and any physical hold would have ever been able to express.

-Everything I didn't tell you is because I can not… But know this… Understand and always remember this, my Adriel… You will be the next Hero Of The Fox… You will be the Ultimate Protector of this Kingdom. You will be stronger than your own Existence…-

And Adriel was listening every single word and still held by the power of his father's Soul, he felt his own body releasing energy…

And he smiled...

-I love you...-

Those words came out from his mouth without him really realising he was saying that, but definitely feeling every single letter that was part of the full composition of that real and honest confession he expressed to his adored father.

-I love you too, Adriel... Go... And remember... One last thing...-

Adriel felt his father's energy going down all at once, the connection with his Soul was slowly vanishing...

-Tell me... Please, tell me...-

-Remember this... Stay real... Never change for anybody... Respect the Nature... The Nature, Adriel... Respect the Nature... That will make all the difference... That will make... All the difference...-

And with those final words he interrupted the connection with his own Soul, a sudden spark of energy hit Adriel in the chest, not to hurt him, not at all, but just to push him away, away from being close to his father that in that meantime got back in the same kind of lost and hugely confused expression he had on his face when Adriel entered inside that enormous room at the beginning of their meeting.

-Adriel... Adriel... Adriel... Adriel... Why are you here? I can see you... Adriel... Are you staying here, Adriel? -

He was talking to him, but Adriel's father was looking inside the nothing, unable to really feel the presence of his son inside the room.

Adriel didn't want to look at him like that, but once by the door he gave a rapid look at his then once again lost and disorientated father.

The man let himself falling on the sofa and then he started to giggle by himself.

Adriel left the room, closing the door behind himself and he then walked back inside the kitchen where his mother was still sitting reading her book.

-What are you reading? -

His mother looked at him.

-Go to bed. Tomorrow is coming. -

-But now is still today. What are you reading? -

Adriel's answer surely got his mother unprepared.

-Good answer. -

And she closed her book so to be able to make the cover visible.

-A book about the Kingdom Of The Scorpion? -

Adriel was just not sure why his mother would have been interested in reading a book about the meanest Kingdom of the Regions Of Darkness.

-Yes.- Adriel's mother answered, dryly.

The boy got serious.

-I don't like the fact you are reading a book about a Kingdom part of the Regions Of Darkness…-

His mother gently laughed.

But she didn't even think, not even for less than a second, to consider to answer to her son's proud statement.

-You don't even know what the Meeting is, don't you, Adriel?-

The boy felt a bit in embarrass by the fact he was not in fact aware about what the Meeting really was about and he somehow didn't even give extreme importance to the fact his mother smartly changed the matter of the conversation in a way he was definitely not expecting it to happen.

-Well, why don't you tell me? I am pretty sure you know what all that is about. -

-I surely do. But it is not me the one that have to tell you. -

Adriel was disappointed.

-The Commander didn't want to say… And you as well…-

His mother put her book on the table and looked at her son.

-Understand this, Adriel. The Commander doesn't say much not because he doesn't want to, but because he can't… That is very different. And me… If the Commander can't tell you that, I certainly cannot be the one that says that to you.-

-You are my mother. -

Adriel was feeling terribly alone in that moment.

The feeling was painful.

-Yes, Adriel. I am your mother. And only God knows how much I would love to tell you every single thing and even more than that. But… You will understand…-

-Everybody is saying this to me, today…- Adriel replied with huge despondency.

-Because you will. - His mother then said.

Adriel walked few steps and kissed her mother on her forehead.

He then walked away, directed back into the corridor with the intention to go upstairs to his bedroom to have his rest before the unbelievable day that was waiting for him the morning after.

-Adriel. -

His mother called while he was still at audible distance.

He looked at her from the corridor, through the door that was getting into the kitchen.

-Don't worry, my love. - She said.

And she smiled at him.

-You are not alone. You have never been. And you definitely will never be. -

The boy had to resist from starting to cry once again and he barely managed to nod with his head and to wave his hand at his mother and at her words.

He finally ended in bed, and he just had the time to take his boots and his trousers off that he then found himself with his head on the pillow, tired, very tired, in need of sleep and he lost the consciousness of reality pretty quickly.

He was dreaming serene and away from the troubles of the real Life.

He was alone, walking in a field.

Nothing was around.

Nobody was part of the scene.

The Moon was high in the sky.

He stared at her magnificent figure.

-Who put you in there? - He asked directly to her without expecting any kind of answer that in fact didn't come.

He kept walking and suddenly it was dark.

The Moon was not there no more.

He was trying to understand where he was but all he was able to see was darkness.

-Hey!! I can't see!! I can't see anything!!-

He was literally walking with his hands in front of his face, just in case he was going to feel something, but, instead, he felt someone.

-Who are you?! I can't see you!!-

No answer came out from the someone's mouth.

-Hey… Who are you…-

He then moved his hands very fast, and he grabbed the not visible but concrete presence that was in front of him.

He grabbed one hand with his one and with his other hand he grabbed what he felt were hair, long hair.

Long and soft hair, like silk.

And the hand he was holding was at the feeling very soft too, but he was also able to feel the presence of rings, one for every single finger.

A very low breathing was coming from the presence in front of him and Adriel felt a feeling he was not usually experiencing.

-Hey…-

But before he was able to say anything else, a bang woke him up.

With his eyes still close he heard his mother swearing something, probably due to her hitting something by accident downstairs in the kitchen that crashed on the floor.

Adriel was conscious but still with his head to the dream he just had.

That feeling he was experiencing while holding that Entity's hand and while passing his fingers through those amazing velvety very long hair…

A kind of sensation he forgot it was actually existing and part of that World.

A sensation that was still surrounding his person even if not inside the dream anymore.

He was still feeling it, there, right there, in the heaviness of the real Life.

The powerful feeling of the absolute awareness that he was way more than safe.

VIII

REVELATIONS

Adriel, Dawako and Crevan arrived in Vixen early. After the strange dream Adriel had the night before, he found very hard to fall back asleep.

When he woke up his mother was still sleeping but he heard his father talking, by himself, from the inside of the massive room that was opposite to the kitchen.

In the Silvery Lands people were usually helping themselves around with the use of horses.

Big, muscled horses, that for some reason, at least in the Silvery Lands, were mostly black coloured but with a long blond and soft mane that was appearing majestic every time those horses were running fast against the wind.

They were a true spectacle of the Nature.

Adriel's horse was called Titan and he was indeed a massive mount.

The Commander and the two boys succeeded in reaching Vixen not long after the Sunrise.

The air was colder in Vixen compared to Renard, even if it was Spring.

There was a bit of morning fog that was gently caressing the walls of the buildings of the Town.

The colours of Renard were not present in Vixen.

All around was all made of marble, white and grey marble, even the footpaths, which it was giving a surreal atmosphere at the Town.

The houses were presenting nothing in particular, but the most of them were black coloured.

Every now and then it was easy to spot few flags outside of a balcony or a terrace, presenting the face of a fox on a fully orange background.

-Wait here...- Crevan said to the boys.

The two of them stopped there as they have been ordered and they looked at each other.

-How is that crazy head of your father, Adriel? Is he still able to recognise you, or what? - Dawako said while Crevan was leaving them in there to disappear behind a corner with his horse.

-He is fine, thank you for your interest, man. -

The way Adriel answered to him, definitely shook Dawako a bit.

He surely was not expecting such a calm and composed reaction coming from the long-haired young man.

Adriel then looked at the few people that were walking around that exact spot where him and Dawako were in that moment.

Those people were not paying any attention to them and probably, even if they knew who they were and what they were up to, they would have not cared anyway.

They were the exact opposite of the people of Renard.

Way more distant and not only that. They were looking very angry every single rare time they were accidentally meeting someone else's eyes.

After not a long while, Crevan came back and someone was following him, right behind, on a horse as well.

A young girl around the same age of Adriel and Dawako was on a bright white horse with a shiny light blue mane and deep blue eyes.

Adriel and surely even Dawako, never seen a horse like that before.

But in any case, it was not the horse's appearance that got the two boys' attention.

The girl that was riding him, had wavy brown hair that were ending just a tiny bit after her shoulders and her eyes were matching her horse's ones.

She was wearing a very exceptional orange dress with no sleeves.

At her neck, a radiant yellow Citrine was giving her an even more special appearance.

She was beautiful. No other words, even way more elaborated than that, would have ever been able to describe the aspect of that girl that was carrying simplicity and a sophisticated aspect mixed all together like no-one else.

Beautiful.

And Adriel and Dawako for once, or maybe for the first time ever since they have met, they looked at each other without any kind of rivalry or without any sort of disrespect for the other one.

They genuinely looked at each other with the expression of who just didn't exactly understand what was going on, but whatever was in fact going on, they would have been agree with that.

-Boys. Come down from your horses and go down on your knees for Princess Lisica, daughter of the King of the Kingdom Of The Fox. Your King. Our King. King Balgair. -

The two young men jumped from their horses and rushed on a bowing down to the Princess that didn't go well.

Both of them ran so fast in their attempt to bow down to Princess Lisica, that they bumped into each other, nearly falling on the ground but somehow managing to keep their almost lost balance.

The Princess giggled a bit without hiding it.

-Princess. This is Dawako Kettu, probably the Warrior that between all the others showed off the best expression of the power manifested with a good, more than good, knowledge of his unconscious self. -

Dawako stood up and smiled to the Princess with his perfect smile made of charm and beauty.

The Princess smiled with a nod of her head.

-And, Princess Lisica... This is...-

-My Princess...- Adriel interrupted Crevan under the surprise of everyone while standing up.

-My name is Adriel Centauri. And I am, certainly, the Warrior that between all the others showed off less than the half of the power, surely because it is that deeply hidden inside of me that I know it will manifest, all at once, and with no way to match it, at the right and proper time. -

That statement made Dawako stop to smile for a moment, before pretending, with another way less convinced smile, that those words didn't touch him at all.

Crevan was absolutely unable to say a word and Princess Lisica gave a very attentive look at Adriel.

-Adriel Centauri...- She said, more to herself than to the young Warrior.

-Well. Good luck to both of you then, I guess. -

She then faced Crevan and she smiled at him.

-Should we go? -

-Absolutely. - The Commander answered without even thinking a second about his answer.

-Wait. We? - Dawako asked.

-Yes, we. - The Commander answered.

-King Balgair asked me to bring his daughter with us, the Princess… You know… She never really spends too much time outside of the Castle… The Meeting is a great excuse to evade from the Castle for a bit, I believe…-

And he looked at the Princess, that stared at him with a firm, feelingless smile pictured on her face.

Dawako spoke to Adriel out of nowhere, totally unexpected, while getting back to their horses.

-I wonder why I have never seen her in all of my days… I mean… I live here in Vixen, after all…-

Adriel was certainly not glad to have a conversation with his rival, but he found himself answering anyway.

-Well, Crevan said she never goes out from the Castle…-

Dawako thought about that answer, and he agreed with a nod of his head, even if still not extremely convinced.

-So… Horses? - Dawako asked to Crevan.

-Indeed. -

-Why not Elixirs? -

Crevan gave an amused look at Dawako.

-If you want to become the new Hero Of The Fox you need to forget about the easy ways, son. -

And, suddenly, horses in position, flexing, and…

On the run!

All together were on their way already, going fast, very fast, through the streets of Vixen.

They left the central location of the Town in less than a minute and they started to head to a great vastity of orange fields that were giving an absolute feeling of Liberty to whoever was going to face them.

-Guys!!- Crevan called the attention of Adriel and Dawako.

He was pointing his finger to his left.

Down there, under the morning sky, there was the Castle of the King, King Balgair, the King Of The Fox, black, almost entirely, with some interesting sides of it shining of a bright, sparky orange.

-What is that shiny orange? - Adriel asked.

-Crystals. - Lisica answered from behind him.

Adriel kept looking at the Castle while on the run.

That was the first time he was out of Renard.

The first time in twenty years.

And he liked it, or at least he thought he did.

His attention got caught by the huge, massive Cross, on the top of the highest Tower of the Castle.

While riding fast on his horse, he managed to spot a quite big Citrine stuck right in the middle of that Cross, the same Gem the Princess was carrying as a necklace.

The only difference, apart, obviously, of the size of it, was the fact the Citrine that was stuck inside the Cross was way less bright than the one Princess Lisica had as jewellery.

Actually, that huge Citrine, was somehow very opaque, which was strange if considering the Sun was already slamming his shiny rays all around Vixen and, mainly, all over the Castle.

They soon left Vixen and the Castle way behind them.

****

They were on the road since few hours already, time where no-one really said much, even due to the high speed they were riding at.

When close to a small village down the road, they slowed down drastically.

-This is the first time ever I am about to go that far from Vixen without my father. - Princess Lisica stated out of nowhere.

The only reason why Dawako and Adriel were able to understand whatever the Princess was saying every now and then, was simply because both of them were very well focused on her lips, moving soft and amiable at every word she was pronouncing.

-Where have you been with your father, Princess? Far away from the Kingdom? -

Dakawo was asking that not because he really cared about the answer, but mainly because he just wanted to admire the Princess moving her honey lips once again.

-It only happened once. And we went very far, indeed. We went to the Kingdom Of The Lion. -

Adriel got curious.

-The Kingdom Of The Lion? But… It is ages away from the Silvery Lands…-

-Well, yes, but I wouldn't exaggerate, though. It is far, yes, but it takes less than what you think if you go with the dragons. -

Adriel laughed out loud.

-What? - Dawako asked.

-Yes, what's so funny? - Lisica asked, audibly and also visibly not very glad about Adriel's reaction to her words.

-I mean… What?! Dragons, you said? -

-Hey, mind your language, son! - Crevan said entering inside a conversation he was not interested being part of until few seconds before.

-I apologise! - Adriel quickly said.

-No, it is ok. - Lisica replied giving a bad but at the same time amused look at the young boy.

-No, I mean it…- Adriel insisted.

-I just… I've just never seen… A dragon, I mean… In all my entire Life and honestly, I was not even thinking they were part of this Existence. -

This time was the Princess' turn to laugh.

-Are you serious?! There's not dragons flying over Renard, sometimes? -

-I guess… I believe Renard is a beautiful Town but not extremely fun… I don't think the… Dragons… Would find it interesting. -

Princess Lisica giggled.

-You are funny. -

And she smiled at him.

The way Adriel blushed would have been able to be seen even by a blind man.

Dawako didn't enjoy any of that conversation between the Princess and his rival.

Especially the part where she said Adriel was funny, then smiling at him.

-It would have been strange if dragons were flying over Renard. - The Commander then said.

-Because the dragons do not leave the location where they live unless they are called by a King or by a Hero.-

Adriel felt more curious and hungrier of information than ever.

-And where do they live, exactly? -

The Commander Of The Fox rolled his eyes. He was rarely keen to talk about secrets regarding The Circle with the boys as he was thinking some of that knowledge about it, would have been a cause of distraction from their upcoming battle, the Challenge, where one of them would have become the new Hero of the Kingdom Of The Fox.

However, he understood that, slowly, it would have been right and important to start to let them understand something more, not too much, not plenty of details, but at least an idea that in that case might have been, why not, even useful for them.

-They live at the extreme limits of The Circle. They live at the extreme West and at the extreme East of our Planet. -

The two boys found the information pretty interesting and the Princess too, as it was obvious by the look she had on her face that she had not a total knowledge regarding that topic, as well.

At the end of all, she was still very young.

Even being the Princess Of The Fox, there were still many secrets about The Circle that she had no clue about.

-I see…- Adriel muttered.

They entered in the Village they arrived to, and they jumped from the horses.

-But why some of them live that far from the others? -

-Because they are not the same. -

The answer sounded very straight, and it was clear the Commander really didn't want to talk about that topic regarding the dragons of The Circle anymore.

Adriel noticed that, but it was stronger than him.

-And… The difference is…-

Crevan felt hopeless and that was a feeling he was hardly experiencing in his Life.

But that boy was getting eaten up by his own curiosity.

Some people were entering inside Restaurants and Bars.

It was almost Midday, after all.

-Fancy a bite? - The Commander asked.

-Before I answer to your LAST question...- He added looking at Adriel that in that moment was already picturing a very upset expression on his face due to Crevan apparently ignoring him.

They entered in a Restaurant and people looked at them once on the door.

It was not a bright place.

The tables, the sits, the pavement itself, everything was black and dark green. The lamps pending from the ceiling were spreading a dirty yellow colour on the site.

-Hello, can I help you? - A girl with round glasses and green hair went to ask to them.

-Sure. A table for four, please. To eat. Please. -

Crevan leaded the group following the green haired lady that sat them on a table in a corner of the Restaurant, far from the ones where the most of the people inside where already sitting at in that moment.

-Is there a Menu? - The Princess asked, amazed by the fact nobody seemed to know who she was.

-Oh, no Menu in here, guys! - The waitress smiled at them.

-Only three things on the Menu. Cheese as a Starter, roasted rabbit as a Main and ice-cream for Dessert. -

Dawako looked at the others at the table.

-Well... Not much to choose from...-

-It's perfect. - The Commander said.

-I think we will pass on the cheese. Four rabbits, please. And... Why not... That ice-cream after that. Oh, and, please, water. Four. -

-Perfect! - The girl giggled.

-You will love it! - She winked at them, walking away.

-Strange place…- Adriel commented.

-Well… It is called The Weird Rabbit, after all…- Lisica pointed out.

Adriel put a hand on the table.

-Commander…-

-Yes! Yes…-

Crevan for a moment felt himself so naive as he thought, even if only for a second, that hopefully Adriel forgot about the conversation they previously started before entering inside the Restaurant, regarding the dragons.

-So… The dragons… At the extreme limits of The Circle, at West… We have the Luminous Dragons. Dragons that if in real need are always at the service of any Kingdom part of the Regions Of Light. -

The water arrived at the table, carried by a different server, a man, skinny and tall, that left the jar of water and the four glasses on the table without a word and, possibly, not even a look at the four people sitting in there in front of him.

-Crazy…- Dawako commented looking at him walking away.

-Everything sounds so interesting. - Adriel said with sparky eyes.

-And… So, at East… What sort of dragons we have there…? -

-At the extreme limits of The Circle… At East…- Crevan restarted his speech.

-We have the Tenebrous Dragons. Dragons at the exclusive service of any Kingdom part of the Regions Of Darkness. -

Those discoveries made Adriel, but not only him, even Dawako and Lisica, very excited.

-So, how come that King Balgair and the Princess were able to attain the service of a dragon? As we live in the Silvery Lands, not in one of the two main Regions of The Circle. -

As much as Crevan was not too glad to have to answer to all those questions regarding the mysteries of The Circle, he actually thought that question was that full of sense that it deserved a clear answer.

-Even the two Kingdoms that are part of the Silvery Lands can attain the service of a dragon. But in that case, it really has to be, literally, a Life-or-Death kind of situation. -

Dawako and Adriel looked at Lisica. What the wondering was about, inside of their heads, were obvious, but Adriel looked back at the Commander Of The Fox and went for a different question.

-I do understand. But. In that case… In that case we are talking about right now… Which kind of dragons would come then, as we are the Neutral Regions? -

Crevan looked at him with a severe look in the eyes.

-It's simple. -

And he literally entered inside of his bright and green eyes.

-The dragons are not listening to the call of the person that calls them… The dragons, at West, and even the ones at East… They listen to the call of the Soul of that calling person… And… Depending on the nature of the Soul of that individual… The right dragon will fly to that Being. -

All of those information fascinated the two boys at the table and even the Princess pretty much.

Dawako was tapping his fingers on the table. Adriel attempted a little whistled melody, failing after three seconds of it.

Crevan was severely looking at both of them.

It was Lisica that finally interrupted that embarrassing moment.

-Yes, yes, guys. The reason why we attained the service of a dragon to fly to the Kingdom Of The Lion was a real and… Critical… Situation… Of Life or Death. -

Adriel didn't look at her. Dawako did.

-I understand... That is personal, I guess...-

-Your guess is correct. - Lisica answered to the not anymore very much smiley boy that, even if compared to Adriel was better able to hide it, he was dying out of curiosity all the time.

After all, both him and Adriel were twenty two and twenty years old, curiosity was a feeling that had to be understood, somehow. Especially considering the Existence they were living in.

The Circle.

A World made of mystical factors that all together were making the biggest sense of any other Dimensional Existence of all of the Universes, but, if even only the half of a small detail was going to be missed, everything was destinated to fall in chaos and eternal confusion.

-Rabbits!!- The girl with the pink hair loudly informed the four at the table.

Even Crevan jumped on his sit.

The rabbits were accompanied with some green jelly something that nobody was able to understand the nature of.

-Enjoy! -

They all looked at their plates.

-I mean, the rabbit smells and looks good... But...- And Adriel moved the strange jelly side on his plate.

-What in the Existence is this? -

The Princess had a bite.

-It is not too bad. Whatever it is. -

They all had a bite of it.

-Oh, hey... Actually... It really is... Tasty...- Dawako appreciated.

They cleaned the plates fast. Before eating they were not even that aware about how hungry they were.

The skinny boy came back to take the empty plates.

-Bread? - He asked with a slow and tired voice.

-Well… Not that we really need it anymore, now…- Dawako said.

-Oh. Ok. - The waiter replied without any real interest, and he disappeared leaving them at their at least then cleaned table.

-He is particular…- Dawako stated.

-Leave him alone, stop talking about him. - Crevan said.

They all looked at him.

-He is not a waiter. I mean. He is. But he is forced to do it. He is a prisoner. -

-What?!-

Dawako looked at Crevan more interested than ever.

-What do you mean, Commander… And how do you know…-

-This is the Town of Aedificator. It is one of the smallest Towns of the Kingdom Of The Fox, but it is probably the less friendly one. It is that small that we refer to it more as a Village. This is the place where the people that come from one of the Kingdoms of the Regions Of Darkness with the intent to cause disorder and even pain to our Kingdom, get imprisoned. -

The confusion on the two boys and the Princess' face was at its maximum level.

-I know what you are thinking. Yes, in here they let them work too, they let them serve the people that they were supposed to hurt, this is part of the punishment, they stay inside their jails, and they make them work the whole day, and then they slam them back inside. It is the way it is. -

Adriel had a look at the girl with green hair that was waiting for new customers at the entrance, while she was playing with her long nails, obviously green coloured, with her expression lost in her own thoughts, whatever her thoughts were.

-So… Even her? -

-No. She is one of us. You can recognize who is not… Who is a prisoner… They don't really talk… They sound tired and without any apparent feeling in their voice when they do… You can easily tell… The vibes… Their vibrations, guys… The energy. Their energy is not only bad. It is sick. -

While they were waiting for their Desserts, Adriel was really lost inside of his own mind, thinking about how much he wanted to ask to the Princess if the dragon that got called by King Balgair did that time come from West or from East.

But he absolutely refrained himself from pronouncing that question as it was not his intention to give out the idea that he was thinking King Balgair's Soul might have been obscure.

The ice-cream arrived at the table, carried from the girl with round glasses.

-How was your rabbit, guys? -

-Delicious. - Crevan said.

-But we were all wondering what that… Very jelly but hey, very tasty side was…-

-Oh. That is Molecula. -

-Which is…- Dawako said trying to do not sound too much intrusive.

-Just a type of musk that grows all around this Town. Very full in proteins. You came with your horses, I recognize you, Commander. I believe you all are in a journey. You will feel full and with enough strength for the next day and more with that. -

She smiled and she walked away.

-She recognized you and not me, Crevan! - The Princess laughed.

-Well, don't take it personal, my Princess... I am out here more often than what you think. -

-I'm not taking it personal at all! I was ironic, I mean... They hardly know who I am in Vixen... I'm never out...- She concluded with the shadow of a bit of sadness on her face.

They finished their Desserts and they stood up.

-Wait, we need to pay. - Adriel said.

-No, we don't. - Crevan said.

-Don't be silly, Adriel. As the Commander of the Kingdom Of The Fox, Crevan doesn't have to pay in places like Restaurants or Boarding Houses. -

Adriel found that a bit unfair, but he thought that, after all, he would have probably be entitled of the same privilege once he would have become the new Hero of his Kingdom.

They were already outside, about to get their way to their horses, when the door of the Weird Rabbit opened and the girl with green hair ran to them.

-Wait, Commander, guys! -

She gave them a big smile and she tried to give them something that was pending by her hand.

-Take. -

Crevan took what it seemed to be a decent sized black leather bag that was making the content not able to be visible.

-This is Molecula. You might need it. You have enough of it for the next days, so you should be all right in case you are out of food. You eat this and you will be able to recharge yourself. -

Crevan looked at the bag he was then holding.

-Thank you. This is very much appreciated. -

He gave a pat on her shoulder, and he smiled at her.

-Good luck. - She said.

And she made her way to the door of the Restaurant where she was working, but, before entering back inside, she stopped and she looked at them.

Her eyes were different. The sparkle was different. It was possible to see very vivid the blue eyes behind her glasses.

And she focused on Adriel.

And she then said something with apparently not even a hint of sense.

-The rings… The hair…-

Suddenly it seemed like an expression of pure lucidity got back on her face. She shook her own head rapidly and she went back inside The Weird Rabbit without looking back at them or at Adriel.

Confusion was probably the main feeling that day, apparently.

-What was that. - Crevan asked to Adriel, again, with that then very iconic and very often present severe look on his face especially, for some reason, most of the times when he was talking to Adriel.

-How am I supposed to know…-

-Yeah… How are you supposed to know, right? -

Crevan gave one last interrogative look at the boy and then he went to the horses, followed by the two boys and Princess Lisica.

They were on their horses and about to go, when Adriel's eyes had a motion of surprise.

The rings… The hair…

He remembered… But… How did the girl know…?

-Hey, son. All good? -

Crevan was studying him.

-I'm fine. -

The Commander Of The Fox was not convinced at all by the boy's answer but he decided to do not investigate too much.

They were running again, fast, on their massive horses, strong and incredibly dominant animals that were seeing no obstacles not even in front of a hurricane.

They kept riding and at that speed they were hardly say a word, but they had to when at some point they saw in front of them what seemed to be a huge lake, which it wasn't, but the burnt ground, entirely black, was completely different from the one they were coming from. And the reason why at a first sight it looked like some sort of loch, it was the fact that on the ground there were wavy movements of the air, which it was unusually thick and vaporous.

There were bad vibrations in the air all around that location.

Lisica's horse shook his head with a weird even if not too loud neigh.

-There's something down there... In the middle of that burnt field...- Dawako noticed.

And he was right.

Between the tick and deep wavy air, a massive serpent of a very profound black colour with few spots of his body of the shiniest of the greens, was there, right in the middle of the field.

It was not making a move, totally motionless.

Crevan was contemplating what he was seeing and the way he made the horse standing back was an obvious sign the level of safety was not very high in that moment.

Dawako slowly passed his hand on the hilt of his sword, but the Commander raised a hand as a clear sign to do not do that.

The clouds were covering that location far, but not extremely far from Aedificator and the rain started to fall quite heavily.

-This is bad. - Crevan said.

-Really bad. - He concluded.

Before anybody was able to formulate any kind of question, the great snake finally moved, just a little.

He slowly made a move, facing the four presents.

His eyes were very well visible through the dark smoggy air, yellow with thin pupils of a vivid red colour.

The way it was moving, very slowly, was putting even more pressure on Adriel, Dawako, Princess Lisica and the Commander Of The Fox.

The rain was falling and now a very cold wind started to fulfil the entire scene.

-Crevan, he is coming here!!-

The Princess was starting to feel not only scared but also very disgusted by the view of that huge and lucid serpentine Being moving towards them, even if at that incredible low rate.

-He will never attack us. - The Commander said.

-But we still have a big problem as he wants us to go back from where we came. He doesn't want us to go any further on our journey…-

They were looking at the unbelievable creature, in the wind, under the rain that was keeping the same intensity, falling down hard and heavy on the location and all over the presents.

Adriel wasn't a boy that used to be known for his capability to always think before to act. Sometimes it was just stronger than him, he just needed to act and, eventually, to think afterwards.

And that day was one of those days for him.

He unsheathed his sword, a very regular type of sword, and he looked attentively to the huge serpent.

-Hey, put it away, you don't know…-

- What I know and what I don't know doesn't matter in this moment. - Adriel interrupted Crevan.

-Take a look at this. -

And before the Commander or Lisica or yes, even Dawako, were able to even only try to stop him, Adriel was already several feet away from them, getting in the way of the snake's view.

Crevan raised his sword in the air, and he made it moving fast against the wind.

-Stupid boy!! Come back here!!- He yelled pointing the sword at him, waiting for something to happen that in the end didn't happen at all.

-What…-

Adriel was not hearing or seeing anything else that was not related to the snake.

And he kept walking, until he found himself right on the burnt ground that was already hosting the presence of the black and particularly shiny green creature.

The serpent stopped his slow moving and he focused, very clearly, his eyes on the boy and his black gear, simple, tight and tough that was keeping his arms completely free due to the absence of sleeves on it.

Adriel stopped too.

His mind for once was not busy, it was totally empty and quite serene.

-I don't care who you are, whoever you are. I will slay you apart. -

And he raised his sword concentrating like when during his trainings with Crevan, the Commander, that was looking at the scene with Dawako and Princess Lisica, the three of them totally unable to say or do anything due to the unexpected behaviour of Adriel that, as not able to see himself from the outside, didn't actually know what the others were seeing.

His body was weirdly releasing thick orange vapour, some sort of energy that was coming from his inside, but the act of release was intermittent, very far from being steady or continuous.

And the young man had no clue about it, he was not aware of it, he was not feeling it.

But the serpent probably did.

As a matter of fact, the creature opened his mouth and showed off his black forked tongue, but without a hiss.

The edge of Adriel's sword was starting to attire and cumulate some of the orange energy that then was coming out from Adriel's hidden self continuously and very vividly.

And Adriel was in that moment very well aware of that.

He opened his green eyes and he looked at the enormous Being that was right there, not too far from him, and he stared at him.

The snake's eyes shook a bit.

-Let's test this…- And Adriel screamed while jumping from the ground, fetching the air between himself and the serpent with his sword that released all the cumulated energy that his deep hidden self previously freed out from his body to the top of the blade of his sword.

The velocity the serpent's eyes had in their changing colours definitely seemed coming from a Being of a way superior nature as in the second that Adriel was in the air due to his jump and the energy exploded from his sword's blade, the snake's eyes inverted their colours, getting red with the thin pupils of a bright and sinister yellow and with a glare of them, the energy power that Adriel threw at him got easily and simply stopped, then making it vanishing in the nothing.

Another glare of the eyes and an invisible energy impacted against Adriel's body, making him fall many feet away, literally where the other three presents were.

-Stupid boy, what were you trying to do there? You don't even know who that Being really is...- The Commander said to the boy that just got slammed away from the burnt field with only a glare of the eyes coming from the snake.

-Hands off! - Adriel said pushing Crevan's hands away.

-Excuse me? -

-I said hands off! - The boy repeated with a look full of anger on his face.

-I don't know who that creature is as you say, because you never tell anything, you barely do! Yes, I do not know who that beast is but it doesn't matter as I will cut his head off in the middle of that burnt ground! -

The wind was raging way more than before and the rain started to fall in a sandy consistence.

The whole Environment got blurred for a good bunch of seconds, before getting back to the usual form of it.

And the snake, completely out of nowhere, started to slowly abandon the ground, levitating in the windy air, the thick dark air that was waving like the water of a lake, that was following the creature, leaving the ground as well, surrounding the serpent's figure at that point already far enough from the surface of that location.

-Adriel. You don't have to show anything. Not now... Not in this situation... Not against him...-

They all looked at the snake floating in the air.

-What... What now, then...- An already less upset Adriel asked.

It was obvious that the young boy had moments where he was not able to think with rationality, and in other moments he was perfectly able to understand the nature of every single situation.

And the Commander Of The Fox knew that well. That was the reason why he didn't make a big deal about the crazy and angry reaction Adriel had few instants before. He really would have not permit that to anybody else.

-Now… Now you leave it to me…- Crevan answered.

The big creature started to have a very radiant amaranth Aura all around of his own figure, that made the black wavy air vanish away.

Then there was a brilliant Aura all around him that was making him look like something of a Holy nature shining right there in the middle between the ground and the sky.

The Commander made his sword rotating in the air, the face hard and secure, the chains attached to his gear clattering and producing some sort of ominous sound and his sword quickly turned of a very bright white light and he pointed it to the creature, releasing all of that energy.

The amaranth Aura that was surrounding the incredible Being started then to rotate around him and the energy power Crevan released directed to him, got pushed away in the air leaving the snake untouched and totally free from any kind of hurt.

But Crevan didn't stop to charge his sword with his deepest power and even the Commander, like the serpent, started to be surrounded by his Aura, white, almost transparent, like the lightful energy his sword was capable to release.

The beams that were exploding out from his sword were increasing in power and intensity, but the rotating Aura of the serpent was making Crevan's surely great power look like not much more than the flashy rays of transparent light that in fact they were, and it became pretty clear that Crevan's attacks were not a matter of danger for the creature's Life. Not at all.

But the Life of the four presents coming from the Kingdom Of The Fox was seeming pretty much in danger when then the snake opened his mouth generating a bright purple ball of energy that was crossed by tiny little lightnings that were giving to the whole scene an even more sensation of imminent endangerment.

The ball of energy was getting bigger and bigger and at that point the Commander Of The Fox stopped to throw lights of energy at the monster due to the inefficacy of his own power against what seemed to be the reason of the end of their days.

-Let's just go away! Let's go back, Commander! - Dawako yelled over the raging wind.

-We need to go, NOW!!- Princess Lisica yelled, too.

-It's too late. - Crevan said. His voice not more than a whisper but everyone was able to hear him very well.

-What... How...-

-Yes, Adriel... You decided to attack him. You decided to be the Hero you are not yet and well, most definitely, you will never be. You sent him the message we had no intention to step back, to go back. You attacked him. And that was the end of his peaceful presence. Now, because of your actions, Adriel...-

And the Commander looked inside those then frightened and desperate green eyes.

-Now he will kill us all. - Crevan concluded.

He then looked up in the air, staring at the serpent.

-But why... What was your interest in this...? - He murmured more to himself than to the snake.

At that point the ball of energy reached a size big enough to cancel whatever was in that location, whatever and whoever.

-I am not... I am not the cause of this...-

-What...- Crevan interrupted the stare at the snake to face Adriel, that was keeping his head down, making impossible to see his face, as he was facing the ground beneath his feet.

-I am not the cause of this... You are...-

Crevan was not believing his ears and so Dawako and the Princess.

-Adriel, what are you doing...-

But the Commander's sentence got interrupted by the view of Adriel raising his head and showing his face, the eyes of a bright orange colour and a small pupil that was almost impossible to spot.

And those eyes were shining vividly and with an expression of total control.

-You are the reason why we are in this situation... You should tell us more... To make us ready... We need to know... The mysteries of The Circle...-

He then looked up to the incredible purple energy that would have been released in the matter of few instants, directed to them and the entire vastity of that area.

-Hello, monster. Today you were so close to win. -

Dawako was speechless, Lisica was strangely calm with a sort of expression made of curiosity that was studying Adriel's mysterious behaviour.

Her horse that earlier was keeping stomping his hoofs and producing some very weird neighs, became strangely calm, attentively staring at the scene of Adriel looking up to the huge black and bright green serpent.

-So close to win...- Adriel continued, talking to the Being, while a thin orange smoky vapour was flaming around his body.

-But you didn't. -

And on those words, his eyes turned back to his natural green colour, and he fell on the ground, completely fainted.

-What is going on?!- Dawako yelled.

The guy that normally had his bright white smile as his iconic way to charm was then very far from being that airy, as what was pictured on his good looking face was the expression of fear and confusion due to what just happened to his even more good looking rival.

Crevan went down on his knees to hold the fainted boy.

-I don't understand… What's happening… What's happening… Guys… I don't know anymore…- He said, the eyes unusually wet and red.

-I am sorry. -

And he kept holding Adriel, that was completely unaware that in that very meantime the Existence was still going on even without him being part of it in a conscious way.

It was then a matter of seconds, even less, and the serpent would have made his unbelievable amount of power exploding on Crevan, the Princess Of The Fox, Dawako and the unconscious Adriel.

Wind, raining sand that was affecting the visibility of everything that was around but, somehow, the snake was remaining very well visible, his amaranth Aura still rotating around his figure, even faster than before, his energy ready to finally detonate on the four people coming from Vixen and from Renard, once and forever.

Crevan looked at Lisica and Dawako and then back at Adriel.

-I apologise. Princess. Dawako. Adriel… But this is an obstacle way above my level. -

Crevan, the Commander of the Kingdom Of The Fox, invited Dawako and even the Princess to join him close to Adriel's alive but senseless body, with a gesture of his arms.

They both united with him and the boy that would have been Dawako's rival in the probably breath taking duel that would have been deciding the next and new Hero Of The Fox.

They hugged, they were not looking at each other but not even at the serpent anymore, it was just the end, they were looking at the ground, less thoughts inside of their minds than what they were expecting to have while experiencing such a dramatic situation as the one they were encountering in that moment.

When even shiner shadows of lights illuminated the then very dark cloudy location, the Commander, Dawako and the Princess thought it was just the final bright moment of the serpent's energy before the deliverance of it, but when they kept feeling and noticing the brightness of even more flashes of light which warmness was felt strongly and insistent all over their bodies, they then looked up where the creature was and that's when they saw a burst of white fire flames that were going to hit the ball of energy in front of the monstrous Being's mouth, one after one.

And then his mouth got hit too, one, two, three, four, and many more several times.

The exclamation of surprise that came out from the three inhabitants of Vixen, got followed by an even louder exclamation of pure stupefaction when they turned their head to take a look behind them, realising from who those powerful white fire flames were coming from.

A majestic, sublime fox of the size of a horse was standing tall behind them, throwing those fiery beams of energy precisely directed against the centre of the lavender-coloured sphere of energy produced by the massive serpent Being.

The fox was launching the powerful white fire flames with a slowly and enchanting movement of the paws.

The combination of the fox's slow movements and the extreme velocity the fiery energy was speeding at, then colliding with the snake's mystical power, was striking.

The great fox had a candid white gleaming all around herself and it got even brighter in the meantime the beams that were getting launched by her paws got bigger and stronger, that stronger that the purple sphere up in the sky was reducing hit after hit, apparently unable to get released due to those attacks that were actually also functioning as a stunning defence.

Sooner than what was expected by Crevan, Lisica and Dawako, the energy power of the black and shiny green snake reduced fast until it totally vanished in front of the still opened mouth of the floating beast.

For the first time since his appearance, a loud and frightening hiss came out from his mouth, the forked tongue avidly moving as its only need in that moment was to get the taste of some of whoever's blood, whoever's warm Lifeblood.

The fox loaded a big amount of white energy on her right paw, and she threw it in the direction of the floating serpent and that was most definitely the biggest flame of pure and white fire she had ever thrown since her advent into the scene.

The lightful beam was launched, the impact was inevitable, it was a matter of seconds, it was fast, it was closer to the target, and…

Suddenly the rain stopped, the wind howled away, the serpent was disappeared, and the last, massive, white fire beam instantly ended up in smoke, vanishing into the nowhere, far, up in the sky.

The fox was still there, the white Aura still shining around her figure, staring in front of the little group of people that were still looking at her amazed and confused like probably never before in their entire Existence.

She clearly sent a look at Crevan.

-You saved us…-

But after he said that, the fox looked at the still senseless body of Adriel, still laying in the Commander's arms.

And then she looked back at Crevan.

-Or…-

The majestic animal looked then at the Princess' horse, and she stared at him for a moment, with the horse apparently pleased by that look as his neigh was a lovely sound that reminded a mystic melody.

A move of her tail and, literally out of nowhere, the fox vanished.

An instant after that, Adriel moved and Crevan exclaimed out of joy and surprise.

-Adriel!!-

The boy sat on the ground. He appeared quite not sure about what happened or what it was actually going on.

-Hey, Adriel!! How do you feel!!- Lisica said with what sounded like an exclamation more than a question.

-I'm not sure...- He said looking at her.

He thought he was already feeling better, but that was only an illusion.

His whole body was hurting. His eyes were itchy.

-My eyes... Are itchy...-

The Commander looked at Dawako and the Princess, shaking his head slowly as a clear sign to do not mention anything in particular about when his eyes turned of that incredible orange colour and his pupils were not bigger than the hole of a tailor's needle.

-Hey, wait a moment! - Adriel then said, getting a more focused look on his face.

-The serpent. Where the snake is?! You, Commander, killed him?! Or...- And he looked at Dawako.

-No, none of us did it, man. - The rival answered in a lazy way, but, inside of himself, not too disappointed about the fact the guy he liked less than anybody else on that Planet was actually starting to feel better.

-Well... If none of you did it... Then, who...-

Lisica looked behind him.

-A very unexpected help came to save us, Adriel. -

-A what... Who came...? -

The Princess looked at Crevan.

The Commander looked down.

-A fox of the size of a horse, Adriel. This is all I can say. - And she left giving a severe look at Crevan, heading back to her horse to then caress his amazing long and light blue mane.

With huge surprise of the Commander, Adriel didn't ask anything straight away, but, instead, he showed a big smile on his face, while looking at the spot in the air where minutes before the huge serpent was about to erase all of them.

-Oh well, the fact you are smiling is a good sign, I guess. - Dawako sarcastically said and he then left giving a confused look at his apparently very glad rival.

When Lisica and Dawako were not close anymore, Adriel finally spoke.

-Commander. -

-What. -

Crevan knew too well that at some point some questions would have been leaving Adriel's mouth, but he certainly didn't expect that the nature of the upcoming question would have been that strange and, somehow, shocking.

-Commander… A great sized fox, yeah? And… By any chance… Was that fox able to generate white fire flames from both of her paws? -

The Commander's face pictured an expression difficult to name or to explain, something in between the astonish and the dubious.

-You were senseless the whole time she was in here… How do you know she was able to do that…-?

Adriel looked at him, the big smile still on his beautiful face, his eyes way greener than usual due to the lovely rays of Sun that were getting back all around the previously dark environment, making the whole area appear way more friendly and welcoming than before.

-Let's say I was just supposing she was able to. - He answered.

He then got serious, all at once.

-The truth is… I have never told you, but… I see the same type of fox in my dreams, every Equinox and every Solstice, literally four times every year. -

And he stood up, facing Crevan, looking inside of his eyes, concluding his sentence.

-Since twenty years. -

IX

<u>THE CIRCLE</u>

The whole topic regarding the events of the day remained unspoken, firstly due to the continuously riding fast with the intention to be at the Kingdom Of The Wolf in few days, so long breaks during the daytime were out of question, secondly due to the still very present feeling of perplexity generated by those happenings.

Way after the Sunset, the time to rest finally arrived.

They were finding themselves in an open space where fresh grass was expanding its very pleasant smell.

The vastity of that area was more than decent and it was very characteristic the presence of few trees which leaves were of an incredible deep kind of orange, even if in Spring.

-I like those trees. They look a bit out of Season, though. -

-Their colour is not a matter of Season, Adriel. That is their regular colour. The whole year. They don't even lose their leaves in Winter.-

Crevan was laying his back on the grass and everyone else did the same.

The sky was dark blue, the stars were quilting it with harmony and the sensation of beauty was finally pretty high in the air around the four passengers from the Towns of Vixen and Renard.

There were also those dusty icy grains far away up in the sky, but very well visible during those extremely clear nights of Spring or Summer, where everything that was present in the airspace, and the airspace itself, was looking brighter than usual, or, actually, brighter than what it really was.

-It seems like they are moving... But I think they are steady...- Dawako said looking at them.

-Wrong. - Crevan said with a sleepy voice.

-They are moving and also really fast. -

-You have never been there, Crevan. - The Princess laughed.

The Commander had a moment where he didn't know what to answer, then he murmured something.

-Yeah... Right... I have never been there...-

Adriel was still feeling very energic.

After the events of the day, Crevan gave him a good bit of Molecula and that did really hit well on him.

They only enjoyed some cheese and bread they had with them, they were still pretty full from the lunch at The Weird Rabbit that, they thought, it was not only giving away big portions of food, but that tiny bit of Molecula they used to serve with the rabbit was probably enough to make people feel full until the day after without the need of having dinner.

And Adriel probably had too much of it that day but after all Crevan didn't think he did exaggerate due to the condition the boy was because of what happened to him during the encounter with the huge serpent.

-Commander? -

Crevan looked at Adriel.

-What, now? -

Adriel took a little pause to carefully think about how to formulate his very specific question.

-Would you mind telling us more about The Circle? -

That question found the agreement of Princess Lisica, that left her laying position to comfortably sit and the same did Dawako that in that moment was hating himself very much to find Adriel's question more than legitimate.

-Oh, you are unbelievable…-

Crevan sat on the spot where he was laying an instant before.

-Bring me the Styx. - He ordered to Adriel.

The boy happily stood up and ran to Crevan's horse.

There was a big bag that was carrying some food, the same bag from where they tapped into hours before to get their dinner made of cheese and bread.

Closer to that bag there was the black leather one the girl with the green hair from Aedificator gave them with the Molecula inside.

And right on the left of that, there was another bag, a silk one, with a bottle inside.

Adriel brought it to the Commander.

-Styx. If I have to stay awake the next thirty minutes talking about things I would prefer not to, at least I will do it with pleasure. -

The Styx was an infuse of cinnamon and oranges, mixed with the purest alcohol.

But the secret ingredient was a little stone, a type of stone very easy to find under the ground of the fields of the Kingdom Of The Fox, that had the power to eliminate the property of the alcohol to make the people drunk, but without altering his savour.

Styx was in detail the name of the stone.

-So, what do you wish to know…? - He asked having his first sip directly from the bottle.

-More. Just more. -

Adriel was so enthusiastic that was affecting even Dawako in the impatience to discover more about their World.

The Princess Of The Fox was definitely interested in that kind of conversation too, but she was more calm, without that visible kind of excitement that was in that moment so much alive inside and outside the two boys.

-The Circle. - Crevan mumbled.

-I can tell you I wish one day you will all be able to go to the Regions Of Light, well, actually our Princess has already been there...-

-Yes, she went to the Kingdom Of The Lion... But I don't know much about it... I also know the names of the other Kingdoms... But again, I have no clue about their characteristics...-

Adriel was all ears.

-Well, so you know the Kingdom Of The Lion is at West of the Regions Of Light. Its King is King Lander. One of the strongest Kings I have ever been pleased to personally meet. At East of those Regions, we have the Kingdom Of The Dove. That is the only Kingdom of The Circle that is ruled by a Queen, a Queen without a King. -

-Queen Layleen. - Lisica specified.

-Indeed. If the Kingdom Of The Lion has strength as its main Principle, the Kingdom Of The Dove has, instead, hope. Hope is the main Principle of that Kingdom, which power is way higher than what you will probably ever be able to understand. -

The Styx was keeping giving company to the Commander, that had few more sips.

-You can drink faster, that won't make you drunk. - Dawako laughed.

They all had a nice laugh and then Crevan was ready to keep going with his speech about The Circle.

-In the middle of the Regions Of Light we have their most powerful Kingdom and, possibly, the strongest Kingdom of the whole vastity of The Circle.-

-The Kingdom Of The Eagle. - This time was not Princess Lisica being prepared about some knowledge about their World.

Dawako was the one that mentioned that.

-King Lysander…-

Crevan smiled.

-Correct. The greatest one. We can talk about every single King of any Kingdom of The Circle and their unbelievable and unthinkable skills and countless different powers, countless of them, but there is no King that can say he is a match for King Lysander. -

Crevan looked deeper inside the sky.

-Silverlight…-

-What is that? - Adriel asked.

-His sword. - Dawako answered in total excitement.

-The strongest sword ever made. -

Adriel listened to Dawako without looking at him, but the ecstasy was very high inside of him.

Such a powerful King… And also the Master of the strongest sword ever made in the World. The strongest sword of The Circle.

-And…-

Adriel was ready to expose his next question, but Crevan interrupted him answering straight away without the need to listen to it.

-Freedom. -

Adriel was not expecting Crevan to anticipate his question with the connected answer.

-Oh…-

-Freedom. The main Principle of the Kingdom Of The Eagle is freedom. -

Dawako stood up just a bit due to the need to stretch his legs.

-And then, us. In the middle, the Silvery Lands. -

And Crevan approved.

-Obviously! - And he smiled.

-We are the Neutral Regions indeed, but that doesn't mean we are weak. Actually, it is the opposite. You see... Being neutral means we can potentially join the Forces of one of the two Main Regions if we like...-

-Which puts us at their same level. - The Princess concluded.

-Very much correct. -

Then, even Crevan stood up. The air was very chill and all the four of them were enjoying every single breath of that mesmerizing and crispy air.

-What do you know about the Regions Of Darkness? -

Crevan's question got the two boys and even the Princess with a feeling of surprise.

It was an unexpected question, but Lisica answered before Adriel and Dawako.

-I know the Kingdom Of The Scorpion. - She said with simplicity.

It was the Commander's turn to be surprised, then.

-No, I haven't been in there. - She also said predicting the most logic following question that most definitely would have come from one of the three other people from the Kingdom Of The Fox.

-It was years ago... I was still a very little girl. King Anthares came to the Castle ones. -

The Commander was silently looking at her.

-I know he did. So, you were there. -

-And you weren't. -

The way the Princess pronounced that last sentence left Crevan with not much to say.

There was a strange tension in the air at that point, which was not able to be explained by Adriel or Dawako.

-I was away because your father sent me somewhere that day. That is why I wasn't there, Princess. -

Princess Lisica looked at Crevan, and she walked towards him until she got right in front of him.

-Sure. That is what he said too. -

Unexpectedly, the Commander broke the eye contact, unable to handle it.

He then scratched his short beard and looked at the two boys.

-And what do you know about the Regions Of Darkness? -

Dawako was the first speaking this time.

-The Kingdom Of The Owl. A Kingdom that has its main Principle in Knowledge. -

-Very well. While the Kingdom Of The Scorpion is a Kingdom that is pure destruction, which is also its leading Principle, the Kingdom Of The Owl is based on the more polite Principle of the knowledge of the many mystical mysteries of The Circle.-

-So... They are like the ones that know the most about our Existence...-

Adriel was thinking loud.

-Possibly. -

Crevan indulged a moment on Princess Lisica, that was then not even being part of the conversation anymore, back to her horse, petting his mane.

After few seconds of silence, the Commander then announced.

-Here we are. One more Kingdom is part of those Regions, lands I hope you will never have to find yourself in all of your Life. -

Adriel was being sure his ears were well connected to Crevan's voice, waiting to hear more about...

-The Kingdom Of The Serpent. -

The fascination was probably very well visible on Adriel's face, as Dawako looked at him in a not very good way.

-What is that excitement about, dude? -

Adriel realised at that point his sensations were obvious, but it was stronger than him.

-I have only had the chance to hear about that Kingdom in few occasions... Once from my mother... I obviously don't fancy... Anything... About it...-

-But you really feel somehow fascinated by it. Is it right? -

Crevan asked looking at him.

-Right. -

Crevan smiled, with the surprise of Dawako but even more of Adriel, that was expecting the Commander to get mad over it.

-I understand. It is very common. Normal. Everyone is somehow attracted by it. It is because of its mysterious and unknown kind of Existence. Yes, unknown even to the Kingdom Of The Owl. - He added, predicting that would have been a very possible question coming from one of the two boys, especially Adriel.

-We could say...- The Commander told the two rivals.

-The Kingdom Of The Serpent is by far the most mystical and mysterious Kingdom of The Circle. The most unknow one of all of our Dimensional Existence. -

-Do we at least know their main Principle? - Adriel asked, that expression of excitement still well pictured all over his face.

-Sure, we do know that. - Crevan said.

-Immortality. -

The Commander's final part of the answer succeeded to make an expression of genuine pleasure even on Dawako's face.

The two boys were still assimilating the information Crevan just finished to tell them, when, completely randomly, Princess Lisica came back on the scene, adding something regarding the Kingdom Of The Serpent.

-Why don't you tell them about the particularity of the Castle of that Kingdom, Crevan? -

It was very rare to spot expressions of pure surprise on Crevan's face, but it was seeming like Princess Lisica was always able to make that happen.

Suddenly Adriel and Dawako, avid for more, stared at their Commander without even asking him to talk about that topic just came out from the Princess' mouth, they were just waiting, they were waiting like they were not even aware on which Planet they were living anymore, totally focused on all those secrets about the Kingdom Of The Serpent, completely disconnected from all the rest that was part of The Circle.

-Well. - The Commander said, slowly.

-Their Castle. The bigger I have ever seen... Between all the Kingdoms we have been talking about until now... Dark... Shiny green shadows coming from everywhere and even from nowhere... Their Castle... Invisible... Unless they want you to see it... Because they want you inside there...-

The level of pure fascination in Adriel and then even Dawako's eyes was then reaching a kind of high level that would have been extremely difficult to match.

-The most dangerous Kingdom in this Existence. -

He concluded.

Princess Lisica walked close to Adriel.

-Not only that. Even if you find yourself in there, with the Castle getting visible for you because you are wanted inside for whatever reason, doesn't mean you will be able to somehow remember the location where you found it to try to reach it a second time. -

That sounded a bit too confused to Adriel to refrain himself from questioning his own Princess.

-What that exactly means? -

-It means…- Crevan answered instead.

-Their Castle never appears in the same location. In fact, it doesn't have a location at all. -

Dawako was speechless as much as his rival.

-Incredible…-

And the Commander agreed with a nod of his head.

-You will never be able to find them. If you are in their Kingdom, they will find you. If they want to. -

And after that new revelation from him to the two boys, as the Princess of the Kingdom Of The Fox was appearing to already know enough about that very particular topic, Crevan went back lying on the grass where his bottle of Styx was lying too, but without the Commander having the desire to drink more of that.

Dawako walked his way to his horse to lay down close to him.

Lisica did the same, while Adriel remained there, sitting, not far from Crevan that already had his eyes closed.

The green-eyed pretty boy decided then that maybe was time to lay down for him too.

-Adriel. - The unexpected call of the Commander.

-Yes? -

Few instants made of silence followed Adriel's voice, then Crevan spoke once again.

-I have something to ask you. -

Adriel waited, silently.

He knew there was no need to tell the Commander to keep going on asking him whatever he wanted as he was obviously going to do that anyway.

-When you woke up from unconsciousness… You said something about your dreams… Can you… Can you remind me what you have said, Adriel…? -

It was unusual, but for once it was Crevan starving to know something from Adriel and not the other more common way round.

-I was saying… I do very, let's say… Singular dreams every Equinox and every Solstice…-

-Since twenty years, you also said…-

-Yes. I did say that. -

At that point some silent pause was more than normal due to the kind of topic Crevan and Adriel were facing in their conversation.

In that moment, the air started to get colder.

-You are twenty years old, Adriel. - Crevan stated.

-How can you remember your dreams, even if only in those four occasions every year, when you were one or two years old for example? -

Adriel felt a little upset, as he felt like Crevan was doubting his words.

-I recognise it sounds not very normal. But I do. I do remember those dreams. And actually, in the details. Even if there are parts of those dreams that are just very confused. -

The Commander Of The Fox was listening carefully and with interest.

-So, you are saying you saw a fox that throws white flames of fire in most of your dreams? -

The boy got then a pensive expression on his face.

-Not in most of my dreams. - And he looked at Crevan before finishing his pronouncement.

-I see that fox in every single one of them. -

The more Adriel was answering to his questions, the more Crevan was feeling confused but at the same time with a hint of understanding about something Adriel would have never been able to comprehend.

-And tell me, Adriel... The fox... To who she throws her fiery beams at? Have you ever been able to notice that? -

-I can not see. - Adriel answered.

-The huge fox throws her fiery energy all around and not specifically to something or someone. -

Before Crevan found something else to ask, Adriel spoke again.

-I just always find myself in the same place... A place I don't know... Extremely dark... Nothing around... Not even the sky is present in the location I always find myself in those dreams... The ground dusty and burnt...-

That was something the Commander decided to don't reply at.

Adriel rolled himself on the soft grass, beautiful and green, even if not as green as his eyes.

-I think I will try to sleep. - He said while looking at the dusty icy grains that were seeming so steady but, in fact, Crevan said they were actually, apparently, moving faster than a Being could ever imagine.

It was extremely enchanting the fact they were so unbelievably far but at the same time it was seeming like they really were so close, mainly due to their astonishing brightness.

When Adriel was about to close his eyes under that spectacular and relaxing view, the Commander Of The Fox called his name one more time.

-Can I ask you one last thing? -

That would have been a day to remember, that was for sure. The Commander never had so many questions for him since he first met him many years ago.

He was too tired even to giggle because of that, but he agreed at that last question.

-Sure. -

Crevan had a deep breath.

-Any other particular… Unusual factor… That normally happens in your dreams? -

Adriel had a thought and he answered, the voice suddenly having a very well awake sound back.

-Actually, there is something… But… It is not about what happens in my dreams. It's about what happens every single time, straight away, in the exact meantime I wake up. –

-And… What is that…? -

Crevan waited, then holding his breath until Adriel revealed what that something was.

-Roses. -

The Commander sat so fast that Adriel thought he actually jumped.

-What?!- He asked, a bit surprised by the man's reaction.

-Say that again… What have you just said…? -

The young boy was not sure how to explain Crevan's very strange reaction.

-I said roses. A very strong and intense smell of roses all around in the meantime I wake up. -

The Commander thought very well about the words to choose for the sentence he was about to say, and Adriel noticed that.

-Well... Is your mother in love with roses, maybe? She maybe puts them in your room to give a great smell to it...? I don't understand... What's strange and unusual about that, Adriel...? -

He focused inside Adriel's eyes.

Adriel held the eye contact without a blink.

-Roses in my room, you say. -

Adriel's green eyes flashed for a moment.

-My father can not stand the presence of roses. That is the reason why not even one single rose has ever been seen anywhere inside and even outside of my house. -

X

SLOW MOTION

The Throne Hall was extremely dark.

The few candles around, some of them even stuck on the floor, were the only origin of light inside there.

From some indefinite point the rain was falling down and the sound of it hitting the pavement was very well audible.

A little mouse had a quick run from a wall to another, disappearing through a hole that was leading to who knows where.

A man, a big old man, was sitting on the Throne.

It was a very massive Throne and the man that was sitting on it, even if of a big size, was not enough to fulfil the whole sit.

It was all made out of bronze, and it looked very transcendental.

The man that was sitting on it, was touching his beard, black and white, and he was touching it slowly.

His pale blue eyes were looking at a not very specific point in front of him, like he was thinking lost in whatever was going on inside of his mind.

He was wearing a very heavy armour, dark brown, and his Crown was made out of bronze exactly like the Throne, his Throne.

But the Crown, compared to the Throne, had a very unique particular.

It was simple, nothing ornamental with the only exception of the Gem that was stuck right in the middle of it, a violet Amethyst, that was shining of a mystical and spectral kind of light.

The King stopped to touch his beard.

The sound of the rain dripping down from the ceiling inside the room, was giving to the scene an even heavier sensation of tension and remote.

-My glass is empty. - The King said to someone not well visible due to the lack of light inside the room.

-I am going to fulfil it, Your Majesty. - A low voice answered.

The sound of few steps, some clattering and the unmistakable sound of something liquid hitting the bottom of a glass.

Glass then handed, slowly and solemnly to the King, hailed with a bow right after that.

-Much appreciated, Ulmuka. - The King said.

-It is an honour for me, my King. -

The King sipped something of whatever he was drinking, without breaking the eye contact with that unclear point in front of him.

-The taste of knowledge... Have you ever experienced it, Ulmuka?-

The man looked at his King.

-No, Your Majesty, I have never had the pleasure...-

-Of course you didn't. The nectar of knowledge is a treat sophisticatedly made only for me...-

The King took another sip of his drink.

His glass was made from ebony wood.

Ulmuka remained silent.

-You see, Ulmuka. This is the difference between being a King and being a Commander. -

He moved his head just a little bit, for a moment it looked like he was looking for someone, or for something, but his pale blue eyes didn't really move.

-You are a strong and respected Commander, Ulmuka. Everyone likes you in the Kingdom. Everyone cheers for you. Every time you come back from some mission or some extraordinary duty, everyone in the Kingdom is always waiting for you, impatient to welcome you back home. In our Kingdom you are the people's favourite, no doubts about that. -

The Commander was keeping his silence, looking down to the ground, remaining on his position, with his perfect posture.

-They have never liked me as much as they have always been liking you. - The King kept saying, then clearly moving his head in Ulmuka's direction, still keeping his eyes wide open, not even a blinking coming from them.

-I am sure, my King, the people of our Kingdom... Your Kingdom... I am sure they like you very much...-

The King had an annoyed sarcastic expression on his face after those words.

-No. You are wrong. They do not. -

He said those words in a way that was clearly meaning he was not going to accept any other kind of contradiction.

-Yes, Your Majesty. - Ulmuka said, very rapidly, keeping his eyes down.

-But...- The King kept saying.

-That doesn't matter... Because even if they love you... And even if they hate me... You are the one that fulfils my glass, Ulmuka. -

And he strongly held his glass before finishing his sentence.

-And I am the one that drinks from it. -

Ulmuka gave a bite to his own lip.

-Yes, my King. -

The rain was dripping faster inside the room, still in some indefinite spot inside of the Throne Hall.

-I can't see, Ulmuka. - The Kings said.

-But I can feel. -

He then left the glass falling from his hand, slamming on the ground, close to his Throne.

-My eyes are blind... But my sensations are not...-

Then the air changed. It got colder than how it already was. The rain that was hitting the ground of the Throne Hall suddenly started to fall in slow motion.

Ulmuka had to open his mouth as the air got much heavier to breath and his whole breathing process got slower and very difficult to manage.

At the same time, the King got surrounded by a brown Aura and his hands were the main part of his body that were loading the biggest amount of that gleaming dark energy.

-Tell me, Ulmuka... What the most important Principle of this Kingdom is? -

In that moment even his voice sounded slower and deeper. And far... He was sounding like his voice was coming from another floor of the Castle, echoed, but still very audible, coming from every single corner of the Throne Hall.

Ulmuka, that was still battling with himself to be able to breath, managed to answer, somehow.

-Knowledge... Your Majesty... It is... Knowledge...-

The rainy precipitation that was coming from the ceiling not too far from them, was then taking several seconds before reaching the pavement.

-Indeed. -

A little tremble of the ground.

The mouse that earlier got inside the hole in the wall, was about to attempt another run across the room, but he had to give up due to the surreal and dangerous vibrations that were generating inside the room, and he just ran back through the same way he just came from.

Ulmuka fell on his knees, the new heaviness of the air was suffocating him.

-It… It was ten years ago… Your Majesty… Please…-

The King revealed the angriest expression on his face Ulmuka had ever seen before.

-And it still bothers me…-

Then everything got calm.

The air went back to its regular consistence, becoming easily breathable once again.

Everything that was having a movement went back to its regular motion, including the mysterious rain that nobody exactly knew from where it was coming from, as outside the sky was clear without even the presence of a single cloud.

Ulmuka fell on the floor, finally able to breath normally, but still feeling the pain inside of his chest due to the incredible strength he had to use to be able to at least breath some minimum amounts of air, few instants before, when the whole environment became heavy and painful.

The voice of the King was back to normality too, very clear, present, and right there, right there in front of Ulmuka's tired body.

-Knowledge… Knowledge is everything for the Kingdom Of The Owl, Ulmuka. -

He paused only for a moment, to pass his hand on his beard.

-And after ten long years it is my will to add some very important details to your knowledge…-

Ulmuka was at that point able to breath almost normally, but his hand was still on his chest, while being able to sit, carefully, on the floor where until an instant before was still gasping for air.

-I know you like the boy… But it is important we get sure he doesn't succeed… You need to get rid of that good Soul of yours, Ulmuka… You have to get rid of it…-

Ulmuka was listening very carefully, without saying a word.

-Because, Ulmuka, if your good Soul will make you fail again in the upcoming duty that I will soon order you to do…-

In that moment the King Of The Owl looked down not too far from his Throne, clearly pointing his violent blind eyes at the Commander.

-I will kill you. -

XI

THE COLOUR OF BLOOD

The evening was mildly surrounding the dark Town of Ogle and the blurry sky was impossible to be described with accuracy.

Ogle was a Town where obscurity and fear was around every corner, and it was a sort of vibe that was impossible to do not feel for whoever was about to be in there for a reason or for another.

But if somebody was putting his feet in that unsafe location, he definitely had to have a very important and proper reason to do so.

Even if it was the main Town, Ogle was a place without high or huge buildings. It was a very flat City and full of tight and small little alleys. The crime and the high level of danger in Ogle was well known to the entirety of The Circle and the people that were living in there had clearly written in their faces that goodness or kindness were not two feelings part of their Personalities.

The one and only building that was majestically ruling over the whole Town was the Castle, from the edge of what was probably a mountain, black mountains were the only view around Ogle, but it was not easy to precisely tell where the Castle was standing on as, whatever the surface was, it was completely covered by a massive, giant dark cloud, permanently enlightened by lightings that were not followed by any thunder for the most of the time. Only every now and then, occasionally, it would have been possible to hear a few rumbling thunders coming from there, but they would have not last for more than a decent bunch of seconds.

The Castle was darker than the mountains that were surrounding it.

It was almost dinner time at the Castle, but something was troubling the whole environment.

-I need you to find her. I need you to find her right now, Chrysanthe. -

-I will do my best, my Queen. -

The woman's voice sounded angry, even if her speaking was low and apparently calm.

-Your best is not enough. You have to do way more than your best. Or… We will all be in serious troubles…-

Her eyes were of the same colour of the light, and they were shining in two different intensities of that light, one was pure and pale, the other one was more intense and bright and the two different lightful versions of those eyes were exchanging themselves in an intermittent way.

However, even if light coloured, the Queen's eyes were giving a sensation of danger, a feeling of imminent risk.

Even so, that was an evening where Queen Nova, the Queen of the Kingdom Of The Scorpion, was experiencing a feeling that extremely rarely was growing inside of herself.

Fear.

-I understand, my Queen. I will do way more than my best. - The boy that was standing in front of her, said.

-I will find her. -

Chrysanthe was wearing a tight and black vest and his sword was greatly tightened around his hip.

He was wearing light clothes, his black hair were almost hiding his eyes, of a silvery grey colour.

Queen Nova was an enchanting woman, a kind of beauty incredibly pure and also tremendously cruel, all at the same time.

Her long red hair were seeming to carry the sparkle of fire wherever she was going.

That evening she was wearing a long satin blue dress that was matching more than amazingly with the unicity of her hair.

She looked at Chrysanthe and she spoke.

-Go. -

She then looked severely at the young man bowing down and then disappearing down the stairs that were leading into the Main Hall, where the door to go out from the Castle was.

Queen Nova stayed there, staring then at the stairs and lost deep inside her thoughts.

Chrysanthe had to find her… He had to find that little rebel, the Princess, her daughter… Otherwise when dinner time was going to come, it would have been a very serious problem.

She tried to distract herself walking down the corridor where she was in that moment, to reach the window, having a look outside.

The lights were turned on in Ogle, every house, every bar, every restaurant, every indoor place. Far, somewhere on the mountains, flames of fire were raging, but without burning anything, without even expanding themselves.

The blurry sky was still not able to be detailed. Impossible to say if it was cloudy or clear.

Impossible to say with precision what time it was.

If a clock or anything that was signing the time was not present or in possession of whoever was wondering what time it was, it would have even been impossible to tell if it was daytime or night time.

Because it didn't matter what time of the day it was, or what moment of the night it was, the sky over Ogle and over the entirety of the Kingdom Of The Scorpion, was always the same.

Dark.

Darker than the deepest corners of the Outer Space.

Dark.

But not darker than the Soul of the people that were living under of it.

++

Ogle had a spacious square, very empty, if not for a very huge statue representing a scorpion right in the middle of it.

The statue was entirely made of Black Gold.

The posture of the scorpion, in the position ready to attack with his poisonous tail, was giving to the whole statue a very powerful image and the whole square itself was seeming like to give out very bad and negative energies and for that reason, even the angry and dangerous people of Ogle were trying to avoid finding themselves walking around there, if possible.

However, that evening there was an unusual amount of people gathering around there as, pretty obviously, something very exciting was seeming to be going on.

Chrysanthe made his way through the people that were covering the view of whatever was happening in there, in Acrab Square.

-Excuse me... Thank you... Pardon me... I'm so sorry...-

Somehow, he reached the middle of the square right where the Black Gold statue representing the attacking scorpion was, and what he saw made his blood freezing.

In the middle of the scene there was a young man on his knees without any upper vest, covered only by some old trousers and a pair of broken boots.

He was not simply on his knees, he was bowing down, and the man he was bowing down to was standing tall in front of him, completely dressed in tight leather, with a belt with a big buckle representing a scorpion identical to the one of the statue, and its material was majestic Black Gold as well.

Long dark hair, his face of the most gentle of the features, however, there was something sinister about the light that he was presenting inside of his magnificent green eyes.

-Stand up, dog. I am not your King. -

His voice sounded like an emotionless blow of freezing wind.

-I am not bowing down… I am begging you…- The young man that was kneeling in front of him cried.

-Begging me? - Another vibration of cold cruelty in the green-eyed man's voice.

-I am not your God either. -

The solemnity he used to unsheathe his sword made the presents holding their breath.

With an impressively rapid movement of the sword, that fast it almost seemed like he didn't even move, he succeeded in cutting the poor young man's throat, making a decent amount of blood spilling all over his boots and his tight leather trousers, but the blood didn't leave any sign, no stains, on them.

The people of the Kingdom Of The Scorpion were people that were living everyday with the deep thought inside of their mind that destruction and pain were the only right and legitimate way to not only show their power, but also to fix things and also people that were not living the way their Kingdom was expecting them to live.

There was not a single person in Acrab Square that day that had any clue about the reason why that poor person's throat met the blade of the pretty man's sword.

But whatever the reason was, they were convinced, inside of their mind, that if that young boy's Life found its end it surely was what it had to be done, it certainly was what that boy deserved, they didn't even need to know what the issue was, precisely, because they were sure that the young man was in that moment breathing no more because it was what he deserved, for a reason or for another.

For that reason, after the then dead man's head hit the solid black ground of the square, all the presents started to slowly disappear from the scene, walking away, back to whatever they were doing before assisting to a murder that in their mind had been made all and exclusively because of Justice.

And they were feeling satisfied.

They were feeling alive.

When every single person left the spot, away from Acrab Square, the long-haired man was still standing tall, in front of the dead body of the person he personally murdered only few instants before, the sword still strongly held in his hand, his eyes still pointed on the throat he did cut fast and, in his mind, rightly.

And that was when the permanent dark sky over the Kingdom Of The Scorpion started to bleed all over Ogle, all over Acrab Square and over its majestic Black Gold statue, representing the attacking scorpion.

The tenebrous sky was raining blood all over the man with the sword in his hand and over the young one that found in that evening the last breath of his Life.

And that blood, the one falling from the sky, that blood yes, it was clearly visible on the standing man, mixing with the black of the leather, giving to his stunning figure a combination of black and red that combined with the green of his enchanting green eyes, was donating him a presence and a figure of absolute pre-eminence.

Of cruel and beautiful power.

He then sheathed his sword with the same kind of solemnly beauty he used to unsheathe it not too many minutes before.

The blood was still falling down from the invisible sky, and far, but not extremely far from there, surrounded by the enormous black and lightening cloud, there was the Castle, shining beautiful due to the lightnings that were colliding on its walls, even more black than the cloud it was seemed to lay on.

Few thunders shook the silence that was in that moment screaming loud, louder than the howls of pain that were so extraordinarily audible every now and then in the whole entirety of the Kingdom Of The Scorpions, yells that were coming directly from under the ground, deep and far away from the surface of the Planet.

Chrysanthe was the only alive person, apart of the leather dressed man that was still in the square.

He decided to show himself from right behind the pillar where he was hiding until then, and he spoke to the man that, even if covered by the intense red raining blood, was still perfectly dry.

-Crimson! What are you doing…! -

The man that was standing with his hand still holding the hilt of his then sheathed sword, looked in Chrysanthe's direction and, once spotting him, he made a smile extremely hard to comprehend. It was, in any case, a smile without any type of good feelings, but full of mean and negative vibrations like it was the whole Town of Ogle and the entire vastity of the Kingdom Of The Scorpion, located at South East of the Regions Of Darkness, the obscure lands that were finding their Existence in the South of The Circle.

-Chrysanthe…-

His voice had the same cynical sound it previously had when he was talking to at that point still alive begging young man.

Chrysanthe was keeping himself at a safe distance while interacting with the man that was then waiting for him to speak.

-Crimson, I'm sure that was not necessary…-

The mean man with the deep green eyes, focused his attention on Chrysanthe a bit more and it was hard, literally impossible, to just even try to understand what was going on inside of his mind, the feelingless expression clearly drawn on his enchanting face.

-Your voice is shaking. - He said, answering without any kind of interest, despite of the way he was attentively looking at the man with the grey eyes in front of him.

Chrysanthe, and yes, his voice was shaking, tried to do not appear that extremely frightened, but he was failing, second after second, under the cold, freezing look, of Crimson.

-Have you seen the Princess…? -

Finally, after all of that staring, the man that few minutes before showed himself murdering another man in front of a very full Acrab Square, made a move, leaving his steady position under the rain of blood that was still falling on them and all over Ogle, even if at least the intensity of it was decreasing at every minute.

-You know, my lovely friend… You were talking about what is not necessary… Few instants ago…-

He walked until the distance between him and the man sent by the Queen to look for her daughter, was minimal.

And with a glare of his eyes, with a green little sparkle coming from them, entered deep inside Chrysanthe's eyes, hitting them with beautiful inhumanity.

That glare made Chrysanthe shake on his feet and he ultimately fell on the ground, at Crimson's feet.

-Chrysanthe… The only thing that is never necessary in this Kingdom, is your presence.-

Those words shook the man that was still on the ground even more and the cruel way those words got pronounced was the ultimate hit to his Spirit.

And, all at once, he felt completely unable to stand up, to get back on his feet from his current laying position on the black ground that was characteristic of the square with the majestic statue of the attacking scorpion, as well as Ogle and the entire vastity of the Kingdom Of The Scorpion.

Crimson put, softly, his boot on Chrysanthe's neck.

-One day… One day, Chrysanthe… I will break it…-

And he started to press a bit on it.

A bit more…

And again… Just a tiny bit more…

Chrysanthe was not even able to lament as the heaviness of the presence carried by Crimson had a sort of power, some real obscure energy, that was making him unable even to think, it was like in that moment his Existence went on a total blackout.

The cynical man was enjoying every single second of that moment, but suddenly, all at once, he retreated his boot from his victim's neck and he remained there, motionless, his eyes wide open, his mind somewhere else, but still somewhere around there.

It was literally like his whole attention reached a different target, but this time, compared to Chrysanthe, it was a target that was not visible, not present, at least not in that precise moment.

Then, Crimson raised his head and spoke, loud and clear.

-Show yourself. -

And he didn't have to wait too long.

From behind the huge statue of the scorpion, a young girl with long black hair all tied back up and a white satin dress, showed herself in front of the dominant Crimson and the massively Spiritually broken Chrysanthe.

She walked slowly around the statue, keeping the distance between her and the man that just called her out.

Crimson squinted his eyes while looking at her, the language of his own body speaking clear supremacy over Chrysanthe's figure.

The proud man and the girl were looking at each other from the distance, without a word.

It was Crimson that, at some point, finally spoke first.

-You are not supposed to be out here. -

The girl raised her eyebrows and took two steps or three in direction of the two men.

And those few steps towards them, made possible to have a look at her eyes.

Eyes of an unicity never seen before... Or maybe only once before her...

Red. Pure fire, pure heat. Red. Like the blood that then was barely falling down from the tenebrous invisible sky over Ogle.

-You are not supposed to kill people without a concrete reason. -

Chrysanthe was starting to move once again, slowly trying to sit on the spot where he was currently laying down.

Crimson, even if for literally just a second, had a very genuine expression of surprise on his face, that disappeared straight away to let the most arrogant of his facial expressions show up before his answer.

-There was a concrete reason. Princess. -

The pale skin of the Princess Of The Scorpion, was the timid strong meeting between the fresh colour of the snow and the mystical vibrations of the Moonlight.

Two very special kind of beauty that were never present in the Kingdom Of The Scorpion.

Even her voice was extraordinarily unique... Ethereal...

-There should never be a reason concrete enough to kill a person and especially in the way you just did...-

An ominous silence.

Crimson leaped over Chrysanthe in such a delicate way that it almost seemed like he floated over him.

He then kept walking towards the Princess, that ran back behind the statue.

Crimson stopped.

-Come back here. Now. Don't let me come there, Princess Kirsa...-

No answer back from the Princess Of The Scorpion.

In the same meantime, Chrysanthe was back on his feet.

-Crimson, please... Leave her alone... I will take care of her... Queen Nova sent me to look for her...-

At those words, the mean Being touched the hilt of his sword. That hilt was very particular. The black leather of it, was a perfect match with Crimson's gear. However, it was seeming to be a regular sword, apart of the beautiful silvery ornaments all around the leathered haft.

Without even looking back at him, the green-eyed young man passed a hand through his hair and he spoke with his characteristic feelingless voice.

-Queen Nova sent you here? -

Chrysanthe was not feeling very well yet, still not healed from the dark inner attack Crimson moved against him only few minutes before.

-She did... She did, that's why I am here, Crimson...-

The boy with the most beautiful facial features in Ogle finally turned his head to look at Chrysanthe.

-Then, next time, be sure you just do what the Queen tells you to do... Without putting yourself into my affairs...-

Crysanthe this time didn't respond.

In that moment, the Princess showed herself once again, leaving her hide behind the statue of the scorpion.

-My mother sent you here, Chrysanthe?- She asked.

The young man simply nodded with his head.

Princess Kirsa then showed a little smile, that was revealing more sadness than happiness, and she spoke again.

-Well. I am here. I'm ready. Let's go back to the Castle, then. -

Even Chrysanthe was surprised by those words.

But not Crimson.

Actually, Crimson was not even thinking about Princess Kirsa's words in that moment.

-Crimson... We...-

-Go. -

Suddenly, the long-haired man seemed to be lost inside his deepest thoughts.

Chrysanthe didn't say one more word and the Princess was not facing Crimson at all, only waiting for the apparently more good hearted man of the two to go with her back to the Castle, back to her mother, Queen Nova.

Once Kirsa and Chrysanthe moved the first steps to get on their way back to the Fort, Crimson spoke.

-As the Ultimate Protector of this Kingdom, it is my duty to clean the streets from the dirt. -

His voice was loud. Full of pure and fiery anger.

Chrysanthe stopped to listen to him and Kirsa did the same, as apparently she didn't have any intention to go back to the Castle and to her mother if not with the man Queen Nova sent to find her.

-For you it's easier, Chrysanthe... Your duties as the Leader of this Kingdom are barely relevant... You see... They send you down from the Castle to find their daughter... This is the most they ask you to do...-

The rain of blood stopped completely. Crimson's face and clothes were visibly dry, even if he spent the last several minutes under of it.

Even Chrysanthe and the Princess were perfectly dry and without a sign of blood on their clothes.

But the whole area was a tremendous view and smell of vivid and pure blood.

Crimson looked at both of them, standing tall, with power, with visible pride coming out from all of his great figure.

-But for me… For me is different… It's me they call for the most dangerous missions… It's me they call in case of attack from another Kingdom… It's me they talk to about the deepest secrets of our Kingdom and it's always me they go to for any serious situation regarding the Kingdom Of The Scorpion and its protection. -

Few thunders fulfilled the silence that followed Crimson's words, coming from the great dark cloud that was surrounding the surface where the Castle was.

-I am the Hero Of The Scorpion. And whatever I do, I do it because I can. -

More silence. This time without thunders.

-Understand. - That was the short answer coming from the Leader Of The Scorpion.

The Princess kept her silence.

The Hero of the Kingdom Of The Scorpion gave a mean look at both of them.

-Before you go. Do you want to know why that man deserved to die, today? -

Those words sounded like ice, but they hit like fire.

-If you want to share it with us... Sure, Crimson...- Chrysanthe said, with a clear sound of fear in his voice.

But then something strange happened.

Crimson's eyes changed, his face suddenly became like he was the one in fear in that moment, and that surely was more than a rarity, that was a real unicity.

He was facing Chrysanthe and Princess Kirsa, that then were looking at him, but his eyes were looking at a point behind them, far away from them, from Ogle and from the Kingdom Of The Scorpion, far away even from the Regions Of Darkness, from the Silvery Lands and even from the Regions Of Light. Far away from The Circle.

-He spoke about him, Chrysanthe...-

His voice was different too. Not arrogant or full of anger anymore, not in that moment.

He was the one having his voice shaking in that instant.

And the Leader Of The Scorpion and the Princess of that Kingdom found themselves shocked by what they were seeing and even more by what they were hearing.

A lightening. A thunder. But this time not from the cloud around the Castle, this time was coming from the sky over them, blurrier than ever.

-I had to kill him, you see... The people were listening... They were giving him too much attention... I had to act like he was telling lies... But... I know he was telling the truth...-

Crimson was keeping his stare into the nothing behind Chrysanthe and Kirsa, even if in reality, he was looking at the everything.

-I can see... Even now... The truth in his words... Chrysanthe...-

Another lightening. Another thunder.

Then the Leader Of The Scorpion found the strength to ask the most important question to the Ultimate Protector of the Kingdom at South East of the Regions Of Darkness, at South of The Circle.

-But… Please, Crimson… Tell us… What did he say, exactly…? -

The Princess' eyes were shining, looking in Crimson's direction, avid to know the answer even if she was pretending that all of those information were not of any kind of importance for her.

And Crimson spoke, frightened. Suddenly, alarmed like never before in all of his entire Existence.

-He said…- And he took a deep breath before finishing the sentence, his great green eyes focusing back into the Present in the location where he physically was, looking at Chrysanthe and the Princess.

-He spoke about him, and he said he is watching. And he doesn't want us to interfere. -

XII

THE PRINCESS WITH THE RED EYES

Dark.

Flashing.

Dark…

Flashing again…

The massive cloud that was covering and surrounding the base of the Castle of the Kingdom Of The Scorpion, was sending bad vibrations all over the Town of Ogle and somehow even to the more far Towns like, for example, the Town of Ara.

The Castle was located between the black mountains around Ogle, and the flames that were growing from the ground were high and bright, but they were not burning anything and also, they were not even expanding themselves around the mountains. They were simply steady, stuck on the spot where they were flaming, giving to that darkness a bare touch of light.

Chrysanthe and the Princess Of The Scorpion, were right outside the dangerous streets of Ogle, then walking through a field covered by shiny black coloured grass.

They stopped at some point once the lights of Ogle became tinier.

The Castle was, in terms of view, right over them, but in fact still very far, up between the mountains of the colour of Death.

Not far from there, under the mysterious sky over them, it was clearly visible a quite bright source of light, so they kept walking until they found themselves right in front of it.

It was a very soft kind of light, and it was simply lightful air floating exclusively on that precise spot of the field.

The Leader Of The Scorpion was holding his sword by then and he pointed it at that curious smoky and glossy air.

A little wind surrounded Chrysanthe, quickly disappearing howling away through his arm and, ultimately, through his sword.

Instantaneously, the brilliant air burnt, and fiery flames fell on the ground, generating a unique big fire, without burning the black grass at all.

-After you, my Princess. -

-Much appreciated. -

The Princess walked literally through the fire, but she didn't end up finding herself on the other side of the fiery fount of flare.

Actually, it was impossible to know where Princess Kirsa disappeared, certainly she was not anywhere close to where Chrysanthe and the innocent fire were.

The man stayed few seconds with his eyes pointed on the flames and then he moved few steps towards them, in the end finding himself walking through them as well as his Princess did few instants before.

When he reopened his eyes, the view was totally changed.

The Castle was standing tall right over him, black and shiny despite to the total darkness that was gathering all around of it, except for the flames of the tall fire he came out from.

He had a rapid look beneath his own feet, and he saw what he was always seeing when outside of the Castle.

His own image reflected on the surface of the area where he was standing tall, thoughtful, looking as well at the reflection on it of whatever was present in that spot, even the reflection of the great Castle itself.

An unbelievably massive cloud was surrounding the whole location and its extremely powerful lightnings were the only way to see some light in all that gathering of never-ending darkness.

-Chrysanthe. -

Princess Kirsa was already in front of the huge doors of the Fort that were leading inside of it.

They were closed, still, but in the meantime Chrysanthe walked towards her, the Princess opened them and she disappeared inside.

When the Leader Of The Scorpion entered inside the Entrance Hall, he was amazed, like he always was, about the Spiritual silence that was fulfilling the entire hallway.

The Princess looked up at him without saying anything and she took a deep breath.

She then made her way up using the stairs, and Chrysanthe was following her, slowly.

Once upstairs, the corridor was empty, but the door that was getting into another room on the right side, was semi open.

Chrysanthe pushed it and he let Kirsa entering inside.

They were inside one of the biggest rooms of the whole Castle, with a massive rectangular table in the exact middle of it and completely made out of mahogany.

There were three chandeliers pending from the ceiling, all of them with black candles which burning flames were of a pretty and intense purple colour.

Apart of that, the room was not much illuminated.

But it was illuminated enough to see who was already inside of it.

Queen Nova was standing not far from the door, making very easy to understand all she was doing was waiting for them to finally arrive at the Castle.

And close to her…

-Crimson?!-

Chrysanthe was surprised as much as Princess Kirsa to see the Hero Of The Scorpion already there, as when they made their move to go back to the Fort, Crimson was still in Acrab Square, standing there by himself and his own strength, thinking about the words of the man that he murdered, words that were the absolute reason of his cruel but justified actions that day.

-How can you be that surprised? - His voice was back to its regular mean sound and his unbelievable green eyes were seeming, if possible, even more violent than what they have always used to be.

-I do not need to use the Airy Flames to teleport myself at the Castle, Chrysanthe. -

The way he pronounced the Leader's name, whispered, with anger and denigration, made Chrysanthe feel like that if he was able to, in that moment, he would have given his own Life away.

His entire Spirit was once again getting marked and stained by the meanness of the words of the Hero Of The Scorpion, which was able to destroy somebody's confidence right from the inside… Roughly… Brutally… With that spark in his deep green eyes that was able to cut the Spirit in two, especially the Spirit that was living inside the Existence of people that were good at heart.

Queen Nova looked at her daughter.

Her eyes were a great show of light, and the small black pupils were giving her an appearance of even more danger.

-Where have you been…- She muttered at the Princess.

Kirsa was not even looking at her mother in the eyes, not because of fear, but simply because she didn't really want to look at her.

-You are not answering…? - Queen Nova tried again, without any success.

She stared at her daughter few more seconds, looking at her avoiding her look and she felt her own Aura about to explode out of her body, but she concentrated at her very best and she, somehow, managed to remain calm. Angry, very angry. But calm.

-We better get ready. - She then said, the voice shaking because of the upsetting way her daughter was acting with her, but trying to keep her solid and powerful presence firm but at the same time serene.

The Hero Of The Scorpion gave a look at Chrysanthe that was enough to make him understand what he had to do.

The Leader disappeared out of the room, leaving the door open, while Kirsa walked all down the huge room to end up sitting far away from where the big dinner table was, right on the floor, the head leaning on the wall.

Queen Nova called her louder than how she intended to do.

-Kirsa! I swear, I am going to punish you harder than I have ever done before, you little rebel…-

Before she was able to say anything else, Chrysanthe entered back inside the room, followed by three servants.

One of them was a tiny old man, all dressed in black with aged and dusty clothes, while the other two, a man and a woman, were dressed cleaner, but not better.

It was darker in the room as the purple flames that were coming from the candles on the chandeliers were getting thinner.

Queen Nova raised her eyes to look at them, to stare at them, only few instants each and suddenly, after a flash crossing her very luminous eyes, the candles' flames strongly increased their brightness, even if the room itself was remaining mainly of an obscure type of luminescence.

The servants started to prepare, quickly but impeccably, the great mahogany table, to make it ready for dinner.

Nothing exciting, just more than enough to fulfil an empty stomach.

Vegetables, fruits, beef and chicken and a decent amount of bread, that was all.

Not a lot of choices but in a sufficient quantity.

The young servants positioned themselves close to the windows not too far from the table, standing in silence, waiting.

The old one, left the room for a good couple of minutes, possibly more.

When he appeared back, he spoke, a grasp and shy voice.

-Queen Nova…-

The eyes of the Queen flashed on him, looking down due to the short height of the man.

-What, slave? -

The Princess, from her spot far from the table, turned her head to be able to have the view of her mother speaking to the short old man.

She felt the fire inside of herself burning through her boiling blood.

-Queen Nova… My Queen… The King is coming. -

The cynical look inside of the Queen's eyes disappeared instantly, to reveal a kind of alarmed look that was almost impossible to normally see on her beautiful face.

-Everyone! At your standard positions! -

She gave a look down the room to her daughter.

-Kirsa, please!!-

But the Princess had already put her head back leaning on the wall, feeling comfortable, more or less, in her tiny little spot on the floor far from all the other presents in the room.

She didn't even move a finger in response to her mother's call.

The reason why Queen Nova didn't insist more than that, was due to what everyone that was there heard.

Few steps were audible from outside the room, from down the corridor.

The door was wide open after the old servant entered back inside a minute before and everyone remained silent, standing in there, Crimson close to a chair on the right of the sit that was at the head of the table and Chrysanthe close to the chair positioned on the left of it.

The old little man was in front of the table, not a movement, not a blink of his eyes.

Nova was the closest one to the open door, holding her breath, her lightful eyes still with a strange and unusual sort of alarmed feeling inside of them, rigidly standing in there, waiting.

Kirsa was not paying attention to anything that was happening, able to hear the steps too, but totally disinterested in that and simply lost deep inside her thoughts.

The candles were giving a fiery light to the room otherwise swallowed by the absolute darkness.

Outside of the windows the lights of the Town of Ogle were barely visible, but what was easily noticeable, were the Airy Flames on the black mountains all around the Castle.

One… Two… The people inside the room were counting every single step that was coming from the outside corridor, it was a long corridor, and the walking steps were slow and deep.

Three… Four… It was seeming like every single person in there stopped to breath, as the only detectable sound was maybe the timid falling of the rain, black rain, that was starting to fall over the Castle and Ogle.

Five... Six... The steps were closer then, way more audible...

Seven... Eight... It was a matter of how many seconds, then? How many instants left?

Nine... Queen Nova was then releasing her long held breath by slowly and softly blowing out of her mouth all the air she previously accumulated.

Ten.

The steps stopped.

Right before the entrance, so that nobody was able to spot anyone's presence, yet.

Nova was forcing her eyes to don't start to tear due to the effort she was putting in trying to appear relaxed, but she was completely failing in that attempt.

Kirsa was still motionless and with her mind somewhere else, very far from the room, the Castle, the Kingdom Of The Scorpion and also very far from the Regions Of Darkness.

Everybody, except her, held the breath one more time.

Then another step... And a second one... And all at once all the purple flames that were coming from the chandeliers' candles started to shake like if a quite strong wind entered in the room where everyone, everyone except the Princess, was waiting.

And after the initial shake, all of the flames vanished, blown away.

The air became heavy and unhealthy.

And then, right there, in front of the entrance, in front of the open doors, he appeared.

King Anthares was standing there, tall and muscly, long dark hair that were laying down on his back, a straight beard which end was touching his chest, covered by his massive black armour that was shining of a strange purple light even if there was not a single source of light of any colour in that moment inside there, with the only exception of the Airy Flames that were raging with no danger outside of the Castle.

His Crown was an absolute masterpiece, the white gold decorations that were fulfilling the black base of the Crown were not representing anything in particular, but were somehow making sense anyway. It presented many crests and all of them were high and pointed.

Stuck in the middle of it, there was a stunning black Topaz.

His bright red eyes were shining like fire and his black pupils were very small.

Everyone remained silent. Somehow, they managed to restart to breath, even if slowly, still in a state of uncomfortable stress.

The King Of The Scorpion moved few steps inside, studying all the presents, focusing his eyes on all of them, the Hero, the Leader, the two young servants close to the windows and the old one that was standing in front of the table that was ready for dinner.

He then pointed his eyes on his wife, Queen Nova.

In his eyes there was no love able to be seen. There was no presence of care or kindness of any genre, not even a little hint. There was not the bare shine of a single feeling of that type, not at all.

Only violence.

And power.

Queen Nova felt breaking inside, once again, like it had been forever.

Then the King took a look down to the room.

An extremely quick expression of concern crossed his uncharitable eyes of the colour of blood, eyes that got their usual light of cruelty straight back right before he finally spoke.

-Welcome.-

The floor trembled.

Suddenly every single flame that previously got blown away by the appearance of his dark presence, restarted to flaming once again on every candle but this time instead of the purple colour they previously had before blowing away, they had a very vivid red light.

Every single person in the room bowed down.

Princess Kirsa didn't move, looking straight to the wall in front of her.

All the others remained on their knees, the head down, looking at the floor.

-Up. -

His voice was warm. The voice and the eyes were probably the only two characteristics of the King Of The Scorpion that seemed to have a bare presence of warmness.

The Hero and the Leader stood up.

The Queen didn't move.

King Anthares looked down at her.

-I said... Up.-

Nova started to speak with a heavy shaking in her voice.

-I have to apologise, Anthares. The girl... She is... She is...-

-She is what? -

Anthares was staring at his wife with a look of his eyes that would have been able to set the whole World on fire.

-She...- Nova tried again.

-She is a twenty years old girl. - The King interrupted her.

-And you are her mother. It is your duty to be sure she behaves the way she should behave. But…-

And the King took one very deep breath, which was a very common characteristic of his personality.

-You keep failing. -

A powerful thunder shook the air inside the room and outside the Castle, down to Ogle and in all of the Kingdom Of The Scorpion.

The rain was still falling, then very heavy, and it was able to be heard very easily.

Crimson was looking down during the words his King was pronouncing to Queen Nova.

Chrysanthe, instead, was looking at the scene with his eyes well pointed on them.

-And now. Up. - King Anthares ordered one more time to the Queen.

Queen Nova didn't reply, and she stood up, the eyes still very well focused on the pavement.

The King spoke.

-We should all take our sits. -

The Hero Of The Scorpion sat straight away, while Nova walked slowly and full of thoughts inside of her head, heading to her sit at the other end of the table, opposite to where the chair of the King was.

Chrysanthe took his eyes off from Anthares for the very first time since the painful conversation between him and his wife had its start.

He then took his sit, opposite to Crimson.

The King slowly walked to his chair at the head of the table, to his great black chair, bigger than all the others, and visibly more comfortable. Even the Queen's one was not different from all the others. Wooden, hard, and very much uncomfortable.

The old servant ran behind the King's chair to let him sit, bowing down right after that.

Everyone remained in silence.

Kirsa was looking at her own nails, her mind still busy and confused by the thoughts that suddenly found a way deep inside of her conscious self.

The servants, in the meantime, were starting to fulfil everyone's plate with a bit of everything on it, without forgetting to be sure even the glasses of the presents at the table were full and ready for all of them to drink from.

King Anthares moved his eyes on everyone at the table, before speaking.

-Yarden will not join us, today.-

-May I ask you why, my King? - The Hero asked.

His voice, normally so cold and proud, was always much more controlled when talking to King Anthares.

The King looked at him.

-Because the Commander Of The Scorpion is not in the Kingdom, today. -

The last statement of the King was clearly not accepting any other form of additional questioning regarding that precise topic.

Crimson knew that very well and he didn't ask anything else.

The King looked at everyone at the table once again and he ordered.

-Eat. -

They were eating only since few minutes, when the King pointed his eyes on the young waiter that was back standing close to the window with the young woman.

-Here. Come here. -

It was not even sounding like an order. It was more like the way somebody would speak to a dog.

The waiter walked fast to the table.

-Yes, Your Majesty… Always at your service…-

The King looked at him.

-Why are you shaking? -

The waiter instantly felt overwhelmed.

-I don't… I don't know… My King… I can't… I don't know why…-

-Why is your voice breaking? -

-Your Majesty… I am… I am just… Frightened…-

-Frightened about what? -

The calmness of the King's voice was making him sound even more dangerous.

-Please… I am not able to answer… Your Majesty…-

The waiter's eyes started to tear a bit, silently.

The King kept staring at him.

-Is that girl your wife? -

King Anthares asked, clearly referring to the young waitress.

-Your Majesty… Yes… She is my wife…-

-Do you have kids together? -

Everyone stopped eating.

A thunder from far outside the Castle, from the great dark cloud that was surrounding it, a thunder definitely heard from all the inhabitants of Ogle.

Chrysanthe raised his eyes to the King.

-I have asked… If you have any kids together…- The King of the Kingdom Of The Scorpion repeated.

-No, we don't… Not yet, Your Majesty…- The young man said, few tears still crossing his face, with the slightly try to show a smile due to the nature of the topic.

King Anthares didn't smile back.

What he did was keeping on looking at his servant, the eyes pumping blood, a look that was not promising anything good.

And, ultimately, he spoke.

-Brilliant. -

The man looked at his wife and then back at the King.

-Brilliant…? My… My King…? -

Anthares' eyes did shine strangely.

-Yes. Brilliant. -

The servant was visibly confused.

-I don't… I don't understand, Your Majesty…-

He then gave another look at his wife that during all that conversation remained silent, her scared big eyes pointed on her husband, even more confused than him.

-I beg your pardon, my King…- The young waiter said.

-I apologise about me asking something to you, but I have to… What do you mean by that, Your Majesty? -

Anthares was not upset at all about his servant questioning him about something. Actually it was like he was hoping the poor young man was going to ask him the reason why he expressed himself in that way regarding the fact the two servants still didn't have kids together.

He then spoke, absolute and hard.

-Because that means no child will cry, tonight. -

Everyone looked up at him.

Kirsa, for the first time since she isolated herself in her lonely spot at the end of the room, she moved her eyes to look at her father.

The King looked at the waitress, the young man's wife.

The man spoke with a whisper of hope that was leaving his Soul, looking up at the King.

-Your Majesty...- He cried.

King Anthares didn't take his focus off from the man's wife, that was shaking few feet away from the table.

She was not even able to open her mouth to say anything, she was not even able to start to cry.

The King raised his right hand, that got circled by a very pale black gleaming.

It was like a foamy vapour that was floating around his hand.

-My... My King...- Chrysanthe said with a speechless thin sound of his voice.

It took a moment.

The King shook his hand, the pale black vapour of energy left his right hand at an incredible rate, speeding in the waitress direction, only stopping once in front of her face.

The girl held her then heavy breath, her eyes were humid and sore, looking in front of herself, where the obscure floating energy was, in that moment almost completely motionless.

The flames of the chandeliers' candles reached an even more vivid intensity of red, and they also increased in size.

The King spoke, directly to the shivering girl.

-Anything to say? -

The frightened girl just started to cry, silently, without any noise, unable to take her eyes off from the energy born from the King's hand.

Without being able to say a word.

-Very well. - Anthares said, every single person looking at him and at that pale dark power that was still in front of the young girl's face.

Princess Kirsa was then standing, still down at the end of the room, but not sitting anymore.

Then, with a last look of hate and disgust, the King pronounced words that succeeded in making even Crimson's dark heart tremble.

-Thank you, my darling. The reason of my happiness is the view of your desperation. -

Another rapid movement of the hand from the distance and the vapour entered inside the woman's nose.

She had a little gasp and then her eyes turned white.

-ZOHARA!!!!- The man tried to run to her, but he realised that he was unable to move. Instead, he felt forced, inside of himself, to bow down to the King and he was suddenly stuck in that position, being only able to move his neck and so his head.

-ZOHARA!!!!-

But Zohara was already gone. Maybe less than five seconds before. Maybe just in the same meantime her husband was screaming her name to the absolute nothing.

Her body fell on the black cold pavement, her eyes still open and white.

Her whole skin went from being of the colour of a rose to being grey as ash.

Her lips from being delicate and soft to being dry and green.

It was an absolute Soul breaking view to handle.

-NOOOOOOOOOOO!!!!- The younger servant's scream of pain that, then able to move once again, ran to the dead and tumbledown body of his wife, forever gone from her own and also his Existence.

Forever gone from his Life.

-My love… My love… My darling… My sweet Zohara… My little darling… No… Why…-

The man raised his face, entirely crossed by his very own tears, his eyes into the eyes of the King Of The Scorpion that was smiling for the first time since he appeared inside the room that evening.

Only a little smile, but more than enough to make him appear even more cruel than when he was tremendously serious.

-What did I do…? What did she do…? - The man cried to his King.

-KILL ME!!!! KILL ME TOO, PLEASE!!!! I AM BEGGING YOU!!!!-

And he let fell himself on his own knees screaming even louder.

-KILL ME!!!!-

It was an absolute hurtful scene to look at.

The King Of The Scorpion moved his hand, this time his left one, and by doing so the voice of the heart destroyed young man was not able to come out from him anymore, remaining stuck inside his throat, nearly able to choke him.

-What makes me feel good… And what really gives me a reason to smile… It's not to cause death, my dear friend. - Anthares said.

-What I really find astonishing is to create pain and agony to someone in the way that better works in that very particular situation. You see…- He continued looking at his servant with pure and real meanness.

-Your wife was very scared about Death. Because she was loving her Life. With you. -

He took a deep breath and he kept talking.

-But your situation is different. Now that she's gone and she will never come back to you... You want to die... And you honestly want to... I know it... I can feel it...-

He looked at the chandeliers, while continuing with his speech.

-And this is the reason why I will not kill you, young man. This is the reason why I will let you live. Because you are not afraid to die. You are now afraid to live. Your desperation is not caused by your being in front of the coming of your Death. Your desperation is caused by your being in front of a long Life without your beautiful Zohara, that will never come back to you and that will never give you the pleasant feeling of a hug, that will never come back to give you the sweetness of a kiss and that will never come back to give you the happiness that comes with the universal experience to have kids together. -

The man was in pain, his voice still stuck inside his throat, uncapable to scream, uncapable to cry out loud that feeling of despair he was experiencing, that feeling of desperation that was King Anthares' only reason to smile.

For some unknown reason, Anthares was then starting to feel raging inside of himself.

A black gleaming Aura circled his whole figure.

-Your pain is my satisfaction. And if your pain is caused by the thought of a long Life without your beloved wife, then it is my will to be sure you will live, it is my will to be sure that you will live longer than anybody else in this Kingdom. -

The Aura around him, his Aura, got more luminous, even if the colour was darker than the night.

-To give you Death would give you in this moment something way better than Life. Death would give you peace. And serenity. But, unfortunately for you, my dearest friend, I'm not Death. I am King Anthares. And to give you peace and serenity is the last thing I want. -

The King Of The Scorpion stood up from his sit.

-You asked me to kill you. My letting you live is my way to kill you. -

The King then looked at Chrysanthe.

He stared at him and the Leader Of The Scorpion understood straight away.

He stood up and he went to grab the man that was suffering, in agony, a man with a Soul dismantled to dust, a man with a heart that instead to stop beating was then beating even harder, faster, pulsing, pumping, about to explode.

-You know where to bring him, Chrysanthe. -

The King was strangely staring at the Leader of the Kingdom Of The Scorpion, still.

Chrysanthe nodded with his head.

-Bring him where he deserves to stay, where he will spend the rest of his Life. His very long Life. - King Anthares said.

Chrysanthe bowed down and he then grabbed away the man still muted by the energy power generated by Anthares.

However, he was still able to cry, with a terrible and disturbing expression of pain shown on his face.

The Leader Of The Scorpion was about to leave the room with the once servant with him, when the King called.

-Chrysanthe. -

The grey eyed man turned his head to his King.

-Your Majesty…-

The King looked at him.

And he blew his breath out of his nose, breath that came out in the form of a dark smoke slightly similar to the lethal vapour that not too many minutes before ended the Life of the innocent and lovely young girl called Zohara.

-There is, by any chance, something you don't particularly like about my methods, Chrysanthe…? -

Instants full of negative pressure and discomfort followed those words.

The Leader Of The Scorpion was genuinely not able to answer.

He tried to, obviously with the intention to lie to his King, but he found himself not able to say a single word.

Then, the King spoke, once again.

-From now on, Chrysanthe… Do your best on trying to do not stare at me the way you have done in a couple of occasions, tonight…-

The strongest and most noisy thunder of that day followed the words of the King, that at that point was producing that then very misty black vapour from his nose at every single blow following his breath.

The Leader didn't have the strength to look at his King in the eyes and he kept his head down.

But he then found himself able to speak again.

-I sincerely apologise, Your Majesty… If I have done that… Which I did as you are saying that… It was not intentional… Or for any particular reason…-

The King stared at him, still standing tall in front of his great chair.

-I am sure you are sincere in your apologies, Chrysanthe…-

Anthares' red eyes shone of an unnatural light.

Chrysanthe bowed down once again and he then left the room carrying the devastated man with him.

The once servant's expression inside of his eyes was empty… Lost… Forever.

The King then looked first at the Hero Of The Scorpion and then at his wife.

-Eat. -

They ate in silence.

At some point, Crimson noticed the plate with still plenty of food where Chrysanthe was earlier eating.

-My King…-

-Chrysanthe's time with us has already ended for tonight. - King Anthares said.

-And he knows that very well. -

His black Aura was then completely disappeared, the candles' flames were back at a normal size and to their regular purple colour.

The rain outside the Castle stopped.

Everything in that moment was strangely calm.

The whole vibrations inside the room were a huge amount of very surreal energy.

Once they all finished their food, Anthares focused his attention to the only servant left in the room, the little old man.

-You. Here.-

The old man ran to the table.

-Your Majesty…-

King Anthares was touching his beard, while looking at his servant bowing down to him and remaining in that kneeling position.

-Tell me. How many times did I even only raised a hand on you? -

The servant answered pretty quickly.

-Never, Your Majesty...- In his voice the fear was obvious.

And even Crimson and Queen Nova were not quite sure about the nature of that question coming from the King Of The Scorpion to the old man.

-Correct. And do you want to know why, my lovely friend? -

The voice of the King got lower and somehow he sounded like it was coming from a tomb.

The servant shook.

-Yes... I would... I would like to know... Your Majesty...-

The King spoke.

-Because you represent nothing to me. You represent less than nothing to me. That is what you exactly look like to my eyes. And your being that... Valueless... Doesn't generate any kind of feeling inside of me. Surely not compassion. But, somehow, I don't even feel pleasure by thinking to cause you pain. -

The King drank from his goblet, made out of black gold. There was the great image of a scorpion in the position to attack on it, which was, instead, made out of white gold.

-You do not deserve my Mercy. Well, nobody does... But you do not even deserve my cruelty, which is quite singular... Basically, old man...- And his cruel little smile reappeared on his face.

-You deserve nothing. -

For the first time since the arrive of the King Of The Scorpion in the room, Queen Nova had a smile appearing on her beautiful face.

The words of the King to the penurious servant, seemed to cheer her up.

The fact her behaviour was very much controlled and remissive when the King was present, wasn't changing the fact that Queen Nova was an absolutely cruel Being.

In the Kingdom Of The Scorpion, in terms of cruelty, she was second only to her husband, King Anthares, the King Of The Scorpion.

The servant, still on his knees, didn't reply at all.

He would not have dared, of course.

Then, all of a sudden, the King took the plate from where Chrysanthe was previously eating and he put it on the floor, close to the old servant.

-Eat. -

Nova's smile disappeared.

Crimson was shocked.

Kirsa, that in that meantime was back sitting on the floor, looked into her father's direction.

The servant raised his eyes to his King.

He was probably afraid it was a test.

King Anthares then specified.

-On the floor. -

The old man then started to eat, slowly, then faster, hungry, starving, with his hands.

He was ripping pieces of meat with only his hands, and he finished his meal pretty quickly, under the expression of disappointment of the Queen and the shock on the face of the Hero Of The Scorpion.

Once he finished, he raised his eyes back to the King.

-Now. Clean everything. And disappear. -

And that was exactly what the then not anymore starving servant did.

Queen Nova was disgusted.

She was feeling a lot of anger raging inside of her.

Once the man closed the doors behind himself, the remaining people in the room were only King Anthares, Queen Nova, Crimson and, down to the big room, Princess Kirsa.

The Princess, that previously looked at her father with great curiosity while giving food to the old servant, was then looking at her own knees, with her body clearly there, on the cold pavement of the place that during that evening saw many different events going on, but with her mind totally far away from there, completely lost in extremely deep thoughts about things she didn't even know, thinking about Legends she never really understood.

-Nova. - The King interrupted the misty silence.

The Queen looked at him.

And the King looked back at her in the eyes, his boiling red eyes colliding with her flashing ones.

His nose was now reproducing that unreal black vapour while breathing.

-There is anything that bothered you, tonight? -

The Queen didn't break the eye contact.

-No. No, of course not, My...-

But she got strongly interrupted.

-Two things I have to tell you. The first one is... Don't you ever lie to me. And the second one is... Whatever I do...- And then even the dark Aura all around the King's figure appeared once again.

-Whatever I do... Don't you ever think I am wrong. -

A strange shine crossed the King's red eyes and in that moment Queen Nova had to interrupt the eye contact.

The way she looked down to the table, was way more satisfying than a verbal answer of acknowledgment of the King's words for Anthares.

The King of the Kingdom Of The Scorpion stared at her for few more instants, his Aura still well visible all around him and he then focused on something else, something not visible in front of him, apparently looking into the nothing.

His black Aura instantly disappeared.

-Take Kirsa. - He spoke, clearly to his wife.

-Leave me alone with Crimson. -

Queen Nova didn't hesitate a moment.

The last thing she wanted in that moment was to give to the King another reason to get upset, again, for the second time in the same night.

She silently stood up from her chair and she walked, slowly, down the room, to meet Kirsa's eyes.

Her eyes. At the view so perfectly identical to her father's eyes, but… Somehow… They were also so different…

They were yes, red like raging fire…

But at the same time they were also red like a rose…

-Kirsa. Let's go. -

-No.- The dry answer coming from the Princess.

Queen Nova's expression suddenly changed from severe to alarmed.

-Kirsa… Please…-

That last please, in some way, moved the Princess.

And that was Kirsa's particularity.

The Princess really had something different.

Something that all the members of her family and the most of the inhabitants of the Kingdom Of The Scorpion didn't have.

She saw her mother right in front of her, she felt her voice, the sound of it, the sound of fear.

The type of voice somebody speaks through when in a situation of particular danger, when even every single external detail that happens all around of them has the power to be the cause of their damnation.

Or of their salvation.

The Princess stood up.

She walked past her mother and she kept walking, directed to the doors.

Nova followed her, in silence, confused.

While passing close by her father, Kirsa stopped.

The Queen stopped too and in that moment she felt her own blood freezing inside.

Kirsa was staring at her father.

The King gave the look back to his daughter.

But the kind of collision that happened between the eyes of the King Of The Scorpion and his daughter's eyes felt way different than the exchange of feelings he previously had with his wife.

Red eyes into red eyes.

Fire on fire.

Blood on blood.

Power and… And what? What the main feeling that was coming from the Princess' eyes was?

Anthares didn't know.

She was the only one that he was not able to read. The only one that was able to make him blind, unable to not only read her eyes but also to read her mind, something the King Of The Scorpion was incredibly great at.

It did last more than a year, but in reality not more than five seconds.

The Princess turned her head away and she walked out of the room with her mother right behind her, Queen Nova, that was very much relieved by the fact her daughter didn't try to do or say anything able to generate even more anger inside of the King.

The doors were closed once again.

Anthares and Crimson.

The King and the Hero.

The last two people remaining in the room, after a very turbulent night.

The atmosphere was not particularly tense at that point.

The kind of relationship between Anthares and his mighty Hero, was pretty much close to perfection.

It was probably due to the cynical nature of Crimson's personality, not extremely far from King Anthares' one.

His cruelty, his being very much passionate about destruction and pain to cause to others and also his meanness and love for power, were all qualities very well seen by the King, making him someone in a very high position, definitely not respected, but at least accepted by the King Of The Scorpion.

And, as confuse as it might sound, that was not a bad thing at all.

The King did not respect anyone. But he accepted only one person, truly and with intention, and that person was Crimson. The Hero Of The Scorpion.

-Crimson. -

The King looked at him, speaking calmly to him.

-I haven't seen you much, today. -

The way the King was speaking to the Hero, was different from the way he normally used to speak to anybody else. It was not confidential, but not even distant. It was not focused on complimenting him, but not even focused on denigrating him.

Crimson looked at his King.

-I know. I was just being sure people... Our people... Your people... The inhabitants of this magnificent Kingdom... Were behaving...- Crimson answered.

-I was being sure everyone down in Ogle is doing everything to make sure this Kingdom is and stays the way you want it to be, My King. -

The Hero looked then back down.

Anthares studied him for a moment.

He then pointed his eyes on the Hero's sword, laced tight to his belt.

-And tell me, Crimson. Were they behaving? Or not? -

-Your Majesty...- Crimson got a little bit worried for some reason.

-Your Majesty... I...-

-There is something you have to tell me. - The King interrupted him.

-I'm... I'm not sure...- The Hero Of The Scorpion was then visibly uncomfortable.

The King spoke, this time less calmly.

-Mine, Crimson, was not a question. -

The green-eyed man noticed the change in the King's voice.

And he was well aware of the fact there was no reason to even only attempt to try to hide something from Anthares.

He knew better than anybody else the capability of his King to read people's emotions. He was also able to read their minds, but that was requiring him to sacrifice a huge amount of energy that was normally taking a while to get fully restored, which was forcing him to carefully decide if that process was deserving to be made or not.

-I have killed a man, today. - Crimson said.

Anthares, staring at him, didn't seem surprised.

-What has he done? - The voice of the King got deeper. And mean.

Crimson felt that change of the atmosphere in the room.

He took a breath and spoke.

-I was only walking around Acrab Square, when that man saw me and he started to talk about him, my King…-

Anthares had a quick but visible expression of surprise on his face. Visible if anybody was actually looking at him, but Crimson was not facing directly his King in that moment.

-Him… You mean…-

-Yes, Your Majesty…-

King Anthares stood up.

Crimson then finally looked at him.

-And… What did he say about him…? -

-He said…- Crimson noticed the King was looking at him, but his eyes were somewhere else, like his mind was too.

He was physically there, but Spiritually he wasn't.

-He said that he is watching… And… He doesn't want us to interfere… You know… My King… What is supposed to happen soon… In the Silvery Lands…-

But the King didn't answer back.

He was then standing there in front of the table and with his mind he was in fact somewhere else.

He was travelling with his Spirit, his eyes were in that real moment still focused on Crimson, but without really looking at him.

They were not looking at anything that was related to the room where they were. Anything that was related to the Castle.

He was inside Crimson's mind, to look for the face, the image of the man the Hero killed that same day, few hours before.

He saw Ogle, and he saw all the people gathering in Acrab Square.

He saw the invisible sky over the biggest Town of the Kingdom Of The Scorpion.

And then, right there, not far from the black gold statue of the scorpion, he saw the scene that was showing Crimson and, on his knees, the man that was about to meet his Death in a matter of instants.

Anthares closed his eyes in front of that vision, both in his physical presence inside the Castle and in his Spiritual form down in Ogle, back into the events of the early evening.

He focused very deeply.

He was able to feel it. His Soul… The King was in direct connection with the poor man's Soul.

He memorised that very strong connection in the deepest location of his own mind and by doing that he would have then been able to recognise that Soul.

He would have been able to recognise that Soul wherever that Soul it was going to be, maybe just somewhere in the Universe, maybe already inside a new Being.

When he reopened his eyes there was not Ogle or its inhabitants, his people, anymore.

There was not Crimson or that man.

Actually, there was nothing around him. Certainly nothing that resembled the Kingdom Of The Scorpion or even the Regions Of Darkness.

He was in a place that was darker than the night, where the alternation of cold and heat was giving to the location an atmosphere of uncomfortable pain.

A mental pain.

Screams. Very far. Far away, yet so close.

The fiery eyes of the King were looking around. Impossible to spot anything due to the completely absence of light. Not even a hint of it.

More screams. They then sounded closer, like only few feet away from King Anthares.

The air was strange.

The screams were then more like if someone was crying in pain. And in fear. It was hard to handle the heaviness of those feelings of sadness and desperation.

Even, incredibly, for King Anthares, that usually enjoyed those type of feelings coming from people.

But where he was finding himself in that moment, was somewhere at the extreme limits of The Circle, located somewhere around Southeast.

Those feelings in there, were a lot to deal with even for the King that had in destruction the main Principle of his Kingdom.

Also, those screams, those feelings coming from them, making the air even more hard and dark and difficult to breath, were certainly not coming from any people.

But that was something, however, that King Anthares knew very well. Or, at least, well enough.

The bawls were then far again.

King Anthares took his sword.

It was too dark to even see it.

-I feel you. - He said.

He raised his sword in front of himself.

-Come to me. -

King Anthares got surrounded by his heavy black Aura.

At some point, the most of it concentrated on his right arm, the one that was holding the sword.

The screams were then very much audible.

A lot of crying. A lot of begging.

Then the red eyes of the King had a shine.

His breathing was generating that black vapour, from his nose and from his mouth.

The blade of his sword had a red flash and it then started to generate some sort of energy, red as well, that floated in the air.

Then, suddenly, the red vapour seemed to start to get a spheric form.

But the truth was that it was not actually taking any form.

It was simply revealing something until that moment invisible at the eyes by floating around of it, separating it, whatever it was, from the rest of the darkness.

The revealed object, or subject, had in fact a spheric form. And it was then red lightening at different levels of intensity.

Anthares' eyes were confounding themselves with all of that red gleaming.

The sword's blade went back to normal.

The King was standing in front of that sphere, his Aura completely disappeared.

After staring at the sphere a few more seconds, the King yelled out loud, grabbing it with his hands.

Countless of flashes of many different colours lightened in front of his eyes.

Green… Red… Blue… Yellow… Black, purple, orange and then black again. Then black to blue. And green, once again.

The same sequence for hundreds, thousands, millions of times and all of that in only few instants.

Then the blue appeared once again and this time it stayed.

It only started to change of tone.

Anthares was surrounded by a completely blue environment.

All around and above.

His eyes were wide open.

Focused. Steady.

The blue colour all around him, became lighter. It then happened to turn light blue, of the most candid kind.

It then all happened very quickly.

The whole then light blue environment surrounding the King, trembled and it then suddenly concentrated all in one bright little gleaming right in front of the King's eyes, leaving the whole of the background completely colourless.

Few instants.

And that last and small gleaming exploded in every possible and even impossible direction, showing something that made shock and fear the two main feelings that the King Of The Scorpion was able to experience at that point of that whole magnificent event.

Chants.

Latin Chants.

"Vita nostra brevis est…

Brevi finietur...

Venit mors velociter...

Rapit nos atrociter...

Nemini parcetur..."

("Our life is short...

It will end soon...

Death comes quickly...

He snatches us brutally...

No one is spared...")

There, right there, not only looking inside the red eyes of the King, but also stabbing them, commanding over them, killing them, winning over them, there were the most beautiful and bright light blue eyes the whole Existence had ever witnessed.

The most proud and powerful eyes a Human Being had ever encountered in all of his numerous, countless and different Lives.

The black pupils were small, intense, and full of Eternity.

No other details of the face were visible, due to the white and blinding light that was then surrounding the whole empty location.

More Chants.

"Vita nostra brevis est...

Brevi finietur...

Venit mors velociter...

Rapit nos atrociter...

Nemini parcetur..."

A strong, unreal, smell of roses.

The superior light blue eyes penetrating inside and through the scared red eyes.

Wind. A very strong wind.

A flash.

A hit.

Dark.

+++

-My King! -

Crimson was calling the King loudly.

Anthares was laying on the pavement of the room where they had dinner that same evening, inside his Castle, in the Kingdom Of The Scorpion.

The King moved a little.

-Crimson…-

He then tried to sit on the floor, but he growled and remained laying down on the floor.

His armour was completely destroyed on the right side and the skin was visible and of a strange dark green colour, like he got hit by something.

By someone.

His hands, on the palms, were burnt.

Fuming a little.

His sword was on the floor too, not too far from him.

Crimson waited.

And King Anthares spoke.

-It is true, Crimson… That man was telling the truth…-

Crimson was shaking.

-Your Majesty...-

Anthares grabbed Crimson's arm.

-He is watching. Find Yarden. Tell him there is a change in the plans. By my order. We are not going to the Silvery Lands anymore. -

XIII

THE BRIGHTEST LIGHT IN THE SKY

It was evening in the Kingdom Of The Dove.

Queen Layleen was walking serene on a big outdoor terrace outside the highest tower of her Castle.

A mesmerizing white and pink Castle.

That night the Queen's thoughts were slightly different, though.

Normally, she was fantasising about what to do to make the people of her Kingdom happier and relaxed and also how to make the Kingdom Of The Dove a better place where to live, how to make it brighter and welcoming.

The evening sky was stupendous, dark already, but fulfilled by millions of stars.

But the beauty of that stunning Spring starry sky, was nothing compared to the unique awesomeness of the Queen Of The Dove.

Layleen. The blue-eyed Queen.

The merciful Queen.

Those were the two names the people of the Kingdom Of The Dove and whoever was from a different Kingdom of The Circle, were using when referring to her.

Queen Layleen took a breath.

That night her thoughts were troubled. Disturbed.

She was keeping walking up and down the magnificent white grass that was beneath her feet, in that outdoor side of the highest tower of the Fort.

It was like she was waiting for someone.

There was no Moon that night.

Few steps came from the inside of the tower.

The Queen turned her head, waiting.

The steps became more audible, then one guy appeared in front of the open door, not far from her.

A good looking guy, carrying a shiny armour of a white colour.

-I was waiting for you. - The Queen welcomed him.

The guy went on his knees.

-I know. I've felt it. - He replied.

The Queen smiled at him, and he stood up.

-I have to talk to you, Brayleigh. I need to know your opinion about something that is disturbing me since a little while. -

Brayleigh looked at his Queen.

-Naturally. Everything for you, my Queen. As always. -

Queen Layleen looked at the sky over them.

-I didn't want to talk to Ailana and Evangeline about this because they would say I think too much. And maybe they are right. But I really need someone's opinion and who's better than you for something like this, after all? -

The armoured guy nodded with his head.

-I'm listening. -

Brayleigh leaned himself against the wall of the tower.

-You know, few nights ago it happened again…- The Queen started.

-I've heard about that. Evangeline told me. - Brayleigh answered.

Layleen gave a little bite to her lips.

-We all know very well there's something not quite right in all of this, I mean, it is pretty obvious. But... This time it was different. This time it was definitely different, Brayleigh. -

The guy stared at his Queen, waiting to hear more about what Layleen had to say.

But the Queen didn't continue the conversation straight away, so he spoke.

-What does it mean? In what sort of way it was different from all the other previous times, my Queen?-

Having Brayleigh questioning her, gave her a reason to keep talking about that, trying to win over her own overwhelmingness.

-Even if strange, at least the other times I was, somehow, aware that I was inside of a dream. But... Not this time. -

The guy left his leaning position against the wall to stand straight in front of Layleen.

-Do you mean this time it was a very realistic one? Is that what you mean, my Queen? -

The Queen looked at him with a shine inside her eyes that was something in between excitement and fear.

-No. No, Brayleigh. It was not a realistic dream. Not at all...-

And then her eyes left the shine of excitement to only show, loud and clear, the only feeling of fear.

-I was there. I was there, Brayleigh. That was reality. -

Few seconds of silence followed that very strong sentence.

Brayleigh broke that mystic silence.

-How do you know, if you don't mind me asking, that what you experienced last time, was... Reality...?-

The Queen looked at him in the eyes.

-I know. -

The Queen's response didn't leave any space for any other kind of questioning regarding the fact that time she was sure she experienced something way more than a dream. Something that was, in some way, happening in reality.

The guy looked at the white grass, thinking.

-So… What would you like me to give you an opinion about, my Queen? I mean…- And he really gave her a very intense stare with his eyes.

-You already seem pretty sure and final about the nature of your last… We should call it… Experience…-

The Queen stared back at him, in all of her greatness.

-The opinion I want from you is not about my dream. - She said.

-Brayleigh. As the Hero Of The Dove, do you feel our Kingdom is, somehow, in danger? -

Brayleigh didn't answer back straight away.

He waited few instants, then he said, firm and clear.

-No.-

Another pause.

-No. I don't feel our Kingdom is in any kind of danger, my Queen. Why this kind of question? From what this concern is coming from? -

The Queen moved her eyes away, all around the location where her and Brayleigh were having their very particular conversation.

-In my last dream… Or whatever it was… It happened something that never happened before in the previous ones. -

She was then breathing heavily.

-I saw, for a moment, for a matter of seconds, the face of someone I've never seen before. The face of that someone that in my previous dreams was calling me, telling me to join him... To go with him...-

-You saw him? - Brayleigh's attention raised quite exponentially.

-How did he look like? Was he maybe the King of one of the three Kingdoms of the Regions Of Darkness? -

Layleen started to walk up and down once again like she was doing before the arrival of the Hero Of The Dove.

-No. I've just said... He was someone I've never seen before. We know all of the Kings of the Regions Of Darkness. -

The Hero thought about those words, then he tried again.

-Maybe... The King Of Darkness...? Nobody from the Regions Of Light, or from the Silvery Lands ever seen him. Never. Only who rules in the Regions Of Darkness personally knows him. -

-Thank you, Brayleigh. - The Queen responded.

-Uh? - The Hero said, surprised.

-Thank you. - Layleen repeated.

-That was my feeling. - She then concluded.

Brayleigh had another thought.

-But... Why... What would it be the reason...? I mean... In the far possibility we are right...? -

-Oh, that I don't know. - The Queen said.

Now both of them were looking at the sky.

The Hero Of The Dove smiled at the view of that unbelievable show of lights.

The Queen then had a look at the huge purple Cross that was standing tall and magnificent on the top of the main tower, focusing on the Amazonite that was stuck in the exact middle of it.

-Do you know why the Amazonite is the Gem symbol of our Kingdom? -

The Hero didn't expect that question.

-Because… It represents Hope? - He answered.

Layleen thought about that answer.

-Maybe. -

And she then looked back at Brayleigh.

-But it actually was my father's favourite gemstone. -

Queen Layleen put a hand on Brayleigh's shoulder.

-Thank you, Brayleigh. -

The Hero of the Kingdom Of The Dove, looked inside her warm blue eyes.

-You didn't even tell me anything else about what you have seen apart of that face, this time. -

Layleen smiled at him.

-You don't need to know. -

Brayleigh bowed down.

-Have a good rest of your evening, my Queen. - He said.

The Queen smiled one more time.

Once the Hero left her company, disappearing after the open doors that were leading back inside the Castle, the Queen started to walk up and down again.

That was a sort of action she was doing pretty much, that day.

The sky was still amazing, luminous, unbelievable.

But when the Queen looked back at it, after the several times she already did that evening, the plenty of stars that were decorating that gorgeous and vibrating sky were not the matter of her interest anymore.

She was then looking at the sky over her for a reason way deeper than the simple, yet astonishing, beauty of it.

She was then looking at the sky for one reason only.

Queen Layleen looked then again at the green Amazonite stuck in the middle of the great Cross.

Staring at it she then followed the direction, the exact direction, that the gem was pointing at into the tremendous vastity of the sky.

She tried to focus at the very best of her capabilities and then she saw what she was looking for.

She found what she was craving to see.

The most shiny point of the whole deep and endless sky.

Every single star was then only a pale little fount of light if compared to it.

It was actually looking as an incredibly brightening star but, at the same time, it was also pretty clear that it wasn't.

Even the kind of light it was radiating in the sky was not quite ordinary.

It literally looked like the brightest diamond in the World had been stuck in the sky, spreading the purest light to every single corner of the Universe.

Layleen's eyes got wet.

Few, then many tears crossed her face.

They were falling like shiny little crystals, coming directly from the most beautiful blue eyes in the whole Regions Of Light.

She did bite her lips while crying, trying to contain the suffering, failing.

She tried not to be loud.

Even if she was in the highest spot of the Castle, way distant from all the other locations inside and outside of it.

The Queen looked with more intensity.

The shiny point, from far away deep in the sky, seemed to be pulsing.

Like a heart of light.

And like that the Queen's heart was pulsing too.

Full of emotions, feelings and sensations that made her cry even more, then finally loud, but with her eyes still well pointed on the brightest light in the sky.

And while doing that, compared to other times before that night, Queen Layleen was not able to smell any roses around and above.

The only smell she would have wanted to feel inside her blood and inside her Soul in that moment.

XIV

BLEEDING TOGETHER

The light coming from the Stars outside of the three windows were the only fount of luminescence inside the small room, otherwise completely swallowed by the darkness.

It was cold. A kind of cold not able to be handled by any regular Being.

There was an Altar, and suspended over it there was a shiny and big Cross.

The Cross was black, and an incision was visible in the middle of it, but due to the only natural brightness that was coming from the sky outside, it was not possible to understand it in the details.

There was a massively pleasant smell of incense all around.

In front of the Altar, few steps down from it, there was a pew and a kneeler.

His naked upper body was sweating, generating a golden light all around him.

It was not his Aura. It was another form of Energy impossible to be defined.

The little drops of his sweat were crossing his body slowly, reflecting the light coming from the Stars through the opened windows.

Everything was perfect in the appearance of his figure.

His body was built to ultimate greatness and his hair, long, falling on the whole length of his back, were luminous and of an icy kind of blond, with the only exception of a long but thin part of them, on the right side, where they were presenting a candid black colour.

The long headscarf he was wearing was nearly transparent, but entirely covered in ultra-small fragments of white crystals.

His eyes were closed. The hands were in praying position, a ring on every single finger.

Two different pairs of long and shiny pendants as earrings were slightly visible through his hair, his head was down.

He was not pronouncing the prayers.

He was formulating them inside of his mind.

The muscles, the posture, the whole presence was not of a regular Being.

There was silence.

The incense's smell was slowly starting to fade away.

The brilliant brown eyes opened. A glare. The incense was back fuming, more than before.

His breath started to sound deeper. It was taking time between the breathing and the releasing of the air.

He was at that point sweating even more.

The air was freezing.

The Cross, made of an unknown material, started to bleed.

And he started to bleed too. No cuts. No wounds.

His skin started to produce blood instead of sweat.

He slowly stood up.

He went closer to the Altar, looking at the Cross that was silently bleeding suspended over it.

The golden light surrounding him, expanded even more and it became extremely brighter.

It was blinding.

His feet left the ground.

He solemnly levitated until he was right in front of the Cross, directly facing it.

He then spoke, his voice yes Human, yet so out of that World.

-Impeterie. Terie. Merie. Roatecai. Sempeterie. -

("Power. Yours. Mine. Together. Forever".)

The flash of light that enlightened the whole room did last a second, but it felt like an eternity.

The unbelievable gleaming surrounding him was then motionless, only simply staying steady around his spectacular figure.

The Cross turned light blue, strongly radiating in front of him, its light colliding with his luminous power, generating the unique combination of millions of colours that didn't exist.

Then, all at once and without any possible way to predict it, the strongest wind ever started to rage, howling loud but with the room remaining silent, like the wind and the room were somehow part of two different Dimensions.

But two different Dimensions happening in the same place and at the same exact time.

The wind was that strong it was almost possible be seen as a concrete presence.

But the smoke coming from the incense was still floating in the air calmly and slowly.

His hair were moving, but not because of the wind.

They were moving due to the electrical Energy that was still coming out from his body, still bombing all around him.

Many flashes. Many different sounds. First the scream of a woman. Then the not well audible voice of a boy. Then laughs. And then distorted voices, where it would have been impossible to understand even just a single word for any regular Human Being.

And then the voice of the woman, again. Scared. Terrified.

The boy's voice, once again, too.

-I'm ready! -

Then more distorted voices. More laughs. More screams.

Then Chants.

Only Chants.

Latin and melodic Chants.

They were seeming like they were coming from some location around there, actually extremely close.

One last massive flash.

And then everything went back to normal.

The wind ceased.

The Cross was still there, pending suspended over the Altar, of its usual shiny black colour, not bleeding anymore.

He was with his feet back on the floor.

He was standing in front of the Altar.

Not bleeding. Not sweating.

The golden gleaming was gone.

His eyes staring at the Cross.

The starry night was once again the one and only fount of light inside the small and then warm room.

His look was serious. And strong.

He was not angry.

He was proud.

He was perfectly able to feel his own power running inside his blood, inside of every single vein of his body.

He was perfectly able to feel the superior power he had.

The unmatchable greatness that was making him who he was.

He kept looking at the Cross.

He then bowed down to it.

And he stood up again, speaking with his very particular voice, directed to the Cross that he earlier faced while floating in the air.

-It will soon be defined. -

And, with an unusual little sparkle in his eyes, he concluded.

-The Destiny of The Circle. -

XV

THE SACRED ANIMALS

The location where Adriel Centauri, Dawako Kettu, the Commander Of The Fox and Princess Lisica were finding themselves at, was of an entirely yellow colour all around, with some spots through the grass that were presenting a sandy ground.

Every now and then, the light wind was happening to carry with itself a small amount of sand that was going to end falling on the already mentioned grass.

It was a way warmer location compared to the one where they spent their last night sleeping under the starry and luminous sky.

That afternoon was brilliant, the Sun was radiating its rays all over those lands and the whole area around them.

It was quite singular how they were never encountering any other person around those fields, which was maybe also something that was meaning the people of the Kingdom Of The Fox were all populating the Towns and villages, without really adventuring themselves around the more desolated locations of the Kingdom.

Princess Lisica was touching the sand on the ground, and she was letting it fall again down on it, the breathe gently caressing her beautiful facial features.

Adriel was petting his horse, Titan, and Dawako was standing with Crevan looking at what they had in front and around of them.

-Yellow. A lot of yellow. - Dawako said, more as a loud thought.

-And wet. - Crevan added.

In fact the air, even if nicely warm, had a light characteristic to be quite wet.

Adriel looked at the other two men and he smiled.

-Much better than the dry and misty air we had surrounding us when we encountered that monster. -

They all agreed without a verbal answer.

Lisica's horse was peacefully walking around them, enjoying the touch of the soft grass, but by himself, without sharing his time with the other three black and blond maned horses.

-Your horse... You actually never told me his name. - Adriel went to talk to Lisica.

The Princess looked at her beautiful bright white horse walking not far from where her and Adriel were, his light blue mane moved by the calm wind.

-Destiny. -

Adriel looked at the horse with his mouth semi open.

-That... That is a beautiful name...-

-Oh, I didn't give it to him myself. - Lisica answered.

-And who named him, then? King Balgair...? -

-Not even. - The Princess kept looking at Destiny.

-Someone gave him to my father. And my father gave him to me. As a present. But he was already named like that and we didn't change it. -

Everything sounded a bit mysterious, but Adriel asked nothing more.

Crevan called Adriel and the Princess.

-My Princess! Adriel! Come to join us, please! -

Dawako and Crevan were preparing few sandwiches and the good looking boy with his wonderful bright smile, was sticking some Molecula inside of them.

-This will make them even more fulfilling. -

Adriel didn't complaint.

Everyone of them learned very quickly how that very particular vegetable was in fact extremely useful for their energy during their long journey.

They were all happily eating, when Crevan looked at every single present and he decided to speak.

-I think I still have to tell you few more things about The Circle. -

Adriel nearly bit his own tongue. It was unusual for the Commander Of The Fox to be the first initiating some sort of conversation that was involving something about The Circle, especially if it was something related to its unbelievable secrets.

-Yeah… I mean… I know sometimes I dodge these kinds of conversations, but… Maybe… I can tell you just a bit more… For you to be ready…-

There was something strange in his voice, in the way he was talking.

It was like he was saying those words, definitely very felt, but also using them to hide something higher than that.

-So. Last time we spoke about all the different Kingdoms of The Circle, the ones in the Regions Of Light, the ones part of the Regions Of Darkness and, of course, our Silvery Lands.-

He took back his Styx.

Sipping it, he continued, while Dawako, Lisica and more than them Adriel, were attentively listening, ready to discover even more about their unusual World.

-Every Kingdom has a Hierarchy. - Crevan said.

-A King. A Hero, which is the Ultimate Protector of the Kingdom. A Commander, still in command of the other Warriors, the Army, of the Kingdom. -

By saying that, he proudly looked at the then cloudy sky.

-Then, there is a Leader. The Leader of a Kingdom still has a huge and important role as the one that reports suspicious activities around that Kingdom and he also have the duty to ensure the quality of Life of its inhabitants and so their level of happiness. -

Adriel was listening, still munching the piece of sandwich he had in his mouth since Crevan started to talk.

-We then have a Kingdom's Guardian. -

This time was Dawako's turn to appear the most interested one.

-I have never heard of such a figure…-

-Of course you didn't. - Lisica interrupted.

-His identity is secret. Only the King, the Hero, the Commander and the Leader know who he is. Not even my mother or I know his actual identity.

Dawako looked at Adriel, in that moment without his usual bright smile.

-So many things we don't know, man…-

Adriel didn't look back at him, but he nodded with his head.

-Everything correct. - The Commander said taking back the lead of the conversation.

-The reason why his identity is that secret, is due to the fact that the Guardian has the knowledge of aspects of the Kingdom that are ancient and unknown to the most. The Guardian knows things of the Kingdom that not even the King is aware of. -

The Princess had a look at her horse.

The beautiful light blue mane caressed by the air.

-Let's see how smart you are now. - Crevan said.

-Who wants to tell me who comes after the Guardian? Who is next in line? -

Everyone had some little thinking.

-The Army? - Adriel tried.

-The blacksmiths because of the weapons they make for the Army?- Dawako exclaimed.

-The people. -

Lisica's answer made Crevan smile.

-The people. Exactly. All of them. No-one above anyone else, everyone at the same level, whatever they do… A farmer, a Barman, a waitress, a warrior, a painter… The people. That's who is coming right after the five figures we have already named. -

That was, in some way, a sort of emotional answer.

But the two rivals and the Princess were still waiting for more.

-And finally, after the people, there is one last step. One last step only. The seventh level of our Hierarchy. -

Silence.

The atmosphere was a bit heavier in that moment and they all had to breath a bit deeper than usual, while, at the same time, trying to hold their breath due to the excitement about what the Commander was about to reveal to them.

And, ultimately, Crevan spoke.

-The Sacred Animals. -

Adriel didn't say anything in response. Nobody did.

Then, the Princess spoke first.

-Please. Keep talking. -

And that day, Crevan had not the slightest intention to stop talking about The Circle.

-The Sacred Animals... Holy Beings put in our Dimension... In our Existence... To maintain the balance... The order... To look after us when nobody else does... Capable to change the course of the events...-

Adriel then promptly interrupted the Commander Of The Fox.

-Put in our Dimension... And in our Existence... By who...? -

Crevan did expect that question, but he stupidly hoped, even if only for a moment, that no-one was going to come up with that.

-Every Kingdom of The Circle has been created under the skills and characteristics of a specific animal...- He said, completely ignoring Adriel's question.

-The Sacred Animals are the first ones of their Species. -

-Well... But...- Dawako said, trying to formulate an accurate question under the look of Adriel, at the same time upset and speechless by the fact Crevan totally ignored his question.

-You just explained to us the whole Hierarchy of the Kingdoms of The Circle. From top to bottom...- Dawako continued.

-How the Sacred Animals can be at the bottom of this Hierarchy? I mean... They are the ones and only that keep the balance and the control of the Kingdom, in such a Holy way, after all...-

This time the Commander was very happy to answer to that question, making Adriel even more upset and unhappy.

-Fair point, Dawako. And here we are, even due to your appoint, at the ultimate explanation of this Hierarchy. -

Crevan used his fingers to picture in the air the shape of a Pyramid.

-Imagine our Hierarchy as a Pyramid. At the top we have the King. Then the Hero, the Commander, the Leader... The Guardian, the people... And the Sacred Animal at the bottom. -

He then kept picturing his invisible Pyramid in the air, but reversing it.

-Now, imagine putting this Pyramid upside down. -

Everyone was listening in some sort of solemn silence.

-The biggest and most spacious spot of the Pyramid, that earlier was at the bottom, now is at the top of it. And that is where the Sacred Animal is located. The ultimate hope of any Kingdom. The ultimate form of salvation. We then have the people at the second level. The people are the ones more in need of their Sacred Animal, because regular people always feel the need to have someone or something where to place their final hope in and the Sacred Animals represent that kind of hope. Also, there is no-one the Sacred Animals care about more than the people. The ones in need.-

Crevan then sipped his Styx to then concluding that long but very revealing sentence.

-Remember. A King is not enough to make a Kingdom. There is no Kingdom without the people. -

Everyone was sincerely fascinated.

Even Adriel, that for a moment forgot the fact that he was still upset with the Commander Of The Fox, that purposely didn't answer to a question that was then finding a comfortable space inside Adriel's mind.

-The Guardian is then at the third place. As we already said, the one that knows the most of the Kingdom's secrets, even regarding the Sacred Animal. The Guardian is the one that really can help in solving situations where nobody else would be able to find a way. -

Everything, until then, was making sense inside everyone's mind.

Crevan was very clear in all the aspects of his explanations.

-The Leader. The fourth most important figure of this upside down Pyramid. He is the one that physically and spiritually take care of the Life of the people of the Kingdom, being in direct contact with them, something no-one else does, not the Commander, not the Hero and certainly not the King. And as we have already said this is not something possible to be done by the Guardian, due to the fact his identity is secret and also, his knowledge is not sharable with regular people. Some of their knowledge is not even possible to be shared with the King. -

The Commander stopped for a moment just to be sure, once again, that everyone was following without any problem in the understanding of his very important and unique speech.

Nobody spoke, so Crevan restarted with it.

-The Commander. It's simple. No Kingdom is a Kingdom without an Army and warriors to raise up and to make grow to perfection. That's why the Commander of a Kingdom is important. To empower the forces of that Kingdom. -

Everybody noticed the pride in Crevan's words, but they all thought it was more than legitimate.

Dawako asked something that sounded in fact a bit strange.

-So, are you telling us the Hero, the Ultimate Protector of a Kingdom, is close to the bottom? -

Crevan laughed.

-Yes, Dawako. The Hero is, in the Hierarchy of the original Pyramid, the one that comes right after the King. In our upside down Pyramid, he is instead close to the last level of the Hierarchy. You want to know why? -

No answer was needed. They were all ears.

-Because without all the other roles we have just mentioned, all above him, a Hero would not have any single reason to exist. Because he would not have anyone to be the absolute strongest for.-

That sentence did hit hard. Pleasantly hard.

Adriel felt his blood running hot and fast inside of his veins, Dawako showed his perfect smile and Lisica as well was absolutely stunned by that amazing explanation.

Then Adriel spoke and everyone looked at him.

-That's why in this Pyramid the King is at the bottom of the Hierachy. -

Crevan looked deep inside of him, before the green-eyed boy completed his sentence.

-Because without every single other figure above him, a King would have no reason to be a King. -

Dawako had a laugh.

-Well, absolutely... But I guess at this point of the Commander's explanation, we are all able to understand that, thank you, Adriel.- He then concluded showing a radiant smile at the Princess, that didn't smile back.

-I believe you miss the deepest part of all of this, Dawako. - Adriel then said, looking hard at the rival.

-It is pretty clear to me. It is actually very simple... The roles and the power of all of these figures don't change. The importance of all of these individuals will never change. A King will always be a King, in any single kind of way you rotate the Hierarchy. As the Hero's greatness remains the same, he is the Ultimate Protector, the strongest warrior of the Kingdom. The Commander...-

And Adriel gave a look of gratitude at Crevan.

-How a Kingdom would have its Hero if there would not be a wonderful and strong Commander to raise him up, as well as all the other warriors of the Kingdom, generating an Army strong enough to face everyone...-

The Commander Of The Fox felt emotional inside of himself, but he succeeded in not showing it.

Adriel continued.

-The incredible and pure presence of the Leader. The importance of the Guardian, who holds the deepest secrets of the Kingdom and of the entire majesty of The Circle. The people, the ones that really make our Kingdom. And...-

He took a deep breath.

-The Sacred Animals. The ultimate help, the ultimate hope, the ones that can change everything, even the destiny in any type of event... For all of these figures their role or importance never change. It stays exactly the same. -

He stood up.

-Because...- And he then concluded.

-Everyone helps everyone in The Circle. Every single one of these individuals is important for all the others. We all help each other. We all support each other. King, Hero, Commander, Leader, Guardian, regular people, and even the Sacred Animals. At the end of the story, none of these figures would have any reason to exist without all the others. -

A very light rain was falling on them, but it was not strong, it was a very lovely feeling over their skin.

No-one said anything in response of Adriel's words. Surely, Dawako was not smiling anymore. They were all thinking about those words. Those right and strong words.

Crevan stood up too and he looked proud at Adriel.

-Indeed...-

Then, suddenly, the Commander went serious.

-Is everything fine, Crevan? - Lisica asked.

The Commander Of The Fox didn't directly answer to that question, but he kept talking.

-And here we come to the unpleasant event we had to experience very much against out will. -

The light rain did already stop, and now the Sun was back shining through the few remaining clouds.

-The enormous snake we encountered…-

And Dawako interrupted.

-No way!!!-

And Adriel and Lisica understood too.

-Yes…- Crevan looked at the area around them.

It happened to be Lisica the one to say those words.

-The Sacred Animal of the Kingdom Of The Serpent. -

Crevan's silence was louder than any answer.

Adriel was lost inside his mind, once again.

-But why…-

-It is not easy for me to understand the reason why. - Crevan said.

-However, whatever the reason is, it is quite obvious the intention was to do not let us carrying on in our journey to the Kingdom Of The Wolf. -

Dawako stood up.

-But… So, if that was the Sacred Animal of the Kingdom Of The Serpent… The fox…-

-Correct. - Crevan confirmed.

-That was our Sacred Animal…- And he looked in the eyes of everyone of them before concluding.

-Tokala. -

-She came to save us…- Adriel was once again thinking out loud.

It was not his intention to share his personal thoughts, but somehow it was like he was not able to keep them silent inside of his mind.

Crevan jumped a bit on the spot to keep warm. The air was starting to get colder. The conditions of the weather and even the temperature, were pretty unusual in the location were the inhabitants of Vixen and Renard were at that point of their journey.

-But... There is one thing I can not quite understand...- The Commander said.

Lisica stood up too, then none of them was still sitting on the yellow grass anymore.

-And what is that? - She asked, curious and genuinely interested in the answer.

-The Sacred Animals don't really interact with each other... Unless there is a particular situation... An immense kind of event...-

-Well...- Adriel said.

-We were basically about to get killed by the Kingdom Of The Serpent's Sacred Animal... I guess that was more than a fair reason for our... Tokala... To appear...-

Crevan looked at him, then he gave his back to them.

-It's not only that... Every single Sacred Animal can be evocated or in some very particular circumstances can appear only in relation to one person...-

Dawako felt inspired and spoke.

-I understand! The King! And it was quite strange, as our King was not there...-

-Wrong. - The Commander strongly interrupted him.

-The person related to the Sacred Animal, is not the King. -

Crevan then faced back all of them, and he declared.

-It's the Hero. -

XVI

THE DREAM

A lot had been revealed in the past few days, that was the thought that welcomed Adriel to the new morning, thinking in particular about the conversation of the previous night, but too many questions, actually even more than before, were finding place inside of his already busy mind.

Why the Sacred Animal of the Kingdom Of The Serpent showed up, trying to interrupt their journey to the Kingdom Of The Wolf?

And how was it possible that Tokala, the Sacred Animal of the Kingdom Of The Fox, appeared even if in a situation of Life or Death, as the only figure being able to generate a connection with the Sacred Animal in every Kingdom, was the figure of the Hero? And it was certainly not a secret that the Kingdom Of The Fox still didn't have its one, not yet.

So, what actually happened that day?

Did Tokala act by her own choice?

Did somebody else send her to save them?

Also, his main thought was the fact he was seeing Tokala in his dreams every Equinoce and every Solstice, since twenty years, and he didn't even know, before the day she showed up, about her real existence or even about what she was representing.

Every single thought regarding that, was not only making his mind painfully full, but also, it was making Adriel live in a complete state of tremendous confusion.

It was also making him feel angry, somehow. A lot of different feelings were all colliding with each other.

Sometimes there were moments he was also feeling sad.

What if he was not going to succeed? What if Dawako, was in fact better than him, as he previously already showed up amazing skills and hidden energy power and more than once?

Yes, he was always repeating to Crevan and to himself that he was going to win, that his power didn't really show up yet just because he had the belief it was there, hiding deep inside of his Soul, ready to come out from his body when it would have been really needed… Because too great to simply being generated through his sword in some very useful but somehow simple trainings.

And he was really feeling like that.

But what if he was wrong?

The Hero Of The Fox.

To become the new Ultimate Protector of his Kingdom, was his greatest obsession.

However, between the many colliding feelings he was experiencing that morning, Adriel didn't have the slightest trace of one feeling in particular, inside of himself.

Fear.

He was happy, he was confused, he was upset, he was melancholic…

But he was not scared.

Not at all.

-Adriel Centauri. -

The low voice that called his name, roughly woke him up from his thoughts.

-Lisica! Oh, I mean, I deeply apologise, I really mean it… I mean… Princess…-

Lisica laughed.

-You can call me Lisica if you like…-

The encounter of their eyes did last for not more than a second, but it seemed like it did last forever.

-Oh… I am not sure I could do that… But… I will try…-

Another giggle came out from the Princess' mouth.

-What's the matter? -

Adriel didn't understand that question.

-What do you mean…? -

Princess Lisica looked at him with an expression between the severe and the amused.

-I see you. Don't try to hide yourself to me… You are an open book… I can tell something is disturbing your mind…-

Adriel felt caught. Dawako and Crevan were already awake too, but far from them, fixing stuff on their horses.

Destiny, as always, was walking in a sort of solemn way by himself, away from the rest of the crew.

And Adriel spoke.

-Princess. I have so many things inside my head… I cannot find a proper explanation to anything that is occupying my mind these days…-

And he looked again at the Commander.

-Yesterday a lot has been revealed, but somehow that made everything even more unclear, if possible. -

Lisica took a deep breath and she nodded with her head.

-I understand. I feel the same. As the Princess of this Kingdom, I thought I knew enough, but I have realised how much I actually don't know. -

Adriel looked at her. She was really feeling similar emotions to the ones he was experiencing through that journey they were in.

-I know it's not a nice feeling, Adriel. -

-No. It is not. - He agreed.

He took a moment to think about something to say and he then somehow found the words to let the Princess know about one of his biggest thoughts.

-Even my dreams… How come… How is it possible… I have never known about Tokala's existence before the encounter with the Sacred Animal of the Kingdom Of The Serpent…-

-Oh, right!!! Your dreams!!!- Lisica yelled out loud.

Both Dawako and Crevan looked in their direction.

-Hey! What is going on in there? - The Commander Of The Fox asked from the distance.

-Nothing! It is all good, I am sorry, Crevan! - The Princess said.

The fact she said she was sorry to Crevan was way more suspicious than the fact she said a very obvious fake "Nothing" to start her sentence.

However, somehow it worked, as the Commander and Dawako went back to their being busy to get ready to restart the journey.

-Adriel…- Lisica extremely lowered her voice that much that Adriel then had issues to hear what she was saying.

-Do you… Do you remember… Adriel, what did you dream last night? -

Adriel was confused.

-I cannot remember… Why…? -

Lisica took his arm.

His heart missed a beat.

-Last night… It was strange… You woke me up. - She said.

But Adriel was barely listening to her.

He was facing something way more difficult than the apparently serious topic Lisica was so avid to talk about.

He was fighting with the strong instinct to take her hand and to exchange a touch he was dreaming about, but with open eyes, since the first time she showed up in Vixen and in his very own Existence.

Ultimately, he somehow managed to answer.

-How did I wake you up…? -

-It was strange. - She said.

-You were sweating. You were talking to someone, but it was impossible to understand who you were talking to. -

-We will go in ten minutes! - Crevan exclaimed in that moment.

-And… What was I saying…? -

And his eyes instinctively went in direction of the Commander and Dawako.

-No.- Lisica promptly said.

-They were very much asleep. -

She then finally left the held on his arm.

But his heart was still beating fast.

-I'm not sure… What you were saying was very confused… But I remember you were talking about a sword… And you were asking… To whoever he was… How to make the blade being able to absorb the light of the Sun… And you were keeping saying "Too many clouds, too many clouds!" and still you were sweating very much. -

-Five minutes! - Crevan impatiently informed.

Then it happened as a matter of pure instinct, he actually didn't really mean to do that, but somehow, he did.

It was Adriel that took that time the Princess' arm.

-Lisica. Please. Tell me more. What else was I saying? -

The Princess Of The Fox looked at his hand. Strong but tenderly holding her arm.

-You didn't say anything else… Well, no, wait… Apart of the very last thing you said… Yes, you said one more thing…-

Adriel waited.

-I'm ready. - Lisica said.

-What? You are ready for what? - Adriel asked, a bit panicked about the fact Crevan would have call them very soon, ready to go.

-No. You said, "I'm ready", that was the last thing you said while you were dreaming. -

Silence.

Adriel left the Princess' arm, interrupting the holding of it.

-Enough talking for this morning? -

Both Adriel and Lisica jumped due to the surprise.

Behind them, Crevan was looking at them.

-How did you…-

Crevan laughed.

-Maybe one day you will be able to do it as well. -

-But you didn't…-

-I have heard every single word. Yes, even from the distance. - He said interrupting Lisica's words.

-So… You know…-

-I know what, Adriel? I was very much asleep, indeed. But as I have said… I have heard this whole conversation between you two…-

Adriel didn't even think before speaking.

-I guess you know… Who I was talking to…-

That question didn't surprise Crevan at all.

-Yes. I know. -

Adriel's eyes got a shine crossing them.

-And I also guess you can not tell me…-

-No. I can not. -

Adriel looked behind him, to the yellow landscape that was brilliantly showing itself all around them.

-Fine. I guess… I will have to accept that…-

-You have to, young man. For now. -

Adriel was then fighting against a new instinct.

He was really feeling like he really wanted to go home.

The thoughts he had in the morning were already more than enough to handle with.

Then he had that new revelation about something he said while being asleep, inside of a dream he was not even able to remember.

He really didn't need that.

-Now it's time to go. - Crevan said.

Adriel, even if against his will, followed the Commander Of The Fox and Lisica did the same, but at some point she stopped.

She was like looking for something, she was literally busy in the clear intent to find something around there, searching with her eyes all around the area.

-Is everything fine? -

Crevan stopped too, looking at her.

Adriel was not able to understand what was happening as well.

-Crevan. - She then spoke.

-There's any roses around here? -

The Commander's eyes had a quick expression of surprise that promptly disappeared.

-Why do you ask? -

-Because…- She kept saying.

-I have noticed it last night, during Adriel's dream… I can't be wrong… There was a very strong and… Intense… Smell of roses… But I can not see any of them around here…-

With that being said, the Princess kept looking around, but not walking away, as waiting for one more answer from the Commander regarding her very singular question.

-I know you have been around here already, Crevan… Where are they…? -

And Crevan didn't make the Princess wait one more second for an answer.

-Nowhere, Princess. - He stated.

-There's no roses around here. Not even one. And yes, I indeed know this location very well. And actually…-

He took a pause and, the eyes pointed on both Adriel and Lisica.

-And actually, not even a single rose ever grew up around these lands. -

XVII

THE DRAGONS' TREE

For all the rest of the day, Adriel had been very thoughtful regarding the conversation he had with Lisica about the dream he apparently had the previous night, but that he was not able to remember not even in a small part.

And Crevan, appearing out of nowhere right behind them, that apparently knew who he was talking to in his dream, but avoiding to tell him who that person was.

"I'm ready."

That's what he said at some point in his dream, Lisica said.

Ready for what?

And again. Roses. Smell of roses all around, she said.

As he was smelling in all of his dreams every Equinox and every Solstice since twenty years. And even when he was waking up, then back to Reality.

Where they were finding themselves at that point of the journey, was somewhere where the sky was dark blue, like about to get ready for its nightly best colour, but in fact, it was still early afternoon when they arrived in front of that beauty of a view.

-Weird... It looks like is about to be night time. But it is still very early...-

Dawako was admiring the sky.

Up there, like always when the sky was clear, those billions of small chunks of ice and dusty rocks.

They were so far but yet so incredibly visible.

-Something you don't know…- Crevan said.

-Our World is very singular…-

As always, Crevan being so mysterious, was annoying Adriel a little bit.

They were riding their horses on old roads, where the fields all around were visibly burnt. Even the smell in the air was a mix of wood and ash.

-Everything looks burnt in here. - The Princess was the first one mentioning that.

-A long time ago…- The Commander responded.

-A massively epic battle happened in here. Since then, the whole environment around here has never been the same anymore. -

Lisica thought about those words.

-Two very powerful warriors, then…-

-Oh no, Princess. - Crevan said.

-We are not talking about two Human Beings. -

It would have been legitimate for one of them to question Crevan regarding that statement, but something caught Adriel's attention.

-Hey! What is that? -

There was a huge and massive trunk not far from where they were, but the strangeness of that was the fact the trunk was the only remaining part of what, a long time ago, was a tree.

The trunk was going up and up until reaching its final top, broken, no branches, nothing was part of it anymore.

And, even more singular, was the colour aspect of it.

Black, very black, with some soft brilliant dark blue smoke that was calmly airing around of it.

-There it is…- Crevan's words.

-Such a long time I didn't see it…-

They all stopped, looking at it from their spot on the empty and lonely roads.

-The Dragons' Tree. -

No roots were visible.

Adriel jumped from his horse.

-I want to see it closer. -

-No, you don't! -

Crevan jumped from his horse too, taking Adriel by his arm.

-Why not? - The boy asked.

-There is something we should know about it, maybe? -

The way he pronounced those words, was full of sarcasm.

-The reason why it looks like that is just another result of the epic battle I have mentioned to you earlier, regarding the unusual appearance of the environment around here. -

Crevan tried to dodge Adriel's sarcastic look at him.

-I want you to tell us what that battle was about. -

Those words left Adriel, Dawako and mainly Crevan, very surprised.

The Princess was looking at the Commander.

-It can not all be a secret around here, Crevan. You have to tell us something, sometimes. What that battle was about? -

Crevan felt hopeless for a moment.

-Princess…-

-No, Crevan. -

The authority that was fulfilling those words, made the Commander Of The Fox without anything to reply.

-I am the Princess of the Kingdom Of The Fox. I am the daughter of King Balgair. The King you serve. What I am asking to you, is to stop to try to deny important answers regarding The Circle, mainly because some of those answers might reveal to be hugely important in whatever we will find ourselves in, during this journey, and also during our everyday Lives. -

Adriel and Dawako were moving their eyes fast between Lisica and Crevan, enjoying every bit of that moment.

-Unless. - The Princess then said.

-Unless you really have a fair and proper reason to avoid talking to us about something in particular. But this cannot be happening every single time we have a question for you regarding something about The Circle.-

The way the Princess Of The Fox was speaking, was very intense.

-My dear Princess… Adriel… Dawako…- Crevan thought about what to say and the way to say it.

-Yes. Yes, there is something. There is something going on, something that has always been going on and always will, there's so many things you don't know. And yes, Princess Lisica, I serve your father, King Balgair, and you should then also know that it is actually part of my duties to do not say much regarding the mysteries of The Circle. By his order. -

He took a breath. He was feeling tired. And melancholic, for some reason.

-Please… Believe me when I say that maybe… Probably… For sure… Not even me I am totally, completely aware of all of the mystical secrets of our incredible World. -

That was a very felt answer. Straight from the deepest side of his heart. Directly from his Soul.

-Just remember this. - He continued.

-Whatever happens. You should never stop in the process to elevate yourself. Every single day you should always find the time to close your eyes and know a bit more of your inner self. The more you'll do that, the more you'll be prepared and ready when the time to prove your power will come. -

He then relaxed a bit more, looking at the icy and rocky materials far away in the sky.

-Work on yourself. All of you. The best you've got is not enough. You have to go deeper inside of your Soul to attain the ultimate result, the one you really need to achieve. -

Lisica's eyes were wet.

-Honestly? This was all I wanted to hear. -

Adriel and Dawako looked at each other without saying a word.

Crevan's words had a lot of meaning. A very deep one.

-Now. - Crevan said with a new found smile.

-We should go further. -

They all agreed, and they were all ready to restart their journey and so they did.

They were slowly leaving the location where they were, the black and smoky tree about to be left behind from their view.

Adriel had one last look at it.

Even if Crevan's speech moved him inside and he found it very emotional, he was still very much interested on the secret that he was hiding regarding that tree.

He was about to succeed in letting that thought disappear from his mind, about to move his look away from the mysterious tree, when something caught his attention.

He was not totally sure he actually saw it. Maybe it was just an impression.

He made Titan slowing down.

Lisica noticed that.

Destiny, for the first time in a long time or maybe even for the first time Adriel was able to remember, shook his head with strength, strangely, and he stomped his hooves on the ground with energy.

-What's the matter? - The Princess asked at Adriel, but at the same time giving a surprise and confused look at Destiny.

Adriel kept looking directly at the tree.

-I don't know… Maybe it was just an impression… But… I think… Someone did fly away from where the tree is…-

Lisica opened her eyes in an expression of pure surprise.

-What… You've seen what?!-

Adriel let his horse stop and Lisica did the same.

Destiny was keeping acting in a very unusual and strange way, still stomping his hooves on the old road, but even harder, producing some very weird sound with his mouth.

The green-eyed young man then looked at his Princess.

-An Angel. Lisica, it was an Angel. -

XVIII

THE WALK

Not much difference was able to be spotted up in the sky and around when the night showed up.

The location where Adriel, Dawako, Crevan and Lisica were finding themselves in that precise moment, was still part of the Kingdom Of The Fox, even if they were starting to get not that far from their final destination, the Kingdom Of The Wolf.

The sky was of a dreamy dark blue colour, even if it was still early afternoon.

Adriel was looking at Destiny. The Princess' horse was motionless standing away from all of them, his brilliant light blue eyes lost into the nothing.

-Hey. -

Adriel turned his head.

-Hey. -

He didn't even mean to give such a dry answer to Lisica, but in that moment he would have not been able to reply in any other different way.

-I apologise…-

-No, don't worry. -

She smiled at him.

-Have you spoke to Crevan? -

Adriel looked at her with an interrogative expression.

-Regarding what? -

-Oh, come on, you know about what. -

And Adriel perfectly knew about what, indeed.

He very well knew what the Princess was talking about.

-No. No, I did not…-

Princess Lisica tried to sound not too much intrusive, but she anyway expressed her very personal opinion.

-I think you should. -

Adriel looked surprised at her.

-Really? -

-Yes. Really. -

He didn't really know what to say about that.

-But why…-

Lisica smiled at him once again, softly.

-Not every single why you have inside your mind needs a because, Adriel.-

And with one last, deep, great smile she concluded.

-Do it. -

Emotions. Vibrations. Feelings. Sensations. Few different words with basically the same exact meaning.

But that inside of Adriel's brain, heart and blood, were all pumping very differently and definitely in an absolute separate way.

-I will. - He said, looking back at her.

-Today. - He specified.

They walked down the fresh green grass that was leading to where Crevan and Dawako were talking and laughing.

-Hey, you two. There you are. - Crevan said.

Dawako, for once, didn't show his iconic smile. Actually, it was happening quite frequently those days, since the journey started.

-Commander. Would you like to come to have a walk with me? -

Crevan's eyebrows gave him an expression of pure surprise.

-A walk? -

Adriel felt a bit impatient. Few minutes earlier, he was way far from even thinking to talk to the Commander Of The Fox regarding that very delicate topic. Then, he suddenly felt like to tell him everything about what he saw, was all he wanted to do.

-Yes. A walk. -

Adriel's voice and attitude didn't give to Crevan the possibility to say anything else as, still surprised and maybe then even a bit gently confused, he slowly stood up from the grass.

-Great. Let's go, then. For a walk. -

They left Princess Lisica and Dawako behind, but before leaving them out of sight, Adriel gave a last furtive look at them.

Crevan noticed that, but without mentioning anything about it.

-So… Young man. Tell me. What the meaning of this walk is about? -

Adriel got brought back to the present, there, with the Commander Of The Fox.

-Commander. I wanted to talk to you…-

Crevan laughed.

-Yeah, I think I understood that. But… What about…? -

Adriel thought about the words to say.

-About today. When we left the Dragons' Tree. -

Crevan this time didn't laugh.

-Oh. And what about that? -

Adriel's breath was slow.

-I think… Well, I know… I saw somebody in there…-

The Commander was not even smiling anymore.

-You saw somebody in there? Well, you need to speak straight and clear if you want me to understand what you are talking about, Adriel. -

Adriel, completely out of nowhere, felt something very strange.

The palms of his hands suddenly started to feel very hot.

He tried to do not focus on that and he kept his conversation with the Commander.

-Yes. I saw that… Somebody was there close to the tree… And…-

Crevan was waiting, holding his breath.

-And…? -

-And he flew away. -

He said it fast but clear enough for Crevan to understand every single word of that very unexpected kind of statement.

-He flew away? - He said, looking very seriously inside Adriel's green eyes.

-Yeah. He did. -

Crevan tried to remain relaxed, but every single part of his body was in that moment failing in that attempt.

The Commander of the Kingdom Of The Fox opened his mouth, about to say something, but then Adriel spoke before he was able to.

-He was an Angel. -

-What?!- Crevan's voice broke while coming out from his mouth.

-An Angel. I saw him very clearly. He was an Angel. -

Adriel was ready. He was ready for a probably confused and most definitely upset reply coming from Crevan but, even if the Commander was looking at him in a sort of serious but not upset way he never did before, his calm and soft answer surprised the young green-eyed man from Renard.

-Well. Let's be glad you didn't see a Devil, then. -

-Commander…-

-Another time. It's all good. Now it's not the moment for this. - Crevan said.

He then kept the eye contact with Adriel, and he spoke with feeling.

-Please. -

Adriel felt that.

And he also understood.

He understood that what he saw was way more than real.

He understood Crevan knew a lot more than what he was trying to show every single time they were talking about the many different topics of The Circle.

He also understood that, for once, maybe Crevan was right regarding the fact he didn't want to talk about it in the details in that moment.

That was an extremely exceptional kind of topic. Something completely out of the World, something he didn't even know was possibly part of the reality, part of the Existence.

And Crevan's answer… An answer that opened an even more mysterious kind of revelation…

They both walked down the fields and before they were able to spot Lisica and Dawako once again, Crevan asked.

-Only Lisica knows, right? -

Adriel looked at him.

-Yes. -

And, for the first time since Adriel revealed what he saw hours before that same day, Crevan smiled at him.

-Obviously…-

Adriel was not too sure if he liked that answer or not.

He decided, inside of his busy head, that he probably didn't.

Once they started to be able to see them again while getting back, Crevan had still something to say to Adriel.

-Don't say anything to Dawako. Please. -

The way he asked that, made Adriel understand there was seeming to be a very particular reason why the Commander decided to make that request.

-Sure. Not a problem. -

He was learning, step by step and very slowly, to refrain himself from asking all the reasons why.

It was way far from being easy for a curious Being like him but, somehow, he was starting to learn how to refrain his insane need to get an answer for every single type of matter.

Dawako was sleeping under a tree and Lisica was awake, contemplating the eternity of the sky.

-Adriel! Crevan! - She said once being aware they were back.

Crevan looked in Dawako's direction.

-Yes, he started to sleep almost at the same time when you two left. -

Lisica explained that before Crevan was able to say anything.

Adriel stretched his arms.

-I think that I will, for once, follow his example… I feel quite tired.-

The Commander sat close to the Princess.

-Goodnight, then. -

The young man found himself surprised by that quick answer.

-Alright…-

He then looked at Princess Lisica.

-Goodnight…-

She smiled and she winked at him.

Once Adriel reached another close tree where to lay under, Crevan took Lisica's arm.

She didn't feel surprised by that reaction at all, and she also spoke before the Commander Of The Fox.

-He told you. -

Crevan looked at her with intensity.

-Yes. Damn, yes. He did. - He then lowered his voice the best he was able to.

-I had to act like I was not too impressed… Like it was somehow explainable… Which it is… But also, is not… I mean… He saw…-

-An Angel. - Lisica finished his sentence.

-An Angel. - Crevan also said.

They remained silent for few instants.

Dawako was snoring not far from there.

Adriel was laying down another tree close to where the horses were.

Except one of them.

-Where is Destiny? - Crevan asked.

Lisica didn't look preoccupied at all.

-Don't worry. Sometimes he does that. -

-He does what? -

The Princess looked around.

-He is here. But you can't see him. -

For once, it was Crevan that would have loved to ask questions.

But before he would have even just been able to try his luck with that, something got all of their attention.

Few very pale light blue lights flashed few feet from them.

Very luminously. Very rapidly.

-What…-

But before Crevan even had the time to stood up, Adriel's voice reached them as a loud scream, strong and clear.

-I'm ready!!!-

They both stood up and they ran in his direction.

He was there, laying on the grass under the tree and he was moving his head quite a lot, like he was deep and fully inside of his own dream, living it through his reality.

And then again.

-I'm ready!!!-

-Adriel! - Lisica was about to grab him, but Crevan stopped her.

-Don't. -

The Princess Of The Fox looked at him with anger.

-He is somewhere he doesn't have to be! We need to wake him up! -

But the Commander kept his hold on her.

-Please, no. This is… He is not somewhere he doesn't have to be… Actually… He is far deep inside a very unique and Holy process… That doesn't have to be interrupted…-

The Princess' expression of anger got replaced by pure shock.

-Holy process…?! How do you even know the nature of what is happening inside of his head…? -

Crevan then brought a finger close to his own nose.

-Princess...-

And in that moment Princess Lisica didn't really have many words to say.

-Yes...-

Completely out of nowhere, an unbelievably intense smell of roses started to fulfil the whole area.

An area where there was only grass and trees, where green was the main colour and where there was not the slightly sight of the presence of not even a single rose.

Then the atmosphere changed, it got heavier and then lighter again.

It got windy. And warm. Way warmer.

The mysterious light blue lights they previously saw, flashed once again, more vividly, more strongly.

Lisica started to feel very bad, almost like she had the need to scream.

The Commander was suddenly on his knees, his hands on his head, unable to stop the tears that were crossing all of his face.

Then Adriel opened his eyes.

The smell of roses vanished.

The wind was there no more.

The temperature was back to normal.

Lisica was once again feeling perfectly fine and Crevan was back on his feet, close to her, feeling great but confused and they were both looking at Adriel.

In the same meantime, only few feet away from them, Destiny was serenely moving his head visibly trying to smell the air.

It was looking quite strange, but it seemed even stranger once he stopped doing that to literally stare his incredible light blue eyes on Adriel, that was then looking at the Commander Of The Fox and the Princess.

-Adriel, you were dreaming… Again… The same…-

But the young man didn't even listen to what his Princess had to say, and he sat on the spot, looking straight into Crevan's eyes.

-Commander. -

The level of vibrations in that moment, was deeper than the Outer Space.

-Yes, Adriel…? -

Adriel stabbed Crevan's mind with his brilliant green eyes, and he expressed himself clearly… Calmly… With one simple statement.

-I'm ready. -

XIX

UNCONSCIOUS POWER

The following morning the breathe was mild and pleasant.

-What a great day to get even closer to our destination!- Crevan stated, stretching his arms and legs.

Dawako was exercising and Lisica was watching, completely disinterested.

Adriel was looking at his own sword.

Just a normal, regular sword, nothing special.

He then gave a look at Crevan. He was feeling in a weird mood that morning.

Certainly, the events that were happening since the beginning of their journey were not helping his peace of mind at all.

-Commander. -

Crevan looked at him.

-Yes? -

Adriel didn't reply straight away.

-What, Adriel? - The Commander Of The Fox insisted.

But the young man was just keeping his eyes on him.

-Well… Is everything ok with you…? -

Then, finally, Adriel spoke.

-It is. I was just wondering… Shouldn't we train at least a bit every now and then…? All together, I mean…-

What the Commander didn't really need that morning, just after waking up and more important with the Kingdom Of The Wolf still to reach, was Adriel questioning him about the reason why they were not taking some time to train. And all together.

-Adriel... Don't be silly. We just need to speed up our journey a bit... Plus, not less important, you and Dawako will soon be rivals. I don't think some fighting training would be a good idea...-

But Adriel was not interested in those words.

-Me and him will be not rivals. -

And he then gave a challenging look to Dawako, that was there looking at the scene.

-We are already rivals. -

Crevan looked at Lisica in search for help.

The Princess stood up from the grass.

-Actually, Crevan. I was wondering the same...-

The Commander's eyes got full of surprise after she said those words.

He quickly realised that any single try to avoid all of that, would have been a big failure.

-I see. You want to train? You really want to do this? Now? Before restarting our journey? Are you very sure about that? -

Adriel smiled at the Commander.

-Positive. -

Dawako's laugh broke the intensity of that moment.

-You are absolutely crazy, man. -

He walked closer to Adriel.

-Let me tell you one thing, Renardian... If you really think I will TRAIN with you... And also giving you an idea of my power...

You really are sick in the head…Well…- And Dawako's expression became very malicious.

-I am sure it would not even be a particular surprise… As it is a characteristic that runs pretty much in your family…-

Lisica brought her hands on her mouth.

Crevan gave a look at Dawako full of a feeling that had no name.

Adriel's hand went slowly on his own sword. He kept her on it, not a word.

And it happened faster than the wind, his sword was out, a rapid movement of his legs and he was already on Dawako.

The young man from Vixen had to dodge one, two, three times, and he did it pretty well, considering Adriel's speed was elevate and with the only goal to hurt the rival.

Dawako unsheathed his sword too and he clashed his blade against Adriel's one.

They were moving quick and also very well. Impossible to define who was handling the battle better only based on their capability of moving and managing their skills with the swords.

Maybe Adriel was even faster.

But Dawako was seeming way more solid and concrete in his fighting, with more experience.

Adriel was pure instinct.

Dawako was unbreakable resistance.

Adriel jumped quite high, and he threw a flying attack directed to Dawako's neck, but the boy from Vixen blocked the attempt and he took his turn to attack the opponent, with a long series of attacks that were all finding Adriel's blade in their way, making impossible for Dawako to hurt the green eyed man from Renard.

-Hey…- Lisica said to Crevan.

-Yeah…- The Commander said straight away.

-But... Crevan... They are...-

-Trying to kill each other...-

Dawako kicked Adriel in the leg, and he went for the attack, this time directed straight to his face, but Adriel was still well balanced and able to stay stand with confidence and so he succeeded in his defence, putting his blade right in between his own face and Dawako's sword.

But since few seconds, it was seeming like the usually smiling young man was getting stronger and stronger, giving the impression that Adriel was slowly losing the control of his own duel.

-Crevan, you have to stop them...- Lisica said.

-Crevan, you have to stop them right now! -

But the Commander Of The Fox was not even able to move.

-I can't... I just can't...-

-What?!- The Princess screamed.

-What do you mean you can't?! Of course you can, Crevan!!!-

Crevan was shaking on the spot.

-Something... Something is making me unable to move...-

-What?!-

Princess Lisica was looking at the Commander and she realised the way his boots were literally seeming to be one thing with the ground.

And he was shaking, he was sweating.

-Crevan...-

-I don't know what it is... I have not the slightest idea of what's happening... But one thing is sure...- And he looked at the Princess.

-One of those two...-

But before he was able to finish the sentence, a yell of pain reached their ears.

Adriel was holding his shoulder, his fingers of a vivid red colour.

Dawako's blade was presenting their same colour.

-I've got you…- Dawako said, his smile back on his face.

-STOP!!!- Lisica ordered, but Adriel and Dawako were not able to hear her.

-Hey…- She said more to herself than at Crevan.

-We are not here…-

And she touched the air that was surrounding her and the Commander.

-I can touch it…-

Crevan was speechless.

-One of those two…-

-We have been put inside a different Dimension… But still somehow part of our original one?! Like, we are living the events of our original Dimension, but unable to interact with it because in fact trapped inside of a different one?!-

-I wouldn't go that far. - Crevan said.

-It really is what it seems like but, in fact, is not. None of those two have the power or the skills to do something like that… But it is a very legitimate resemblance of it. -

Adriel was in that exact meantime on one knee, Dawako talking right above him.

-You wanted a training fight, Adriel? You really wanted it, yeah? Come on, then… Stand up… Train with me… Fight me…-

The laugh he put after those words was even more painful than the words themselves.

-Don't worry. I would never hurt you more than this, Adriel. After all, when I will be the new Hero of the Kingdom Of The Fox, I will definitely need to have someone that can be able to bring my sword. -

He laughed again.

Adriel was still on one knee, the hand on his bleeding shoulder, his eyes and his face impossible to be spotted as facing the ground, making his long brown hair the only possible view from everyone else's perspective.

-But to do that for me, all you need is your left arm, Adriel...- Dawako continued.

-I just want to be sure you will never be able to hold a sword again...-

He raised his sword.

Lisica screamed.

-HEY!!! NO!!! STOP!!!-

But her loud yell remained trapped inside those invisible limits that somebody generated above and around them just to be sure they would have not been able to interfere with that very unpredicted clash between the great Being from Vixen and the rebel young man from Renard.

Then, Adriel's voice made everyone silent.

-I'm sorry. - That was indeed what he said.

But his voice sounded lower than his regular one and also very heavy.

Dawako laughed.

-You are sorry? This is nice to hear... But... I am still decided to cut your arm off. -

And he positioned himself ready to deliver the final attack, his grey Aura flaming low and slow around him.

-I'm sorry. - Adriel repeated.

And he then added.

-But my Destiny doesn't allow me to surrender. -

And the eyes that Dawako saw in the meantime Adriel raised his look at him, were not Adriel's regular eyes.

There was not the pure and vivid green that were such a big characteristic of the young man from Renard.

There was, instead, fire.

Adriel's eyes were red like exploding fire.

-What the…? - Dawako stepped back.

Adriel stood up.

An unbelievably shiny orange Aura was surrounding his figure, then standing tall in front of Dawako, his posture giving out pride and strength.

Dawako felt heavy on his own legs, unable to properly move.

-What…- Lisica was shocked.

Crevan even more.

-This is… Insane…-

-What… What are you doing?!-

Dawako's voice was not that confident anymore.

His hand, the one holding the sword, was shaking.

But Adriel didn't reply, his look hard and firm on his rival, standing there, not a move, not a blink of the eyes, still fiery and then very shiny, red like the pain.

Dawako got overwhelmed.

-What are you doing?! Listen… I was not really going to cut your arm… I was bluffing… To make you quit…- His voice broke.

-I swear… I would have stopped there…-

His grey Aura disappeared, his whole energy got sucked away and his hand got senseless, the sword hitting the ground.

And then, before any other word was able to be said, Adriel's Aura got higher and more intense, orange, full of flames firing all around of it and all around of him.

It happened fast.

A glare of his eyes and a huge amount of invisible energy hit Dawako right in the chest, sending him down on the ground, slamming on it several feet away from where he initially was.

And it ended there.

Adriel's eyes visibly turned back to their original green colour, closing right after, his Aura instantly vanishing, his body collapsing down on the green grass of those lands.

Lisica and Crevan felt it. The invisible barriers that were separating them from the actual Dimension they were supposed to be in were vanished too, making them free to move and interact, once again, with their actual Dimensional Time.

-Adriel! - The Princess ran fast to him.

Crevan stopped by Dawako.

-What were you doing in there, you stupid boy...? -

But Dawako was senseless, unable to hear the Commander Of The Fox, talking angry over him.

It started to lightly rain.

Lisica then noticed something unusual.

Destiny, her horse, was walking slowly around her and Adriel, leisurely circling them, but his light blue eyes...

His eyes were not considering the Princess Of The Fox at all.

They were, instead, pointed at Adriel, attentively, in the quite obvious attempt to check what was happening to him, closely checking on him.

Crevan walked down to the scene, without a word.

He looked at Princess Lisica, and she gave the look back.

Both of them unable to understand what was going on.

And then, completely out of nowhere, Destiny raised his head to the sky and he made the loudest and most melodic sound Lisica and anybody else had ever heard coming out from him and the rain became snow.

And Adriel opened his eyes.

-Adriel! -

-Hey, boy! -

Adriel looked at them, from his laying position on the grass.

He didn't say anything.

He slowly sat, massaging his eyes.

-My eyes… What happened… They are itchy…-

The Princess and the Commander looked at each other.

-You…- The Commander said.

-You did something with your eyes… You were… Fighting with Dawako…-

Adriel's eyes pictured a clear and angry expression of surprise on his face.

-Ah! Dawako! Where is that bastard! He wanted to cut my arm! -

Right. His arm. Everyone's look, even his one, went right on his shoulder.

It was bleeding no more.

There was a visible scar, completely healed.

-This doesn't make any sense…- Lisica mumbled.

-Not at all…- Crevan said.

But the sound of his voice was saying something else.

Adriel stood up but his balance was not stable.

-Hey, careful. -

Lisica grabbed him by his waist.

He looked at her and he kissed her on her lips.

Crevan stepped back, his hands up.

The Princess looked at him.

And she kissed him back.

But that time they didn't break the connection between their lips.

Not for a several amount of seconds, seconds that made that kiss taste like forever.

When they interrupted that exchange of sensations, none of them said anything.

They both left each other's contact and Adriel's eyes went on a very shocked Crevan.

-What about my eyes... What happened with my eyes...? -

Destiny was running around them, apparently full of energy.

The snow was still falling but in a very small amount.

The Commander Of The Fox had to concentrate very hard to be able to have a normal kind of conversation pretending to ignore what he witnessed less than a minute before.

-Your eyes... They were not of your usual colour... They were red... Red like fire...-

-What?!-

Lisica went close to Crevan. Her heart was still beating at a high rate, but she tried to hide it.

Her emotions were loud and confused.

-Yeah... I saw your eyes too... They were... Interesting...-

But in Adriel's mind there was then only one question.

One simple question.

-So, how did I end up on the ground? And...- He gave a look down feet away from where they were talking.

-Why Dawako is senseless on the grass down there if I was in the same state too? -

The Commander looked at Dawako.

And then back at Adriel.

-Because you hit him. A glare. From your eyes. A visible hit, right in the chest. You sent him down to the ground several feet away from you. -

Adriel was visibly shocked by those revelations.

-And then, right after that, you collapsed on the grass too. - Lisica concluded.

Adriel massaged his eyes once again. His eyes then went on Destiny.

-He seems so happy today... He normally doesn't hang around anyone when we take our stops through the journey...-

The Princess gave a look at the Commander.

Crevan's eyes penetrated hers.

And she understood.

And she also agreed.

As much as she wanted to say everything, every single detail to Adriel, she was also understanding that maybe at that point, for once, it would have been more cautious to save that last part, the one regarding Destiny, for another time.

After all, not even her or Crevan were actually sure about what they witnessed regarding the stunning horse's behaviour.

His light blue mane was moved by the air, welcoming every single snowflake that was falling from the violet sky.

In that moment, a little noise came from not far from their spot.

-Dawako! - Crevan said.

He went towards Dawako, that in that meantime not only was back being awake, but he was also sitting on the spot where he was laying down, senseless, until few instants before.

-Crevan... Princess...-

But the Princess was far from being in the mood to be sensible with him.

She, instead, jumped in front of Crevan, facing the usually charming and smiling young man from Vixen.

-What were you thinking there?!- She yelled at him.

-That was unacceptable! When we will be back in Vixen, I'll be sure to address my father about your actions. Personally, I even think you shouldn't be allowed to take part to the duel to become the next Hero Of The Fox, anymore...-

Dawako was unable to reply. His mouth was semi open, his eyes scared and in shock.

And he then responded with something that was not even related to the strong words the Princess just finished to pronounce.

-He is not normal...- And he looked at Adriel, staring at him.

-How did you do that... How did you do that?!- He screamed, but not with anger, but with fear, standing up and pointing his finger at him.

-He is the one that shouldn't be allowed to take part to the duel... That power... What was that... With a glare from his eyes...? That is not fair... I can't... I refuse to battle against a cheater... The position should be mine... I deserve to be the new Hero of the Kingdom Of The Fox...-

-You wanted to cut his arm!!!- Princess Lisica yelled at him.

Dawako spoke calmly but weirdly, like he was aware of what was going on around him, but somehow, he was in a mental state where his Soul was having difficulty to recognise the Dimension where he was.

And Crevan noticed that.

-I would have never do that… I would have never… Believe me… Believe me…- He said looking at Lisica first and then at the Commander Of The Fox.

Crevan looked at Princess Lisica.

-Unbelievable…-

The Princess gave him the look back.

-What's happening…-

And Crevan looked back at Dawako, that was then pressing his hands on his chest, like trying to be able to feel something in particular, not on it, but inside of it.

And Crevan spoke.

-He shook his Soul. -

Adriel's speechless silence ended with him facing the Commander.

-What have you just said…? -

Crevan looked at him, with an expression that was something in between the shock and the curiosity.

-You shook his Soul… Your attack with the eyes… Direct to his chest… It entered inside his inner self… You literally shook his Soul… And he is now in a mental state where he perfectly knows where he is… But, somehow, he cannot recognise the Dimensional Time of his Existence. To make it simple. He knows what is going on. But he doesn't feel like he actually belongs to this Dimension. -

Adriel was looking at Dawako with the most surprised of his expressions.

-Will he go back to normal? -

-Eventually. - Crevan said.

-Yes, I would say. But he might need a bit of time... Until his Soul recreates its own balance with our Dimensional Existence. -

At that point it was starting to feel a bit difficult to entirely follow that very exceptional concept formulated by the Commander Of The Fox.

They all went back to the horses and after a very little matter of time, they were all ready to go.

Dawako was silent, but gently caressing his horse.

Crevan was close to Adriel, while Lisica was kissing Destiny, petting his superlative light blue mane, so brilliant under the rays of the Sun, that ultimately showed up once again through the clouds, putting an end to the previously falling snow.

-So.- Crevan said.

-How did you do that? -

Adriel looked confused at him.

-What do you mean, Commander? You perfectly know... I don't know how I did that... But...-

And he looked at the Commander Of The Fox with more intensity.

-Are you somehow telling me that you are not able to do that? -

Crevan looked at him quite amused.

-Able to do what? To use my eyes to generate some sort of incredibly powerful energy that almost everyone else is able to generate only through the blade of a sword? -

He looked at the warm and lovely sunshine.

-No, Adriel. I am not able to do that. The most of the living people of The Circle are not able to. -

Adriel looked at Lisica.

He was so much deep inside the topic regarding the kind of power he expressed that day, unconsciously, that he forgot for a little while about what happened earlier, in front of Crevan's eyes, while Dawako was still laying down on the ground, senseless.

-It is pretty obvious somebody is able to do that, though. - He then said out of nowhere.

-Crevan took a moment before to answer.

-Yes. Of course. But let me tell you one thing. Those extremely few individuals that are able to generate that kind of energy that you made manifest earlier today, know exactly how to do it, which clearly also means they perfectly know what they are doing in the meantime they are doing it.-

Adriel's mind was working hard. He was a very hard thinker, after all.

A known but extremely rare power...

A power that only few really knew how to properly use.

Generating energy from the individual himself, not through a sword, or any other kind of weapon...

A kind of power not granted to the most.

But a kind of power that had been mastered to the detail by the very few inhabitants of The Circle that were capable to use it.

The same kind of power he gave birth to but without knowing how.

And why.

It was feeling strange for sure.

But also exciting at the same time.

XX

SACRIFICE

-Princess? -

Princess Lisica looked at Crevan.

-Yeah? -

They were all back to their journey, the lands where they were going through were empty and not even the slightly spot of a small Town or village.

Crevan put his eyes on the Princess' horse.

-I remember… I think I remember you might have told me about Destiny… King Balgair, your father, gave it to you, right? -

Lisica thought about those words.

-I don't actually remember as well if I have told you or not. But yeah, indeed, he gave him to me. Why? -

The Commander kept looking at the majestic horse.

-No… Nothing, just curiosity…-

Two or maybe three minutes after, the Princess spoke again.

-Actually… To be precise… Someone gave him to my father, firstly. And then, he gave him to me. As a present. -

Crevan, that was not expecting Princess Lisica to go back to that conversation, seemed surprised.

-Someone gave Destiny to him… Did he ever told you who? -

-Absolutely not. -

The honest answer of the Princess Of The Fox, came out in a way Crevan understood that was the real truth.

-And, also only due to my very own curiosity… When did he give him to you? -

Lisica looked at some indefinite spot in front of her in the act of thinking.

-Only two days before he told me I would have been joining you in this journey to the Kingdom Of The Wolf. -

Crevan thought about the Princess' response.

-Interesting. -

Less than five seconds after, something else flashed inside of his mind.

-I'm saying it is interesting, because I could swear I have never seen Destiny before…-

Lisica's reply didn't take long to come out from her mouth.

-Of course you didn't. -

Crevan looked confused.

-What do you mean? -

Lisica looked at him, innocently, but also very serious.

-Whoever gave Destiny to my father, that happened not more than a week and a half ago. -

Crevan's mouth opened a little.

-There is something wrong? What about all of these questions about my horse…? -

The Commander quickly tried to compose himself.

-No, nothing. Again, it's only due to curiosity I'm asking you about him… I was only wandering…-

When the snow started to fall, totally out of any kind of possible prediction, the conversation ended.

It was very strange, as the temperature was still the same, nicely warm, definitely not the kind of temperature that could bring snow.

Dawako, that was seeming to get back to be himself minute after minute, questioned the Commander.

-Commander, how this is even possible?! The temperature didn't go down, but it is snowing! -

Crevan looked all around and ultimately up to the sky.

-This is not snow, Dawako. - He stated.

Adriel stopped Titan, his horse.

-Wait a moment…-

He looked on his gear and he noticed and realised that whatever was coming down from the then dark sky, was certainly not snowflakes, nothing that was attaching on his clothes or all around the location they were finding themselves in.

The tiny little round atmospheric phenomena that were falling down from the sky over them, were actually pretty solid and they were bouncing on their gears as they were bouncing also all around the area.

-This is Silver! - Adriel exclaimed.

-What?!-

But Dawako didn't say anything else as he was able to realise that Adriel was right.

It was Silver what was falling down from the dark and luminous sky over them.

The young man from Vixen, that in that moment seemed like he was finally back to totally be himself, started to try to catch some of it.

-Hey, look here, everybody! I can't believe it... Silver falling from the sky! You should get some, too! This is not something that happens everyday!- He exclaimed, while laughing.

Adriel stared at the image of his rival catching some of those little round silvery phenomena.

-I don't think this is something that is meant to be taken...- He said.

Dawako looked and laughed at him.

-You don't know what you are talking about! The Circle is incredible, full of things we don't know but that we are discovering day after day since we got in this journey. There is nothing bad on taking some of this... It's like if you pick little rocks from the ground! -

And he kept moving his hands in the air, putting whatever he was able to catch inside a big empty bag he was carrying on his horse since the beginning of the journey.

Adriel noticed that it was looking the exact same of a bag, empty as well, that was right on the back of his horse, bag that he never put there, but that he always thought was there because the Commander put it, just in case of need.

Crevan and Lisica were looking at the scene, really not impressed by the silvery rain, the Commander because he was obviously aware of that extraordinary phenomenon and maybe the Princess knew about that too as she was seeming way far from being surprised or excited about that.

Adriel said, more to himself than to anybody else.

-I just think... This is a masterpiece of the Nature...-

Dawako laughed louder than ever before, even if at that point he was seeming to be satisfied enough about the quantity of Silver he had been able to catch.

-And what that is supposed to mean? -

Adriel severely looked at him.

-It means that Nature is where this Silver really belongs. -

And suddenly, as surprisingly as it started, the Silver precipitations ceased.

They all looked up.

-Well, this is weird…- Dawako said.

Nobody said anything.

Adriel was staring at the sky.

-We should move on. - Crevan stated.

-Yes. We should. - Princess Lisica agreed.

The Commander looked at his Princess and he felt grateful.

He perfectly knew she was not really aware about the most of the events that were happening during those days through their journey, but somehow she was able to find the way to back him up, still far from understanding him, but always ready to help him in trying to distract Adriel and Dawako from their thoughts, sometimes also very deep.

They restarted their expedition, and the silence was the reigning noise around them in that moment.

Until, at some point, they found themselves at the beginning of an extremely sandy land.

It was not a desert. It was a regular land, but with sand all around, over the otherwise brilliant green grass.

The temperature became colder, in a matter of seconds.

-Where are we? - Adriel asked.

Crevan looked around.

-Not too far from the Kingdom Of The Wolf at this point, young man. -

Dawako started to cry, silently.

-Hey, what's happening? - Adriel asked.

It was singular how, all of a sudden, Adriel was checking on the rival.

Their almost fatal training duel was only one memory away.

-I don't know…- Dawako sounded very surprised and confused.

-I don't know why I am crying… I just… I just can not avoid it… But… I feel something inside of me…-

They all stopped, jumping down from their horses.

-Dawako, what's wrong? - Lisica was very preoccupied.

-I feel…- Dawako tried.

-I feel extremely sad… And…-

He looked at all of them and he concluded.

-Hopeless. -

One huge explosion.

Plenty of different ones right after the first and main one followed.

They all looked up in the sky and what they saw was something that left them without even the strength to scream or produce any sort of exclamation.

An unbelievably massive black dragon was above them, covering a great part of the infinite sky.

He yelled out loud and his wings opened even more, making his appearance even more colossal, enforcing the vibrations of his bestiality.

-Commander!!!- Lisica screamed.

Crevan jumped in front of them.

-Stay behind!!!-

He took his sword and he cut the heavy air making it rotate fast.

The sky was on fire, fire that was not even coming from the dragon's mouth, but that was literally exploding out of his body in the form of an extraordinary fiery type of energy.

The darkness that were gathering in the sky were then in that moment hugely enlightened by the madness of fire that was getting released out of the dragon's massive figure.

-That is…-

The green eyes of the young man from Renard, spotted the brilliant golden eyes of the Tenebrous Dragon.

-Yes… Indeed…- Crevan said low but clear.

In that very moment, a strong wind started to howl, and it made their capability to see hugely difficult, due to the sand previously laying on the grass that was then starting to be one thing with the wind, raging all around the location where the unbelievable event was happening, in the Kingdom Of The Fox, then extremely close to the Kingdom Of The Wolf.

Adriel and Dawako were shoulder to shoulder, the swords out, while Princess Lisica was holding Destiny strongly.

-What are we going to do?!- Dawako asked loud at Crevan.

The wind was then so strong that it was very hard to hear whatever anyone was saying, with the addition of the explosions of fire that were raging out of the dragon's body, generating a situation of ultimate chaos.

-I have no idea. -

Crevan's answer made everyone's blood freezing inside of their bodies.

The Tenebrous Dragon was staring at them, flying in the sky, clearly in control, in that precise moment, of all of their Lives.

-Step back. -

Crevan's words hit straight on Adriel and Dawako.

-Commander…-

-STEP BACK!-

Adriel and then also Dawako, followed his order.

-Now, listen to me. Very carefully. -

They were all paying attention.

-I will be honest with you. I don't know why this monster is here… I don't even know why he is clearly waiting for us to attack him before he does… Literally… I have lost it… I've lost the logic of many of the events that are happening since we started this journey…-

The way Crevan was speaking, made everyone uncomfortable.

There was something in his voice. Something that was sounding way far from being positive and optimistic.

-However…- He continued.

-If what came to my mind will work…-

And he turned his head, looking at them.

-You will have to continue by yourselves. -

Adriel grabbed his arm.

-What are you saying?!-

-I'm saying…- Crevan replied, gently moving Adriel's hand away from his arm.

-That even if I will succeed… Which is extremely unsure… That will be too much for me…-

Another great loud roar coming from the sky, this time also followed by a thunder without a lightening.

-We fight together. -

-No, we don't. - Crevan responded back, pushing Adriel away.

-You all stay away. Back off and let me do what I have to do. Simple as that. You will realise if I will be about to win or if I will be about to die. If you will realise that I will be losing, run. Run with your horses as fast as you can, disappear from the fight. Reach the Kingdom Of The Wolf. I know once you'll be there you'll be fine. -

And he looked at the sky.

-He will not follow you if you will be already there. -

At that point, it was clear to Adriel, to Dawako and even to Lisica.

That statement was not meant to meet any sort of answer back.

It was just the way it had to be.

The way things had to go.

No questions.

No objections.

Adriel took Lisica by her wrist and gave a pat to Dawako.

And he spoke, looking at them, the tears in his eyes.

-Let's step back. -

-But…-

-LET'S STEP BACK!!!-

The Princess Of The Fox didn't reply anymore and Dawako, head down, followed them, away from Crevan.

An incredible explosion and even more fire erupted out of the giant dragon, that then pointed his eyes on Crevan, focusing attentively on the Commander of the Kingdom Of The Fox.

Crevan gave the stare back.

-You might even win. But I will not make it easy for you, that is more than a sure thing…-

He held the hilt of his sword.

The grip he had on it was not strength.

It was hope.

The Tenebrous Dragon roared loud, and a flashing circle of fire appeared right behind him, rotating on itself, throwing flames all around the location, also howling all around and above dancing with the sand and the wind.

A powerful wind of fire was then raging all around the sandy land where that epic and unique event was happening.

Crevan's body got bright, releasing a pale grey Aura all around of himself.

The dragon's golden eyes had a shine, mean and sinister.

Crevan's sword released a white misty vapour.

Suddenly, through the raging wind of fire, Destiny jumped in front of Adriel, Lisica and Dawako and he then started to run around them, circling them, multiple times, increasing his speed every single time.

-What is he doing...- Dawako was following every single movement of the majestic horse.

-I am not sure...- Princess Lisica admitted.

Then, out of nowhere, after another of his circling runs, a very pale light blue smoke started to took form, surrounding them, putting and leaving them inside of this circle of smoky energy generated by the power of the speed of Destiny's runs around them.

-He is...- Adriel was admiring the amazing light blue mane of the magnificent horse that was keeping running, circling them, and by doing so the energy surrounding them was getting thicker and visibly stronger.

-He is building a protection of pure energy for us...-

Crevan yelled at the Tenebrous Dragon, and he whipped the air with the sword, throwing a white lightening of power in the dragon's direction, that in response smashed the air with the huge tail, directing part of the fiery wind to collide with the attack coming from the Commander Of The Fox, dismantling it.

Another roar. Another thunder without a lightening. The Tenebrous Dragon's eyes made a glare and Crevan's sword turned boiling hot.

The Commander screamed in pain, and he threw the sword away on the ground, going down on one knee, holding his hand, crying in pain.

-Commander!!!- Adriel exclaimed.

Destiny finally stopped his runs and he remained standing right in front of them, his look directed to the scene that was seeing Crevan on his knee and the Tenebrous Dragon flying up in the sky, ready to throw one last final attack to end the Commander of the Kingdom Of The Fox.

Adriel's hands started to burn a bit.

That sensation…

Again…

Lisica noticed him looking at his own hands.

-Adriel, what's wrong? -

-Nothing. - He promptly answered.

But, obviously, that very quick reply didn't convince Princess Lisica. At all.

The three of them were apparently very safe inside of the energy circle Destiny generated with his runs.

The wind of fire was raging, but when colliding on the cloudy energy that was protecting them, it was changing direction, leaving all of them perfectly untouched.

What was very strange was the fact that even Destiny, even if out of the protecting circle, was getting untouched by the powerful fiery wind.

In that moment, for the first time since his appearance, the dragon opened his mouth to show little lightful flames that started to collide all together with each other, then giving birth to a decently big sized ball of fire.

Adriel's hands started in that moment to literally fuming.

He tried to hide them.

-Crevan!!!- The Princess exclaimed out loud.

But the Commander, once again standing tall under the Tenebrous Dragon, was still holding his own hand that was strongly releasing huge amounts of smoke due to the burnt caused from the boiling hilt of his own sword.

The pain was loud.

-Destiny. -

Lisica and Dawako turned their head, looking at Adriel.

The boy was literally calling the horse, talking to him.

-Destiny… I am not sure… I don't really know you… But since we started this journey… I have the impression, I have the strange but strong feeling… That you actually know me…-

The horse kept standing in there in front of them, not a move.

-I know it sounds crazy… I know you are not even my horse, you are the Princess' horse… But… I have the sensation that…-

He stopped, thinking about how to end his statement to the horse, that, even if motionless, was seeming like he was actually listening to every single word said by the green-eyed boy from Renard.

-I feel you, Destiny. I don't know what I feel. But I feel. Every time our eyes collide… You are way more than a horse, right? So please, if you can… And I know you can… If there is a way… Even only one way… Save Crevan, Destiny… Save him…-

A little pause, the tears were signing Adriel's beautiful face.

-Please…-

And the horse by the light blue mane did it again.

That incredibly melodic sound coming out from his mouth.

Once again.

But this time it did last more.

It did last longer.

Such a melancholic sound that was spreading hundreds, then thousands of different vibrations that colliding with the Life of the Planet, of the Galaxy and, ultimately, even of the whole Universe, was creating an unknown kind of feeling never experienced by any regular Human Being before.

The whole Atmosphere shook.

The time started to go slower.

Crevan was then loading some great amount of energy concentrating it entirely on the hand that didn't get burnt.

The Tenebrous Dragon noticed that, but the increasing in power in his then great sphere of fire, was going very slow too.

The whole power of Time was in that moment getting altered by the mystic and unspecified power that was getting revealed by Destiny.

Crevan yelled and his whole body was then flaming of that grey energy that in that precise instant was then mixing with his Aura.

It was not even easy to spot him in the details of his appearance as all of that amount of power was suddenly blurring his image.

Destiny was still spreading that lovely sound all around, everything was slow and surreal.

The dragon was completing the perfect size of his ball of fire, but still, for him Time was going slower.

Yes, for him.

In fact, in that moment only, Crevan and even Adriel, Dawako and Princess Lisica, noticed they were actually able to move at a normal kind of motion once again.

But not the Tenebrous Dragon.

Time was at that point only affecting the dragon's Existence.

For him everything was still proceeding at an unbelievably slow rate of speed.

And in that moment Crevan flashed of a very blinding light.

-What is happening… What is he trying to do…- Adriel mumbled.

And Dawako looked down.

-I know what he is doing. -

-Say what?!- Adriel exclaimed.

-Tell me… Tell me, Dawako… What is he trying to do…? -

Dawako looked at Adriel.

Then at Princess Lisica.

And then back at the scene that was picturing the Commander Of The Fox and the Tenebrous Dragon.

Crevan, surrounded by that even more thick and dense energy, the dragon that even if slowed down by the Time being affected on him was then about to complete his in that moment enormous ball of fire.

Even his wings and his tail were moving very slow, but somehow giving him an even more epic appearance.

And then Dawako answered.

-The Commander Of The Fox… That dragon… It clearly is something above his and most of the people of The Circle level… So… He has one only way to try to defeat him…-

Adriel put both of his hands on Dawako's shoulders.

-Which is…? -

Dawako looked back at him.

-Making all of his hidden power explode, the power of the whole of his Existence and beyond that. Which it might kill the dragon. But that will definitely kill Crevan himself. -

Lisica brough her hands on her mouth, almost to try to don't scream.

Adriel's eyes didn't see anything for a moment.

Destiny's melodic and divine chant stopped.

The horse was then watching too, but he looked more tired than ever before.

And the dragon's time motion went back to normal, making him ready to attack.

And Crevan was ready too.

-Wait!!! Crevan!!!-

It was the first time Adriel called the Commander of the Kingdom Of The Fox by his name.

The tears in his eyes.

His hands were now visibly fuming and under the view of Dawako and Lisica.

-Adriel… What is happening to your hands…? -

But Adriel was not listening.

His eyes were brighter than ever, and his expression changed.

He was serious. But apparently very relaxed.

His hands were fuming even more and the smoke that was coming out from them was white, a very dense and vivid kind of white.

He literally walked through the protection barrier that Destiny built few minutes before by running in circle all around them for multiple times.

-Hey, wait! -

Dawako quickly tried to run behind him, but he got pushed back by an invisible energy even before he was being able to feel a little touch of that thick and strong powerful energy that was then protecting him and the Princess Of The Fox inside.

Lisica was not talking at all, but she was then looking at her horse.

Destiny was still observing the scene in front of them, his electric blue eyes never blinking.

-Princess! How did he…-

-Now I understand. - The Princess said.

-What… What did you understand…? I am not able to understand anything else anymore…-

And Princess Lisica answered to him, without moving her eyes away from Destiny.

-Destiny… When he altered Time…-

Dawako felt even more confused.

-Yes… But why he did stop to sing before the Commander was ready to attack the dragon before the ball of fire was ready? I don't understand… Now both Crevan and the Tenebrous Dragon are fighting in the same Space and Time…-

Lisica's eyes got wet, and she smiled while looking at her unique and extraordinary horse.

-Because it was not Crevan the one Destiny was giving time to. -

Those words had the same effect of a thunder.

And Adriel was then walking, calmly, slowly, towards Crevan.

But his walking that slow was not due to another unusual control over Time.

It was just the serenity he was feeling inside of himself, consciously not aware at all about what he was doing.

But unconsciously, deep down inside the most hidden spot of his Spirit, he was feeling the unmistakable sensation of victory.

The glorious awareness that he was about to sort everything out, and in a matter of seconds.

The dragon's eyes spotted him, and he remained steady floating in the still fiery air.

Adriel stopped his walk once in perfect line with Crevan.

The Commander Of The Fox looked at him.

-What are you doing… Go back there! -

Then he noticed Adriel's hands.

-What are you…-

-I am amazed by the incredible and also noble power you intended to use to beat this creature. - Adriel interrupted the Commander.

-However. I will not let you do that. And not only because I will not permit that…-

He then focused on the huge ball of fire that was floating in front of the Tenebrous Dragon's incredibly short face.

And he concluded.

-But mainly because there will be not even the need for that. -

Adriel closed his hands in fists and the ground trembled.

Crevan's mouth opened but without being able to say anything.

The dragon's golden eyes had a glare, and the incredible beast released the fire.

It all happened very fast.

Crevan closed his eyes, and his Aura and his energy became one and he concentrated, but before he was able to do anything, Adriel hit the Commander's chest where the heart was located with a gentle but still strong punch, and suddenly Crevan's huge amount of power vanished, leaving him there, on his knees, without the smallest sign of all the energy he accumulated until few instants before and not even the slightest sign of his own Aura.

He was completely drained.

-Adriel...-

But Adriel, the green-eyed boy from the second biggest Town of the Kingdom Of The Fox, was already focused on the ball of fire that was about to collide with them and that location of their Planet, and that was when, with a glare of his eyes, slowed down the speed of that fiery sphere, but that was nothing about to control Time.

He was not controlling Time, but he was controlling the events that were happening inside of it.

And not only that.

It was actually extraordinarily easy to understand.

Adriel was controlling the Tenebrous Dragon's power.

And while the sphere of fire was still, even if slower, about to make its impact with everything and everyone that was down under there, Adriel opened his arms, his hands still closed as fists.

And an orange Aura exploded out of him, and he then finally opened his hands, raising them in front of himself, up, in direction of the fire.

A pale but very intense energy of the colour of the Sun got released from the palms of his hands and it slammed against and then through the sphere that solemnly opened, cracking, the dismantled little flames of fire that were still falling on the Planet, but that by the time they were about to touch it, they were all vanishing in the air, air made of a wind that was not made of fire anymore, the sand still hovering in the air, but without any kind of confusion.

-He… He dismantled it…- Dawako said.

Princess Lisica noticed that in his voice there was more fear than admiration.

Crevan was still on his knees, with not much energy left, breathing with difficulty, but still able to pay a lot of attention at what it was happening right in front of him.

What happened right then, left everyone shocked.

The Tenebrous Dragon left his spot in the air to fly down to the ground to then be right in front of Adriel, that remained steady in there, looking up to the enormous and dark creature.

The two clearly penetrated each other's eyes.

Strongly, deeply, in a very intense exchange of vibrations that made the temperature boiling.

The air was steamy.

And then Adriel let his bright orange Aura disappear.

The dragon made a sound with his mouth that was almost certainly something in between the disappointing but also the acceptance.

And with one last and less intense look at Adriel's green eyes, he turned his head, he opened his huge wings and with a noisy slam of his tail on the ground, he left the surface of the location where everything was happening, getting back into the sky, flying away, first slowly, then speeding up, with another weird sound that this time was clearly not about any kind of disappointing feelings, but definitely of total acceptance.

Few instants after, the Tenebrous Dragon disappeared from the view.

Destiny moved his legs for the first time since a while, and by doing so the protection of energy he previously created vanished in the most complete nothing.

Crevan stood up, muddled and thoughtful. His energy and health condition completely restored.

Lisica ran to him, hugging him, holding him strong and with vibes of care that high that made Crevan's eyes producing more than only few tears.

Dawako ran there too, going in Adriel's direction.

-You… You are… Particular. -

Adriel knew that that "Particular" meant "Amazing".

His hands were back to normal, and they were not fuming anymore.

-Yes…- He then said.

-Very particular…- He concluded, hiding a quick smile that Dawako couldn't notice.

They were then all gathering there, Crevan completely back to his full health but still drained of words to say.

But he ultimately hugged Adriel.

In that hold there was way more than a simple "Thank you".

Lisica looked at Adriel in the eyes.

And Adriel felt it.

He felt that feeling that never had the need to include words to be able to be felt.

He felt even more than that, that more that he would have not been able to define it with any word part of his knowledge.

He smiled at her.

Destiny was back walking calmly around that location, but very far from them and from all the other horses.

The sky was seeming less dark after all the fire that did enlighten it until only few minutes before.

-So…- Crevan finally spoke.

-Adriel… Now, it has been a Hell of a thing… I don't think anyone, even if heavily curious, really wish to talk about all of this right now. Let's give it few hours… We will have time to talk about what happened… Your eyes again… And now your hands…-

By saying that, the Commander gave a look at Adriel's hands.

-But one thing only I have to ask. -

Adriel waited, even if he already knew what the question was going to be.

-How… What happened… When you and the Tenebrous Dragon looked at each other in the eyes… I mean… How did you…? -

But Adriel interrupted him straight away.

-I don't know. -

The fast answer was far from being able to be accepted by Crevan's intelligence, but the Commander decided to ask no more.

-Alright… Anyway… Whatever it was… Well done…-

Those words sounded maybe a little bit banal, but for Adriel were meaning a lot.

They were meaning that the conversation was over and that Crevan already gave up on asking him something regarding the behaviour that the Tenebrous Dragon had once he was standing in front of Adriel.

Not that he actually had an answer for that, because he really did not.

But, inside of his mind, and even inside of his whole body, a very uncomfortable and disturbing thought was starting to born and without any possible way to stop it.

It was only a thought.

But a very valid one.

An extremely terribly valid one.

And even the only idea that the thought then stuck inside of his mind might have had a sense and an unmistakable logic, it was making him feel fear over fear.

He was genuinely scared.

Scared to be right.

XXI

THE BLACK HOLE

The lake that was boiling hot in the middle of the dark forest was bubbling, black and red.

It was seeming like the centre of the Planet was opened to the World and everyone was able to see inside of it.

But, as just stated, that was just a lake.

Around of it, a small amount of people were standing right in front of the magma-coloured water.

There was no sky. Not the slightest presence of stars or anything that was usually part of a night sky.

The air was however very clear and dry.

Even the temperature was mild, with the only exception of the closest area to the lake, where it was instead hot and at some points almost suffocating.

The people's identity was unclear.

Somehow, their figures were appearing blurry, not defined.

Nothing was sure about the whole scene.

Between them, however, there was one individual that was attracting the eyes more than anyone else present in there.

He was appearing majestic with his perfect posture, perfect body, a shiny pair of leather trousers worn inside heavy boots.

His chest was naked, muscly, greatly built.

At his waist a belt with a massive buckle of an unknown material, red like fire and flames were seeming to rage inside of it, behind the thick surface that was giving to the buckle a spheric and clear appearance.

It was strange and sinister how a very slow motioned vapour was fuming from the middle of his chest to right up to his face and head, covering him entirely, making impossible to spot any characteristic of his facial features.

Between all of the few presents, he was the one closer to the lake.

There was another man, covered in a huge and furred cloak, the hoodie was hiding the most of his face, but from under that it was very possible to spot two brilliant green eyes, that bright they were actually giving some source of light around the spot where he was standing.

There was then an incredibly short individual, covered under his cloak as well, his breathing was low and heavy.

Close to him there was the Being that more than all the others in there was presenting that very strange blurry presence, it was literally impossible to even define the nails of his fingers.

At last, what was appearing to be a woman, due to the size and shape of her body, was standing close to the man with the brilliant green eyes, her many rings the only visible thing out of the shadowed but shiny dark blue cloak she was wearing all over her red leather gear.

They were all clearly waiting for someone.

Freezing and frightened cries were audible from far away.

Everything was dark and burnt all around.

Even the ground and the grass. Both dusty and burnt.

The not existing sky was burnt too.

The whole atmosphere in there was very tense.

The Being that was presenting an astonishing body but also that mystical vapour that was making impossible to try to define his whole appearance, was the only one that was keeping his vibrations calm and relaxed.

His fingers were moving a little, the long black fingers touching each other.

Two crows were looking at the scene from a safe spot up on a tree, even if not too far from there.

Even if, in all honesty, nowhere around that location really seemed to be deserving to be called safe.

The Being with the great flaming buckle, moved few steps towards the still very much boiling and bubbling lake.

The silence around there was mysterious and somehow also very fascinating.

The vapour that was hiding his whole identity increased in quantity and soon all of his figure, even the parts of his body that were clearly visible until few instants before, became entirely impossible to be seen.

Trembling of the ground, the lake's magmatic water shook too.

All the presents were looking at the scene, without a movement.

A low and cavernous roar echoed all around and above.

The very much blurry Being was giggling from under his hoodie.

The shortest of all of them was instead breathing with difficulty, but in a very ecstatic way.

The individual that was presenting those incredibly luminous green eyes from under his covering, didn't appear to have any particular reaction, while the female Being was motionless, the perfect matching of her clothes giving her vibes of beauty and perfection even in the impossibility to spot her defined facial features.

The water started to bubble even more.

It was even possible to hear the boiling noise of the lake.

And then, unexpectedly, all at once, the vapour of darkness that were hiding the whole figure of the Being that between all of them was seeming to be the most powerful one, vanished.

The presents held the breath.

There, in front of them, and in front of the lake, in the middle of that dark and burnt forest, there was someone, or something, that was in any possible kind of way different, extraordinarily different not only from the ones that were standing in that location in that moment, but also way different from anybody else.

His body wasn't much different from the way he was looking earlier, muscly and visibly strong, a dark white kind of skin, his leather trousers, the boots and his belt with the flaming buckle, all of that was still there.

There was something rolled up around his waist and right over his mentioned belt.

The long black nails were the ending of his hands.

But something that wasn't visible earlier that then was the most visible characteristic of his body, was the big pair of black wings that he was presenting on his back.

Then, from the chest, that was where his figure was changing completely, separating him from looking like any other Being not only of The Circle, but of the entire Universe, known and unknown.

A large ruff of coarse long hair on his chest, black, that was then becoming white at the throat.

His face had the appearance of a mouflon and huge horns of a sickle shape on his head were completing, entirely, his superb appearance.

He opened one hand, waiting.

The brilliant green-eyed present walked slowly towards him.

He put a hand underneath his own cloak, and he took a sword out of it, but not his very own one which was still tight at his waist.

He then put, leisurely, the sword on the open hand of the Being with the mouflon face, that closed his hand on the hilt.

A meek wind started to fulfil the air.

The face hidden individual got back to his previous position, leaving the powerful presence of that unbelievable Being by himself, there, in front of the boiling hot lake.

When he then threw the sword directed into the lake, it would have been expected for it to fall down inside the water, but that was way far from what actually really happened.

The sword, thrown away with incredible strength, flew all over a great size of the lake, to then stop and remaining suspended right in the middle of it, all up above.

It stayed there, steady, motionless.

The horned Being closed the hand he used to throw the sword in a fist and that is when the sword then suddenly fell down into the lake, disappearing deep inside the magmatic water.

Silence.

Then, a huge underwater bang.

All the presents stayed there, not a move, maybe only a little shake of the legs of the shortest of the presents.

The centre of the lake opened, wide, revealing a big Black Hole.

One, two, three, four and then, ultimately, five shadows, or entities, got spit out of it, vanishing, disappearing in the obscure nothing, producing very deafening sounds similar to screams, screams of pure and honest desperation.

Someone, or maybe something, made a noise that resembled a growl, but that was not a kind of growl related to an animal.

Suddenly, all at once, all the presents rapidly got closer to the lake, that was at that point the spot where the Black Hole appeared.

Black Holes normally cause the falling of objects inside of it due to the extraordinary power of their gravity energy.

But that was different, and not only just because it appeared in exact centre of a lake in the middle of a forest, on the surface of a Planet, far away from the Outer Space.

That Black Hole was also different because it was not possessing any kind of gravity and everything and everyone around there were not facing any danger in terms of getting lost inside of it.

However, something spectacular was happening.

It was the hair first, then revealed to be long and dark, a Crown that was presenting the most fiery red colour that the Existence had ever been able to see, a Crown that was shining vividly and where the magmatic colour was in continuous motion, making obvious the understanding that both the Crown and its possessor were clearly not part of that World.

Then the face, then the shoulders, the muscly arms and the hands, obviously the whole naked upper body, only covered by a heavy cloak made out of an unknown material, but of a silver colour.

Then the legs, the leather material of the trousers as well as the boots where they were put inside.

The eyes were closed.

He literally came out from the centre of the Black Hole in the middle of the lake and then, once completely out of it, he levitated right over it, and he remained there, floating in the air, with the wind too scared but also too respectful to even only try to touch and disturb the figure of that great Being.

He remained in a very solemn position, his arms and hands open.

One of the characteristics that were stealing the view about him, was his pair of earrings.

Two amazing pendants with two black opals that were radiating rainbow rays all around.

All the presents were still standing, amazed.

Then, unexpectedly, the big Black Hole closed, and the lake went back to its original appearance, the black and red water, bubbling due to the hotness of it.

The man that came right out of it, was not wet at all.

His hair were perfectly dry too.

His remaining floating in the air spread vibrations of pure fascination.

He was pure beauty.

Even if pure is a term that was way far from being appropriate for the Being we are talking about in this moment.

There was silence.

More than ever before.

A wolf howled at a Moon that was not there, from very far away from that remote location that was finding itself deep inside the lostness of the darkest and the deepest area of The Circle.

The stunning man opened his eyes.

It was like he had two gems of the same kind of his pendants instead of eyes.

Two brilliant black opals, that was what his eyes were looking like and, like his earrings, they were giving away beautiful rainbow lights, giving him an appearance of colourful darkness.

Everyone bowed down.

Everyone except the Being with the aspect of a mouflon.

He remained on his spot looking at the man that appeared right from deep inside the Black Hole and he was looking at him straight into his eyes.

The other presents stood up once again.

And suddenly, every face was perfectly visible.

Every single line on everyone's face was clear.

The woman appeared to have beautiful facial features, her amazing red hair all tied up and her eyes were of the same colour of the light.

Her beauty was genuinely astonishing.

The Queen of the Kingdom Of The Scorpion, was standing there, between all the other presents.

She was visibly calm, but very concentrated.

The man that was closer to her, with the shiny green eyes, was caressing his own long hair of the colour of silver.

He was young.

And he was looking very imponent in his posture and presence.

The green of his eyes was not natural. It was more like his real eyes, whatever colour they had, just turned into that unbelievably brilliant kind of green due to an unknown reason.

The man that until few minutes before was presenting a completely blurry appearance, was very serious, finally visible, tall, grey hair and a small beard, apparently without any particular expression of excitement on his face, his eyes pointed on the mysterious man.

Everyone, clearly in a status of solemn respect and devotion, was looking at the man with eyes like black opals.

At last, but certainly not least, the short man was allowing to see his grey eyes, but not much more, still hiding under his cloak and his hoodie.

Flames of Darkness were coming out from the horned and most majestic Being between all of the individuals that were looking at the man that was still levitating over the boiling lake.

An incredibly strong smell of Sulphur was surrounding the whole area.

Even if he was the only one that didn't previously bow down when the mystifying man made his appearance on the scene, he actually was the one that was looking at him with more attention and intensity than anybody else in there.

The beautiful man floated slowly in the air.

He directed himself close to the ground and when close to that, the Being with the mouflon's appearance stepped back a bit, not too much, just enough to let the man having a spot where stepping his feet on.

-Welcome. -

His words came out with solemn intensity.

Nobody answered back, but they all kept their eyes on him, perfectly aware of the fact they really didn't have to.

-To have you in here, all of you, in this beautiful forest of mine, is always exciting. -

He moved few steps.

He went right in front of the man with the luminous green eyes.

He looked at him deeply and emotionless.

-Your eyes... They make me feel well...-

He moved his fingers close to the eyes of the young man with the hair of the colour of the silver, that was keeping his respectful silence.

-Tell me. How is he? -

And the man finally broke his personal silence.

-Not fully recovered, yet...- He said, then looking down at the ground.

The mysterious Human Being with only a cloak to cover his otherwise naked upper body didn't answer back.

He then moved on until he reached the Queen Of The Scorpion, looking at her with a sinister and malicious smile and he took her hand.

His pendants shook a bit when he started to shake his head, a totally insincere expression of sadness and pain on his face, one hand still holding the woman's hand, the other hand on his heart.

-It is truly heart breaking for me to know your daughter still doesn't show any kind of inclination to the few but extraordinarily important Principles that make the greatness of these Regions, our Regions… But I have hope, Nova… I really have…-

He left her hand, hand that she then brought to cover her mouth, the eyes closed, in a state of serious silent and internal affliction.

When he reached the man with grey hair, his expression really changed.

A lot.

His cloak was then moving due to the breath that was in that moment fulfilling that location.

A very hot breath.

He looked at him with his black eyes, not even a tiny hint of white was left in there anymore, or maybe it never been in there.

Those eyes that were then studying the tall standing man in front of him.

It was difficult to spot any kind of emotions on his face, but the way he was looking at him, was spreading vibrations of danger able to be felt from every single Being that was present in that moment on that scene.

When he then left the man in there, without saying a word, but finally interrupting that stare so full of everything, they all released the air they previously held inside due to the huge amount of uncomfortable tension.

At that point, the last in line was the short man.

The one that was still hiding himself.

The hoodie was covering the most of his face.

The great and clearly powerful man looked down at him.

-Answer. Will they make it? -

His voice was pleasant to hear, but it always had that hint of obscureness that was making his real feelings impossible to understand.

The short man kept looking down and he answered.

-Yes. -

The man with the mean dark eyes was caressing his own cloak.

-Yes, you say...-

He then looked back at the Queen Of The Scorpion, but without leaving his position.

-What happened to Yarden? -

Queen Nova looked at him, not too sure about how to say what she was about to say.

-He didn't go. Anthares made Crimson find Yarden and he ordered him to stop him. -

The impenetrable man stopped to caress his own cloak.

-Explain why. -

Queen Nova was feeling overwhelmed.

-I don't know... I really don't... Anthares didn't tell me the reason why... He just told me he ordered Crimson to do that... And...-

Queen Nova stopped.

-And? -

She took a deep, painful breath, and she concluded her sentence.

-And he was shaking. -

In that moment, for the first time, the man with dark long hair had an expression of pure surprise on his face.

He didn't reply anything about that topic, and he brought his attention back to the short man.

He looked at him with huge disgust.

-You will find out why. -

The hiding little man had a shy exclamation of surprise.

-Me…? Yarden… He is a member of the Kingdom Of The Scorpion…-

The pretty man's laugh that followed those words was sincerely emotionless.

-I know of which Kingdom Yarden is a member of. -

The other presents all had a genuine but nervous little laugh.

-But it will be your duty anyway to discover the reason why Yarden has been ordered to interrupt the mission he had to victoriously complete. -

As much as all of that was not making any sense inside of the little man's mind, the decision to agree to that seemed the obvious best choice to take.

He bowed down, his head nearly about to touch the black grass.

The clearly superior man closed his eyes.

The air got even more hot, and the time seemed to get slower.

It was unclear if it did last seconds, minutes, or maybe more.

He reopened his eyes.

Everything was seeming to be calm, the two crows that were previously on a tree not too far from the scene were gone.

But, out of nowhere, two very strange entities of a dark colour without a clear and defined appearance, were there on the scene, behind the man with the tenebrous black eyes.

They didn't make a move, they were just standing in there, steady, behind him.

-Send him back. -

The order of the mysterious man to those two new presences.

They both nodded, slowly, with their heads.

Then he closed his eyes again.

The same feeling. The air got roasting. The time changed.

Not clear if a short or long time was the result of it, but surely was the fact that when he reopened the eyes and that feeling left, the two unclear entities and the short man were not there anymore.

At that point, everyone was standing right in front of the man with the two black opals earrings, that was then facing all of them.

The Being with the mouflon's face in front of all of the presents.

-The greatness of these Regions is huge. - The man said.

-I am entirely sure you all are well committed in keeping our pride… And our dignity… At extremely high levels…-

With the only exception of the horned Being, all the others started to timidly nod their heads, in sign of agreement with the man's words.

That was the exact moment when the great looking man with the dark long hair walked towards the tall and imponent Being with the big black wings.

He pointed his black eyes inside the yellow ones of the majestic creature.

-It's the time over? -

The creature stared at him.

He nodded his head.

The man then passed a hand through his own hair, and he faced the other presents once again.

-I want you all to listen to me very carefully. -

He looked at all of them.

One by one.

-I don't want any of you or anybody from your respective Kingdoms to go after them anymore. -

He stopped straight away, clearly to make sure everyone was really listening to his words with a massive amount of solemn attention.

-I want you to focus on another matter, now. -

His eyes had a sinister shine, rays with the colours of the rainbow got sent all around for a very small amount of seconds.

-Let's move our focus, more than ever before, on the purest Soul of The Circle, the most candid presence of our Dimensional Existence… The most beautiful creature the Regions up North have ever seen…-

His voice was reaching a new and higher level of real excitement.

-Bring me those blue eyes where every man's desire can swim deep inside…-

He then walked one step closer to his listeners, the expression on his face picturing the evil and the implacable.

And then, with a whisper that sounded louder than a yell, he ultimately finished his sentence.

-Bring me the Queen. The Queen Of The Dove. -

At that point, always with the only exception of the winged creature, everyone else went on their knees.

Nobody spoke, initially.

Then, while still on his knees, the young man with hair of the colour of silver and the incredibly luminous green eyes, spoke.

-Please, don't worry… We will bring her to you…-

And his green eyes had an even brighter flash of light in the meantime he finished his sentence to the man that was powerfully standing in front of all of them.

-Your Demoniac Majesty. -

XXII

LANDSCAPES

The lands of The Circle were lands presenting a very unique kind of landscapes.

The shiny Regions Of Light were presenting unique colours that would have been visible even at the eyes of a blind person.

The Kingdom Of The Lion was presenting a red coloured landscape, the grass, the trees, the leaves... The contrast between the clear water and those red lands were the stunning view every single one would have had in front of his eyes if finding himself in there.

The Kingdom Of The Dove was the absolute and candid encounter of white, white and, if possible, even more white.

The whole nature in there was presenting the purest of the colours everywhere, all around and above.

When walking through fields of that colour and full of amazing violets, every person with a warm heart would have been feeling like being in the sweetest of the dreams, a dream that they all would have loved to exchange with their personal reality.

The Kingdom Of The Eagle was where the metallic and silver colour was reigning all around, even if most of the nature in terms of leaves or grass where mainly light blue.

It was then normally, for example to see stunning silver-coloured trunks with a great amount of enchanting light blue leaves.

Light blue like the mountains all around, while the water was of a very dense bright grey colour.

In the Silvery Lands, everything was more ordinary.

In both of the Kingdoms of those areas, the Kingdom Of The Fox and the Kingdom Of The Wolf, the green grasses and leaves and the many different colours of other nature's presences were still, however, giving a strong feeling of harmony and happiness, even if the colours of the Towns of the Kingdom Of The Wolf were definitely colder than the ones of the Kingdom Of The Fox, which also had the particular factor of its beautiful yellow and orange enormous fields.

In the Regions Of Darkness was unusual to see the Sun. Strongly uncommon. But not impossible.

The temperatures where, anyway, cold most of the times and the grey and cloudy atmosphere characteristic, for example, of the Kingdom Of The Owl, was not the most welcoming of the experiences.

The Kingdom Of The Scorpion was pure darkness where black was the main colour in most of the still fascinating nature's aspects of the Kingdom.

The many fires on the mountains, not capable of any harm, were one of the very few, and maybe the most vivid one, sources of light, in a Kingdom where it was even impossible to see the sky due to the thick and heavy gathering of the darkness in literally the whole entirety of those lands.

The Kingdom Of The Serpent was where everything was green.

But not a regular kind of green.

The green colour that was characteristic of that Kingdom, was ultra-shiny, almost unnatural, with a sort of luminescence all around, yellow and white, like an infinite number of microscopic lights that were making appear the already astonishing landscapes even more mystical.

The Circle had a very particular type of air, that sometimes was changing in heaviness and without an apparent logic.

When that was happening, it was always becoming quite difficult for every single Being to breathe in a serene and pleasant way.

The precipitations and phenomena, including strong winds and strange changes of the temperature, were pretty common.

In The Circle, one day was during 20 hours.

Old Legends were saying that the Planet, billions of years before, had its year duration of 600 days, that then reduced down to 365.

Even more Legends were talking about when the Planet actually had plenty of Satellites, but that since many Lifetimes, that was a factor that had been changed by some Divine Force, by someone superior, someone above anybody else.

And that was when, apparently, following those sayings, the Planet started to present one unique Satellite called Moon.

The infinite amount of very tiny chunks of ice and rocks floating and speeding in the sky it was one of the most significant characteristics of this unbelievable Dimensional Existence.

The view of that, though, was easier to see and admire when the evening and then the night were making their appearance on the scene.

The Circle.

A World lost in spaces and times.

A World part of a Dimension completely different from any other Dimension of the many Universes that were fulfilling the unique gift of Life.

The Circle.

A mystical World where nothing was able to be easily understood.

But also a World where what was not easy to be understood always had an honest and Universal explanation.

XXIII

INSIDE A DIFFERENT DIMENSION

-Why do you always look at the stars, my Queen? -

The Queen Of The Dove was at the outdoor space right out from her beautiful Castle not too far from the very high top of the higher of the Towers.

-My dear Evangeline...- Layleen said, looking at the Leader of the Kingdom Of The Dove.

-I wish I would be allowed to tell you the reason why...-

The Queen looked then back at the brilliant starry sky.

-But please, believe me when I say I really can not...-

Evangeline's eyes opened in an expression of true excitement.

-Oh, it is like some kind of secret? -

Queen Layleen smiled.

-Something like that. - She answered, keeping her beautiful blue eyes pointed up to the Infinity.

Evangeline remained in silence.

After few instants, she then felt the need to talk.

-I will leave you alone, if you prefer...-

Queen Layleen didn't interrupt her stare at the sky, but she smiled once again.

-I prefer you to do whatever that makes you feel good. If you want to stay here with me, I am glad about you staying in here. If you want to go, then, please, feel free to go. -

The pure honesty of that answer was so beautiful that Evangeline felt she really wanted to stay there a little bit more with her Queen, but, for some reason, she decided to do something different.

-Your presence and your words are always more than enough to make me feel good, my Queen. But I think I will go. -

Layleen stretched her arms.

-Are you going to sleep? -

The Leader Of The Dove looked down.

-No… I will go to read…-

The Queen looked lovely surprised.

-I don't think I have ever seen you reading anything… What are you reading these days? -

Evangeline didn't look up to face her Queen.

-Oh… It's just a book…-

The Queen's eyes got thoughtful for a moment.

-I see… It is some kind of secret…-

And she smiled at her.

This time, Evangeline looked at Queen Layleen and she gave the smile back at her.

-Well… Something like that…-

Few seconds of embarrassed silence and then Evangeline, after bowing down to the Queen, took her way back inside the Tower, to then get back in the downer floors of the Castle.

Layleen kept her eyes on her until she was able to see her no more.

-Reading… It is such a long time I don't read something…- She said to herself.

People were very noisy not far from the Castle, down to the almost fully marbled Town of Umbriel.

She was able to hear the people's voices from the high spot of her Castle where she was at.

Then, all at once, her mind went all completely dark.

And then she was back there, outdoor, out of the highest Tower of the white and pink Castle of the Kingdom Of The Dove, and totally aware.

-Oh… What's happening…-

And then again, her mind blacked out, more darkness than before gathering all inside of her obscured mind, to then being able to see once again the ground where few minutes before she was standing at with Evangeline.

She was slowly going down on her knees.

Her head was pulsing.

-What is this…-

When, for the third time, the view and the environment changed and all of her sensations got possessed by that unnatural and painful dark energy inside of her mind, Queen Layleen went completely down on her knees.

In that moment, even if in a state of pure pain and confusion, she was perfectly aware of her being awake and of her living that extraordinary situation.

She obviously didn't know what was actually happening, but at the same time she was able to live that very particular moment with unmistakable awareness.

She was lost somewhere inside of her own mind, but she was awake, conscious that that exceptional event was really happening to her and in that exact moment.

In front of her, nothing was visible.

-Hello?!- She called.

-What is happening to me?!-

Few steps became well audible.

A voice. Calm and firm.

-Don't worry. -

Layleen recognised the voice.

It was definitely more natural and relaxed, not echoed all around like it normally was, but it was that voice.

That same voice that she heard so many times, four times every year, every Equinox and every Solstice, since twenty years.

-You…-

-Yes… Me…-

Wolves were howling from very far away from that unusual level of consciousness, a level of consciousness lost in some remote area of Layleen's mind.

-Who are you? And where are you? I can feel you are here. - She said.

And the mysterious voice spoke once again.

-I am here. But you can not see me. -

As always. Queen Layleen has never been able to see the person that was speaking to her in her dreams.

And again, not even in that moment and the Queen Of The Dove was feeling scared and completely unable to understand how to handle that very overwhelming situation.

-But… This is not the Equinox… Or the Solstice… This is the first time I find myself inside this type of dreams in a regular day of the year…-

The temperature became warmer.

-This is not a dream. - The voice answered, before continuing the last part of the sentence.

-But this is not even Reality. -

Those words sounded very confusing to her, even more than mysterious.

-So… If this is not a dream… But this is not even Reality… Then, what is this? -

Few instants full of silence followed that question.

Then, the answer.

-This is something in between, my dear Layleen…-

The Queen Of The Dove overthought for more than an instant.

-Something in between… How can an answer like that be clear enough to make me understand…? -

Silence again.

Then the voice spoke.

-It was not meant to be. -

The darkness of that situation was profuse.

-What do you want? - She asked.

She was fighting against the tremendous instinct to scream, but somehow she perfectly knew that nobody would have been able to hear her.

-The question is… What do you want…? Tell me, my Queen…-

But Queen Layleen was already travelling inside of her own mind.

She was, in fact, thinking about what she really wanted.

That hug. That sensation. Once again. Only one more time…

-Oh, I see…-

Two extremely shining eyes flashed not too far from Layleen.

The Queen noticed that.

But she didn't move, she didn't even give too much importance to what she just saw.

She was just able to feel the tears crossing her unbelievably beautiful face.

-I should tell you, my dear Layleen, that this is a Dimension I've brought you in where I can't touch you. - The voice said, sounding a bit more loud.

-But at the same time, it also is a Dimension where not even him can find us…-

The Queen of the Kingdom Of The Dove, finally spoke again.

-You know him…-

The same struggling and mellow silence that was so common when talking to that mysterious entity, broke the air.

Then, again, even louder than before.

-I know him in a way you will never be able to equal… Nobody will ever be able to…-

The kind of rage that was getting over that mysterious voice, surprised Layleen a lot.

More than a lot.

And then Layleen cried. She cried out loud.

-I just want him to hug me… One more and last hug… I am not asking anything more than that…-

And the Entity that was hiding in the darkness, laughed.

A laugh completely empty of any type of real feelings.

-He doesn't care... He doesn't want to... He is selfish... He is vain... He is arrogant...-

Layleen was then crying even more. But more silently.

-So why... Why does he always come...? To protect me... To save me... Even last time... He always comes to save me...-

She wiped her tears away with her hand, before then finishing her sentence.

-From you. -

This time there was no silence getting involved in between the Queen Of The Dove's question and the Entity's answer.

-This is what you don't understand, my Queen... Every single time he comes to take you away from me, he doesn't come to save you, Layleen...-

A serene wind was then caressing the Queen's cheeks and the voice finished its pronouncement.

-He comes to save his name. -

The Queen suddenly stopped to cry.

-Why are you here, now? Why did you bring me here? -

The air and the scene got blurry.

-Because I wanted to see you, Layleen... That's the one and only reason why I have brought you in here...-

-But I can never see you, right? -

-Not now... Not yet... But soon... Sooner than what you will ever be able to think...-

The whole environment changed once again.

From being completely dark and unsafe, it became all totally white and incredibly luminous around the Queen Of The Dove, even if with still the same sensation of sadness.

-I know you like this kind of atmosphere way more, Layleen… White and bright…-

Even if the whole scene was the exact opposite of the one before, the man or whoever was talking was still impossible to be seen.

The Queen didn't seem surprised at all by that.

-Yes, I do. -

-I know. I know you do… Look at this white environment all around us, Layleen… Enjoy this luminescence… Find pleasure in the comfort of this stunning brightness…-

A little pause.

-Because, my beautiful Queen…-

And everything went back to normal, Layleen was on the floor of the outdoor of the highest Tower of her enchanting and lightful Castle.

The sky, the stars, everything was back to their regularity.

Everything except her mind, still not completely clear from the voice of the mystic Entity, that pronounced his last words with an extraordinary amount of cruelty, right in the exact meantime Layleen was reopening her eyes to the view of her Kingdom around her.

-Because, my beautiful Layleen, very soon all you will be able to see will be only darkness. -

XXIV

LION-LIKE

-I have never asked you before, Your Majesty, why in here the most of the Nature is red? -

-Because red is the colour that better represents our inner selves, Gurion. Strong. Passionate. We do not live between the flames of Hell, but we live with the fire in our eyes, and that is why our Kingdom has always been, and still is, one of the greatest in absolute in the whole vastity of The Circle. -

The red leaves on the trees around the two talking men, were lightly moved by a very calm and warm wind.

They were finding themselves in a very open space.

The combination between the red grass and the many different kinds of wonderful and colourful flowers, was giving birth to an extremely unique spectacle for the eyes.

The Kingdom Of The Lion was unique.

And its King, King Lander, was unique too.

And beautiful.

King Lander was beautiful.

His long red hair and his green eyes were, in fact, a breath-taking view, very difficult to handle.

His name was meaning "Lion-Like".

-But, King Lander, who made possible to have a different kind of Nature's colour in every single Kingdom of The Circle? I mean, mine is only pure curiosity...-

King Lander passed a hand through his incredible hair, then letting them to be moved by the air, allowing them to dance in the wind.

The King Of The Lion didn't respond straight away.

Gurion waited, while looking far away in the Present, letting his eyes following the direction of the invisible wind.

King Lander than looked at him.

-He did. -

The man kept his eyes busy on the unbelievable landscape that was existing in front of him, in front of them, and he repeated the words of his King.

-He did...-

King Lander smiled.

-Yes, my friend. He did. None of the Kings of the Kingdoms of The Circle can actually turn their Nature's characteristics and colours in the way they want. -

The King had a little laugh.

-But...- Gurion finally raised his eyes to his tall King.

-Have you ever met him? -

The King Of The Lion, gave Gurion the look back and he calmly said, with a note of solemnly pride in his strong and secure voice.

-Yes. I did. Twice. -

Gurion was a young boy, but his eyes, very dark, were suggesting that he was hiding a very delicate story deep inside of them.

-And... How is he? Is he... Amazing? -

King Lander was walking slowly around that open space where they were together, starting to make his way up the hill.

The young man was following his King step by step.

-He is way more than amazing. - The King stated.

And, after few seconds spent thinking about how to best describe the Being him and Gurion were talking about, he then made an even more revealing statement.

-He is… The Ultimate Standard Of Perfection. -

Gurion was fantasizing inside of his carefree young mind, and he then took a dreamy look at the then pink and red sky.

-Maybe one day I will be able to meet him too…-

King Lander looked in the same direction up in the sky where Gurion was not even really looking, while lost deep inside of his thoughts, made of fantasy and hope.

-Maybe…- The King answered, lowing done the usual strength in his voice.

Gurion smiled, but this time in a well visible melancholic way.

The top of the small hill they were walking on, was getting closer.

The two men stopped for a moment.

-I am happy about how the things went. -

King Lander introduced what was appearing to be the beginning of another kind of conversation, with a topic clearly far away from the previous one.

-I am happy too. - The boy answered, and he then looked at the top of the hill, red as blood.

-Very happy. - He concluded.

They then restarted walking and in a matter of few instants they were on the top of the hill.

And that was the moment where both men smiled, happy, full of energy and full of hope in their Souls.

In front of them there was Neon, the main Town of the Kingdom Of The Lion, and focusing very much, they were able to spot the Castle.

An entirely red Castle, with flames and fire all around of it.

An extremely huge green Cross made out of an unknown material on the top of the highest of the Towers, with a great Ruby stuck in the middle of it.

And the King left his young friend behind, only few steps behind, and he reached the very top of that hill, standing tall and imponent right in the middle of it.

Even if not extremely close, if attentive enough, people were even able to spot the figure of their King, far, but still visible to whoever was lucky enough to spot him from the streets of Neon.

King Lander closed his hands in fists, and he got tense with his muscles.

The greatness and the beauty of his red armour was shiny under the Sun and his Crown was pure Gold, big, a lion's head at every side of it with tiny little Rubies as eyes.

The most of the shininess was in fact coming from those beautiful Gems more than from the rest of the Crown itself.

He closed his eyes and he clearly concentrated. Really hard.

And then, all of a sudden, a pale but very well visible vapour of energy appeared all around him, the colour of a warm kind of yellow that then turned orange and then red before, ultimately, all of those three colours were surrounding him all together, all at once.

The dark red clouds that appeared in the sky, came down fast and then faster, covering most of the then golden coloured sky over the Kingdom Of The Lion, but without covering the Sun, that remained free and warm over them and their lands.

The combination between the dark red clouds and the staggering Sun, was giving to the Town of Neon a completely different atmosphere.

Also, something very singular happened to the people of Neon too.

Suddenly, they all left whatever they were up to, just to give a better look at the far figure of their King, standing tall on the very top of what was called Ruby Hill.

The expressions on all of their faces, changed.

Few instants before they were all calm and their faces were smiley and relaxed, giving the genuine impression that nobody of the people living in that Town would have ever been able to hurt someone.

But then, in that precise moment, those same people were presenting the purest kind of anger on their faces, some sort of absolute strength that was able to be felt in form of extremely intense vibrations, boiling energy that was coming out from their bodies and from their minds.

The same people that only less than few minutes before were peaceful and shy, they were then confident and very well aware of the fact they were not only strong, but also, they were dominant.

Like nobody else.

King Lander was their source of energy.

He was the one and only reason why those people were able to suddenly feel invincible, second to nobody else in The Circle.

And then, they were also able to see him more focused.

Their eyes were having a different skill in terms of greatly focusing on people or things, in the meantime they were experiencing that kind of condition of their inner selves.

They moved few steps, getting closer in the direction where the King was, even if still far from him, and they were walking with very serious expressions on their faces, moving with an extraordinary kind of confidence, knowing very deep inside of themselves that whoever would have been trying to step in their way would have been defeated, with absolutely no other options in terms of epilogue.

Then, they stopped.

And they stared.

Waiting.

Waiting in silence.

A rumble coming from a thunder.

A very warm breath.

And then some precipitations started to fall down from the sky.

It was not rain. Definitely it was not snow.

It was nothing usual.

Actually, it was very unusual.

Flames were falling down from the sky.

Fire flames big enough to enlightening the whole area even more, going to combine themselves with the rays of the Sun, still shining up there, between the darkness.

And King Lander finally opened his eyes.

So green.

So pure.

Extremely strong.

Extraordinarily unique.

And he roared at the sky, he roared so loud that the sound of a second thunder resulted to go completely unnoticed.

A roar that he yelled while facing the sky, while facing the fire that was falling down, fast, final, but a fire that would have never been burning those lands, a fire that would have never been hurting the people of the Kingdom Of The Lion.

His people.

A fire that was actually the purest of the many essences of those people's Souls.

And the most ultimate of the essences of the Soul of the King.

And they all bowed down to that roar.

They all bowed down to the roaring figure of the King, that was then opening his arms under the rage of the tempest of fire, that was standing tall, powerful, on the most Sacred spot of their Town and of their Kingdom, the spot that was known as Ruby Hill.

They were all bowing down to their King.

And the King was giving them the strength to be deserving to be the people of the Kingdom Of The Lion.

And Gurion was bowing down too.

Only few steps away from his King.

Because in that moment, every single Being in Neon and even every single Being in the whole Kingdom, too far to be able to see the King, but close enough to feel his Soul and to be able to see the fire, was doing the same exact thing.

They were all bowing down to their King.

They were all bowing down to King Lander.

XXV

DARK PARTICULARS

It was an awesome Spring day.

The Sun was very warm and there were no clouds bothering the great blue sky.

The Kingdom Of The Wolf was seeming a bit more shiny than what it usually used to be, especially in the Town of Shaw.

Adriel, Crevan, Dawako and Princess Lisica were trying their very best to try to get through the impressive amount of people that were walking and running all around.

-Come here, you silly boy! -

A mother was yelling at her child that, running, found himself on the floor after bumping right into Adriel's legs.

-Oh no, don't cry! - Adriel said, as the kid started to scream out loud due to the collision with the hard and pale white ground.

-Oh, don't worry! He is just a little Devil…- The woman said, while helping her son to get back on his feet.

-How many times do I have to repeat to you to don't run around the Town?! You see, you are always do that anyway and then there you go… You are causing troubles! -

-There's no troubles going on in here, really…- Crevan stated, getting interrupted straight away.

-Yes. There's troubles going on in here. - The woman said, with her whole expression changing all of a sudden.

From seeming cute and peaceful, she then was seeming to be angry and also very sinister.

A strange brightness crossed her eyes for a moment.

-Well…- Crevan said, also noticing a very uncomfortable change of the atmosphere.

-We really have to go…-

The woman looked at them.

The kid, that in that meantime completely stopped to cry, was looking at them too, very well focused on all of them.

Especially Adriel.

They were standing in there, staring at them, in silence, very strangely and somehow like they were not even real.

-Let's go…- The Commander said to the others of the Kingdom Of The Fox.

Adriel didn't move.

-I am wondering…- He said.

Everyone looked at him.

-I am actually wondering… What kind of troubles are you talking about? - He asked to the woman.

But both her and her son didn't move from their stare.

-Adriel, let's go…- Dawako said, grabbing Adriel's arm.

But Adriel hit with a straight punch Dawako's arm, that felt the pain.

-Adriel!!! Are you mad?!-

Adriel looked at him.

-Don't you ever touch me…- His words came out like they were not actually coming out from him.

Another very rapid shine crossed the mother's and the son's eyes.

A red light, but way too fast to be noticed.

Way too quick to be seen.

And the kid spoke.

-He has a mean nature. -

-Yes, he has. Everyone has. - The mother added to her son's statement.

-He is bad. - The kid said in a way that was more like singing a song.

-Yes, he is. - The woman agreed, once again, then looking deep inside Adriel's eyes.

-Everyone secretly is. - She added.

Adriel coughed.

-What? What was that? -

-What was what? - Dawako answered with another question.

-You hit me…- The usually smiling boy from Vixen concluded.

Adriel looked at him like if Dawako was out of his mind.

-What are you saying? I didn't touch you, you are crazy. -

Nobody spoke.

It was obvious there was something going on.

However, what was really happening was very far from being able to be understood easily.

Then the kid laughed.

-Look, mom! The guy that got hit is envy! -

-And jealous too! - The woman replied.

Dawako got red on his face.

-I am what?! I can not be envy or jealous of him! I am better than him, way better than him! And I am also even better than Crevan! I am the best between these people around me! -

The Commander Of The Fox didn't seem touched by that very weird behaviour coming from Dawako.

Adriel remained focused on the scene, not a move.

Lisica was very much confused.

-Mom! He is so proud! - The kid seemed even more excited than before.

This time, the woman didn't answer straight away, but she kept staring at Adriel even if in that moment was Dawako the matter of the conversation.

-He is not proud. - She then said.

And then, finally bringing her attention on Dawako, she made one last, final statement.

-He is scared. -

Few moments of silence.

Few instants of thick and heavy silence, until someone called the Commander Of The Fox's name.

-Crevan! Crevan, this way! Such a long, long time…-

Everyone looked in the direction of where that voice was coming from.

A man not even taller than Princess Lisica, was walking fast towards them.

-Ixanthi. - Crevan said.

-Nice to see you…-

The Commander of the Kingdom Of The Fox sounded way more formal in the way he spoke to him.

-Crevan! Crevan! Everyone is waiting for all of you at the Castle, Crevan! Every single one! -

He then gave a look at Adriel, Dawako and Princess Lisica.

-I didn't expect to see the Princess of the Kingdom Of The Fox. - He said, a serious expression on his until then extraordinarily ecstatic face.

Then, suddenly, the smile appeared back on his face, a kind of face extremely difficult to read.

-It is an extremely pleasure to have you here in the Kingdom Of The Wolf, Princess Lisica. I do hope your father, King Balgair, is in a great health. -

Lisica didn't expect to be known in there, in the Kingdom Of The Wolf, by somebody she never met before.

-He is fine… I guess…-

Ixanthi kept the smile on his face.

-You will apologise the fact I am not bowing down to you, Princess, but as a Resident of the Kingdom Of The Wolf I am entitled to bow down only to the Royalties of my Kingdom. -

-Oh, I know that. - Lisica said.

-Every single person of every single Kingdom of The Circle, bows down only to the Royalties of his Kingdom.-

-Yes! Well said! - The short man gladly exclaimed.

Suddenly, his voice became surprisingly low.

-With obviously a couple of exceptions. -

Adriel spoke.

-Exceptions? -

Ixanthi looked at him.

Something not clear, flashed in his eyes.

Then, completely ignoring Adriel's question, he also gave a look at Dawako.

The young man from Vixen, spoke too.

-What exceptions…? -

The short man then moved his attention on the Commander Of The Fox.

They were looking at each other.

Eyes in the eyes.

-Don't think about it. - Ixanthi said.

-But…- Dawako tried.

The power that made his voice unable to keep coming out of his mouth, was unknown.

Sure was that in the meantime he tried to answer back, his voice remained stuck inside of his throat.

-Now. If you would please follow me…-

Ixanthi gave his back to them and he slowly started to walk, but Adriel's exclamation really made him stop straight away.

-Wait a moment! Where are that woman and her son gone?!-

Adriel's question got everyone's attention.

Ixanthi, remaining calm and apparently not interested in that topic at all, smiled and he restarted to walk, once again, sure the guests coming from the Kingdom Of The Fox were going to follow him.

But he was very wrong.

-You are right! - Dawako said, answering to Adriel.

All those events going on and the arriving on the scene of the short man called Ixanthi that really seemed to know Crevan quite well, literally caught everyone else's attention that much that all of them, even the Commander, totally forgot about the woman and her son, that until few minutes before were standing in there, staring at them, talking to each other and about topics honestly very hard to understand.

Certainly, they were not there anymore.

They were gone.

And nobody noticed that before that moment.

-That's weird. - Lisica stated.

-It is…- The Commander Of The Fox agreed, serious and concentrated.

The Town of Shawn was very busy and nicely vibrant, that day.

-Should we go? King Adalwolf is waiting for all of you…- Ixanthi said.

They all started to move.

Not a speech.

They were walking since not a very long time, when Ixanthi faced Adriel.

-Are you excited to meet King Adalwolf, young man? -

Adriel didn't expect that question coming, so he had to answer pretty quickly and without thinking too much about how to choose the words.

-Oh, well… Yeah… I mean… Yes, sure… Actually, I am also very excited to be here… I have never been out of my Kingdom…-

The short man seemed satisfied enough by the way that answered was formulated by the young man.

-And you, Dawako? Are you excited to meet the King Of The Wolf? -

Dawako seemed to be very far away with his mind, but he somehow managed to give an answer.

-Oh? What? Oh yes, sure… I guess…-

Ixanthi then focused his eyes on the Princess, that was walking carrying Destiny with her.

-And you, Princess? How do you feel about it? -

The Princess Of The Fox took few moments to give an answer.

-If I feel excited about meeting your King? Sure... Very excited...-

This time the type of answer that the man received didn't seem to please him.

However, nothing had been said in response to that.

He was short, as already mentioned, very difficult to guess what his age could have been, due to the combination of very young details of his image, like the eyes and the skin, apparently so fresh and full of energy.

But few other characteristics of his appearance were putting many doubts about the nature of that Being.

For example, the hands that were coming out from the black vest, were seeming very old. Full of wrinkles and spots that were seeming burnt and aged.

Even his hair were denoting vibes of elder, white and grey, even if very well presented.

His yellow eyes were impossible to read.

They were heading to the Castle on the top of Moon Hill.

The Castle was white and shiny, and the hill was green and lovely at the sight.

Then, Dawako stopped walking.

All at once, all of them did.

-What? - Crevan asked.

Dawako was focusing on his left.

-I'm really not sure...-

Ixanthi gave a deep and attentive look at him.

-Have you seen or heard anything, young man? -

His calling Dawako "young man" put some more questions regarding the man's true age.

Dawako spoke, with a vibration of pure curiosity in his voice.

-I'm not sure, but… There…-

He pointed his finger to a spot not too far, a fountain with the form of a wolf, that was giving shots of water from his mouth.

The fountain itself was absolutely stunning.

But the view of the water coming out from the wolf's mouth, was seeming a bit singular.

-I know, it is quite creepy, I do agree…- Ixanthi said with a smile without happiness.

-No. Not the fountain. There… On the back of the wolf. -

Dawako pointed his finger even more vehemently and then, finally, everyone noticed what he was pointing his finger at.

On the wolf's back there were two crows, very close to each other, steady, and they were without any kind of doubt looking at them.

Crevan focused on them.

The two crows were completely motionless.

Ixanthi spoke.

-They are just two crows, young man. -

Dawako looked at the short man.

-The crows are not the point. -

Nobody asked anything, as clearly waiting for Dawako to say more than that.

-Their shadows. - He said.

The day, that earlier was very warm and shiny, did suddenly became grey and way colder.

And, considering that, those two crows were seeming to carry in fact something very unusual with them.

Even if the Sun was in that moment long gone, their shadows were clear and vivid on the freezing and stony ground.

But that, even if out of any logic, was not even the main detail that made everyone, everyone except Ixanthi, stare at them, the mouth open in a genuine expression on their faces that was describing only one type of feeling.

Total confusion.

-Wait a moment...- The Commander of the Kingdom Of The Fox said before anyone else.

-Oh, Lord...-

Lisica was not able to say anything more than that.

Adriel looked at Ixanthi.

The short man was looking at them looking at the crows.

A smile full of mystery and something else impossible to define.

And Dawako spoke.

-They don't match. - He said.

And, in fact, not only the two shadows should have not even been there.

The most shocking part of that view was the fact the two shadows were not resembling the figures of the two crows at all.

They were, instead, long and big, and they were resembling something or someone similar to two Human Beings, which was not even possible either, due to the shadow of the apparent pair of huge thin wings behind them, with a spiked kind of form on the top of them.

Destiny started to crazily stomp his hooves, producing strange noises with his mouth, shaking his head quite strongly.

-They look like… Their shadows, both of them, they resemble the form…-

Lisica started the sentence, but Dawako, staring at the crows and at their not matching shadows with no Sun, ended it.

-Of two Devils. -

XXVI

LUMINOUS CONNECTION

It was a peaceful night in the Kingdom Of The Dove.

Queen Layleen was walking around the Castle. Her Castle.

A Castle that was that beautiful that she was never tired to look at, from the outside and even from the inside.

However, even if unbelievably shiny from the outside, there were not many sources of lights inside Queen Layleen's Castle.

Actually, it was quite dark.

The Queen was alone that night.

Ailana was already sleeping.

It was very late.

Evangeline was still out, somewhere in Town, under Layleen's order.

She sent her to visit someone in particular, due to her strong need to have the answer about a very important and delicate topic.

And that was the reason why she was still awake, not even tired, thinking and overthinking to that very huge obsession she had inside of her mind.

She was, as most of the times, somewhere near the very top floor of her Fort, very close to the stairs that were leading to the outdoor space she loved so much on the top of the highest Tower.

She stepped right in front of them.

She was tremendously tempted.

She gave a bite to her lips.

A little bite.

But a very sinful one…

She looked behind herself.

No-one was around inside the Castle, at that time.

She finally stopped thinking, even if only for a moment, and she took her way up the stairs.

Every single step she was taking, she was then thinking that it might have been better to go back.

But it was way too late, by then.

She didn't even realise, and she was already half the way up.

There were then not many steps left to take, but she started at that point to walk them very slowly.

Then, finally, she found himself in front of the door that was leading outside on the open space on the top of the highest of the Towers of her magnificent Castle.

Her forehead was sweating.

She tied up her long dark hair even tidier and she caressed her cheeks, softly, while staring at the door in front of her.

Her hands were cold.

She pushed the door, a heavy dark brown door, and in that moment a fresh smell of Spring, directly from the vibrations of the night, reached her senses.

Once she was finally outside, she remained amazed.

The sky was a Universe of stars.

Brilliant and never-ending stars that were not only enlightening the Town of Umbriel, but that were actually enlightening the entire Kingdom Of The Dove.

But there was no Moon that night.

She loved the Moon.

It was her favourite way to get rid of all of her constant overthinking about everything.

Looking at the Moon.

Because while she was doing that, it was always feeling like she was always getting all the answers she needed. All the answers to all of her many questions.

But as that night the Moon was not there, she kept thinking, even if enjoying the breath-taking view the sky was donating her with also a touch of silent romance.

Then, the natural instinct to raise her eyes up to the Infinity, looking in the right direction, searching for that particular spot… That particular source of ultimate light…

And the Queen of the Kingdom Of The Dove didn't really do anything to only even try to refrain that instinct.

She raised indeed her eyes up to the sky, deep inside of it.

The stars, plenty of them, became a great and confused amount of lights, they were seeming like one unique enormous source of light, due to the powerful kind of concentration the Queen was putting in her searching for what she was precisely looking for.

And, ultimately, she found it.

It was there.

Her melodic blue eyes ecstatically focused on it.

It was really there.

Between the stars.

Between the countless Constellations that were shining inside the infinity of the Universe.

But that very specific point was even, possibly and most definitely, at the extreme limits of any Universe.

The only way for her to spot it, was the Universal Connection she had with that specific point far away above the skies.

A kind of connection that was even stronger and definitely deeper than any extraordinarily magnificent kind of Soul Connection.

The most luminous light above everything and also above everyone.

It was not a star.

It was nothing the sky was normally presenting in its mystical and Divine appearance.

Layleen looked at it with even more attention.

-Are you watching? - She whispered.

-Are you looking down at me? -

The silence was stabbing her heart.

She didn't obviously expect any kind of answer, but she was dreaming about it, with her eyes wide open.

She had a last look up above.

-In any case... Thank you...-

And she interrupted the stare at it.

She interrupted the connection.

Slowly, she walked back to the door that was leading back inside the Castle.

Once she disappeared back inside her Fort, something quite unusual happened.

But it was way too late for the Queen Of The Dove to see it, as she was already gone.

The giant Amazonite stuck in the middle of the big Cross on the top of the highest Tower got brighter than ever, but that was not the main incredible factor that was happening in that moment.

What really shocked Evangeline, that was going back to the Castle in that precise instant, was the amazingly radiant, thin, laser of energy that became a concrete connection between the Gem and the stunning shiny light that was the matter of the obsession of the Queen Of The Dove.

And it was seeming to be transparent, but the truth is there was some sort of light blue coloured dust.

In all honesty, it was seeming like the dust was in reality Crystals' dust.

The view of that incredible event was powerful.

And totally impossible to define.

What was happening?

Certainly, Evangeline didn't have the right answer.

Actually, she didn't even have a wrong answer to give.

Everything was genuinely impossible to be defined in any known way.

And then, all at once, everything just terminated, going back to normal.

The Amazonite in the middle of the Cross, lost that temporary brightness it acquainted only few moments before.

It was then yes still sparkling, but in a very natural way.

The connection between the Gem and the highest and brightest point in the Universe, vanished.

Evangeline saw everything.

She was more than speechless about what she just witnessed.

She tried to then look deeper inside the sky, but she didn't spot anything.

She knew exactly what she was looking for, but she also knew very well she would have never been able to see it.

Evangeline moved few steps, but she had to stop again pretty quickly.

She would have not been feeling like to bet everything she had in her Life, but she was also pretty sure about what she saw.

-Hey!!!- She yelled, literally.

But she was well aware of the fact she was way too far to be heard.

She just yelled by instinct, without expecting to receive any answer back in response.

She knew she saw someone walking by the doors, around the main entrance of the Castle, but that was not the biggest of the questions inside of her mind.

Whoever he was, she knew who she did see was not someone ordinary.

She ran right to the doors of the entrance, it took her few minutes to reach that spot, and she took a look around.

No-one.

The absolute nothing.

Everything was very calm and chill.

Warm.

Evangeline initially gave up on her thoughts, thinking that maybe she somehow really imagined she saw somebody walking around that same exact spot where she was then standing, covered by doubts and thoughts.

-Interesting...-

She thought for a moment at what she definitely knew she saw for sure not too many minutes before, witnessing to the absolutely real and magnificent event of the connection between the Amazonite stuck in the middle of the massive Cross on the top of the highest Tower and the mystical point in the sky that was reigning above the whole Humanity…

Over the whole Existence…

She was about to open the main doors, then she saw it.

She really saw it.

On the candid white grass, there was something.

And that something was of the same colour of the grass, but it was easy to spot, as not tiny at all.

Evangeline picked up the white feather from the ground.

She looked at it… And she was trying to swallow, but her throat was blocked due to the emotion.

It was extremely soft at the touch.

She waited in front of the doors. Thinking. Looking around.

Holding the feather in her hand.

That big white feather.

And she concluded she was right about what she saw few instants before.

When she saw, even if only for a moment, that presence walking around the Castle, in front of the main entrance.

And not a regular kind of presence.

That someone she saw, was different…

The image of that someone was very much alive inside her eyes…

The figure of that man.

And his heavenly and huge pair of wings.

XXVII

THE POWER OF HOPE

In the morning, Evangeline didn't talk much.

She didn't sleep well at all, and her mind was still busy thinking about the many things she saw the night before.

Ailana was keeping looking at her while they were both walking around Umbriel, but she was choosing not to actually ask anything, even if it was clear that the Leader of the Kingdom Of The Dove had her mind troubled, that morning.

They were waling silently, when an old man got his way towards them.

-Good morning, Ailana! Evangeline…! What a beautiful day today, don't you agree? -

The two girls stopped.

-Good morning to you, Sabath. You look well. - Ailana said with a smile.

-I am! And finally I see the two of you… Such a while… How is the Queen…? I hope everything is amazing with her…-

-It is. - Ailana rushed that topic.

Evangeline looked at her, with a questioning kind of expression on her face.

Sabath noticed the very quick answer coming from the Commandress Of The Dove.

-Well…- He then said.

-I hope you will then remember to bring her my best greetings…-

-Sure, we will. - Ailana answered once again, but this time in a more calm way.

The Commandress and the Leader gave their back to Sabath.

-One moment! Please! -

The two women turned their head.

-Yes? - Evangeline spoke.

-Evangeline… Ailana… There is one more thing…-

The man was then looking less confident than few instants before.

-Apparently… Someone, today… Not me… Saw…-

-Saw what? - Ailana asked, a bit worried by the way the man was then talking, like if he was about to say something extremely bad.

-Someone, today, saw Ulmuka. -

Ailana opened her mouth, speechless.

Evangeline spoke for her.

-Ulmuka? -

-The Commander Of The Owl is here?!- Ailana finally spoke.

-Indeed. - Sabath concluded.

Ailana grabbed Evangeline's arm.

-Let's go. - She said, firmly.

-To the Castle. -

They ran away, leaving Sabath behind, the man looking at them disappearing from his view, directed to the Fort of Queen Layleen.

They reached the mesmerizing Castle very quickly and they entered.

Everything was apparently calm.

-Queen Layleen! - Evangeline called.

Ailana hit her in the stomach.

-Ouch! -

The Leader Of The Dove looked up at the Commandress.

-Why?!-

-Are you crazy?!- Ailana whispered to her.

-If he is here, we don't need him to know we are here too…-

-Right…- Evangeline answered, still massaging her own belly.

They both took their swords.

They ran up the stairs, trying to reach the fourth floor, where the Throne Hall was.

Once there, the doors were closed.

Two massive doors where a white gold dove was stuck in, pure and candid.

It was on the left door.

On the right door there were quite big letters, white gold as well, that were giving birth to the word HOPE.

They didn't knock on the doors.

Ailana opened the doors slamming them with a massive hit with her foot and they both jumped inside the room, swords ready, but what they saw shocked them.

Ulmuka was there.

But that was not the shock. They knew they would have found him there.

The real shock was the view of him sitting on the steps that were leading to the Throne of the Queen of the Kingdom Of The Dove, that was talking calm and serene with him.

-What's happening in here?!- Ailana yelled, still shocked by the view she was having right in front of her and Evangeline, quite speechless as well.

Ulmuka turned his head to face the two women that just entered in the Hall Of The Throne.

-Queen Layleen...- He said.

-Your Protectors are here...-

He smiled, maliciously.

The Queen Of The Dove was sitting on her Throne.

A great Throne made out of marble. Candid. It was that white that the Sunlight was looking dark compared to the light that Queen Layleen's Throne was spreading all around.

-Hello, Ailana and Evangeline. -

Queen Layleen welcomed the two girls.

-Ailana. - The Queen said, giving a sign to her to move in direction of the Throne.

Ailana obeyed and walked few steps until she was quite close to Ulmuka, that remained sitting on the steps that were leading to the Throne of the Queen Of The Dove.

-Ailana, my darling. You already know...-

-Ulmuka. Yes, I know this man. - The Commandress said.

Ulmuka gave a look at Queen Layleen.

-I wasn't aware of the fact it was allowed to your people to interrupt you like that, Queen Layleen...- He said with a tone of pure maliciousness in his voice.

-I cannot imagine if it would have been happened with King Mongwau...-

-There's many things that make me and your King very different, Ulmuka.-

Queen Layleen was not smiling anymore.

She was, instead, looking at the Commander Of The Owl with a very severe look pictured on her face.

Evangeline was still waiting on the entrance by the doors.

-Sweet little thing down there...- Ulmuka called her.

-Come to join us, please...- He concluded, finally standing up.

Ailana went face to face with him.

-Don't even look at her, man. -

-Oh... What a lovely view...- He said, looking at Ailana directly in the eyes.

-A woman like you... So strong... So proud... So full of confidence...-

-What do you want, Ulmuka? Why are you here? -

-Enough. - Queen Layleen stood up from her Throne.

The Queen Of The Dove was very angry.

-Ailana. Step back from him. -

Ailana was very far from wanting to obey to her Queen's order, but she did as Queen Layleen requested, even if visibly reluctant.

-Yeah... Step back from me...- Ulmuka said, mocking and smiling at the Commandress.

Queen Layleen gave a look at Evangeline.

The young Leader of the Kingdom Of The Dove didn't move a muscle since she entered inside the room.

Ulmuka was dressed in grey.

A light grey vest, with black boots that were presenting few holes here and there.

His eyes were on Evangeline's hair.

He was smelling them with his eyes… He was pulling them… He was pulling them with his mind…

-My dear Evangeline. Come here. - Queen Layleen said.

The young girl moved her feet walking down the room, reaching Ulmuka and Ailana right in front of the Queen, few steps above all of them.

-This is the first time you meet someone from another Kingdom, right? -

-Yes, my Queen. -

-Oh, I feel honoured…- Ulmuka commented, the same malicious smile pictured on his face.

Ailana had the impulse to step right in front of the Commander's face, but she incredibly succeeded in the attempt of refraining that very natural kind of instinct, remembering Queen Layleen inviting, ordering her, to step back from Ulmuka earlier on.

-This is Ulmuka, Evangeline. He is the Commander of the Kingdom Of The Owl. - Queen Layleen said.

-In the Regions Of Darkness. - She then concluded.

A little silence followed the Queen's voice.

Then, she spoke again.

-Ulmuka. This is my brand-new Leader. The Leader of my Kingdom. - The Queen said, then facing Ulmuka directly from her spot, standing tall right in front of her Throne entirely made of the greatest kind of marble.

-Impressed. - Ulmuka commented.

-Very impressed. -

-You should be. - Ailana interrupted.

-Evangeline has an extraordinary potential. And a good knowledge of herself. That means she can produce a very good quality of energy…-

Ulmuka snapped his fingers.

-I was thinking…- He said, completely ignoring Ailana's words.

-I was thinking… Queen Layleen… Why don't you tell your Protectors the reason why I am here today? -

Ailana was disappointed by being ignored like that, but at the same time she almost felt glad that Ulmuka asked that very particular question to the Queen, as she had to admit to herself that she was extremely curious to understand the reason why someone from one of the Kingdoms of the Regions Of Darkness was there, in the Kingdom Of The Dove, at the Court of Queen Layleen.

The Queen looked out of the window.

-Apparently… Ulmuka is here to warn us. -

Ailana laughed.

She laughed louder than ever.

Evangeline remained serious.

Strangely serious.

-Forgive me, Queen Layleen. - Ailana said.

-But I can't believe you are actually believing he is here to warn us about whatever it is. -

The Queen looked at Ailana.

-You do need to believe in something… Or someone… Sometimes.-

Ailana saw that.

It was extraordinarily quick, but she saw that.

A strange sparkle in the eyes of her Queen in the meantime she was pronouncing those words.

-I apologise, my Queen. -

Ulmuka laughed.

-It really is hilarious how in your Kingdom they go from interrupting you while you are speaking to then looking at the ground asking for forgiveness...-

He looked at Queen Layleen.

-It doesn't work like that in the Regions Of Darkness. -

-Not even in the other Kingdoms of the Regions Of Light. - The Queen said.

-But in my Kingdom I want my people to feel relaxed, to feel comfortable even when they are in front of me, talking to me. I am their Queen. And they know that very well. I don't need them to remind me who I am in every single moment. -

Ulmuka this time didn't say a word.

He snapped his fingers again.

-I came here because the Regions we are part of is a detail that is not relevant at all in this actual situation. - Ulmuka replied.

-We are all part of The Circle. -

He took a pause.

-Queen Layleen... The Kingdom Of The Fox... We are sure... They want to join the Regions Of Darkness. We still don't know yet if straight away or only once they will have their new Hero...-

Ailana was not able to succeed in trying to refrain herself, this time.

-What kind of absurdity is that? - She replied to Ulmuka.

-That Kingdom is the weakest Kingdom of The Circle. And you want to make us believe you are interested in letting them join you in the Regions Of Darkness? -

After a little pause, she said more.

-Also...- She almost whispered to Ulmuka.

-What kind of joke is this? Why would you come to say that to us? You should be glad that one of the two Neutral Kingdoms of The Circle is actually trying to join your side… Am I wrong? -

Ulmuka smiled.

-You said it right. They are the weakest. Nobody wants them. Especially with a completely new Hero. Imagine without…-

-What are you trying to say? - Ailana asked.

-He is trying to say…- Queen Layleen jumped in the middle of the conversation.

-That the Kingdom Of The Fox is not only the weakest Kingdom of The Circle. They also, at the moment, don't even have a Hero. However. They will have their new Hero very soon. On the night of the Summer Solstice. -

-And…- Ailana tried to speak.

-And…- Ulmuka mocked her, before getting serious once again.

-And to avoid them having a new Hero, would keep them at a level where they could not even have the right, certainly not the privilege, to ask what they really want to ask to the King Of Darkness. -

-They are the weakest…- Ailana repeated.

-But we don't know the level of these new guys that are about to battle for the Role of Hero Of The Fox. If the winner is strong enough, they might be entitled to a Meeting with the King Of Darkness. And we don't want that to happen, in our Regions. We truly and deeply believe the two Neutral Kingdoms should remain like that. - Ulmuka said.

-For the balance of The Circle. - He concluded.

He snapped his fingers.

-Exactly the same way King Lysander did when he denied the Kingdom Of The Wolf to become part of the Regions Of Light a very long time ago. - He added.

Finally, Ulmuka seemed done with his talking.

Evangeline moved few steps closer to the Queen.

She didn't say anything, she just looked at her.

And the Queen smiled at her.

-So, the reason why Ulmuka is here today, is because he thinks I should join him only for few days in the Kingdom Of The Owl, where we could plan how to stop the Kingdom Of The Fox from having their new Hero. Like...-

And she caressed her own beautiful dark hair.

-Like, for once, being on the same page for something that would be a matter of importance for both sides. - She said.

-And for The Circle. - She also added.

-Exactly! - Ulmuka exclaimed, weirdly excited.

-Exactly like that. Not even the other Kingdoms know that I am here... Not even the King Of Darkness... I am here only for the interests of the Kingdom Of The Owl...-

-How do you know that to join the Regions Of Darkness is what the Kingdom Of The Fox wants? -

Ailana asked a very smart question.

But Ulmuka was ready for that.

-Our knowledge... Make us able to see things clearer than anybody else... We entered... Well... King Mongwau entered... Inside of King Balgair's mind... As he was feeling... He was feeling something coming from that way...And he saw... He saw his thoughts...-

And he lowered his voice.

-He saw his plans. - He concluded.

-Very well. - Queen Layleen said.

-Everything sounds very interesting. Honestly. It really does. - The Queen smiled at Ulmuka.

-However. - She then said.

There was silence following the Queen's voice.

-I don't think I will come to the Kingdom Of The Owl, after all. – Ulmuka's voice sounded disturbed.

-I don't quite understand… Queen Layleen… I thought… I thought you were agree that it might be a good, a great idea, to cooperate for once… For our Kingdoms… For our Regions… And for The Circle…-

The Queen was suddenly looking at the Commander Of The Owl with a really severe look, penetrating inside his grey eyes.

-Oh, don't get me wrong… I do agree… Believe me… I really do…- She said.

A little pause, and she then concluded.

-But I stay here. -

Suddenly, Ulmuka's voice changed.

It was deeper. Like coming from a tomb.

-Are you? -

The windows exploded. Pieces of glasses everywhere.

-ARE YOU?!-

And Ulmuka got surrounded by a brown and grey Aura, that was misty and dusty.

Ailana and Evangeline stepped right in front of Queen Layleen.

The Queen Of The Dove was calm and concentrate.

She was looking at Ulmuka but, in fact, she was not.

She was, in reality, looking far away. And while doing that, she got protected by a shiny and semi-transparent veil of energy. Electric.

-She is fine. She can not get any hit. - Ailana said.

-Let's get him. -

Ulmuka yelled, the sword in his hand.

Ailana and Evangeline were ready.

Ulmuka moved fast and he went attacking Ailana, that stopped the hit with her sword.

The Commandress Of The Dove responded back with multiple attacks that got, however, dodged by a very fast Ulmuka.

Evangeline jumped inside the action, trying to hit the Commander Of The Owl from behind.

But again, Ulmuka was extremely fast, and he did not only dodge the attack, but he also responded back with an elbow hit right on Evangeline's stomach.

-Coward! Little coward! Trying to hit me from behind! - He laughed.

He then delivered two very powerful hits generated by the only movement of the sword in the air, that went to hit both Ailana and Evangeline, pushing them back.

-You know in The Circle our two Kingdoms are one the counterpart of the other one, right…? - The Commander Of The Owl said.

-But… The difference between you and us…- He kept saying.

-The main difference between you and us is that you built your Kingdom on Hope. We built our Kingdom on Knowledge. -

While saying that, he cut the air with the blade of his sword and both the Commandress and the Leader of the Kingdom Of The Dove, got their swords slammed away.

-Hope is an abstract way to believe things will always be fine, but realistically based on nothing, only based on thinking the good luck will come to fix your issues... You all think Hope is something that can end Darkness, but no, it can not. Peace... That word doesn't exist in the real World. -

In the meantime, the Queen was still standing in front of her Throne, physically there, but visibly far away with her Spirit.

The electric transparent energy that was clearly protecting her, separating her from all the events that were happening inside the Hall Of The Throne, was still there, strong and vivid.

-But Knowledge...- Ulmuka kept saying.

-Knowledge is something concrete. Something you discover... Something you study... Something you learn... Something you can teach... Something you really know... It's not something based on events, it's not something you have to pray for. -

His voice was then louder, and it was echoing all around the room.

-Knowledge. You earn it. And you make it yours. Forever. -

Ulmuka raised his sword, strongly held in his hand and he literally loaded it.

His Aura got concentrated entirely inside the blade, that turned dark brown.

It was shining and then the hilt started to tremble inside Ulmuka's hand.

In that moment, Queen Layleen came back with her Spirit inside the room, her figure still protected by that circling energy, lightful and electric.

-Liar. - She said.

He looked at her.

Before he was able to release all of his power through his sword, a kind of power that was coming right from the deepest inside of his

Being's vibrations and sensations, Queen Layleen made her energy protection vanish and her blue eyes turned all completely white.

Ulmuka's sword suddenly got all of that energy loaded in the blade entirely blown away and that got him very unprepared.

-What...-

He looked at her once again.

Her then white eyes with no pupils and with no colour, were giving her an expression that was extremely hard to tell if it was Angelic or Evil.

Sure was that it frightened Ulmuka.

And, completely out of nowhere, the Commander Of The Owl realised that his sword was not in his hand anymore.

-Hey! My sword... Where...-

And then he saw it.

His sword.

In Queen Layleen's hand.

-How... How did you...-

The Queen's arm flashed and, after that instant of light, Ulmuka's sword was just something then part of the Past, as the only thing that fell down from the Queen Of The Dove's hand, was dust.

Burnt dust.

-What?!- Ulmuka yelled.

Queen Layleen was then about to speak.

Calm, again, but with something raging inside of her Being.

-You keep talking about the differences between you and us. -

She was then caressed by an invisible energy that was moving her white dress and her dark hair, tied up in a high tail.

-The real difference is that we actually recognise the more than useful usage of the biggest of your beliefs. Knowledge. -

Ulmuka was listening, breathing deep and heavy.

Sweating very much and not due to the few exchanges of sword hits with Ailana and Evangeline.

-Knowledge is indeed something incredibly impressive to attain, but it also is, as you said, concrete. And that is your limit, Ulmuka.-

The Commander of the Kingdom Of The Owl, was not able to say a word in front of the view of that Form of the Queen Of The Dove that he never saw before, with those white eyes that were deeper than the Darkness, her perfect hair moved by an energy not visible at the eyes.

She continued in her speech.

-Nothing that truly and genuinely comes from the Soul, is concrete. Nothing. It is, instead, always something fully abstract and universally mystical. Secret. Eternal. -

Outside the sky got darker than ever before in the Kingdom Of The Dove.

-Hope is not based on having some good luck. Hope is not only about praying for the events to get better or the same events to get perfectly fine. Hope is a word you can locate without any doubts close to the word Life. -

She then stared with her invisible eyes at Ailana and Evangeline. And then back at Ulmuka.

-To hope means to be in love with Life. -

She opened her arms.

-I am pretty sure you have no clue about the meaning of love. You maybe, barely, might have a slightly idea of what Life actually really is. But…-

And her smile felt sinister.

-But I am also very sure about the fact that today, right here and right now, you will start to learn the real meaning of Hope. In fact...-

White and thin lines of the same transparent electric energy that was surrounding her, started to flow down from her fingers.

-I am sure you will be hoping someone will come to save you... You will be hoping someone will come to help you to avoid what is about to happen to you in ten seconds... And if you still will not be hoping for that...-

And the smile vanished from the Queen's face.

-I will make you to. -

An incredibly loud electrical noise started to be extremely audible, coming from the entirety of the Queen's figure.

Ailana and Evangeline were standing up witnessing that unbelievable greatness that was coming out from Queen Layleen's presence.

Ulmuka stepped back.

-This power... It is way more than what I knew about you... In all honesty... There is no way for me to compete with you, that is for sure...-

Ailana was looking at her Queen in a way that was easily able to be called admiration.

Pure and total.

Queen Layleen raised her open arms a little bit more.

Behind her, a pale but still well visible rainbow lightening appeared.

She stared at the Commander Of The Owl and she said, calmly, but apparently without any known kind of emotions in her voice.

-Farewell. -

The rainbow light vanished from around the Queen's body, only to be then very well visible all unbelievably concentrated around her hands.

-Not so fast...- Ulmuka murmured.

He snapped his fingers.

That was the fourth time he was doing that.

Suddenly, the air changed.

Everything inside the room, the whole Castle, and even outside of it, was not lightful anymore.

Everything was misty and blurry.

The whole environment was not the one it regularly was.

It was not right.

Every sound was seeming like it was coming from extremely far from there, and the whole intensity of those sounds were altered in countless ways.

And it got very cold.

The Queen Of The Dove didn't move a finger, staring at Ulmuka with her eyes with no colour.

She was perfectly aware of what was about to happen.

-I'm wondering...- She said.

-What's the real reason why I am requested in your Regions... I mean... If one of them is here... It has to be a very extraordinary kind of matter...-

Ulmuka laughed.

-Don't even start to worry. You are wanted alive and well. -

Something in between a rage of dark wind and a huge and loud screams of desperation, all together, happened to manifest behind the Commander of the Kingdom Of The Owl.

An indistinct figure made his way out of that phenomenon, floating then in front of Ulmuka, taking a more concrete form second after second until presenting his whole and real essence once right in between the Commander and the Queen, on his full and well defined form, in every single detail.

Black, furry boots over black leather trousers, entirely covered with chains and a tight belt that was decorated with many little stones, red and orange, that were radiating a raging fiery kind of light.

The tail was ending like the edge of an arrow, and the horns were small, but thick.

The huge pair of black wings he was presenting were moving slowly. Little claws were at the top of them.

The eyes were all completely red, not presenting, like Layleen's eyes in that moment, any pupils.

The skin was of a dark kind of white.

Evangeline screamed.

Ailana yelled.

-Queen Layleen!!!-

But the Queen was not paying attention.

She was still looking at Ulmuka.

-Interesting. -

Ailana and Evangeline got ready to interfere, but the Queen stopped them.

-Do not make a move. -

Both women arrested their action.

-But…- Ailana mumbled.

And suddenly, Queen Layleen's power, her unbelievable rainbow energy that was all loaded in her hands, vanished.

Her eyes got their majestic blue colour back, the transparent electric energy that was surrounding the entirety of her figure was there no more, and while sweating she fell on her knees.

Yes, her, the Queen Of The Dove, she fell on her knees.

And in front of the new Being that appeared by Ulmuka's side.

-Queen Layleen… Oh, Queen Layleen…- The Commander laughed.

-I knew you were going to be difficult, and that's why I had to be sure there were not going to be too many issues in the process to bring you to the Regions that never see the light. -

-That's the reason why you brought a Devil to help you…? - Layleen said, sweating, finding difficult to breath properly.

The presence of the Devil in the room was making her weaker second after second.

-Indeed. And now… It's time, Queen Layleen…- Ulmuka announced.

The Devil didn't even move, but somehow Aialana and Evangeline got unable to leave the spot where they were standing at.

-Hey!!!- Evangeline exclaimed.

-She screams too much to be a Leader…- Ulmuka mocked her.

-NO!!!- Ailana was fighting with all of her body, but there was no way she was able to break the power that was keeping her and the Leader Of The Dove unable to move.

And, finally, the Devil spoke.

-Layleen. -

The sound of his voice made everyone's blood freezing.

Even Ulmuka's.

It was sounding like many different voices all at once, making a unique one.

-You are coming with us. And...- He said, cutting the air with his tail.

-There is absolutely nothing you can do about it. -

Those last words hit the presents even more, words that echoed in the Hall Of The Throne.

Queen Layleen was then about to touch the floor with her face.

-He... He will...-

-What are you saying? - Ulmuka asked.

-He...- The Queen said again, then almost at the maximum level of her weakness.

-He will punish you... All of you...-

Ulmuka lost his smile.

-You are getting silent, now...- He replied.

However, by the way his voice shook while pronouncing those words, it was clear that suddenly some thoughts inside of his mind were for some reason making him scared.

-He will... Believe me...-

The Queen was at that point coughing at every single word she was pronouncing.

The Devil spoke.

-Do you think he cares? -

Then his voice was whispering in Layleen's ears.

-So tell me why he is not here... He is never here... If he cared, you know very well there would have not been any kind of way me and Ulmuka were still here... Right? -

That voice... It was like if the wind was suddenly starting to get access under Layleen's skin, inside of her blood, raging, making her whole body and also her whole Spirit cold and disturbed.

Then, something appeared inside of Evangeline's mind.

Ailana noticed the change of expression on the Leader's face.

Even if unable to move, they were both still able to use their facial muscles and they were even able to talk.

-Ailana…-

The Commandress didn't answer, as a way to let Evangeline say what she was thinking about.

-We will be safe…- She whispered to the Commandress Of The Dove.

-What are you talking about? - She responded back to Evangeline, whispering as well.

-Brayleigh is not in the Kingdom, you know that, and even if he was here, he would have not being able to…-

But Ailana interrupted her own saying by herself.

Evangeline was pointing her own eyes at something that was pending from her belt, something the Leader Of The Dove attached to it as an ornament.

Ailana remained speechless.

A big white feather was the item that was pending from Evangeline's belt.

-Where did you…-

But Ailana got her hair pulled back by Ulmuka.

-What you two are talking about?! Stop talking. You will come with us too! -

The Devil flapped his wings and he looked at the Queen, that was lying down on the floor.

-Ulmuka. - He said with that voice that had the sound of many different Worlds.

-You take them. They will be able to move once again once in the Kingdom Of The Owl. I will get the Queen. -

Ulmuka collected all the instructions.

-Great. -

The Devil flashed of a dark kind of light.

-It's time to go. Layleen...-

What he did was a gentle movement of his tail and all at once his figure, his body, was not there anymore.

But, somehow, he was then right in front of Layleen's laying body, without being clear how he managed to do that.

He was about to take the Queen by her hand, but right before he was able to touch her, to grab her, a quick flash of light hit the Devil on the entire size of his body.

He growled.

Ulmuka ran to him.

-What was that?!- He said.

But the Devil raged on him grabbing him by the neck.

-Don't stay on my way...-

His hands got very hot, and the long black nails of his fingers were pushing against Ulmuka's skin.

He left him on his knees, the Commander Of The Owl gasping for air, his neck then presenting burnt spots where the Devil's hand was pressing on it only few instants before.

Ulmuka stood up with difficulty and without a word.

He was lightly touching his own neck, in pain.

The Evil Being was searching in the air...

Evangeline laughed.

Ulmuka got nervous.

-What are you laughing about? -

The room then started to have flashes of lights all around, very fast and luminous.

Flashes of lights that were colliding, clashing, with the misty darkness the Devil brought there with him.

And Evangeline laughed again.

She then looked into Ulmuka's eyes.

So deep that the Commander Of The Owl had to break the eye contact for a moment.

And, with a big bright smile, she said.

-You have failed, Ulmuka. -

Ailana smiled too at those words and added, looking at the Commander.

-Once again. -

An extremely uncommon wind started to howl very strongly on the Devil and Ulmuka, but the particularity of that was that, instead, was not disturbing Queen Layleen, Ailana and Evangeline.

Not at all.

And the Devil perfectly knew what was happening.

And because of that, he screamed, he screamed so loud that some dark energy blew off from his body, boosting the air with a strong smell of Sulphur.

Ulmuka grabbed both Ailana and Evangeline, he was very strong, so he was able to handle both of them very well.

He started to make his way to the doors, but once in front of them and about to put his hands on them to push them, opening them, the doors disappeared, ultimately becoming two tough walls.

-Hey!!!- Ulmuka exclaimed out loud.

Then, all the flashing lights stopped.

The wind stopped too.

Some of the misty and negative energy in the air brought by the Evil Being, even if still present in the environment, was very much reduced.

Queen Layleen was drained from her energy, but she somehow managed to get back at least on her knees, leaving the laying position she was presenting herself until few seconds before.

It was very dark in the room.

Even due to the very black clouds that were covering the entire sky over the Kingdom Of The Dove outside of the window.

To waste time was not something that was in the Devil's plans.

He vanished from the spot where he was standing at, and he reappeared right behind the Queen and he would have been able to grab her if it wasn't for the incredible event that left everyone shocked.

A sonorous bang and all at once, that extremely dark room, became the brightest room of every single Castle of The Circle.

But this time it was not about flashing lights, it was steady, and the wind that was then back to howl inside the Hall Of The Throne, was a real pump of energy and it was clashing itself against the invisible negative Evil's vibrations that were hiding in the unseeable domains.

But what really left Layleen, Ailana and Evangeline in ecstasy, was the same view that was at the same exact time leaving Ulmuka and yes, even the Devil, in a state of pure fear.

The view of the reason of all of that light, the view of the shiny source of it, that, very slowly, was defining itself more and more, until presenting the then perfectly detailed figure of a man of a warm and soft kind of skin, with gentle long and light brown hair, that were caressing his shoulders.

His eyes had the colour of the bluest of the skies, even more intense, if possible, than the stunning ones of the Queen Of The Dove.

He was wearing a light white vest in one unique piece, but interrupted by the wearing of a huge brown leather belt, with a buckle that was presenting the yellow gold image of a rose.

His boots where white as well as the vest and they were of a fantastic shiny kind of material which nature was unknown.

And, as the ultimate detail to complete the then majestically defined appearance of that luminous Being, a very big, strong, white and mesmerizing pair of wings.

There was a supermassive amount of energy all around him.

White and slightly light pink.

Evangeline looked at him completely ecstatic.

-Ailana…-

Ailana found the way to answer to her, but her eyes totally captured by that amazing view.

-Yes…-

Ulmuka was petrified, unable to move even just his eyes away from the Angel.

The Evil Being was then not behind the Queen anymore, but right in front of her, looking at what was happening in front of him.

And in that moment, right as the Devil did only few minutes before the appearance on the scene of his Universal counterpart, the Angel vanished.

Few instants after, a matter of less than a second, he was standing right between the Queen Of The Dove and the obscure Entity.

The horned Being realised it before then turning his head and his whole body to be able to face his natural opposite.

The Angel was staring at the Devil.

It was overwhelming.

Those candid blue eyes, clearly so kind, but in that precise moment picturing on his beautiful face one of the meanest expressions any Being in the Universe would have never been able to replicate.

Ulmuka tried to punch the walls where not a long while before the doors were, leading out of the Hall Of The Throne.

He started to scream while banging on them, but that was not working at all with no surprise not even for him.

It happened in a very magnificent way when, even if still standing there, an exact copy of the Angel appeared behind Ulmuka, even if in a more abstract form compared to the Original, and he just opened his arms to generate a decent release of light that clashed into the Commander Of The Owl, that instantly fell on the floor senseless.

And, as quick as it appeared, that copy of the Angel vanished, lost in the infinity of the unknown.

A very gentle movement of his wings and the Angel was there, calm, but very serious, looking inside of the Devil's eyes, red as the most raging fire from Hell.

Queen Layleen crawled away, close to Ailana and Evangeline, then able to move once again.

They were feeling a very singular warm sensation inside their blood.

-Queen Layleen… How are you feeling? - Ailana asked.

-I feel fine… Just… Tired… Drained… But I am here…-

Then she looked at the Angel.

-How this happened? -

Evangeline didn't answer.

And Ailana didn't as well.

Not many feet far from them, very close to the Throne, the Devil's tail moved like a whoop, and he held his sword strong.

A moment after, he was attacking his enemy with few rapid and superb fencing attacks that the Angel dodged without even having a sword with him.

He kept dodging several times until, on the last attack attempted by the Devil, he blocked the blade between his two hands.

And the even more intense stare that he gave to the Evil Being in that moment, made the Devil shake.

-What do you want?!- His many voices spoke.

But the Angel didn't answer.

He was not talking at all.

But what he did, made the black winged Entity yell due to the pain.

The Angel moved the blade of the Devil's sword away and he punched the air with an extremely soft movement of his fist and an invisible bomb of energy exploded right over the Devil's chest, making him fall, slamming on the floor.

His eyes had a very intense and bright red light crossing them.

He took his sword back.

And this time, the Angel opened his hand, giving birth to a new and different energy all concentrated on his palm, from where the hilt of a sword started to take form, until even the whole length of the blade was then shiny and concrete, ready for the real battle.

It happened so fast.

They both flown in the air, making their blades clashing and slamming against each other, the Devil's sword, black, even the blade was black.

The Holy Entity's one, instead, with a stunning white gold hilt and a transparent blade that was releasing white vapours at every clash.

And at every clash, the blade of the Evil Being's sword was seeming to release small pieces of ashes.

The Devil loaded some dark energy through the blade and he released it against the Angel, that simply put his sword in front of himself looking at that obscure power not even being able to reach and touch the transparent blade, as its run was ending right on the way to it.

The Angel let his sword down and, while floating in the air, he kept confronting the creature from Hell staring at him deep inside of his Devilish eyes.

And the Angel smiled.

Certainly not the type of smile that somebody makes when feeling happy about something.

It was more of a smile of pride, a smile of pure and cynic supremacy that was making the Holy Being spreading away, all around and above, vibrations full of anger and meanness.

The sensations everyone was getting from him, were in that moment obviously pure but also brutal at the same time.

And then, like a lightening, the Angel exploded down at a supersonic speed, targeting the Devil that then generated an incredible amount of dark Aura that surrounded all of his great figure.

At the moment of the impact, the time stopped.

And the Devil somehow managed to move himself from the spot of the imminent clash, but once the time restarted his regular course, the Angel was not there anymore, before reappearing right behind of his rival, unleashing a powerful bomb of white energy that collided on the back of the Evil Entity, that got hit away smashing against the opposite wall and falling with a huge thud on the hard and cold floor of the Throne's Hall.

The Devil's hundreds of voices released an unbelievable proof of the pain he was suffering.

Because, in fact, that bomb of energy released from the deepest inside of the Angel's essence, did not only work as a greatly efficient way to hit his antagonist, but also, it was still burning.

It was still burning the inside lost Soul of the Devil, that was screaming with angry desperation.

-Let it stop! Let it stop!!!-

The Angel walked, slowly, in his direction.

-Let it stop… I am telling you… Let it stop…-

His hands were on his horned head, the eyes were closed and he was drooling due to the agony he was experiencing in that magnificent instant that was the greatest meeting between perdition and salvation, both raging in the whole environment at the same time.

The Angel was very close… Only few feet away, marching with absolute greatness in the Devil's direction, that was then suffering on his knees.

-I can't handle it anymore!!! Let this pain stop… I am asking you… PLEASE!!!-

And in the same moment the Evil present yelled the word "Please", clearly acknowledging his defeat, the effects of the Angel's white energy bomb ceased, and that kind of ultimate pain suddenly left the empty inside of the inner self of the Devil.

The Holy Entity was in that moment standing tall in front of his defeated rival, looking at him with an expression of arrogant pleasure.

-Thank you… Now… I will leave… Don't worry, I'll leave… I will leave now…-

The Devil was saying, with very low voice, without even having the strength or the audacity to look at the Angel in the eyes.

-I'm going… I'm going now…-

He then raised a hand, slowly.

-And you will come with me. -

Before even having the reaction to move himself away, the Angel's arm got caught by the hand of the Devil, that instantly pressed his fingers with his long black claws on the unadulterated skin of the Holy Being.

But his laugh that followed his fast and nasty move, didn't last for long.

He was indeed pressing on the Angel's arm, holding it with absolute strength, but something was definitely being strange.

The Angel was feeling nothing.

He was there, accepting the hold of the Devil, but without accepting the pain he would have never been able to experience.

He, instead, closed his eyes, and once he reopened them, with a glare, he generated another explosion but this time of pure light, that was not focused on harming the enemy, but more on breaking the hold of the Devil on his arm.

The Evil Being was again entirely on the floor, finally looking up to the one that was standing over him, staring at him like he always did since he appeared in the room, the huge white wings moving slowly and with Celestial grace.

The Aura all around the Angel's figure was that spectacularly shiny that was enlightening the whole place even more, making the Hall Of The Throne that white that it was almost painful for the eyes.

Ulmuka was still on the floor.

-I'm not impressed…- The Devil mumbled.

The Angel disappeared to then reappear in front of Queen Layleen, Evangeline and Ailana.

He was giving the back to them.

His posture was clearly defining the fact he was there exclusively to protect them.

The Devil stood up and, panting, but strongly on his feet once again.

His eyes began to shine strangely, visibly trembling while a smoky form of energy was coming out from them.

He was seeming like he was loading some sort of power he would have been about to release in a matter of instants.

-Oh, this looks very bad! - Evangeline screamed.

In that moment, everything including the brightness spread by the Angel, turned of an intense kind of red, that quickly took possession in terms of colour of the whole environment.

-What's happening?!- Evangeline screamed again.

This time the Angel turned his head to look at the Leader Of The Dove deep inside her eyes.

He was serious and severe.

And, still looking at the young girl, he put a finger on his lips, as an order to do not talk anymore.

Layleen looked at her Leader and she winked at her.

Ailana was only standing there, confused, looking at the Evil enemy that was finally ready to make his power explode against them.

But, even if slightly confused, the Commandress was calm.

She was somehow felling secure and safe.

She was feeling like there was nothing to worry about.

A blur of the environment, a weird acoustic noise and the change of the Atmosphere.

Suddenly, nothing was clear anymore.

Dark.

Entirely dark.

And nothing else.

When everything slowly restarted to be visible, everything was calm and the whole room was warm and silent.

Ulmuka was not there anymore.

Not the Devil and not even the Angel.

Layleen, Ailana and Evangeline slowly walked to the window and they looked outside.

And what they saw was not the view they normally had in front of them when looking outside of the Castle.

There was not Umbriel, there was not the Kingdom Of The Dove.

There was nothing, actually.

Only a colourless background where raining Crystals were falling, unclear to realise where they were coming from and also over where they were going to hit themselves on.

-Where are we...- Evangeline was shocked.

Ailana interrupted her.

-Don't talk. -

Evangeline looked at her Queen, that pointed her finger to a very bleary point not too far, a scene that was confused through the falling Crystals.

It was a scene located in a room they all recognised as the Throne's Hall of the Castle of the Kingdom Of The Dove.

The grainy image of a horned Entity that released a dark energy from his eyes and the whole of his body, but a dark energy that collided against a luminous and semi-transparent Cross that was floating and radiating right in front of a bright Being, his dark brown hair moved by the raging force of the clash between those two incredible powers and his hand opened in front of him, controlling the extraordinary power of that Cross made of pure and unbeatable light.

The Evil individual got blown away.

The bright Being stayed there, motionless, the huge pair of wings moving a little, just to caress the then gentle and pacific air.

Everything was happening there, but somehow, somewhere else located in another Dimensional Existence.

Then, everything got extremely shiny.

White.

A soft howl of the sweetest of the winds.

A lovely melody, like immensely far away Latin Chants that were echoing deep inside the ears of the Queen Of The Dove, Evangeline and Ailana.

When they reopened their eyes, they were inside their Castle once again.

There was not too much light, but there never was inside the Fort of Queen Layleen, after all.

Everything was seeming normal, perfectly untouched.

The doors that were leading outside of the Throne's Hall, were semi open and a nice and fizzy air was coming inside the room from the open window.

-I have never… Experienced something like what just happened to us…- Evangeline said, almost whispering it.

Ailana looked at the Queen.

-Queen Layleen. -

The Queen looked at her.

-Yes? -

Ailana waited few seconds before saying what was fulfilling her mind in that moment, but then she ultimately found the words.

-Those Crystals... That was definitely...-

But the Queen interrupted her with the only power of her beautiful smile.

Because those Crystals they earlier saw falling down while inside the most mystical of the Realities, were in fact what Ailana was thinking about.

Those Crystals were the proof of the Supreme Existence of a superior power, an unknown power, or at least unknown to the most.

A power that was carrying the purest essence of the Eternity, an Eternity that was part of an extremely higher Level in the Hierarchy of The Circle and of the entirety of every single Universe.

A kind of extraordinary energy not even the most Evil of the Beings would have ever been able to escape from.

XXVIII

THE SAD FATHER

-My daughter… My beautiful daughter…-

The old man dressed in his Golden vest, was crying.

His silent suffering was the only sound in that tiny little room, full of nothing, only few benches and chairs and just a Cross of a great black colour on the wall.

-My daughter…-

The blue eyes of the man were not visible due to the tears that were running fast all over his face.

He decided to leave his laying position, standing up from the floor.

He wiped his eyes with his hands, and he walked out of the room.

The corridor was fulfilled of tiny little Crystals that were floating all around the place, accompanied by an amazing and misty black vapour that was actually more like many little clouds that were not making possible to spot the floor and they were covering the old man's legs to the knees.

The contrast between those many colours coming from the Crystals and the black consistence of those small clouds, were giving a surreal and mystical atmosphere to the whole environment.

The man walked down the corridor, caressing the black clouds at the height of his knees and the clouds were caressing his hands back.

Far away, Latin and beautiful melodic Chants were being sang by voices that were barely able to be associated to any known Being of the Universe.

The pure colours of their voices were not a type of sound known by the mortal World.

In fact, those voices were owned by Entities of the same Dimensional Existence of the Human Beings, but from a totally different World.

A higher Level of the Eternity, however, part of that same Reality.

But for the old man there was nothing more common than those Chants.

He was hearing them everyday, for almost the entire duration of the day.

But he was not bothered by them in any way.

Those melodies were so beautiful and Divine that was impossible to get tired of them.

He pushed a golden door and he entered inside another room.

The air was different inside there.

He touched his beautiful necklace, an amazing Cross, a white gold one, with in the middle a very dark stone, that was seeming to be of some sort of turned off colour.

The room where he was finding himself inside in that moment, was only a tiny bit bigger than the one he was crying inside before.

A great smell of incense was spreading in the air inside the room.

There were three huge windows and the night outside of them was bright and peaceful.

Floating through the quietude of the night, there were little Crystals of the size of a single grain of sand that were dancing in a wavy way with the calm and warm wind that was pleasing that unknown side of the Universe.

But the ones that were falling down to the ground, were not attaching.

They were simply vanishing. In little smokes.

A wooden Cross was inside the room, suspended over an Altar.

There was a pew and a kneeler right in front of it.

The old man bowed down in front of the Cross and then he put his knees on the hard kneeler's cushions.

He was in a praying position and the tears slowly restarted to fall down from his eyes.

But those were different kinds of tears.

They had a different taste.

And a totally different meaning.

That was the reason why he was also smiling.

The gratitude to who saved his daughter and even him.

A very long time before.

And that Saviour then just entered in the room, smoothly, without a noise, being surrounded by the most explosive of the silences.

The frequency of Time changed.

It was never about Time when it was about him.

It was always about control.

Total control over everything and everyone.

Absolute control over Time too.

The old man felt the lightful presence.

And he pointed his eyes on the floor, without raising them to the identity of the luminous individual.

-Something is disturbing your peace of mind, today. -

The deepness and the firmness of that voice made the air visible and concrete for a moment.

Time stopped completely.

The rest of the Existence was in a state of stand-by without being aware of that.

Once Time would have been brought back to his regular course, no-one in the entirety of the Universe would have ever been able to notice or even to know that their Lives had been put in some sort of temporary stop for several minutes.

The minutes where the conversation between the old man and the one that a long time before gave to him and to his daughter the chance to keep existing and maybe living, saving both of them from their Destiny, a Destiny that wanted them spiritually slaughtered apart, with their Souls being taken and murdered forever without any way to keep one day living in another, different Being.

But as for Time, even Destiny would have never been able to handle the challenge with the one that that day entered in the room where the old man was kneeling in front of the great suspended Cross over the Altar.

But the real truth was that if, as for Time, Destiny would have even only tried to challenge him, the chances for Destiny to succeed against the Universal superiority of that Being, would have been way below the level of the impossible.

The old man gently touched his eyes to wipe them from the tears.

-Your Unique Majesty…-

-Tell me. What is it? - The man with the multicolour voice asked.

The old man kept his stare down to the pavement and answered.

-I believe you already know…-

-I do. - The straight answer of the tall man, the white vest covered by another even whiter gear, more similar to an armour.

The black cloak heavy and shiny.

-Of course I know. But I want to hear it from you. -

The shorter man left the kneeler.

He was standing up, in front of him, and he was trying to find the words, his eyes still very well pointed to the warm and shiny pavement.

-I... I miss her. - He finally said.

-Who do you miss? - The other man asked, patiently waiting for the old man to tell him everything that he already knew.

-I miss my daughter, Your Unique Majesty. -

The answer was truly felt, real, unbelievably honest.

No answer came out from the other man's mouth, this time.

But the sad father was able to feel the ambient changing around him.

The room got warmer.

And suddenly, outside of the windows, the night disappeared to leave the sky to the day and the heaviest Sunlight any Being would have ever been able to experience.

The sky was deep blue but, at the very extreme highest top of it, there was a strange ultra-luminous radiating expansion of the already mentioned sky, brighter, way brighter, than the Sun.

Then, the clouds started to run fast in the sky, that fast that it was extremely difficult to spot the shape of any of them.

But the Crystals were keeping falling down.

But a lot slower. That slow it was so easy to see all the colours that were mixing inside of every single one of them.

-Your Unique Majesty...-

And the tall man spoke.

-Do you know why God is the greatest? -

The old man thought about an answer to that incredibly random and definitely very much unexpected question.

-Because… He lets every single one free to decide which way to take, right or wrong, and in any case He will always be present and keen to help if needed? -

-You understood the matter of my question. - The other man responded.

-But. Your answer is wrong. -

The heartbroken father touched the Cross that was the pendant of his beautiful necklace, and the dark stone that was stuck in the middle of it, had a quick but very bright shine.

And the extraordinarily luminous Being, noticed that.

And he spoke again.

-Don't feel embarrassed. - And he gently caressed his own soft and very long hair, straight and blond, of a kind of blond extremely close to a very icy white.

A thin part of his hair, on the right side, were of a very luminous kind of black.

-I didn't expect you to give me the right answer. As if you were able to, that would have made you entitled to be exactly where I am.-

And in that moment, was night once again.

The biggest Moon of the last few months was up in the sky, countless of stars enlightening even more a sky that was somehow giving even more light than what the Sun was able to give during the day.

And the Time that had been previously frozen, was then in the Past.

The regular course of it restarted and the rest of the Universe was back to its normal motion, without any kind of clue about the fact everything had been in a state of stand-by for great amount of minutes.

In the room was still very warm.

The old man looked outside of one of the windows.

Where the only one man that was making the Universe vibrating more than any Nature and more than any power, more than any energy, more than any Being in the eternity of the Existence, was in front of, looking outside as well.

And the suspended Cross over the Altar, trembled.

And the Universe did too.

And the image of the man with the long blond hair vanished, leaving the old man by himself, there, in the small room.

The short man with the Golden vest, almost screamed for the surprise when he saw what outside was happening.

Following the vanishing of the luminous Being, every single Crystal in the air was, slowly but amazingly, becoming a rose petal, so that the whole sky, the whole air, the whole ground and the whole location, were all a magnificent show of rose petals, mainly red, but also few white ones here and there, giving to the whole environment a very strong but absolutely stunning smell of roses.

XXIX

THE DEEPEST FEELING

Once Lisica, Adriel, Crevan and Dawako found themselves inside the Castle of the Kingdom Of The Wolf, what really impressed them was the incredibly freezing cold air inside the Hall at the entrance.

-Hey. - Dawako bumped his elbow into Adriel's ribs.

-What. - Adriel pushed his arm away.

-Look…- Dawako answered pointing his eyes to Ixanthi.

Adriel's surprise was real.

While they were all freezing by the coldest Hall they have ever been in all of their Lives, Ixanthi was sweating like someone that was staring at the hottest Sun ever, wiping his sweaty forehead with his hand.

-Weird…- Adriel agreed.

-This way, please, this way… Follow me! - The very short man exclaimed.

He leaded them floor after floor, until he finally stopped in front of a massive door.

He looked at all of them.

-Are you ready? -

They all looked at each other, Crevan taking the lead of the speech between the ones that were coming from the Kingdom Of The Fox.

-Sure. -

Ixanthi opened the door.

They all entered inside the Throne's Hall.

It was very spacious.

Nobody was there waiting for them, certainly not the King, as the Throne was empty.

-Are you feeling good? -

It was a long while Adriel wanted to talk to Lisica about what happened between them, but somehow he always felt too insecure to do so.

-I do. And you? - The answer felt cold, almost like the Hall at the entrance of the Castle of King Adalwolf.

-I think I feel good, yeah…-

He took a pause, then he spoke again.

-I think we should talk… At some point…-

The Princess looked away.

-The King will be coming in no time. - She answered, reaching a level of coldness that then was really close to match the temperature of the Hall at the entrance of the Castle of the Kingdom Of The Wolf.

Adriel got the hit.

He didn't really know what to think.

After that kiss, the Princess Of The Fox didn't really interact with him anymore, not even for a simple chat.

He really didn't know if he had to convince himself it was due to some sort of embarrassment she was feeling for what did happen or if maybe she was avoiding him, regretting every single second of that for him incredibly meaningful kiss.

-Yeah… He will come in no time…- He repeated, looking at the floor.

-Silence. - Ixanthi said.

Everyone was listening.

The man spoke from a little Altar not far from the Throne.

-Now. I know. As residents of another Kingdom, you normally should not have to bow down when the King comes. But. Because of the reason why we are here today, as a sign of respect for the other King of the Silvery Lands, I am going to ask you kindly to bow down to the King when he will be here in a couple of minutes.

We will do the same when King Balgair will reach us here. -

At the hearing of her father's name, Lisica expressed herself with a little exclamation of surprise.

-My father is coming here?!-

-Yes, indeed. - Ixanthi answered.

Then Crevan spoke.

-We can do that. -

In that same meantime, Adriel was lost in his thoughts.

-Wonderful. - The man without an age replied.

A bell from some church not too far, informed everyone of the time.

It was Midday.

Ixanthi then declared.

-He is coming. -

Behind the Throne, not too many feet away, there were steps that were leading somewhere upstairs.

Adriel noticed for the first time since he entered in the room the huge word written in the grey stone of the Throne, that was also the main Principle of the Kingdom Of The Wolf.

Loyalty.

Some steps got audible from somewhere upstairs.

Crevan was looking at the last few steps where, in a matter of seconds, King Adalwolf would have been about to appear.

And those few seconds passed fast and all at once the whole figure of a big man, old, with long black and white hair and beard, appeared inside the Throne's Hall, presenting himself in all of his Majesty.

-Your Majesty. Princess Lisica, Adriel Centauri, Dawako Kettu and Crevan Oberon from the Kingdom Of The Fox. - Ixanthi exclaimed.

He took a little pause, then he restarted.

-Kingdom Of The Fox. King Adalwolf. The King Of The Wolf. -

After those final words, the residents of the Kingdom Of The Fox bowed down.

But once on their knees, Lisica, Crevan and Dawako noticed something.

They noticed that not all of them were bowing down to King Adalwolf.

One of them was still standing tall, looking at the King from a safe distance.

-Adriel! Down! - Dawako whispered, whisper that sounded extremely audible due to the echo that was a huge factor in the Hall Of The Throne.

But Adriel didn't consider Dawako at all.

Ixanthi looked at Adriel.

-Adriel Centauri. I am asking you, with extreme kindness, to bow down to the King. -

King Adalwolf was standing there, not a word, his eyes pointed on the boy that was refusing to bow down to him.

-He is not my King. -

Adriel's words came out strong, hard as a stone.

The King kept staring at him, still not a single word, not even a movement.

Ixanthi quickly tried to do not let any silent of embarrassment being part of the extraordinary scene that was happening in front of his eyes, and more calmly than ever he spoke again.

-I know... But... Adriel, we spoke about that already... It has been said that...-

-I know what has been said. - The green eyed boy interrupted, leaving everyone shocked still in their bowed down position.

Crevan was sweating.

-What is wrong with you...-

-It has been said...- Adriel continued.

-That because of the extraordinary Event we all are here today, we were all going to greet your King...-

-And we were going to do the same with yours...- Ixanthi concluded, a very audible taste of anger in his voice.

Adriel looked at him.

He was not even paying attention to King Adalwolf, that in the meantime was still standing there, far away from being shocked, surprised, or even irritated about what was happening inside his Throne's Hall.

The way he was looking at Adriel, was a proper studying of every single detail of him.

It was almost sinister.

-I barely know King Balgair. I don't mind what you do or what you don't do when he will show up. -

The arrogance in the voice of the boy from Renard, was amazing.

-Enough! -

Crevan stood up and faced Adriel.

He went face to face with him.

-Enough… Adriel… What's going on inside that silly mind of yours…-

Crevan's voice was shaking.

Adriel noticed that.

He then finally gave the stare back at King Adalwolf.

He then pointed his attention back to Ixanthi.

-You bow down to our Princess, then. -

Crevan nearly chocked himself, Dawako fell from his kneeling position and Lisica stood up.

Ixanthi didn't reply.

But his expression visibly changed.

A shine of cruelty crossed his eyes.

King Adalwolf was then touching his beard, thinking about something, maybe about Adriel's words. Or maybe not.

-Pardon me…? - Ixanthi slowly replied, trying to hide his real feelings.

-Princess Lisica. She is a Royalty in our Kingdom. She is the daughter of the King. Bow down to her. And I will bow down to your King. -

Crevan ran few steps closer to the Altar close to the Throne, where Ixanthi and the King of the Kingdom Of The Wolf were standing.

-I am so sorry… I am deeply sorry…-

The man that had features of his appearance that were making extremely difficult, almost impossible, to define his actual age, opened his mouth ready to reply to the Commander Of The Fox, but before he was able to say anything, a deeper and stronger voice spoke.

-Do it. -

It became pretty clear that everyone, even Adriel, didn't really expect anything like that.

Ixanthi slowly turned his head to his King.

-My King...-

King Adalwolf deeply looked inside of his yellow eyes.

-Do it, Ixanthi. Do what the boy is asking. -

The King Of The Wolf's words were final.

The short man gave a last look at his King.

He then looked at Adriel. The fire in the eyes.

And Adriel not only saw, but also felt the anger coming out in form of strong vibrations from the Spirit of Ixanthi.

Princess Lisica's face was impossible to read.

Ixanthi moved few steps towards the Princess.

-Princess Lisica. - He said once he was not too far from her.

And he went down on his knee, bowing down to the Princess of the Kingdom Of The Fox.

He didn't stay down for long, but in the meantime he was on his knee in front of Lisica, a little amount of black vapour came out, pale, from all around his figure.

Adriel was the closest one to the scene, while all the others were all a bit too far to be able to notice that very particular detail.

Ixanthi was then back to his standing posture, with no trace of that strange vapour anymore.

-I did what you asked, young man. - He said, faking a calmness that was visibly not real.

-Now, if you please...-

Adriel didn't say a word, moved few steps towards King Adalwolf and once in front of the steps that would have been leading to the Throne where the King was still standing in front of, he bowed down.

Adalwolf spoke.

-Stand up, young man. -

Adriel did as the King Of The Wolf said.

-Do you know… Which one is the main Principle the Kingdom Of The Wolf puts his most sincere belief, young man? -

Adriel didn't need to think too much about the answer, answer that he already knew and that was also hugely written on the Throne.

-Loyalty. -

-Indeed. - Adalwolf finally moved few steps.

-But do you know what Loyalty really means? - The King questioned Adriel once again.

-I guess…- The guy from Renard thought about the answer a little bit more, this time.

-I guess is the highest level of respect someone can show to someone else…- He said.

King Adalwolf looked well deep inside Adriel's green eyes.

And the King's eyes focused even deeper inside Adriel's Soul, reaching the most intimate connection between his Soul and his heart.

-Obviously…- King Adalwolf mumbled.

Adriel was confused.

-What… Is it the correct answer? -

The King looked at Lisica. Then he looked at his Throne.

The stony Throne that was starring all over the Hall.

The King moved forward to it, and he sat.

He gently caressed his Crown made out of Titanium and he then spoke again, his shiny yellow eyes pointed on all the presents, including Ixanthi.

-I want everybody out. - He said.

Once everyone started to move, more confused than ever, he concluded.

-Except Adriel Centauri. -

There was a bit of mess following that order.

Dawako didn't refrain himself.

-Your Majesty! Allow me to remind you I am a contestant too for the Role of…-

-I know. - The King interrupted him.

Dawako didn't enjoy a second of that situation.

-Now, everybody out. - He repeated.

He was, however, incredibly calm, and he put his eyes back on Adriel.

Nobody said anything else.

Crevan gently took Dawako by his arm.

The guy from Vixen looked at the Commander.

-What is that about? - He asked, still visibly and audibly disturbed.

Crevan answered without looking at Dawako in the eyes.

-I don't know. But. He rules these lands. We have to please his request. -

Princess Lisica was following them outside, looking at the marble pavement, thinking about who knows what.

Ixanthi was the last one about to exit from the Hall Of The Throne, but before doing so he gave a look at Adriel.

Adriel's ears stopped to be capable to hear anything for few seconds, before then getting back to be able to even hear the far singing of some birds outside of the Castle of King Adalwolf.

The door closed behind Ixanthi and finally in the room there were only King Adalwolf and Adriel.

The King Of The Wolf and one of the two contenders for the Role of new Hero Of The Fox.

The two studied each other for few seconds.

Or maybe not. Maybe even for a minute or two.

Then the King spoke.

-Loyalty. -

Adriel was listening and the King continued.

-I thought what you did earlier for your Princess was one admirable act of Loyalty, you know… Loyalty to your Princess…-

The intensity of the way the King was looking at Adriel, was concrete in the air. It was visible.

-But…- He kept saying.

-I was wrong. - He concluded.

It was Adriel's turn to speak.

-I don't understand… You were not wrong, Your Majesty…-

King Adalwolf smiled.

-Yes. I was. - He said.

-And I tell you why, Adriel Centauri. I've been penetrating inside your Soul to the deepest and purest connection between your Soul and your heart… I saw it…-

At that point, Adriel was just genuinely curious.

-And…? -

-And I saw that very clearly. Actually, I was even able to feel it…- King Adalwolf kept saying.

-That was not Loyalty, right? That was not an act of Loyalty to your Princess… Am I right, Adriel? -

At that point, Adriel's eyes started to get wet, the overwhelming voice of the King pumping inside of his head.

-And what was that, then…? - He slowly asked, his voice not more than a broken whisper.

-If not Loyalty, King Adalwolf, what was that you felt inside the deepest side of my Soul? What was that you felt as the highest emotion I have for my Princess, if not Loyalty? -

Adriel looked at the King, that took a goblet from a little table on the right side of his Throne.

-Love. - The King simply said.

-What you did earlier for your Princess was not an act of Loyalty, Adriel. - He continued.

-That was love. -

He sipped something from his goblet, his yellow eyes inside the green ones of Adriel.

-A pure, Universal act of love. -

XXX

THE MEETING

In the Kingdom Of The Wolf, the weather was going from being warm and sunny, to getting cold and snowy.

Even that day, in the space of few hours, the people of Shaw experienced a great warmness at the shores of the lakes right outside of the walls and the streets of the Town, and then they all had to run searching for a shelter due to the strong snow storm that hit the biggest Town of the Kingdom Of The Wolf.

When the ones coming from the Kingdom Of The Fox, accompanied by King Adalwolf and Ixanthi, walked inside the closest forest from the Castle, away from the vibes of the Town Life, the Sun was already back in the sky, not a single cloud running in the deep blue.

They reached a spot not far from a little lake, where they finally stopped, and the King Of The Wolf spoke.

-I have understood that you two, Adriel Centauri and Dawako Kettu, know a very little about The Circle, which is honestly quite strange if we think that one of you two might become, potentially, the new Hero of the Kingdom Of The Fox. -

Nobody replied, so the King kept saying.

-However. I can see why it had been decided, by the higher Levels of your Kingdom, to keep you away from many of the most incredible secrets of our World. What I can not see…- And he looked at Crevan, the Commander Of The Fox.

-Is if it was the right decision to take. -

Crevan didn't say anything, but he looked at Adriel and Dawako, instead.

Then, the King moved on a side, giving a sign to Ixanthi.

The short man moved few steps closer to the ones from the Towns of Vixen and Renard.

-I'm aware of the reason why it might have been decided to adopt this method, Crevan. - He said with a very strange smile.

-But. The Hero Of The Fox is a very important factor not only for your Kingdom and also, not only for the Silvery Lands. As for every Hero of this Dimensional Existence, the importance of that Role goes way higher than that. -

Ixanthi was suddenly extremely serious.

-How do you think these two young men can lead a Kingdom shoulder to shoulder with the King Of The Fox, if they are not even aware of how The Circle really works? -

And he stared at the Commander Of The Fox, waiting for him to speak.

The Commander thought about Ixanthi's question.

He tried to study his eyes, but they were very enigmatic, impossible for him to read.

-There is a time for everything, Ixanthi. -

The man probably older than what he really seemed, fired Crevan with his eyes.

-There is a time where the real truth has to be told too, Crevan. -

This time, the Commander Of The Fox didn't reply.

He remained there, silent, lost in something way deeper than the most confusing of the thoughts.

Few steps became audible from not too far from where they all were standing at.

-Someone is coming our way…- Dawako stated looking around, as even if perfectly able to be heard, it was not possible to define from which direction they were actually coming from.

Ixanthi looked at his King.

-He is here. -

And the King Of The Wolf nodded with his head.

-Yes. -

Few steps and even fewer instants after, an imponent man covered by his black and orange armour was standing in front of all of the already presents, the long cloak presenting a deep black colour, while his eyes were orange and mysterious, long brown hair and a short beard that was embellish an already quite fascinating face.

The new arrived was also wearing a big Crown made out of an unclear type of material, but what was sure was the fact that all around of it there were many little Citrine Crystals that were radiating very warm vibrations all around.

The Princess Of The Fox felt way better at that view.

-Father! -

And she ran to hug and hold the King's waist.

-Lisica, my love… It is so powerfully great to see you…-

-King Balgair. The King Of The Fox. -

Ixanthi announced the King like if nobody was really actually aware of who they had in front of them, with also maybe a little vibe of vexation in his voice.

Adriel, Crevan and Dawako, bowed down.

Both Adriel and Dawako never really met the King that closely before.

Their feelings were a bright collision between excitement and fear.

King Balgair gave a caress on Lisica's cheek, and he then walked in solemn silence towards the small man and his King, the King of the Kingdom Of The Wolf.

Once in front of them, Ixanthi went on his knee.

-A mesmerizing feeling having you here, in our Kingdom, King Balgair… I bow down to you as a form of deep respect for the reason why we all are here today, for the Meeting, for your Kingdom, our Kingdom and for the Silvery Lands. -

He pronounced all that statement before standing back up and concluding his sentence.

-And for The Circle. -

Ixanthi sent a strange look in Adriel's direction.

The boy kept the stare back, with innocent arrogance.

King Balgair looked at Ixanthi.

-Thank you, Guardian. -

All the presents apart of King Adalwolf, Crevan and, obviously, Ixanthi himself, had an instinctive exclamation of surprise.

Crevan spoke without looking at Adriel, Dawako and Lisica.

-Yes. -

They were in shock.

The three younger presents in that tiny little forest not far from the Castle of the King of the Kingdom Of The Wolf, were all in shock.

They were barely able to formulate any kind of question inside of their mind to eventually try to ask, as the huge surprise outclassed their capability to reason with clarity.

King Balgair was then face to face with King Adalwolf.

The two of them studied each other's eyes, the wolfish yellow of Adalwolf's eyes colliding with the fox-kind orange ones of Balgair.

After few seconds where no-one was sure about what was about to happen, the two Kings encountered themselves in a distant but still somehow felt hug.

-The Slyest of the Kings…- Adalwolf said with a smile.

-And the most loyal of them…- The answer of Balgair, but without a smile.

The King Of The Fox then faced the presents that were standing there in front of him, King Adalwolf and the Guardian of the Kingdom Of The Wolf.

-I feel extremely proud. - He said.

He then looked at his daughter.

-I feel extremely proud because the way to reach a Kingdom from another is itself crossed by many other ways that not everyone is capable to overcome. -

He looked at the Commander Of The Fox.

-Thank you, Crevan. I knew with absolute perfection that my daughter, as both of these two boys in here, would have been under strong wings in this unusual and certainly different experience for all the three of them. -

Crevan bowed down, without a verbal reply to those words that, anyway, made him feel very well.

When he looked at the two contestants from his Kingdom, the King this time didn't say anything.

He only stared at them, for a bunch of split seconds, and he then ultimately brought his attention back to the Guardian Of The Wolf.

-When will everything start? -

Ixanthi smiled with pleasure.

-Very soon. -

Somebody screamed.

-Well, what now…? - The expression of the Guardian.

Everyone looked in the direction where the yell came from and they all got surprised when a tall, thin young man showed up through the trees, jumping in the scene, panting and out of breath.

-I have… I have made it… On time…-

King Adalwolf roared.

-You! Damn little boy…-

King Balgair looked first at the boy, then with calm and deep voice delivered his question to the King Of The Wolf.

-Adalwolf. Isn't this boy…-

-My son. Yes. You saw him last time when he was about fifteen. - Adalwolf answered.

-What are you doing in here, Cobalt? - He then asked to his son with magma in his eyes.

Cobalt quickly gave a little pat on his clothes, visibly dirty and consumed and he replied to his father.

-I knew the Meeting was today… But it just came to my mind while I was at home… And I thought… I really wanted to see the way it works… I have never seen it happening before…-

He was clearly overwhelmed, and it was obvious he was in a state of deep and unhealthy stress.

-I hope you don't mind, father…-

-Of course he minds. -

Everyone looked at Ixanthi.

The Guardian Of The Wolf was walking his way towards his King's son, with the strong intention to confront him face to face.

-Of course he minds, and I actually mind too, Cobalt. - He said once close enough to the boy to be able to hear his deep and heavy breathing coming from him.

-But... I am the Prince Of The Wolf... I have the right to...-

-You have no rights in here... Prince...-

The words of the Guardian of the Kingdom Of The Wolf came out like lightnings in a sky full of emptiness.

And they hit the Prince's Spirit like blades cutting through the veins.

Cobalt looked at his father, without saying a word.

His eyes were tearing.

His mouth unable to create any sort of sound.

-Go away. - Ixanthi said.

-Go away...- This time whispering in a way Cobalt would have been the only one between all the presents able to hear.

The Prince Of The Wolf turned his back.

He looked one more time back at the man that for all of his Life always saw as his King, but never as his father.

Even if he had been dreaming for the opposite to be, since forever.

The King Of The Wolf didn't even blink his eyes, waiting for the young man to leave the scene, waiting for the one that was seeing more as a disgrace than as a son to abandon that piece of green with the little lake where one of the probably most Legendary moments in the History of the Silvery Lands and of The Circle, was about to happen.

Cobalt made his way on his way back, directing himself towards the trees he came from.

-Wait a moment. -

It was seeming like that day would have never been fulfilled enough of surprises.

When Ixanthi brought his attention to who spoke, his eyes had a shine that radiated surreal vibrations to the whole environment.

Princess Lisica walked few steps closer to Ixanthi while looking at King Adalwolf's son, that in the meantime interrupted his way out from the spot, giving the look back at her, surprised as much as Ixanthi and his own father were.

-He will stay. -

Ixanthi rolled his eyes.

-It is something that runs in the blood of the people of the Kingdom Of The Fox? - He then asked with audible sarcasm in his voice.

-The habit to go to other Kingdoms and try to make their own Rules in there? -

He then looked at Cobalt.

-Go, you damn boy, go! Do you think the Princess of another Kingdom is going to change the King's decision?! Go! Go away! -

-You need to put your voice down. -

Dawako got shocked at the view of Adriel walking to reach the Princess Of The Fox, directing his words to the Guardian Of The Wolf.

The fact Ixanthi seemed uncapable to reply to the green-eyed young man from Renard, showed a clear sign of how unexpected and also quite astonishing those words felt like.

Princess Lisica looked at Adriel.

And she smiled at him. She smiled at him after a very long time.

-Pardon me…? -

Ixanthi's response finally broke the silence.

-I am sure you heard me. - Adriel answered with firm voice.

Crevan was seeming strangely ecstatic.

Dawako was still speechless.

King Balgair was observing the scene, while King Adalwolf moved few steps towards what was happening in front of him.

The Guardian stared at Adriel.

And he laughed.

-You clearly have the attitude of a Hero, I will give you that...- He said.

Adriel smiled at him.

-I wish I was able to say the same about you having the right attitude to be a Guardian...-

Lisica brought a hand to cover her mouth.

Cobalt was looking at Adriel like he was looking at someone or something not real.

Ixanthi raised a hand.

Suddenly, a deep black coloured vapour smoked away from it.

-Stop. -

Silence became once again the most noisy sound in that small location where nothing was present with the only exception of the grass, the trees and the little lake.

Ixanthi looked at King Adalwolf, that was then standing right behind him.

-My King...-

-Stop...- This time, King Adalwolf's voice sounded more like a growl.

The Guardian stared for few more instants at his King, then he looked down to the ground, his hand back down, massaging his own waist.

-I apologise... Your Majesty...-

The King Of The Wolf growled again, away, giving his back to Ixanthi, that then faced Adriel.

His face was visibly forced to remain relaxed, but his eyes were unable to lie.

The Guardian of the Kingdom Of The Wolf, was burning in anger.

-We should… I should take note of your advice… Maybe I was getting… A bit too heated… I should apologise…-

Adriel looked at him and he replied quite fast.

-Why don't you want him here? What has he done to be treated like that? -

Cobalt was still there, standing by the trees, looking at Adriel like he was looking at some Deity.

Ixanthi closed his eyes and took a very deep breath.

-Cobalt… The son of the King… With this time all due the respect… I can not answer to that…-

Adriel didn't go against the Guardian's statement, but he still looked back at the tall and thin boy, then shaking in front of them.

Adriel stared at him until his eyes connected inside Cobalt's ones, and something happened.

He saw a grey landscape, made out of some sort of spongy ground.

He was not even able to see his feet or his hands, he wasn't able to see anything that was part of himself.

Only some luminous radiations that were apparently coming out from where he was, or at least, from where he was supposed to be.

Not far, some more luminous rays were enlightening the otherwise quite misty location.

He tried to make an exclamation, but nothing came out from him.

But the air around him became visible in the form of wavy vibrations that then diffused themselves all around and above the area.

The other bright fount was getting closer.

Only light, that was all he was able to see.

Nothing was able to be felt, apart of a light sensation of warmness.

And the wavy vibrations that were the actual air happened again, but this time were coming from the other bright source of light, directed to Adriel's impalpable presence.

And it hit him like a stone right in the middle of the stomach and from the inside.

And he saw yellow eyes.

And black amounts of smoke that were going to hit some abstract form of energy lost in the air, and yells of pain and cries of sadness and unlimited desperation that were disappearing in the Eternity of the Existence.

And then, right when Adriel's inexplicable form was about to act in a way unknow even to his deepest inner self, something happened again, but this time was something that made him hear his own exclamation of pain.

Adriel was back in the little forest in the Kingdom Of The Wolf in all of his consciousness, his legs, his hands, his body, his regular and concrete appearance back to what it always used to be, touching his own hair, on the floor, a huge pain inside of his head.

When he reopened his eyes, Cobalt was there no more, and everyone was looking down at him.

Even the two Kings were closer than where they previously were before his strange experience, studying him from above.

Only Ixanthi was still standing where he already was.

He was there, motionless, but what Adriel saw was something that did last less than a second.

He was sure he saw that.

Or maybe no, he wasn't sure at all... After all, he did just reopen his eyes after some incredibly weird vision and feeling of himself in a completely different Dimension and without even the possession of his own body.

But, if he had to choose, he would have been declaring that what he saw was absolutely real.

For less than a second, he saw the eyes of Ixanthi entirely of a deep black colour, not a single spot of white, not the slightest sight of the pupils.

When he focused better on him, his eyes were already back to their ordinary appearance since several seconds, but his stare wasn't changed in any possible detail.

And it was obvious that his feelings were all about displeasure.

-Are you feeling good, young man? -

King Balgair was looking right over Adriel.

-Yeah… I guess…-

Crevan helped the boy to get back on his feet and he looked at him.

-What happened to you? - He asked.

Adriel looked back at him.

-I really don't know…- He replied.

-I saw things… I was there… But my body… It wasn't there… But I had feelings… And light… A lot of light coming from wherever my indistinguishable presence was… And more light coming from somewhat or someone else… Unseeable as well… Commander, I don't know… I really don't know…-

Adriel's hands were holding Crevan's arms.

The Commander Of The Fox, was looking at the green eyed young man, trying to find even more deep inside of them.

Dawako was having a quite chat with Lisica and the two Kings were then back to Ixanthi, and they were lost in some sort of conversation nobody knew about what.

Crevan pulled Adriel to himself, and he whispered to him.

-And then what? -

Adriel's expression got surprised.

-What do you mean? -

Crevan shook him in an energic way, impatiently, and he whispered again at his ear.

-What happened after that? How did you find yourself back in here, in the forest? -

Adriel was extremely confused.

-What... I wasn't here...? -

This time, Crevan hit Adriel in the stomach with a light punch.

-Of course you were here, physically, stupid! You were standing staring at Cobalt and then you fell down on the ground right on your back. What I mean is, what happened in the meantime you came back with your consciousness in here? Do you remember anything about right before finding yourself back here in the forest between all of us? -

This time, Adriel understood the Commander's question pretty well, without any kind of confusion.

-Actually... I do. - He answered, looking at Crevan in the eyes.

-And...-

King Balgair and King Adalwolf were visibly about to finish their strange conversation with Ixanthi, their way to still be busy talking, but starting to slowly have few steps away from each other, was a clear sign that in a matter of seconds they might have been done with their sayings.

Dawako and Lisica were also still talking, apparently quite busy laughing and giving pats of an unknown kind of nature at each other.

Adriel tried his best to don't focus his attention on that view.

-I felt pain. A lot of pain. Inside of my head. That's all. But yeah… It did last only few seconds, but it was hitting hard. It was pumping extremely hard. -

The rain started to serenely fall over the forest.

-It's raining…- Dawako stated, looking up to the sky then grey and cloudy.

-The weather in here is something else…- Lisica mumbled.

King Adalwolf looked at the sky too, and he then closed his eyes.

He was enjoying every single second of that peaceful sensation, the feeling of the calm falling rain tenderly colliding with the strength of his face.

King Balgair looked at his counterpart.

And he smiled.

-Do they like each other? - Adriel asked completely out of nowhere to Crevan.

The Commander Of The Fox looked at his King.

-You know… I have never been too sure…-

And he then gave a pat on Adriel's back.

-But, personally, I think they do. But they will also never admit that. -

Adriel walked few steps on the then humid grass of the forest, and he then looked at Lisica.

She looked back at him, with an interrogative expression.

He literally looked away and he then pointed the whole of his attention on Ixanthi.

-Where is Cobalt? -

The Guardian didn't answer.

The green-eyed boy was about to say more, but the Guardian Of The Wolf looked very annoyed.

But not with him.

-What is wrong with him? -

Adriel, and also Crevan, had a look to try to realise who Ixanthi was talking about.

And when they did, a pure expression of surprise pictured the faces of both of them.

Destiny, the amazing horse of the Princess Of The Wolf, was standing there, completely motionless, and he was staring at the Guardian Of The Wolf with severe intensity.

-What is wrong with that horse? - Ixanthi asked one more time.

-His name is Destiny. - The Princess specified with a sort of anger in her voice.

-However…- She continued.

-The reason why he is staring at you really is unknown to me… Maybe he likes you…-

The way the Princess' voice switched from anger to sarcasm, didn't pass unnoticed by the Guardian.

Ixanthi's eyes, once again, got crossed by a very sinister shine.

The wet air got heavier.

It was so common in the Silvery Lands, actually, it was common everywhere in The Circle.

And it also was extremely common to experience the strong winds that suddenly were starting to howl totally out of a sudden, like the one that began to hit the forest not far from the streets and the walls of Shaw.

-Hey! This is strong! - Dawako exclaimed.

But while everyone was struggling in the attempt to do not fall due to the strong wind that then completely blown the rainy clouds away, leaving the scene to the brilliant Sun, Destiny was still there, not the slightest move of a muscle, staring at the Guardian of the Kingdom Of The Wolf.

Then, all at once, it all stopped.

The wind was gone.

The air was light and fresh.

The enormous blue sky right over them, the Sun caressing their skins.

King Balgair approached his daughter.

-Hey, Lisica…-

The Princess' eyes got suddenly wet.

It was always a very emotional feeling hearing her father pronouncing her name.

They were living together inside the same Castle in the Kingdom Of The Fox, but she was rarely seeing him.

And she was usually speaking with him even less.

-Hi… Yes…- She said in a strong and deep state of shyness.

The King looked at her eyes.

Very different from his ones, but the exact copy of his wife's ones, Lisica's mother, the Queen Of The Fox.

Queen Sinopa.

-What's happening to Destiny? -

The question of the King hit strong and clear.

Lisica didn't even try to hide it.

-It is the whole journey he acts very strangely…-

The King's eyes got a light of surprise crossing them.

-Oh really… And what has he done… What was strange about his behaviour through the days of your journey…? -

The King Of The Fox was seeming extremely curious, very much interested to know more about Destiny's particular behaviour.

-This staring thing… He has done it quite often… And he normally stays by himself, away from us or from the other horses. -

King Balgair was listening attentively.

-However…- Princess Lisica said.

-That's not all…- She kept saying.

Her father put a hand on her shoulder.

-Tell me. I need to know. Please, Lisica. Tell me everything and quickly. -

After saying that, King Balgair gave a rapid look in Ixanthi's direction.

The Guardian was then walking slowly around Destiny, studying him, trying to understand something that apparently was unknown even to one of the few men that knew every single detail about The Circle and its inhabitants.

But Destiny was seeming to be something out of his unlimited range of knowledge of their World.

And that was possibly what in that moment was making Ixanthi literally obsessed with Princess Lisica's horse.

Because inside of his head, there was something very sure and clear.

He was, like the other Guardians of The Circle, aware about everything that was about it.

Every single detail that was a matter of explanation of their Dimensional Existence.

That was leading to a very easy but also annoying and actually quite scary revelation for Ixanthi.

The fact he was not able to give an explanation to the nature of Destiny, was then meaning only one thing.

Destiny was not part of that Dimensional Existence.

-Lisica... Come on... Quickly...-

Balgair was begging his own daughter to talk.

To reveal more about the light blue maned horse.

-He sings... I mean... He makes sounds... Of a very melodic nature... And...-

She would have been about to mention to the King, her father, the episode that saw them involved with the Tenebrous Dragon, but right in that precise moment the King Of The Wolf was walking heading to them.

-Adriel...- She then said.

-What...? - King Balgair was confused.

King Adalwolf was getting closer and closer to them, walking quite rapidly.

-It seems like there is a special connection between them... I don't know how to explain... But sometimes it seems like Destiny is devote to Adriel more than he is to me...-

-Hey! Is everything alright in here? -

King Adalwolf finally reached them.

-Sure. - King Balgair said.

-I was wondering...- He continued.

-When everything will be about to start? -

-Soon. - King Adalwolf responded.

-Very soon. -

And he left them in there, walking back to Ixanthi.

-Let's go. - King Balgair said, grabbing his daughter by her hand.

Princess Lisica felt her heart missing several beats.

After those numerous moments of strange confusion, the whole scene was back to normality.

All the presents were, once again, standing all in front of each other.

The level of tension was still high, but somehow everyone was seeming to try to remain calm.

With no more unwanted and annoying interruptions of any kind of nature.

-You both surely want to finally know what the Meeting is about. Right? - Ixanthi asked, looking at Dawako and Adriel.

It was weird the fact the Guardian Of The Wolf was speaking with an incredibly fake sound of friendly attitude in his voice, pretending Adriel and Dawako to believe even just for a second that he was actually having soft ways to speak to them for real, at that point of their encounter.

None of the two boys answered, but they were genuinely paying a lot of attention to the Guardian, starving for any single sort of information that could have been something new for them to learn not only regarding the Meeting, the reason why they were there, but also about the many different aspects and secrets of The Circle.

-The Meeting will be starting very soon. Sooner than what you think, now. -

Ixanthi kept his stare on the two young men from the Kingdom Of The Fox.

-The Hero Of The Fox...- The Guardian said, with a smile that made Princess Lisica feel uncomfortable.

-There is only one way to see if between you two there is the next and new Hero of the Kingdom Of The Fox...-

Ixanthi opened his arms.

-And there's only two Beings in the whole Eternity of this World, of our Dimensional Existence, that can confirm and decide that one of you two is in fact destined to become the Hero of your Kingdom…-

A thunderous noise rumbled coming from skies far away from there, far away from the forest where the Meeting between the Kingdom Of The Wolf and the Kingdom Of The Fox was about to happen.

-But before we continue…-

Ixanthi's, even while talking, was still find distraction in looking at the horse of the Princess of the Kingdom Of The Fox, that was still visibly focused on the Guardian Of The Wolf.

-Would you kindly bring your horse… Somewhere else… Please… Princess…? -

Lisica was not too sure she actually understood well.

-You want me to take Destiny somewhere else so he can not look at you, Guardian? -

The strength in her voice, that unique way to pronounce every single word with such a great amount of authority but still with more than just a touch of endless grace, was something that was making Adriel forget about everything else, even about the reason why he was there, in the Kingdom Of The Wolf, that day, surrounded by some of the most important individuals of both of the Kingdoms of the Silvery Lands.

Ixanthi answered with calmness in his voice.

-Yes. Please. -

Lisica didn't reply this time, and she walked to where destiny was, only few feet away from all of them, and she stood right in front of him.

-Destiny… Let's go… Let's have a little walk down there, come with me…-

But even if the Princess gently tried to pull Destiny with her by grabbing him by the bridles, the stunning horse didn't move a single step, remaining steady in the spot where he was.

-He doesn't want to. - She declared.

-He doesn't want to move at all. -

Ixanthi was visibly about to lose his composure.

He was looking at the horse like he was a real enemy.

He was looking at him like the horse was actually presenting a true kind of danger.

-Adriel. -

The boy from Renard wasn't sure somebody actually called his name.

But in fact, King Balgair was right there, on his left, talking to him with something less than a whisper.

-My daughter said you have a special connection with Destiny… A strange kind of feeling with him…-

Adriel looked up at his King.

-She said that? -

The King Of The Fox nodded with his head.

-Go to Destiny. And try to do something. If he keeps staring at Ixanthi… You know, the Guardian Of The Wolf… Like every Guardian of every single Kingdom of The Circle… He is very particular…-

Adriel didn't say anything back.

He certainly didn't intend to disobey to his King.

His King, that he actually really met for his very first time and not even between the walls of their Kingdom, the Kingdom Of The Fox.

-Fine. - He ultimately said.

He walked towards Lisica and Destiny.

Ixanthi didn't say anything, but he really looked at the scene with something way more than simple curiosity.

He followed every step Adriel took in Destiny's direction.

Once in front of the Princess, he spoke.

-Your father…-

Lisica didn't even let him finish the sentence.

-I know you can do something…-

And she left him there alone in front of the light blue eyed horse.

Destiny didn't really care about his presence.

He was still pointing his eyes on the small man that had the unbelievably important Role of one of the Guardians of The Circle.

-Destiny…-

The horse didn't even blink.

-Please… We really need to move on… I am sure you want to go back to the Kingdom Of The Fox as much as we all do in here…-

King Adalwolf brought his question to Ixanthi.

-What is happening in here? Is the boy able to speak the Language of the horses? - He mocked Adriel with a laugh.

But this time, Ixanthi remained serious, way far from being unpleasant and sarcastic as he has been the most of the time since the inhabitants of the Kingdom Of The Fox entered into the Kingdom ruled by King Adalwolf.

-I think…- He said.

-I think there is something quite unusual between the boy and the horse…-

The King Of The Wolf looked at the Guardian.

-You think…? You are supposed to know everything…-

Ixanthi didn't move his eyes away from Adriel and Destiny.

-Indeed... I know everything...- He said.

And after a pause that did last a bunch of seconds he then added.

-I do know everything that is related to this World... That is related to our Dimensional Existence...-

King Adalwolf didn't say anything back.

His head clearly got busy, all of a sudden, in the exact meantime Ixanthi finished that last sentence, that was definitely sounding more like a statement.

Adriel then decided to literally face Princess Lisica's stupendous horse.

He physically put himself between Destiny and the Guardian of the Kingdom Of The Wolf, the view of him.

And what happened next, really happened fast in there, but incredibly slow inside the deepest locations of Time.

Adriel's incredible green eyes finally collided into Destiny's soft blue ones.

Their eyes mixed together, in a Dimension far away from the Kingdom Of The Wolf, far away from the Silvery Lands and far away from The Circle.

There was not Adriel. There was not Destiny.

Only energy. Blue energy, very light and luminous.

And even if he was not able to see and not even able to feel his body, again, this time Adriel, compared to the previous experience he had that same day, was completely able to be aware of the fact that he was, somehow, still part of the Existence.

Just in a different one.

He then heard a rumble.

And a whisper, coming from somewhere around and above that great and Mystical environment, that pronounced a short statement, audible and clear.

-He is bad…-

Another tremble shook the limits of that Dimension where Adriel's consciousness was in that moment.

And again, a whisper that had the heat of a Divine breath.

-He is very bad…-

Everything started to get blurry and foggy.

A few more instants, a few more trembles against the limits of one of the most secrets and unknown Dimensions Of Time, and everything slowly restarted to look the way Adriel remembered.

Green grass, green trees, blue sky, the faces of the people he knew and the faces of the people he barely knew.

And Destiny.

Adriel found himself right back on his feet, in the same spot he was when he got lost somewhere inside the most powerful secrets of the Universes.

Destiny was still there, in front of him, and they were still looking at each other.

But this time, Destiny finally moved his legs, he literally gave one last look at Adriel and then he moved his eyes behind the boy from Renard, to then being able to throw his very last but this time rapid look at Ixanthi, that was still there, with his King, assisting at the whole Event.

He produced a low sound, stomping on the grass, to then making his way few feet away, enough to find himself not close to all of the presents anymore, not paying attention anymore to any of them, simply walking around, peacefully, studying the area around him and them, totally disinterested to anything that was then going on between the individuals from the two Kingdoms of the Silvery

Lands, that were still waiting to begin what it was supposed to be one of the most mesmerizing Events that were part of the Existence and, for someone, of the Life that were fulfilling the eternity of The Circle.

Ixanthi was leering at Adriel.

And the boy tried his very best to pretend he was not getting uncomfortable because of that.

Then, the question was inevitable.

-How did you do that? -

The question of the Guardian hit Adriel's mind like an arrow.

-I didn't do anything. - Adriel lied.

Or maybe it wasn't a complete lie, after all.

He surely knew something happened between him and Destiny, once again, but like every other single time he would have never been able to explain what exactly did happen.

-This is a lie...- Ixanthi muttered to the boy from the Town of Renard.

Adriel looked away.

The Guardian Of The Wolf walked back to his King, starting a very frenetic kind of conversation, but to hear what they were actually saying was more than impossible.

In the same meantime, King Balgair walked close to Adriel.

It was a bit surreal for the good looking green eyed young man.

He never really had the chance to ever interact with his King through the first twenty years of his Life, and then, all of a sudden, there he was, in the Kingdom Of The Wolf, having his King walking and hanging around him like they actually knew each other since plenty of years.

-How do you feel, Adriel? -

The question coming from the King Of The Fox, sounded quite felt.

Adriel looked at his King and he then looked down, afraid of keeping the stare with him.

-Your Majesty…- He said, involuntarily ignoring King Balgair's question.

-I have a question…-

The King looked at him, with pure curiosity.

-Try. - He answered.

Adriel looked around himself and after being sure nobody was able to listen to him, he took the courage to formulate the question he was starving to ask to King Balgair.

-If you don't mind me asking… Destiny… Who gave him to you, King Balgair? -

The King attentively studied Adriel, but without wasting any time, he promptly answered.

-I honestly don't mind you asking me that at all. However…-

And he cleared his voice before concluding his sentence.

-It is a very long Story…-

Adriel didn't insist.

The King's sentence was a clear sign he didn't intend to talk about that in any possible way.

But before Adriel was able to bow down and move away from him, Balgair spoke again.

-Why do you ask, though? -

And then, without any refrain, Adriel answered with a straight and clean answer.

-I don't think Destiny is a horse. -

The way the King looked at him, showed a huge expression of surprise but mixed with some sort of nervousness.

But right when the King opened his mouth to say whatever he was about to say to the boy with the stupendous green eyes, King Adalwolf appeared right behind the King of the Kingdom Of The Fox.

-Balgair. - He said.

-It's time. -

And he left, the King Of The Fox following him.

Adriel remained there, left lost inside his never completely clear and serene mind.

He then walked, slower than a slow motion, to reach all the rest of the presents, gathering around Ixanthi, ready and visibly impatient to start a speech.

-The Hero Of The Fox. - He said with unnatural solemnity in his voice.

-The Ultimate Protector and not only of his Kingdom, the Kingdom that base its main Principle on Slyness, the Kingdom Of The Fox, but also one of the most valuable and powerful resources of the Silvery Lands and, ultimately, of The Circle. -

He took a pause to enjoy the view of every single one of the presents, including King Adalwof, his King, and also the King Of The Fox, silently paying attention to every word he was pronouncing.

Words that were coming out from his mouth in a way that was almost hypnotic.

-Finally, The Circle might come back having eight Heroes. The number of Heroes we all need to ensure the integrity and the balance of the Dimensional Existence where we all live in, no matter if part of this Kingdom or another one, no matter if part of the Regions Of Light or of the Regions Of Darkness or, in our case, of the Silvery Lands, the Neutral Regions. -

He looked first at Dawako, then at Adriel.

-I am sure you two can not wait to know how this will all work, right? - He asked, accompanying his words with a smile that was far from being a sign of positive vibes.

The vibrations in the air were trembling and getting wavy and concrete, hitting everybody's consciousness.

Adriel and Dawako didn't move their eyes from the Guardian of the Kingdom Of The Wolf and they held their breath.

-Your mentioned battle to decide and define the next Hero Of The Fox will be not your immediate next step. - Ixanthi said, massaging his short beard.

-Somebody will have to first show up here where we are, look deep inside your inner-selves and state with a clear decision if you two are the real right choice, if at least one of you carries the Spiritual qualities to become one of the most Sacred figures of our World. -

It was then pretty obvious that everyone was waiting for the Guardian to end his sentence.

Lisica in particular was keeping lightly stomping her feet on the grass, without a single trace of patience in her, craving for all the answers.

-The Sacred Animals. -

And finally, one instinctive reaction happened due to Ixanthi's final words.

-Say what?!- Adriel exclaimed.

Ixanthi looked at him with a severe look.

-Yes. The Sacred Animals. The Sacred Animal of our Kingdom, Nashobi. And the Sacred Animal of your Kingdom. -

A very unknow kind of silence fulfilled the entire location.

-Tokala. - Ixanthi concluded.

Dawako looked at Adriel, like Lisica and also Crevan.

But Adriel was then paying attention at Ixanthi's words in a deep state of concentration that was not making him able to have a total view and connection in terms of vibrations, with all the other ones that suddenly started to give looks of something more than curiosity to him.

King Balgair, that in the meantime was caressing his daughter's hair, found himself in a long and ecstatic look he exchanged with King Adalwolf, that then interrupted the stare to then focus back on Ixanthi.

The shortest man between the ones that were in that moment part of the scene in that serene location close to the Castle of the Kingdom Of The Wolf, restarted to speak.

-Yes, my dear friends. - He said with the same smile he presented less than a minute before.

-The Sacred Animals will search for that extremely hidden, or maybe inexistant side inside of your Souls. - He concluded.

He then started to clap his hands, at a very slow rate, his eyes pointed on the two boys from the Kingdom Of The Fox, fulfilled by some kind of sensation that was impossible to detect by anyone of the presents, because unknown.

When he stopped to give that very strange round of applause, he opened his arms once again to give what it was appearing to be the very final part of his solemn speech.

-For the Kingdom Of The Fox! Your Kingdom! -

He kept exclaiming.

-For King Balgair! Your King! -

His voice was then way more loud.

-For the Silvery Lands! Your Regions! -

His voice was a weird encounter of devotion and mystery.

-For The Circle! Your World! -

And he then lowered his voice, still very much audible, but less raging and way more steady.

-And…-

He closed his eyes.

-And…- He repeated.

-For the King. -

A very abstract kind of silence.

And he reopened his eyes.

-The King Of Kings. -

++

Printed in Dunstable, United Kingdom